PRAISE FOR TRIANGLE

"U.S. Navy scientist Jason Parker and other operatives mobilize to secure secrets and technologies left on Earth by a race of aquatic aliens in Clarke's (*Middle Waters*, 2014) sequel."

"The author, a diving scientist for the Navy, continues his series about a steely, Dirk Pitt–style hero who knows his way around deep-water dives, sunken caves, paranormal phenomena, and romance…"

"Superpower rivalry … and suspenseful Clive Cussler-esque, high risk salvage ops… A seaworthy mashup of military techno-thriller and alien contact fare." — Kirkus Reviews

"*Triangle* is a science fiction story full of surprises … chock full of accurate deep-water saturation diving, high-speed small jet piloting, high-level military operations, insightful black-ops descriptions, and even Oval Office conversations that come off as genuine. Clarke nailed these, especially his Navy diver banter! This is a great read from a fine writer!" — Robert G. Williscroft, Author, Submariner, Saturation Diver, Pilot.

TRIANGLE

A NOVEL

JOHN CLARKE

Wet Street Press
Panama City

Published in the United States of America by Wet Street Press, Panama City, FL.

This is a work of fiction. All characters, organizations, and events in this novel either are products of the author's imagination or are being used fictitiously.

ISBN-13: 978-0-9863749-3-7

ISBN-10: 0-9863749-3-8

Library of Congress Control Number: 2017900309

Cover Design by John Clarke

Cover art by Gražina Grei

Acknowledgments

Test readers can have a profound effect on a novel, and Ann Crawford, Shirley Kasser Creech, Andrew David, John Gandy, Maggie Lillo, Rodney Rich and CDR Michael Runkle had a considerable influence. Vince Ferris was my highly experienced cave diving consultant. Richard Garett Morgan, Ph.D., was a patient molecular genetics consultant. Dr. Irina Bryant ensured the believability of "Russian" English and anecdotes.

Inspiration comes on a daily basis from deep sea divers who, with no hyperbole at all, should be called heroes. Their willingness to put their lives at risk on missions that can never be revealed should be an inspiration to us all. They are the finest of the fine, not the least because they seek no notoriety. I hope the heroic spirit of those divers was faithfully captured in some of this book's chapters.

Dr. Michael Lang and the Polar Programs Office of the National Science Foundation provided the opportunity to experience diving operations in Antarctica. Without that, two chapters of this book would not exist.

As always, I am also grateful for the freedom my wife gave me to sit at the computer for endless hours of writing. Being a former 3rd-grade teacher, she has a sharp eye for mistakes. Bravo Zulu to her.

Author photo, Holly Gardner Photography

THE SAMUEL PUTNAM PIECE IN THE FORTEAN TIMES

The following is a summary of the Frogs and their Frogships as recounted by scientists Jason Parker and then-graduate student Laura Smith to the reporter Samuel Putnam. This article is reprinted from its first publication in 2014.

Saying Goodbye

After an earthly sojourn of 10,000 years, more than a thousand spacecraft containing benign and curious creatures of an extraterrestrial origin have departed their deep sea homes for good. Earth is no longer their prison.

One hundred centuries: Their arrival heralded the dawn of the Bronze Age. They had come as refugees from a planetary system wrecked by gamma ray bursts deep in our Milky Way galaxy, and, due to what can best be described as a computer error, once they were here, they lost their way home. Until recently, that is.

Although the aliens bore a passing resemblance to our amphibian frogs, they were far more intelligent than either frogs or men. Through a process that smacks of psychic communication, they were finally able to use information from the Hubble Space Telescope and the Chandra X-Ray Observatory to relocate their ravaged stellar neighborhood. While here on Earth, they had no choice but to wait patiently while our technological abilities grew to a point where we could inadvertently show them the way home: Apparently, they had not brought with them the tools they needed to do the job themselves.

At least a hundred of their generations came and went deep under our oceans, while they remained — for all practical purposes — lost in space.

Although their spacecraft had enormous self-restorative capabilities, they nevertheless had suffered the ravages of time. Every few years the aliens would make exploratory flights, and crashes would sometimes occur. One crash of historical note occurred in Shag Harbour, Nova Scotia, where the majority of the ET crewmembers reportedly survived. After they had made successful repairs under the watchful eyes of the U.S. and Canadian Navies, the craft was able to return to its base in the Gulf of Mexico.

During this final exodus eyewitnesses reported a similar forced landing in Lake Superior, but, in accordance with international agreements hastily signed before the aliens' departure, no nation interfered with those temporarily disabled craft.

As a sign of intergalactic good will, the departing ETs left a detailed and purportedly objective record of mankind's history for the past 10,000 years. Such an unadulterated recounting of human history at least 5,000 years before the advent of written records will be of immeasurable value to our understanding of our world's civilized development. Unfortunately, the ETs estimated it will take mankind 100 years to develop the technology needed to decipher this record.

However, the ETs gave two people a sneak preview of what will prove to be one of the greatest surprises of all time. Laura Smith, a graduate student in oceanography, and Dr. Jason Parker, one of her mentors, learned that the aquatic ET species was not the only one to have sought refuge on Earth so many millennia ago. Another land-dwelling species, a genetic product of those aquatic ones that had been evacuated from their planet, was similar enough to man, anatomically, that they bred with Bronze-Age humans. Over a period of 3,000 to 5,000 years, the DNA of this hybrid species had become mixed with that of our Homo sapiens ancestors and was eventually assimilated into our gene pool. From what these aquatic ETs understand, the land-dwelling alien species no longer exists as a separate species. We have intermingled. The implication of this discovery, of course, is mind-boggling: It means that we modern humans are all, to some extent, star children.

Oddly enough, this is not a new idea. The Osage Tribes from Missouri and Oklahoma believed that to be the case centuries ago. It seems now that they may be right.

The aquatic ETs, which Ms. Smith and Dr. Parker call "frogs" because of their anatomical similarities to our green amphibians, provided a tremendous service to U.S. homeland security. Security concerns forbid any detailed description of what that service was and how it was provided, but apparently in safeguarding their underwater environment, the frogs saved the United States from a potentially devastating terrorist attack.

Mankind could have learned much from our fellow earthlings — as they indeed deserve to be called, since five hundred generations of them have known no life on any planet other than Earth. The recording they left behind as a gift, and that the Secretary General of the United Nations will soon possess, also documents events on our planet extending twenty years into the future: the frogs' precognitive capabilities apparently extend at least that far beyond the present. But since 100 years will supposedly be required to decipher the recording, the next 20-year period they have described will by then have literally become history.

Man can only hope that these ETs' timing of their departure from Earth is indeed based on their serendipitous discovery of their home star system through the use of our space telescopes, as they have claimed. Mankind should sincerely hope that what they have foreseen in the next twenty years of our future has not in fact scared them into hastily leaving our planet.

—Samuel Putnam

CHAPTER 1. LAKE BAIKAL

They say the dead can see their bodies from above before moving on to wherever the dead go.

If that is true, then mining engineer Leonid Nikulov could see himself trapped against the bottom of a mine shaft, filled with 920 meters of deep frigid water that just moments before had not been there. And jutting to within a few feet of his crushed and drowned body would be the smooth metallic surface of an alien spacecraft.

Nikulov, a recent graduate of the Moscow State Mining University, had been hired by the Irkutsker Oblast Gold Mining Company to work with a new mine in a tectonically unstable region. The multibillion-dollar Russian company normally mined gold in open pit mines northeast of Irkutsk in Siberia, not far from the northern border of Mongolia. The company, owned largely by one of the richest Muscovites, had been contracted to attempt their first deep slope mine, perilously close to the western shore of the southern end of Lake Baikal, 90 kilometers east of the regional capital of Irkutsk.

The gold mining company was used to doing everything on a grand scale, so when the Russian government said they wanted a mine with 8 kilometers of large-diameter tunnel reaching 920 meters deep, the company recruited the best engineers academia had to offer.

Nikulov was one of those, relatively inexperienced in actual field experience but blessed with exceptional intelligence, high academic scores, and unparalleled instincts. However, his mining bosses showed their displeasure with the young upstart right from the beginning. While they welcomed Moscow's interest and money in their new operation, they resented Moscow selecting one of their own graduates to replace one of the company's most experienced engineers.

The mining plan involved digging a spiral tunnel from the surface down to the 920-meter level. As was normal for a slope mine, once the miners reached the target depth they would proceed horizontally along an anticipated seam of high-quality gold-bearing rock.

Initially, Nikulov had been concerned about the proximity of Lake Baikal — but the mining plan clearly showed that the gold-filled rock lay in a north-easterly direction from the drilling site, in a line paralleling the rocky shore of the world's deepest freshwater lake. That was to be expected for a rift valley, which in fact was where Lake Baikal lay, so the overall plan made sense, even to young Nikulov and his pregnant wife, Svetlana.

Twenty-two hours before the flood, Leonid and Svetlana were lying in bed. He lay on his side, running his fingers over her rounding belly.

"Are you proud of your handiwork?" she asked him.

"Our handiwork, and yes is the answer."

He turned closer to face her, inches from her face.

"So my kitten, what parts of our little girl will you be working on today?"

"Oh, I don't know. Do you have any special requests?"

"Of course. I request that you work very hard today. No slacking off. I want extra brains in her little head. You can't have too many. And a big heart, so she'll understand when Mama and Papa have to discipline her. And so she'll have extra love for her family when her time comes."

"Anything else?"

"Pay particular attention to her smile today. I want her to have that same smile as her beautiful Mama."

"Anything else?"

"No, that should be quite enough for today."

"Then I better get started. With all that to do, I don't think I'll have time to fix you breakfast. You don't mind, do you?"

They both laughed, knowing this was not the first time they had played that game before.

She did, in fact, fix his breakfast, and he just had time to eat it before heading to the mine.

After an uneventful shift, Nikulov came home dirty but not overly tired. As usual, Svetlana asked how his day went.

"We're tunneling horizontally now. I think we're getting close to the gold-bearing ore."

Looking at her silver wedding band, she said, "How nice. Any chance you could bring me home a souvenir?"

With a wink, he said, "I brought you something even better my bunny, but let me shower first."

At 3 in the morning, multiple water sensors sent alarms to the mining control office, and the company began the time-consuming process of evacuating the mine. There was no emergency yet, but the company called Nikulov, the on-call safety engineer. It was his duty to head down the long and gargantuan tunnel by himself in a filthy, diesel-powered two-person man-trip, a low-slung miner transport vehicle.

As he approached the end of the dark tunnel, the dirt-splattered lights of his vehicle were the only source of illumination. Just as the sensors had indicated, water was oozing from the right side of the tunnel where it straightened and headed horizontally for about 100 meters.

Nikulov backed the vehicle a few meters and turned it so its lights played on the water-slickened wall. He thought he heard a shrill sound, so he turned off the engine to listen more carefully. Then he clearly heard the scream of air being forced through minute cracks in the surrounding rocks, followed by a rumble. Before he had time to react, the wall directly in front of him exploded with a devastating force of over 1,300 pounds per square inch.

The lower portion of the mine was flooded instantly, with a jet of water shooting upwards along the spiraling course of the gigantic tunnel, blasting like a geyser out of the mine opening less than a minute after the tunnel wall collapse.

That geyser quickly dissipated, and the water level subsided to a level equal to the water surface in nearby Lake Baikal.

Stunned, the chief mine operator on duty that night was immobile in his chair for several seconds before hitting the general alarm. The wailing sirens could be heard for miles, but Leonid Nikulov could not hear them.

The operator, hands shaking, placed a call on his satellite phone to the mine owner in Moscow, 4300 kilometers away.

The owner had only one thing to say: "ideal'no," which meant "Perfect."

CHAPTER 2. JASON PARKER

There was mayhem on a Frogship, a spacecraft approaching light speed somewhere past our solar system on an ever accelerating journey towards the Tau Ceti system and beyond.

One of the many vessels in the widely spread flotilla was larger than most. Aside from containing a group of highly intelligent amphibians, it was carrying a contingent of human-like persons who had been subservient to the Frogs throughout their history on both Earth and their home planet, where they were now returning.

Ever since the ships' dramatic departure from Earth, the humans had been isolated in the periphery of the spaceship, separated from the rest of the craft by a glass-like partition. Like a gas-filled aquarium, that wall ensured everyone's safety since it isolated the air the humanoids needed to survive, from the rest of the craft which contained the low oxygen atmosphere the Frogs required. To the alien Frogs, oxygen was as deadly as carbon dioxide is to humans.

But now, after millennia of peaceful coexistence, something was terribly wrong.

An alien Frog watched in horror as a human wearing a helmet on his head, a helmet looking like an archaic and self-made contrivance, grabbed a passing female Frog-child and dragged her into the human's oxygen enriched atmosphere. Through the glass-walled partition, a Frog parent watched in terror as her daughter convulsed and died.

Strangely, the fiendish human then opened the glass door and carried the limp body back to the distraught mother, placing it into her arms. That placement was eerily gentle considering the way the man had just horrifically killed the child.

Another Frog arrived on the scene just in time to grab the edge of the closing door separating the environment of the humans and the Frogs. Even though he must have known that entering the man's environment would prove deadly, he didn't seem to care. Luckily the Frog reached through the opening in time to grab the arm of the murderer as he attempted to retreat to safety, and yanked him back out into the Frog side of the craft. The Frog violently yanked off the man's oxygen-filled helmet and choked him with all the strength in his amphibian paws. The slight amount of blood able to squeeze its way past the man's compressed carotid arteries reached his brain carrying only dark red, oxygen-depleted blood. Unconsciousness and death quickly followed.

Whoever thought extraterrestrials lacked emotion had apparently never met an enraged Frog.

Alerted by some silent, telepathic scream from the despondent mother, a handful of other Frogs, by appearance muscular and Warrior-like, raced in with axes and began pummeling the partition separating the two habitats in the ship, the air habitat of the humans on one side, and the low oxygen habitat of the Frogs on the other side.

Normal Frogs, far weaker than the Warriors, moved quickly away from the scene, to a safe distance. They understood that the Warriors were committed to destroying the robust barrier, allowing the gas environments to mix. The Warriors closest to the shattered wall would die almost instantly from the high oxygen level in the wave of released air. But since the Frog environment was much greater in volume than that of the humans' air space, the oxygen deficient atmosphere would quickly swamp the rebellious humans, killing them, or at the very least, putting them to sleep.

Somehow it was understood by all Frogs that the mutinous humans lucky enough to survive, would never again be free.

As the wall cracked and then shattered, terrified humans retreated to the back edges of the craft, but to no avail. Within seconds, men, women and children dropped to the ground, their brains deprived of the oxygen that kept them functioning. It was like throwing a switch. The majority of the lives would not, could not, be resurrected.

As the most senior surviving Warrior Frog surveyed the human dead, he shook his amphibian-looking head and said telepathically so all close-by could hear, *Such a waste. Now we'll have to make new ones.*

Navy scientist Jason Parker, the witness to this scene, felt like one of the humans. He was suffocating. He sat upright, releasing whatever was blocking his airway and vigorously sucked in the air he desperately needed.

It was 3 AM according to the softly glowing digital clock beside his bed, and Parker was shaking, partly from the horror of what he had seen, partly from the sweat covering his body, now chilled by the cool air in the house, and partly from the panic of not being able to breathe. There is no greater panic.

In stark contrast was the comforting sound of his wife's deep breathing, next to him.

Damned sleep apnea, Parker thought.

Parker, one of only two people on Earth who had close contact with aquatic aliens before their departure from Earth, lay back down, finally able to breathe comfortably. But now fully awake, he could not avoid reliving the most anomalous events of his lately strange life. An occasional bout of sleep apnea was a minor handicap considering the trauma his body had once endured.

In thinking of that trauma, he rubbed the scar on his bare chest, recognizing that he should have been killed instantly by the bullet fired from a Marine's M4 carbine. That round had penetrated from his back to chest and should have obliterated his heart and lungs. But somehow it threaded the needle, so to speak, careening through the safest passage in his chest, and leaving just enough vital organs intact that he could be saved.

The strangest part was that he had not been saved by human surgeons. Rather he was saved by the aliens he called Frogs, in one of their Frogships, deep underwater in Guam.

As the Frogs had later explained, they needed to keep alive both Jason and his Starchild accomplice, Laura Smith, if at all possible. Those two special humans were destined to petition the World's governments to allow the Frogs safe passage. After Parker and Smith helped avert the Earth's fist alien war, the Frogs wished to leave the Earth in peace

Unfortunately, their departure three years ago did not leave Jason in peace. The night's dream had merely been one example of Jason's still troubled mind.

It was a Friday morning, and Sandy Parker had gotten up a few minutes earlier than her husband to put the coffee on.

When Parker finally dragged his tired body into the kitchen, his bloodshot eyes had dark circles around them.

"Good grief Jason, you look like crap," Sandy said. "Have a bad night?"

He shook his head. "You have no idea."

"What do you mean?"

6

"I had an ungodly dream last night. I witnessed murder on a Frogship. A human killed a Frog child and the Frogs retaliated by killing the humans — all of them."

"Humans?" Sandy repeated. "There were no humans on the ships."

"It was like I was there, remote viewing it."

"Can you do that?" she asked.

"I don't think so, not in my sleep."

Sandy stopped pouring her cup of coffee and stared at her husband for a moment. Steam was rising from the half-filled cup, as vaporous and ill-defined as her not so well hidden fear.

"My God Jason, what have they done to you?"

Parker was distracted as he drove his older-generation two-seater Porsche to work that morning at the Navy Diving Center, or NDC, in Panama City, Florida.

What the hell kind of dream was that? he wondered. He could still hear the screams coming from both sides of the shattering partition. Were those really humans he saw in the spaceship?

Seeing too late a familiar stop sign, he slammed on his brakes but still slid into the intersection, narrowly missing a passing grey sedan.

As the driver of the sedan blasted his horn and shook his fist at him, Parker sat there for a moment, and sighed.

Shortly after he settled into his office and fired up his computer, an old friend appeared in his office doorway.

Oh crap, he thought. He'd forgotten about his early morning meeting with the local Naval Criminal Investigative Service agent. *This is not a great time for this*, he thought.

The long-haired brunette from NCIS, Special Agent Veronica Spalding, had visited the Navy scientist Dr. Jason Parker several times before. She was an interesting lady with an easy smile who grew up in Saudi Arabia, and as an adult served as an NCIS agent in both Egypt and Saudi Arabia before transferring to the States.

Ostensibly the purpose of the meeting was to follow up on his periodic security review. Admittedly, in the past five years some very interesting things had happened, a lot of which he could not reveal. It had been classified, after the fact. However, this visit was different. Spalding brought reinforcement.

The lady joining Spalding was a tall, thin, attractive brunette with deep brown eyes. She introduced herself by showing her Office of Personnel Management identification badge, which looked legitimate on casual inspection. She said she was a psychologist. If agent Spalding was there to vouch for her, Parker would trust the woman named Abigail Winters — at least a little bit.

Parker, who was honest to a fault, had weeks before struggled over his response to the following question on his security review paperwork: "Have you had any contact with foreigners outside of your official duties?" And to tell the truth, he certainly had. Extraterrestrial aliens were as foreign as they come. Apparently, his answer had triggered a few red flags.

Spalding's approach to the security interview was casual and perhaps intentionally disarming. However, the way the psychologist's eyes were appraising Parker's face felt unnecessarily intrusive.

Seated before the two of them in his office, Parker subconsciously swept his fingers through his chronically disheveled hair. As he moved, sunlight pouring through the southerly-facing window reflected off his eyes, making their blueness look iridescent.

Parker barely looked his age. He was six feet in height and still boyishly handsome. For a forty-two-year-old, he was still physically fit, suiting his avocations as an active pilot and diver.

"May I call you Jason?" Agent Spalding asked Parker.

"Of course."

"I know you are required to report contact with foreigners, which you certainly did. While we appreciate your candor, I really had to investigate further."

Parker smiled. *Yeah, I bet she did*, he thought.

"On the one hand, we have folks asking what you're talking about, while others are warning me not to ask. But I have to know."

"What is it you want to know?"

"When you said you were contacted by Frogs, I assumed you were being flippant, talking about French nationals. Right?"

Parker laughed. "No, that would be a very disparaging term for my French friends. Actually, I had not thought about that connection, but I see why you might. I was, in fact, talking about Frogs, little green amphibians, except not so little."

So far Spalding seemed to be doing the talking while the psychologist took notes.

8

"OK, Dr. Parker," Spalding said, "you do know that I know, in fact we all know, frogs don't talk."

"That's completely true. They don't."

Spalding looked puzzled but the psychologist sat expressionless. Parker sensed that Winters knew more of the facts than Spalding.

He continued. "The law says I have to report contact, but it also says I cannot reveal classified information."

"We both have a TS rating."

"I'm sure you do," he replied, "but you don't have a need to know."

"Know what?" the psychologist asked.

Parker smiled at her feeble attempt to extract information.

"Agent Spalding, the only unclassified information on this subject can be found in a Fortean Times article published two or three years ago. Search for the author, Samuel Putnam. The title was "Saying Goodbye."

"Yes, I think I read that."

Spalding paused, looking around at the books, awards, and photographs adorning Parker's office.

Finally, she continued. "I'm required to ask, have you had any continuing contact with these people, whoever they are?"

Parker had to think carefully about whether he could safely answer that question. But after a moment's reflection, he thought it harmless. In reality, "they" were not people, although strangely enough, they thought of themselves as humans. But they certainly weren't, not by our interpretation of the word.

And as for contact, he had not heard from them for almost three years. They were somewhere in the galaxy, presumably far from our solar system by now, headed home to their long-ago star-ravaged planet.

His answer was simple and to the point. "No."

Agent Spalding was apparently hoping for a little more than that. She folded her hands in her lap and involuntarily and gently shook her head. "Well damn, I wish you hadn't mentioned this thing you can't mention."

"The law does get kind of complicated sometimes. I just try to keep everyone happy. I'm sorry it's not working for you, Veronica."

The psychologist could not keep silent. "If they were to contact you, where would they be contacting you from?"

"Deep space, somewhere between here and Tau Ceti."

He didn't mean to say that. It just came out.

9

"How do you spell that?" the psychologist asked.

"Don't take that seriously. I was kidding."

"Are you sure?"

Just like a psychologist, Parker thought.

Shaking his head, he said. "I had a really weird dream last night. Tau Ceti, that's what I heard in my dream."

Winters jotted a note down before asking, "Do you hold credence in your dreams?"

Parker glared at her. "Of course not."

Winters looked over at Agent Spalding and asked, "Is it OK if we go off script for a moment?"

Spalding nodded her head towards Parker. "It's up to him. You better ask."

"What do you want to know?" he asked.

"Laura Smith. What can you tell me about her?"

Parker paused. He needed a moment to think.

Sensing his hesitation, the psychologist said, "Take your time."

Why is she asking about Laura? Does she know about Guam?

Parker peered at her, trying to pick up some subtle facial expression that might betray intent. But he got nothing in return.

Well, I have to give her something. I'll try for the shock approach.

"Laura's a smart kid with a brand new Ph.D., and... she believes in reincarnation, and she thinks she's a former Frog, one of the undersea aliens ... from a past life. And she thinks she and I are soul mates from that previous life."

The psychologist sat unmoved, but Spalding seemed shocked, her mouth drooping open.

"We know all that," Dr. Winters said impassively.

There was an awkward silence as Parker looked back and forth between the two women.

"Then, what is it you want to know?"

"Dr. Smith is in a very sensitive position in the government. She's been thoroughly vetted, but there's only one area where we're a little concerned."

Parker was not going to take the bait. He did not speak.

Winters stared back at him, unblinking, while Agent Spalding was shifting her gaze between the two of them. Apparently Spalding had not expected this confrontation.

"What is your relationship with Laura Smith?"

10

Parker smiled. "Ms. Winters, there is no relationship, at all. We worked together, we almost died together, as you might know, but that's all. I'm very happily married to my wife, and Laura is a friend of ours."

"She's a friend of your wife too?"

"Of course."

Winters made another note. As she wrote, Parker turned back towards Spalding. He'd had quite enough of Winters.

"Well, OK then," Spalding said, sounding relieved to break the tension. "I have only one last question. Do you have any international travel coming up?"

"Actually, I'm headed to Brussels in a few days, on NATO business."

"Brussels? Ah, Belgian chocolate — the best."

She rose, and Parker shook her hand. As for the psychologist, he simply said "Nice meeting you," with no handshake included.

"By the way," Spalding continued, "if any foreigners approach you in Brussels, please contact me."

"Uh, Veronica, they're all foreigners," he smiled.

"You know what I mean, anything out of the ordinary."

"OK," Parker answered. "But this is NATO we're talking about. Nothing out of the ordinary happens there."

As they left, Parker quietly closed the door behind them.

I really don't like that shrink. I wonder if it shows?

Then as he walked back to his desk to get started with the day's business, he wondered, *Tau Ceti? Where the hell did that come from?*

11

CHAPTER 3. RUSSIAN VODKA

When Russian Navy officers offer Americans repeated shots of vodka, things rarely end well.

Jason Parker was aware of that risk as the introduction to the Russians, all wearing civilian clothes, moved from their Brussels hotel room to the dining room. He and his accompanying American naval officers had assumed the meeting in the hotel room was part of an intelligence-gathering operation on the Russian's part, but the Americans made sure nothing of substance would be gleaned by their hosts. At least, that was the intent, before the vodka began flowing.

Parker and his officer friends had been attending meetings of the NATO Underwater Diving Working Party held semiannually at NATO Headquarters. Russia was one of the NATO Partners for Peace and had been in attendance at all but the classified meetings. So, diplomacy required the Americans to accept the Russian's invitation for drinks and dinner.

It was not until the Americans and Russians sat together at a large table that Parker and the other Americans learned that one of the Russians was a retired attack submarine Captain.

The Americans were impressed. Such was a job for a very accomplished submariner regardless of which uniform they wore. A Russian Attack submarine was designed to hunt and kill American submarines, but fortunately during the tense cold war years of the 20th century, submarine contacts had not turned lethal, or so it was said by some. Now the Americans were free to show respect for their former enemy.

Another of the Russians, Dimitri Roblenski, freely admitted to having once been a KGB agent. An interesting revelation, Parker thought, but the fact that the Russian would admit it, suggested he was no longer spying. After all, the KGB had been disbanded. All assembled at the table were now colleagues, not adversaries.

It would have been unseemly for Parker to get drunk at this diplomatic meeting, so he let it be known before shots were passed, and refilled, that he would only drink half of each shot and pass the remainder to the other Americans.

For two hours of dinner filled with sea stories and laughter, and seeming mutual admiration, the alcohol flowed. And then the party moved to the bar. It was during the closing session of drinking that Parker noticed the self-avowed former KGB agent was paying close attention to him. Parker had no idea why.

Eventually, the evening came to an end, and the Americans excused themselves to order a cab back to their hotel. The Russians followed them outside as the cab was in transit, and Roblenski stepped in close to Parker. He did not smell of alcohol, which made Parker wonder if the Russian's drinking had been a ruse.

In impeccable English, the former agent said, "America is a powerful country, but we are powerful too."

Parker had not been expecting that political comment, so he paused for just a moment before responding. "Indeed, Russia remains a great country."

The Russian poked Parker on the chest, which in different circumstances would have seemed threatening, but it had been a good night, and Parker took it as simply a Russian way of emphasizing a point.

"No, I said we are powerful!"

Well, it was true that the Russian nuclear missiles were sheathed now, presumably no longer targeting the USA, and détente was still active. However, if it was true what the former agent said, if things were to change politically, those missiles would be a formidable force to contend with militarily. Mutually assured destruction was not something Parker wished to think about on this balmy spring night.

Roblenski looked him straight in the eyes. "We know Mr. Parker, about you and your undersea aliens."

Parker could not resist smiling. That subject had not previously come up at the NATO meeting, and Parker was glad for that. He was tired of answering questions about things which really were incomprehensible.

"I haven't hidden that fact. In fact, it was published pretty widely. And perhaps, if you remember, those undersea aliens were not fans of your supersonic torpedoes."

As soon as he'd said that, he realized that perhaps the alcohol had loosened his lips a bit too much. He couldn't remember if that was classified or not.

13

The Russian's expression did not change. "Indeed, our sources told us that."

Parker said, "Well, I'm glad they're gone, but now we can no longer rely on them to safeguard us from nuclear madness. We'll have to do that on our own."

The Russian smiled for a moment before continuing.

"Dr. Parker, do you really think they're gone? All of them?"

"Of course. Don't you?"

The cab pulled to the curb, and Parker's associates began filing in. Parker looked back at the smiling Russian who simply said, "Lake Baikal. The Frogs love our vodka."

The next day the Americans departed Brussels for the States. Parker's last-minute shopping had provided him boxes of Belgian chocolate for his blond wife Sandy, and the NCIS agent, Veronica Spalding.

Although still jet lagged, one of Parker's first tasks back in the office was to call Hans Richter. NSA's Hans Richter had given Jason Parker a private number to call if something interesting came up after the mass exodus of the Canyoneers, or as Parker called the telepathic aquatic aliens, the Frogs.

Richter had been monitoring Parker throughout the build up to alien disclosure, and the aliens' eventual departure from the planet. Now, the one-eye askew, and sometimes sinister looking intelligence agent, had receded into the background, except to ask Parker an occasional question, clarifying what had gone on back then.

Initially, Parker had every reason to consider the misshapen spook to be the personification of government intimidation. But eventually, Parker came to see Richter as a gifted man entrusted with an almost impossible job of protecting America from unfathomably powerful life forms, creatures not of this Earth.

So in an ironic twist, Richter became a friend, and the closest contact Parker had with the government's black world of intelligence.

As soon as Parker mentioned Russians, Richter told him to call back on a secure line.

Once comms had been reestablished, Richter told him, "The two most senior Russians you talked to are spies and are at this very moment being expelled from Brussels. We've found that one in three so-called Russian diplomats at NATO Headquarters is a spy, and I'd say you got more than your share at your little dinner party."

"Dimitri Roblenski said he was ex-KGB."

"According to the Agency, he was surprisingly truthful. He was indeed ex-KGB. But they have been replaced by the Federal Security Service, and your drinking buddy Roblenski is still a spy. That part I bet he didn't share."

"No, but he did bring up the Frogs, and suggested that perhaps they weren't all gone."

"He did, did he? Well, we have absolutely no evidence of that. I think he was just trying to get into your head."

Parker thought about that for a moment, then shrugged his shoulders in silent admission that Roblenski's ploy may have worked.

"Look, Parker, I want you to keep your wits about you. You're too important to us. Those aliens are in deep space, way outside our solar system by now. All of them, even those on the ship that had to land briefly for repairs. They're history."

"I'm important to you?" Parker asked. "I would have thought I've outlived my usefulness by now."

Richter laughed. "Well, I did just tell you to ignore Roblenski. But, you know, if he happens to be right, we may need you again."

Parker shook his head, before saying, "You know Hans, I get it. This is what you spooks do. You just confuse the hell out of everybody."

"We call it contingency planning," Richter said.

"And subterfuge," Parker added.

On the flight back from Belgium, Parker had been thinking about the lake the Russian spy had mentioned, Lake Baikal. It is a large, deep Siberian freshwater lake, oxygen deficient on the bottom; all the things that would make a good environment for the Frogs. So what if they were there, as Roblenski said, stranded? The U.S. would certainly not have reliable intelligence about what was on the bottom of that 5000-foot deep lake.

"Well Hans, does the Agency have assets near Lake Baikal?"

"Oh come on, Jason. I couldn't tell you that even if I knew. But my hunch would be no. No one gives a shit about Baikal. It's just a big-ass lake. What that Russkie said really makes no sense. Like I said, he's just fucking with you."

"You think so?"

"If you're still curious, why don't you try remote viewing it? I know you can."

"Good grief Hans! I really suck at that, especially if I don't have a location. But I know you did it. I saw you in the De Soto Canyon, from the Frogship."

Richter was silent for a moment.

"Do me a favor Jason, don't mention that again."

"Well, you do have skills."

"Yes, but the same problem applies. I have to have an approximate location, and some idea of what I'm looking for."

Parker asked, "So is there anyone better out there?"

Richter laughed. "I'm going to go now. Out here."

And with that, the line went dead.

Chapter 4. Blind Leading the Blind

"If you could see one last thing, what would it be?"

Just as he did every weekday, Joshua Nilsson was riding a city bus down Walhallavägen Street in Stockholm, headed to his job at the Karolinska Institute. This Monday morning he was thinking about that question, voiced by some unknown girl during his bus ride the previous Friday.

It was a mysterious question from a mystery girl, and that mystery was more excitement than thirty-something Joshua had experienced in years.

It was two months before the NATO meeting, and Nilsson was so far barely a blip on the NSA's radar screen. He was American, but ever since his stay in Sweden had become semi-permanent, he had lost interest in his home country. He knew he would go back someday, but as a blind man, his environment, and interest, remained close at hand.

Nilsson had inadvertently attracted the attention of the Stanford Research Institute, working under an NSA contract. The Institute had sent an employee to monitor him, and it was that person who had asked the question which had flowed throughout his waking and sleeping hours over the weekend.

The greatest irony of his life was that Nilsson's father, a well-traveled man, had repeatedly told his son that he should visit Scandinavia before settling down, just to experience the rapturous beauty of Scandinavian women.

However, almost as soon as he arrived in Sweden, the young man suffered a traumatic loss of vision from a fall down narrow, winding stairs. Female beauty was all around him, but he couldn't see it.

Nilsson's bus stopped once again to drop off passengers and pick up others, then continued its sometimes jerky ride down Stockholm streets. During one of those stops, he heard someone sit down next to him.

"Hi, it's me again Joshua."

It was the girl from last Friday. She sounded pretty, although she could have been butt-ugly. But he doubted it.

John Clarke

In a soft, pleasant California accent she asked, "If you don't mind me asking, have you always been blind?"

He hesitated answering. He'd never been asked that before. It was a rather personal question, but finally he relented. "No, I had normal sight until I turned twenty."

"What happened?"

"Apparently my mother was right."

"About what?"

"Oh, you know, touching yourself."

The girl laughed. "No, that couldn't happen. If that were true, I'd have been blind by age 16."

He couldn't help smiling at that. He was beginning to like this girl who sounded and smelled interesting. She subtly excited him.

"You're not from here. You sound American."

"As do you," she said.

He explained, "I was on a Study Abroad program in my sophomore year at UCLA when I hit my head during a fall and lost my vision, right here in Stockholm. The doctors called it indirect traumatic optic neuropathy. What about you?"

"I'm originally from Michigan, but I've been in San Francisco for a few years."

"And you're here as a tourist?" he asked.

"Yes, but I'm also doing some work for Stanford."

"Well fancy that, two Cali university types meeting on a bus in Stockholm."

If she was going to ask personal questions, he might as well. "What do you look like? You know, so I could recognize you in a crowd."

She stopped talking for a moment, smiling at his dry, self-deprecating humor.

"Well, to be honest, I look sort of like Pippi Longstocking, but with boobs."

He laughed at that mental image. He remembered that during his childhood he and his younger sister watched movies about the energetic and magical Swedish preteen with braided red hair. He loved those movies.

"So you're a red head in a country of blonds. I bet you stand out in a crowd."

"I don't mind. Pippi is quite famous here. So, have you decided what you would want to see, one last time?"

18

"I have, but since you know I'm blind, I'll assume this is a somewhat cruel rhetorical question."

"Assume whatever you like. Have you decided?"

"I have. I'd like to see my parents again."

"Where do they live?"

"They don't. They both died a few years ago."

"Oh...I'm sorry. That's so unfortunate. But, that's not how this works."

"Not how what works?"

She didn't respond for a moment.

Lacking a response, he continued. "Remember, I just told you I'm permanently blind. So technically, nothing works."

"Nothing?" she asked smiling involuntarily, a smile he could not appreciate.

He hastily added, "Nothing visual."

"Would you like it to? To work, I mean?"

"What do you think? Of course I would, but the damage to the visual cortex was too severe."

She placed in his hand a braille inscribed card and gently folded his fingers over it. The card contained nothing more than a phone number. "If you'd like to find out more, give me a call."

With that, she rose from her seat and stepped to the bus door as the bus slowed to its next stop. Nilsson rubbed the card between his fingers as the mystery girl stepped off the bus and the bus pulled away.

Throughout the workday, helping a professor from the Karolinska Institute analyze large masses of data by feeling for irregularities in a 3D-printed data set, he kept reaching into his pocket to touch the girl's card. He didn't know her name, but the phone number was local and was almost compelling him to call.

Which seemed out of place somehow. Why would she have a business card with a Stockholm phone number, in braille no less? Was she stalking blind guys?

His questions expanded in number and became ever more bizarre throughout the day until that evening he realized he had no choice except to call.

"OK, Pippi Longstocking with boobs, I'm curious. Why would you ask a blind guy if he would like to see again, even if for a moment? You know that's not possible."

"Don't be so sure. Have you ever heard of *out of body experiences,* when a person is near death in an operating room or an accident scene and they see themselves from above? Obviously, their eyes and their brains aren't actually up in the air, yet somehow they can see themselves from that elevated vantage point."

"Well, sure, I've heard about that. But I just assumed it was some trick of the brain."

"It's not a trick. It's a form of viewing remotely from your body. Some people call it your 'mind's eye,' but we have a more technical name for it: remote viewing."

"We? You know you're sounding less like a tourist all the time. And how do you know what you say is true?"

"Trust me, I know. Are you interested in knowing how you can do it safely?"

That was a curious request, he thought. Trust someone he didn't know, and couldn't see, who claims that the impossible was possible. But his curiosity and an innate desire to see again, even if only in his mind, was appealing.

What he said next reflected his conflicted feeling. "I guess it wouldn't hurt to find out more." At the same time, he was wondering if he was making a deal with the devil.

"I suggest we meet someplace secure, like my apartment. Why don't you hop on the number 67 bus heading downtown at, oh, seven o'clock and I'll pick you up on the way and lead you to someplace where we can talk privately. I'll even fix you a pizza with lots of feta. You like feta cheese?"

What he would like is some understanding of what in the hell was going on.

"Feta's good, but you sound less like Pippi Longstocking all the time. If you're going to feed me in some secret place, don't I deserve to know your real name?"

She ignored him. "Seven o'clock, number 67 bus. I'll see you soon."

What an unfortunate way to end a conversation with a blind man. He wouldn't be seeing her in return, not at all.

As he later used his cane to navigate his way to the bus stop nearby his apartment, he was half hoping this mystery girl would not show up. The worst that could happen is he'd take another ride down to the waterfront and smell the briny scent of the harbor, mixed with the perfumed scent of those beautiful young ladies his Dad had talked about. There were worse ways to spend an evening.

There always seemed to be an empty seat next to him on the bus, but half way down to the waterfront, he felt someone sit there. It was her.

"We get off at the next stop," she said quietly.

She took his hand, gently guiding him as they stepped from the bus. He felt a little strange not using his cane, but he found her guidance to be pleasant. No one had done that for him since his parents had passed.

They walked only a short distance before she urged him up some unfamiliar steps and to a hall of sorts with an old-fashioned elevator at the end. The elevator ride was noisy but quieter than the street traffic.

Once they were in what he assumed was her apartment, she asked, "Can I get you a drink?"

"Water would be great, no gas."

"There's a chair right behind you. Please make yourself comfortable."

"I thought we were going to a restaurant," he said.

In her apartment, things became very quiet, so he had no problem hearing what she said next.

"Shortly, but I wanted to give a preface to what we'll be discussing."

He was feeling more uneasy by the moment.

"There's a reason why we're showing interest in you."

There we go, the "we" word again. Who are these people?

She touched his hand with the glass of cold water, and he grasped it.

"First of all, you're intelligent and analytical, you'd experienced a lot before your accident, and we've noticed from what you read that you have an open-mind, and you're relatively apolitical. In other words, we think you might be interested in learning more about what we can offer you."

He said nothing for a moment but began to feel very uncomfortable. He did not like the fact that she and whoever "we" were, knew so much about him.

"Thanks for the water, but I think I need to go."

"Oh no, please. I have so much more to tell you. It's all good, really. We're the good guys."

"I don't need anyone's help. I'm quite self-sufficient, thank-you."

"But we do."

"We do what?"

"We need your help."

He was getting exasperated with the ambiguous words. He couldn't read her facial expressions, so her words needed to be better defined if he was to trust her at all.

"Who the hell is *we*? You keep saying it."

"The U.S. government."

Neither of them spoke until he had time to process that statement, and the conflicting emotions he was feeling at that moment.

"Why should I waste my time listening to you? I'm doing useful technical work in Sweden, more useful than I ever could back in the U.S."

"Well that's the thing, you can do this anywhere. That is, if you're as good as we suspect you might be."

"Good at what? That mind's eye crap?"

"Yes. Precisely."

Nilsson sat quietly once again, deep in thought.

"I'm going to give you time," she said, "by leaving you with an audio book of *The Coordinate Remote Viewing Manual,* published by my employer, Stanford Research Institute, better known as SRI. It's fairly dated, but it's unclassified. That's where we need to stay for a while until we have a firm commitment from you."

"Or not," he snapped.

She nodded. "Yes, or not. All I ask is that you digest what's in this book before deciding one way or the other."

"And if I simply pretend I never met you, and we never had this conversation?"

"Well, then very bad things may happen to our country, and you will hold a little responsibility for that."

"Whoa, that's a pretty heavy-handed guilt trip!"

"But it's true," she said.

"So, if I decide I'm interested, I'll just call you?"

"Indeed. Anytime, day or night."

"What's your name?"

"Pippi will have to do."

"Suddenly I've lost my appetite for dinner, Feta or not."

"I understand. What I just said is plenty enough to digest."

He wasn't sure if she realized she'd just made a bad pun or not, but it was sounding final enough for him to excuse himself.

Back in his apartment, Nilsson slipped the USB key into his computer and listened to the voice of a professional audiobook reader. Although the narrator tried his best to use interesting inflections in his voice, the subject seemed rather dull until Nilsson heard the words, "Defense Intelligence Agency."

Is that who I'd be working for?

CHAPTER 5. TRIALS

Pippi's words reverberated throughout his waking hours.

If you could see one last thing, what would it be?

That question from "Pippi" had a greater personal influence on Joshua Nilsson than anything in the CRV manual. As he listened to the reader's words and heard new words and their definitions, he found his mind drifting. It really was a technical document with technical jargon, and therefore inherently boring, except for the subject matter which began to pique Nilsson's interest.

As he heard the word "target" being frequently repeated, he kept thinking, what target would he choose?

As his mind wandered, contemplating that question, his curiosity about Pippi grew ever stronger. And then suddenly, he realized what, or who, his first target would be.

In the hands of a young, sexually frustrated, high-performing remote viewer, viewing can be an exhilarating voyeuristic experience, much to Nilsson's surprise. After a period of relaxation, putting his mind in as dark and unstructured place as meditation could provide, he found himself, or imagined himself, looking around in Pippi's apartment, which was really surprising to him since he had no idea where that apartment was. He simply desired to be with her, and within minutes of concentrating, he was there.

As he explored the apartment, he found nothing that would betray her true employer. Even the books on her bookshelf seemed to be carefully chosen to be as unspecific as possible, a mixture of romance novels, nature books, photography.

He chanced upon a mirror and could not resist looking into it. Of course, nothing showed in the mirror. He was, or imagined himself, invisible.

It was late in the evening, so he expected that she would be at home. Sure enough, he heard a commode flush, and a moment later she walked out of the bathroom completely naked to grab a towel from a closet. She then returned to the bathroom and turned on the shower.

Nilsson was in shock. *Did I just see what I thought I saw? Oh, my God, she has a beautiful body. Did that really happen?*

As he heard her singing in the shower with that seductive voice he had come to long for on his bus rides, he realized he should not be there.

And in the next instant, he was not. He was back in his apartment.

Nilsson did not rest well that night. He kept reviewing in his mind everything that had just happened, and that he had somehow seen even though he was cortically blind. As he reviewed what was happening to him, he became angry, angry enough to confront her when he next met her.

He didn't have to wait long. The next morning she was waiting for him when he got off the bus at the main gate to the Karolinska Institute.

"Good morning Joshua, it's Pippi."

He said nothing to her, ignoring her completely, and started walking through the Institute gate. Surprised at his unexpected behavior, she followed him in.

"It's Pippi. Didn't you hear me?"

He stopped and turned towards her voice.

"You lied to me."

He made no effort to lower his voice. He didn't care who heard him.

"You're not a red head. You're a blonde. A natural blond at that."

Even in sexually liberated Sweden, that comment turned a few heads of those walking nearby.

"Why on God's Earth would you say that?" she asked.

"Because I saw you, and that gun-in-a-holster tattoo on your butt cheek."

"Be quiet. You can't say that. And you can't do that! You viewed me naked? You're not allowed!"

Now about six passersby stopped to listen.

"It's not my fault. You taught me. How am I supposed to know how you'll be dressed, or not, when I RV you?"

"Why in the hell are you RVing me?"

"You asked me what I would like to see if I could see. And you're it."

She glowered at him, incensed.

25

An athletic looking male student asked, "Lady, is this man bothering you?"

She snapped, "No, and you people get out of here. This is a private conversation."

As they started moving off, one of the nearby women muttered, "It doesn't sound very private to me."

He continued, "What do I want to see? I don't have parents or grandparents or siblings. And you're the closest to a girlfriend I've had in years."

"I'm not your freakin' girlfriend!"

He paused. Finally lowering his voice, he said, "You asked me a question, and I gave you an honest answer. I can't do better than that."

"Well, you sure as hell picked a bad time and place to answer."

Nilsson was now angrier than she was. "If you don't like it, leave me alone. I don't want to hear from you again, ever."

A very annoyed Sally Simpkin called her boss Dr. Harry Kincaide at SRI, in Menlo Park, California. It was seven hours earlier there, so Kincaide sounded chipper.

Kincaide was the chief physicist at SRI who had organized and run the remote viewing program for the CIA and DIA, and who had been so profoundly flummoxed when he tested Jason Parker and Laura Smith after the Great Leaving. Their revelation that a device given to the American government by the Frogs before their departure, was nothing more than a training aid for psychokinetic Frog children, had been one of the worst disappointments of Kincaide's distinguished career. Furthermore, his realization that Parker and Smith were the only Americans who could activate the device, had been his greatest surprise.

Now, Kincaide was looking for fresh recruits.

"Sally, how are things in Stockholm?"

"Joshua saw my butt!"

Kincaide, sounding amused, answered, "Is that a good thing or bad thing?"

"Joshua Nilsson, the blind guy."

"Oh, that Joshua. And how do you know that? He's probably making that up."

26

"No such luck, Doc. He described a gun and holster tattoo on my butt."

She chose not to share everything Nilsson had said.

Kincaide was silent for a moment, then he unwisely remarked, "You have a tattoo on your butt?"

Simpkin transferred her anger from Nilsson to Kincaide.

"Thanks for nothing," she snapped. "I'm hanging up now."

"No, wait. I'm sorry Sally. You just caught me by surprise. Let's think of the implications if what you say is true…"

"It is!"

"Then how did he get the coordinates for your apartment?"

Simpkin knew that was a prerequisite for Remote Viewing.

"He must have been in your apartment at some point," he continued.

"He did, but he doesn't know my real name, and I never told him my address."

She paused as the adrenaline began dissipating.

"He's not superhuman," she said in exasperation.

"What if he is? What if he zeroed in on you, without coordinates?"

"He can't do that. No one can."

"Never say never. If he can, then he's the best RVer we've ever had. The best in the world, I would say."

There was dead air on the phone as the young curly-haired Simpkin turned her considerable brain power towards that possibility.

"I can test him. I'll go someplace he's never been, call him up then ask if he can see where I am."

"Yes, that should do it. And if it works, I want to waste no more time training him. Let's make him operational — he's a natural."

"Well, there's only one problem. I chewed his ass out, and he said he never wanted to hear from me again."

"Oh, I see. Well…I trust your considerable feminine charms can win him over."

"May…"

His tone of voice turned icily stern. "Let me put it this way. You WILL win him over. I'm not going to find someone who is potentially the best RVer ever and then lose him just because you got into a snit. Your naked butt is not that important. Do you understand me?"

"Yes sir, I understand."

27

"Call me when you have him back in the fold. And then again when he passes your new test. I have every confidence he'll find you. He better."

"Or what Sir?"

"Let's just say, I don't want him working for unfriendly nations. You taught him something very powerful."

She paused, not liking the sound of that threat, at all.

"Surely you wouldn't."

"That's entirely up to you Sally. Do your job."

The phone went dead.

And now Sally Simpkin had a problem of international proportion.

18 Villagatan was one of the more elegant apartment buildings close to the Embassy of the Czech Republic, and a short walk from the Technical University, KTH, and an even shorter distance from the bus lines that took Nilsson to the Karolinska and back every workday.

But today was not a work day as Sally Simpkin stood at the Art Nouveau entrance of the apartment building, waiting for Nilsson to answer the doorbell.

After a long delay, he finally did.

"Who is it?"

"Pippi Longstocking."

His response was immediate and terse. "No, you're not. I don't know who you are."

She hesitated before saying, "I'm a girl who wants to apologize for the way I overreacted. Can I please come in?"

"Not interested."

"I bring food."

"What kind of food?"

"Wine, cheese, French bread."

The door lock immediately buzzed open.

Once she was in his ground-floor apartment, he laid down some rules.

"You can start by telling me your real name."

"OK, I'm Sally Simpkin."

"Who do you work for?"

"Does it matter?"

"You can leave now."

"OK, I work for the Stanford Research Institute."

"I've heard of that. And why are you in Stockholm?"

She felt very uncomfortable revealing the real reason, but Kincaide's warning was a serious one. One way or another, she had to bring Nilsson onto the team if he passed her next test. But first, she had to gain his confidence.

"Would you believe you're the reason I'm here?"

"I know I'm the reason you're standing here, but what about Stockholm?"

"The same. I came here specifically to do reconnaissance on you."

"You're bullshitting me. Get out."

"No Joshua. What I'm saying is true. I can't tell you how, but the SRI detected that you had a high probability of having certain prescient capabilities."

"Forgive me for being a bit skeptical. Why can't you tell me?"

"I'm not even cleared to know the process. I just took the assignment. It had something to do with a DNA sample you submitted."

"DNA? The only DNA I've submitted was for genealogy research."

"Like I said, I don't understand the process. Genetics is not my field."

"But you're telling me the government has access to my DNA results?"

"Only if you authorized it."

"Well, I didn't. And besides, why am I so special?"

"Results speak for themselves. How many other blind people do you think have seen my ass?"

With that, he had to smile.

"I must admit," he said, "that was a shock."

"For both of us," she replied.

Sally had broken the ice, but she still needed confirmation that Nilsson could do the miraculous and zero in on her wherever she went. After telling him her bosses needed some assurance of his capabilities, she was able to coax Nilsson into a further test, although he remained suspicious of her honesty and true agenda.

Nevertheless, he agreed to another mini-RV session. She walked a half kilometer away to a 7-Eleven, bought a frozen ice cream bar, then called Nilsson.

Against all odds, he got the 7-Eleven, but missed what she was holding — he thought it was a frozen fruit bar. But, as these things go, that was close enough.

Simpkin could hardly wait to get back to her apartment and her secure satellite phone.

"Dr. Kincaide, I think he's ready. He passed my test better than I could have imagined."

"How can he do that?"

"I don't know. He's like a Blood Hound or something. He desires so desperately to see that somehow his brain makes it happen."

"He sounds like a freak of nature."

"Yeah, I guess he is," she said.

"OK, then it's time to go operational. I'll call you back when I have a target."

She added, "The CIA's not going to believe this."

"Nope, they sure won't, if he starts hitting real targets."

CHAPTER 6. COZUMEL

James Cramer was afraid of the dark. At the age of 24, he still slept with a nightlight on.

He knew it was pathological, this phobia with sundry scientific names, but try as he might he could never piece together the events from his life that might have caused this aberration.

Perhaps he had been abused as a young child, in the dark. He couldn't remember it, no doubt because of a repressed memory. Or perhaps as a toddler, the lights had gone out during a storm. Or perhaps he found the experience in the womb to be just a bit too traumatic. Of course he couldn't remember that — no one ever does.

Other than that one flaw, his childhood seemed normal. His parents had learned not to ask him to take out the trash at night. It could wait until morning.

As a college student, his experience with girls was normal and pleasant, although, of course, he always kept the light on. He flattered the girls with his rationale for doing that. What they didn't know was that he was too terrified to turn the lights out.

James Cramer's anxiety was so intense that he had already worked out that, when the time eventually came, his casket would have to be wired opposite to a refrigerator. The light would come on when the top was closed.

He would need a very large battery.

He knew he was a bit odd, but he tried to compensate by wrapping himself in daylight experiences of the highest quality. In high school, he earned a recreational pilot's license: it did not bother him that it was only valid for flight in the daytime. He learned to scuba dive in college but had never made a night dive. He didn't need to.

His present trip to the Isla de Cozumel had brought him close to ecstasy. The tropical sun passed effortlessly through the ever-present azure water currents flowing north, just off the populous western shore. While he skimmed the reefs 80 feet down, being nudged along by the current, it was as bright as summer noontime in Kansas, from whence he had come.

And now he found himself fully in his comfort zone as he stared into a lowering, hot sun, waiting for his chance to prove his manhood one more time. His week of vacation was nearing an end, and after days of diving, he was looking for one last adventure before returning stateside. He would be boarding a jet soon, and to avoid the bane of scuba divers, decompression sickness, he would have to wait at least 12 hours after diving before boarding his flight. And that gave him just enough time to try one more exotic experience in Mexico, tandem skydiving.

Tall clouds were building to the east of the airport, but the staff at the Axolotl Skydiving Center did not seem concerned. They had two more clients to take up before their workday ended.

A tall, thinly built but well-muscled man of maybe 40 years walked up to Cramer in a black skydiving suit. His heavily tattooed left arm visible below his flight suit hinted at a Navy past. His nametag said Brinson.

"Well Cramer, are you ready to do this thing? We're burning daylight."

"Been waiting on you. Just remember, I have a flight to catch tonight, and I've been scuba diving."

"How deep?"

"Last dive first thing this morning was 60 feet."

"We won't be doing your tandem jump high enough for you to worry about. We'll exit at 5000 feet; I'm sure you'll be fine on your flight home."

"Then let's do it."

A Cessna 182 with a side door removed would be taking Cramer, the former Navy instructor and another skydiver up for this trip. Cramer would be completing his first jump in tandem with the Navy man, and after they had left the aircraft, the plane would climb even higher before the last skydiver exited. The last skydiver had a miniature camera attached to his jump helmet.

As the plane took off from the long east-west runway on Cozumel, a breeze was beginning to pick up from the east, from where a towering cumulus cloud was beginning to form an anvil.

"Will we be OK with that storm moving in?"

"No worries, we'll be back before it gets here."

With the large open door in the side of the fuselage, Cramer had to shout into the ear of his tandem partner.

"I was wondering; instead of jumping at 5000 feet, could we do it at 5280 feet?"

"Why?" Brinson said smiling, his skydiving pants flapping in the breeze. "Do you want to be a mile high for your first jump?"

"It's just a little higher, isn't it?"

"You do know that is not what the mile high club is about, don't you?"

"I'm the guy paying, so why don't you humor me? The plane's headed to 6000 feet anyway."

"Well, you have a point, but when we get back, I'll have to add about $10 to the charge. Those are the rules."

"So, you've done this before?"

"Oh yeah, you're not the first to want to jump from a mile up."

Brinson leaned over to the pilot. Cramer couldn't hear what his parachutist was saying, but he assumed he was telling the pilot they'd delay their jump for a bit. However, the pilot shook his head and pointed to the storm that seemed to be getting closer, far quicker than either of them had imagined.

Brinson turned back to Cramer. "We have a little problem, that storm is about to move onto the field already, so we have to head west to stay away from it."

"Over the water?"

"Yeah, but don't worry, we won't be jumping till we're back over the airport."

"How long will that take?"

"As long as it takes. I don't know; depends on which way the storm moves."

Just as Brinson had indicated, the jump plane headed west the short 11 miles across the water until they were just south of Playa del Carmen. However, like some inflating monster, the storm grew, making a return to the Cozumel Airport more unlikely with every passing moment.

The pilot motioned to Brinson, and after a brief consultation, Brinson told the two skydivers they would fly down the coast to the Tulum Airport, about 30 miles away, and make their jumps there. Once the storm had moved on, they'd fly back to Cozumel.

Brinson turned Cramer around and started buckling him up.

"Why are we doing this so soon?"

Brinson laughed, "We have a storm coming, a big ol' open door is next to you, and you don't have a parachute. I'd hate for turbulence

John Clarke

to bounce you out the door, without a parachute. Could mess up your whole day."

Instinctively Cramer moved back from the door even more. "Good point."

Mere seconds after Cramer was safely buckled in, all inside the aircraft were blinded by a lightning strike.

Normally, when lightning strikes an aircraft, the current is routed along the outside of the aircraft, following carefully bonded metal pathways. Unfortunately, the old Cessna, having sat in salt air for decades, had corrosion interrupting the bonding pathways. The result was a flash of heat penetrating into one of the fuel tanks in the right wing. That tank erupted into flames which almost immediately began crumpling the spar holding the wing intact. As the spar twisted from the intense heat, the plane began to corkscrew towards the ground a mile below.

The combination of G-forces and fright catapulted the three skydivers out the open door.

Brinson twisted to confront the air best he could, and once he confirmed they were safely free of the flaming and spiraling aircraft, he pulled their main chute.

Unfortunately, as Brinson and Cramer had cleared the door, the trail of fire from the fuel tank ignited the cover to Brinson's main chute. Looking up and seeing their chute being consumed by flames, Brinson cut the fiery chute free and deployed the secondary.

Normally, that deployment would have been their salvation as they would have floated softly to the earth of Quintana Roo. But that life-saving chute was not opening fully, damaged perhaps by the intense heat that had ignited the main chute. The partially open chute slowed their descent, but not enough to be survivable. And with a man strapped to his front, Brinson did not have the maneuverability he would have liked to try to pop the chute fully open.

At the last moment, resigned to his fate, Brinson flipped onto his back, intending to cushion the inevitable impact with his body. It was as if he were throwing himself on a grenade, hoping to spare his comrades. In this case, his comrade was Cramer, tied to him, with legs helplessly flailing, knowing he was about to die.

The other skydiver's chute opened without incident. With his attention drawn to the drama of the flaming chute, and then the saga of the partially inflated chute, the camera on his helmet recorded the tied duo's impact and bounce. It looked like they bounced maybe ten

34

feet high, raising a dust and sand cloud which obscured their second impact.

As the last skydiver stared in disbelief, the dust cloud drifted off gently, revealing nothing.

Brinson and Cramer were gone.

CHAPTER 7. THE DARK

God, it's dark.
Are my eyes open or closed — I can't tell.
It's coal mine dark.
It's like death dark.
I'm dead.
I'm not dead - I'm in too much pain to be dead.
It kills me when I breathe.
The dead don't breathe.

Where the fuck am I?

James Cramer was able to wiggle the fingers on one hand and felt dirt.

He moved his fingers some more and found he could twist his wrist a little, just enough to touch something he didn't recognize in the dark. It was hard, and cold, and wet.

It had contours that he began to trace with his fingertips, trying to force his shocked and disoriented mind to concentrate on what his hand was exploring.

And then he realized what it was — a hand — a dead hand.

Somehow he sensed he was lying on top of someone, someone who did not move, or speak.

His concussed brain flashed a brief memory, of being in an airplane with an open door. Then seeing flames, and falling.

But he remembered nothing else.

Am I buried? This must be a mistake. I am not dead!

James Cramer was entirely numb except for his ribcage that felt like it was crushed. He was in shock, which was probably the only thing that had kept him from screaming — until he realized he was buried alive — in the dark.

>⊷—

Seven hundred miles north of the hole where Cramer found himself buried, was Panama City, Florida and the Navy Diving Center, made famous by the exploits of Dr. Jason Parker and the Star-child graduate student, Laura Smith. According to science fiction writers, of all the places where alien disclosure was likely to occur, Panama City was not even a consideration. But yet it had happened, several years before.

Panama City is home to military bases, fresh seafood, emerald water and sugar white beaches. Deep sea aliens apparently found something in Jason Parker and Laura Smith, two Panama City residents, that was to their liking.

Monday morning stand-up quarters at the Navy Diving Center started at precisely 0900 hrs. As Jason Parker and others in the leadership filed into the Commanding Officer's Conference room, the Command Master Chief and the Operations Officer, a gray-haired and grizzled Warrant Officer, were talking quietly with each other, with deadly serious looks on their faces. Something serious was up, and Parker leaned over to the Command Master Chief to find out what was afoot. The CMC nodded him off.

At that moment, the Commanding Officer entered with a grim look on his face.

He strode to the head of the table, his usual position, and paused briefly before speaking.

"If you have not heard already, we lost one of our retired members this weekend. Many of you know him well — Master Diver Wayne Brinson."

Shocked gasps and "Oh no!"s filled the room. When the group was silent again, the Commander continued.

"He was presumed lost in a skydiving accident near Cancun, Mexico. All we know so far is that he was doing a tandem jump with a beginner. Their chute failed to open fully, and they were seen hitting the ground."

The Senior Medical Officer, always curious, asked the obvious question. "Why presumed dead?"

"Their bodies disappeared after impact. It is believed their bodies fell into one of the caves in that area. There is no sign of exactly where they impacted. A search is underway, but with the speed they hit the ground, well, it would not be survivable."

"It was witnessed?"

"Yes. Another skydiver caught it on camera. That footage is being analyzed as we speak, but there is no hope for either Master Diver Brinson or his tandem buddy."

There followed a subdued commotion in the room.

"Brinson's family has alerted us there will be memorial services both here and his hometown of Americus, Georgia, perhaps in the next week or so. We'll pass the word to any who wish to participate."

And with that, the tall Commander left the room. He looked somewhat wilted; Brinson had been a friend of much of the Command, and especially the CO.

Brinson had been well liked, a lean and handsome man with dark features, and an extensive parachute jumping history during his years with Explosive Ordnance Disposal, or EOD. As a civilian, he'd taken up wingsuit flying, where he flew like an eagle — something he would rather do than most anything else.

And now, amazingly, he had vanished.

The Executive officer tapped Parker on the shoulder. "Follow me. The CO has a question for you."

The CO was alone in his office when the XO ushered Parker in.

"Jason, please have a seat."

Parker sat at a small conference table, and the XO closed the office door as he left. The CO wanted to be alone with Parker.

"I wasn't at NDC when you had your encounter with the underwater aliens, and I'm certainly not cleared to know the details of that encounter, but there is one thing I've heard about you."

"And what might that be?"

"I'll understand if you don't want to confide in me, but I really want to know just one thing. Can you see distant things through Remote Viewing?"

"Well, that depends. I'm self-taught, and I have had some experience, but frankly, it's not like anything I can verify. I don't think I'm very good at it."

"Would you be willing to try?"

"Let me guess, you want me to search for Wayne Brinson?"

"That's the idea. Are you up to it?"

"I, don't …,"

Mid-sentence, Parker changed his mind. "Sure, I'll give it a try. But I need something to go on. Some approximate coordinates, anything people might have about his potential whereabouts."

"That I can get you. No problem."

"But no promises. Like I said, I don't think I'm particularly good at this."

"Well, we have to try. I'd like to let Wayne's family know we pulled out all the stops to try and find him."

Through the fuzziness of his half-conscious brain, Cramer felt himself being pushed over to his right side and heard the sound of straps being cut. After more jostling, he felt whatever had been beneath him being pulled out from under him. And then things once more became quiet and still as his damaged brain slid back into unconsciousness.

The next thing he became aware of in the inky blackness was the sensation of water on his lips. He realized at that moment that he was desperately thirsty. He parted his lips and felt a stream of water entering his mouth, running across his tongue. He swallowed with eagerness.

Not understanding where the water was coming from, he found his arms had been freed, and he reached into the blackness in front of him and contacted cool, dry skin; human skin perhaps. The thing inside that skin did not withdraw but kept up the gentle flow of water passing Cramer's parched lips.

Cramer reached further, with both hands, and found himself touching something soft. He must be hallucinating, but in the darkness, he imagined that a partially naked female was caring for him.

He could not process why she seemed to be nude, but with his diminished capacity to understand anything, he took this contact in his stride. He couldn't see, and he didn't care, as long as he was being given water.

He sure as hell wished he had a light.

He must have lost consciousness again because at one point he realized that his caregiver, whatever it was, was gone, and he was once again alone in the suffocating blackness.

He remembered reading that sometimes miners trapped underground without light will see phantom lights, flecks of light due to the brain's ability to imagine light when there is none.

So with thoughts of the mental conjuring of light, he stared with interest as a wave of pale blue light seemed to be shimmering, flickering, then fluid like, approaching, like a disjointed, fragmented snake.

As the vision neared, Cramer's fascination with the shimmering light transitioned into palpable fear. The thought that his mind was hallucinating was replaced by a fear that something with energy, and malevolent intent, was approaching.

And then the light reached around to his side, leaving a vile blackness directly in front of him.

He screamed.

Remote viewing, what some call psychic spying or RVing, originated in Russia during the cold war. In response, the U.S. initiated its own program at the Stanford Research Institute. Once the method went operational, the focus of activity was at Fort Meade, Maryland, at the National Security Agency facility.

Strangely, Panama City, the home of NDC, Jason Parker and his wife Sandy, had seen quite a bit of remote viewing activity back in the days of the ephemeral Frog visitations.

"My God Jason. What are you doing now?"

After Parker's previous remote viewing contact with aquatic aliens, Sandy Parker, his wife, recognized exactly what was going on with the drawn drapes, meditation music and Parker's relaxed posture in his Ekkorn chair.

Parker did not answer immediately, then he sighed.

"You broke my concentration."

"Jason, seriously, you're doing this again? You promised me."

"We lost one of our own yesterday. CDR Hope asked me if I could help find him."

"Who?"

"Master Diver Brinson."

"No!"

With that, she fell silent and slipped out of the room. She understood why Parker had to do whatever he had to do.

Remote viewing is like a dream, a dream while you're awake. At least, you think you're awake. You just can't prove it.

Parker worked hard to quiet his mind, to concentrate only on a location in Mexico south of Cancun, about halfway between Playa del Carmen and Tulum Airport, in a clearing nine miles due west of X-Puhá. That was where the surviving skydiver had been rescued, and where the missing skydivers, including his friend, had disappeared into the Earth.

Unfortunately, all he received for his efforts was a blank, black image. He saw nothing but a void. He sensed no presence, no structure, nothing. It was just darkness.

CHAPTER 8. IRKUTSKER OBLAST

The smooth metallic craft lay half in the water of Lake Baikal, and half out. Aeronautical Engineer Anton Volkov could see from the lights hung from the mine ceiling that the metallic-looking surface of the 260-feet wide gray triangle had a satin finish, and no perceptible imperfections to mar its surface. However, along its edges lay a broken row of colored bubbles protruding slightly from the overall contour. They looked like they could have been lights, but their true function was a mystery, just like everything else about the craft.

The craft was as wide as the wingspan of an Airbus A380-800, and the tunnel it resided in was 100 yards wide, a gigantic width for a mine tunnel.

The water level in the capacious tunnel was the same as the level of the nearby lake, but it lay 200 feet below the surface of the mine entrance which had been dug in an isolated and highly secured area east of Irkutsk.

Over a thousand feet behind Volkov lay a much smaller portion of the "mine" tunnel, one heavily protected by impassable doors; impassable without the proper clearances.

The craft was left behind by the Frogs as they departed the planet three years earlier. The best guess of the select few who knew about it was that it had been discarded as being unspaceworthy. After all, it was rumored to be at least 10,000 years old. Whether there were any Frogs still in it, dead or alive, was also not known.

A year after *The Great Leaving*, the craft had been discovered serendipitously during a mapping operation of Baikal. It was nestled in a large natural cave at a depth of 3,000 feet in the rocky western wall of the lake.

To raise the craft to the surface without alerting the ever-present American satellites, a fake mining operation was started using an actual gold-mining company already established in that portion of Siberia, operating two other gold producing mines just northeast of Baikal in the Irkutsker Oblast.

Of course, to preserve secrecy, none of the miners and mining engineers knew why they were digging to a 3000-foot depth. They assumed it was just another deep gold deposit.

They also believed that once they reached their target depth, they would be digging parallel to the lake and the rift valley, which would make perfect sense if in fact gold had been found there.

What they did not know was that when digging on their northeast track, they would intercept the cave containing the craft. The result would be an almost instantaneous flooding of the tunnel, with the unhappy consequence that anyone in the mine at that moment would be killed. But the force of the flooding would also neatly suck the craft into the yawning tunnel.

Humans always die on large engineering projects, but miraculously, only one life was lost when the inevitable flooding occurred. That unlucky soul had been the young mining engineer Leonid Nikulov, whose body would never be recovered. Supposedly, he and the mining vehicle which carried him to the working face of the tunnel was still entrapped in the jumble of broken rock at the 3000-foot level.

Before the mining operation had been planned, deep-sea diving robots, Remotely Operated Vehicles, had tested the buoyancy of the craft and found it neutrally buoyant. That was an extremely lucky happenstance. Although a lift to the surface of a neutrally buoyant craft could be accomplished without too much difficulty, the view of a large triangular craft on or near the surface of the lake would have been detected by the first satellite to fly over the region.

Once high-pressure water flow from the shattered mine wall had pushed the craft inside the corkscrew mine tunnel, it had merely taken time, patience, and a lot of burned out ROVs to maneuver the craft around the spiral tunnel network to reach the well-hidden water surface a short distance from the mine opening. If ever there was a secret submarine pen, this was it.

A tiny cadre of Russian Explosive Ordnance divers, all with the highest possible clearance, had dived below the craft looking for any sign of entry or any lettering, anything to give a clue as to what the Russians should do next with their prize.

The alien Frogs had not made it easy for them.

Anton Volkov, entrusted with perhaps the greatest prize of all time, was as perplexed as anyone. He had crawled over, swum under, and walked or swam around it for the past month without the slightest result. Today he was holding a battery powered black light laser, peering into the shallowest bulbous "light."

In a dream two nights before he had heard the words "black light laser" multiple times. In his sleeping state the phrase became an obsession, and the next morning, to quiet the incessant words reverberating in his head, he requested that the best such laser be flown out from St. Petersburg.

By a pre-assigned signal, he turned the portable laser on and waved a hand for a technician to turn off the lights in the subsurface pen. With the clunk of a high voltage switch, the submarine pen turned to absolute blackness except for the faint violet glow of the laser.

Volkov heard a gasp from at least one technician when they were surrounded by impenetrable blackness.

Volkov peered into the closest bulbous object which at the ultraviolet wavelength seemed transparent. Like an ophthalmologist examining the blood vessels in the back of an eyeball, Volkov moved the laser all around the object looking for some tell-tale marking. But his search was in vain.

Undaunted, he grabbed a mask and snorkel and swam to the next colored bulb. There were nine all total, three on each side of the triangular craft. There he repeated his search and again came up empty handed. On to the next, and again with no result.

What would he tell his superiors if this didn't work? They would ask him why he thought it might, and would he really say, "I had a dream"? He would be sent home in disgrace and told never to speak of the object again.

Or, perhaps he wouldn't make it home, due to an "accident."

Volkov was not a religious man, but as yet another bulb came and went, he was secretly praying to whatever God would listen that his dream was an inspiration, not silliness. He just knew he could in some small way help his Motherland.

His prayer was answered with bulb number 7. In the far back center, he saw the fluorescent glow of figures, hieroglyphics.

"I have it!"

"What do you have?" came a booming voice from out of the darkness.

"I don't know, but it's something, a marking."

"Should we turn the lights back on?"

"No," I have two more to examine.

"Very well," the voice said.

As it turned out, bulb number seven was the only one with any markings.

After the lights were back on, he showed the photograph he'd taken of the fluorescent symbols to the closest political officer. The officer smiled, and said gleefully, "I know what it says. It says *This side forward.*"

He laughed heartily, and those near him who were treating him with deference also laughed.

Volkov, on the other hand, had only one thought, "Idiot!"

Anton Volkov did not think he had enough influence to get support for the next phase of his plan. But like gamblers feeling compelled to keep going after one win, no matter how small, his political bosses were exultant that they had in their possession even a small scrap of unencrypted alien writing.

The next phase of Volkov's plan was to send autonomous vehicles back to the 1000 meter deep cave where the ship had been hidden for who knows how long. If Frogs had been there for a while, they might have left some sign, also unencrypted, that together with the engineering marking on the craft could help them decode the alien language.

That might not help them learn how to open and fly the craft, but it might help them decode the alien code which had been made public shortly after the Frogs left Earth. If the rumors were correct, being able to read that code might bestow inestimable power upon the readers.

Again, the most secure way to reach the cave was through the corkscrew mine tunnel, safe from prying satellite or human eyes. And the RoboRovR remotely operated underwater vehicle with a fiber optical cable connecting it to the surface, was just the small and maneuverable craft to explore the bottom of the tunnel.

There was little flow of water in the flooded tunnel, so the water was still turbid as the RovR neared the bottom, 980 meters, 3000 feet, down. To avoid smashing the RovR's camera housing into the jumble of boulders, Volkov inched the craft forward until almost against the boulders.

45

At this rate it could take forever to explore all the debris, looking for something that might not even exist. He didn't have forever. His lease on the RovR would expire in two days.

For a full two hours, Volkov meticulously inched the RovR from one side of the cavernous tunnel, then moving up a foot and repeating the same maneuver, without effect. The men keeping him company, making sure he didn't somehow harm the spacecraft sitting on the surface, were clearly bored.

Then, at one end of a sweep, he saw something white shining in the gloom. He turned the RovR closer to the object and saw that it was thin and somewhat curved.

Then in horror, he recognized it as a rib; a human rib.

Leonid Nikulov.

"Der'mo."

After pausing a moment to reflect on what he was seeing, Volkov used the RovR manipulators to start moving rocks from around the location of the rib, and as he did more and more bones began to appear.

He might not find any evidence of an alien language, but at least he would be able to recover the remains of a national hero.

All that seemed to be appearing were skeletal remnants with no signs of clothing. Apparently, the tremendous force of the frigid water exploding in at 1300 pounds per square inch ripped off clothes and flesh.

Seeing only what was visible on the video screen, and attempting to operate the RovR's claws quite some distance away, was tiring and slow going. With about half of Nikulov's remains uncovered, Volkov moved a stone from the crushed chest, and as he did, writing became visible on the portion of the stone that had lain hidden. Ironically, Nikulov had received that stone first, the hard way.

Sadly, once Volkov saw the mass of broken bones, he realized that he would not be able to carry the remains back to the surface. Other trips would have to be made, but at least he could now return to the surface with what he had been seeking. He had been vindicated, and more importantly, the hero husband of Svetlana Nikulov could eventually be given a proper burial.

On the surface, as Volkov was examining the wet stone in his hands, the writing looked more like scribbling than anything else. One of the observing guards said, "Frogman graffiti."

The name stuck. From then on that particular stone and its fragment of alien writing became known as the "Graffiti Stone."

Of course, it was the unspoken hope of all viewing that stone that it would prove as significant as did the Rosetta Stone. But only time would tell if that was the case.

CHAPTER 9. LANGLEY

CIA analyst Mark Baisley was staring at his computer screen with intense concentration. He called his supervisor over to his cubicle.

"Sir, I think there's something funny going on in Siberia."

"OK, tell me what you think."

"You know how I've been idly watching the gold-mining operations in the Irkutsker Oblast?"

"I know. You're easily amused."

"And remember how we said we were lucky to be able to watch a new mine starting up near Baikal, and how we commented what an incredible amount of dirt and rock was being pulled out and dumped?"

"Sounds like National Geographic should have been there."

"They're all deep gold mines," said another young analyst who had been attracted to the conversation. "There's a lot of dirt to move."

Mark continued, "And then about a month ago the trucks carrying the mine spoils stopped moving to the dump site, and fewer trucks started transporting to the same processing facility that services all three mines."

"Yes, I remember," the boss said, looking bored already. "And this is oh so interesting from a national security perspective, I assume."

"Maybe. Hear me out. I've started passing the imagery through to Big Ben to do statistics on the amount of trucking and mine product being carried to the processing facility."

"Oh the suspense," his supervisor said sarcastically. "What does Big Ben say?"

"Sir, we all know you don't care much for me, but Big Ben is objective. And he thinks I'm on to something."

"Uh, let me remind you, Big Ben is an *it*, not a *he*."

Baisley responded with emphasis, "*IT* says the pattern of truck traffic is different for the Baikal mine. The truck pattern from the first two mines is identical within a confidence level of 98%, but the southern mine is different with the same level of confidence."

"How is it different?"

"It's not as consistent."

"Which means the mine may not be as good a producer."

"Or the traffic pattern is a ruse, and drivers knowing that, grow weary and not so motivated. Maybe they get sloppy."

"And where does your keen sense of logic take you from there?" the bellicose supervisor retorted.

"Sir, I think they're pulling the wool over our eyes. I think the gold-mining operation is a sham."

"Baisley, either you're going to get yourself assigned to Alaska for wasting computer time, or you're getting assigned to Siberia."

The other analyst asked, "Why do you say that, Sir?"

"Either Mark's very wrong, or he's very right. And if he's right, off to Siberia he goes."

After letting that thought sink in, the impatient boss said, "I tell you what; you two put your heads together, on your own time, and tell me how we can find out if there is gold in those trucks. If you can prove there isn't, on the cheap, then you'll have a lot of peoples' attention."

The next morning, Mark's friend Jeffrey had a wild idea he'd cooked up overnight.

"If you bombard gold with neutrons, it becomes radioactive. Gold changes from the stable Gold 197 to the unstable form Gold 198. 198 then decays to mercury, giving up gamma rays. I know we can detect gamma rays. Problem solved."

"So," Mark asked, "are you going to tell that to our boss, or am I?"

Jeffrey winked. "Let's not."

CHAPTER 10. QUINTANA ROO

The blind remote viewer, Joshua Nilsson, had agreed to help SRI only under the condition he'd be paid in cash, in advance, for his remote viewing attempts regardless of how it turned out.

Sally Simpkin brought the agreed money and also the coordinates for Nilsson's first search as a hired SRI agent. She also brought descriptions of the two people they were looking for somewhere in the narrow northern half of the Mexican State of Quintana Roo. SRI, and the CIA for whom SRI was working, understood that if successful, this would be a body recovery effort.

Nilsson's mind's eye found himself on the grassy surface of a large, roughly circular clearing of an otherwise jungle landscape. The area he had been led to had a lot of crushed and trampled vegetation as if helicopters and searchers had been walking the area.

He had no way of knowing whether he was actually "seeing" this scene or imagining it, but Simpkin's recorder was making a record of everything he said for later comparison with the truth.

Convinced he would find no more clues on the surface than did the other searchers, he willed himself to descend through the soil. At first, he felt thoroughly silly even imagining such a thing. Nothing happened. But then as he looked up, imagining what the clouds looked like, he found his view blocked by soil. He was descending.

"Wow, I can't believe that works. I'm going down, into the soil."

He seemed to descend only a few feet before he began to encounter dark pockets of air. And then the descent ended in what seemed to be a very large cavity, a cave. It was dark as coal, so he could not actually see a cave, but he sensed dirt and sand were not around him.

"I'm not sure how I know, but I think I'm in a cave of some sort. It's dark as hell."

Simpkin decided to give him a few suggestions. She'd never known any RVers who could go underground, so she didn't know exactly what to say to guide him. But her curiosity was egging her on. "Try to look around and see if you see anything."

He smiled, recognizing the irony of what she was saying, to a blind man.

"I have an idea. Please quit distracting me."

"OK, sorry," she said.

"I see glowing, on the walls of this cave. It looks like what I remember of fluorescence, but it's moving. Some of the light is faint blue, some green, and some yellowish. That's strange, there is a lot of it, faint, but moving."

Nilsson had a puzzled expression on his face.

"The walls look alive. What the hell am I looking at?"

"Oh wait, I know. Those are people. My god, they're naked people, several of them, and they have a faint bluish white, fuzzy glow to them."

Simpkin did not believe what she heard, but true to her promise she kept quiet, leaving Nilsson to sort out what he was seeing.

"Oh, I see, the lights on the cave wall are following the fuzzy people."

He panted for a moment, trying to catch his breath.

"Somehow the people are making the walls glow."

Oh, my God, Simpkin was thinking. *He's hallucinating; he's crazy as a bed bug. How am I going to explain this to Kincaide?*

"I'm moving around down here. This seems to be a pretty large cave, not very high, but wide. It's lit fairly well, perhaps by the skin of these people. I swear they are glowing, and that causes the walls to glow...this is weird."

Yeah, he's right about that. I'm so busted — and I convinced them to pay 10 thousand for this crap?

"I don't see anything like the men I'm looking for. But this place is big; they could be anywhere."

Or nowhere, she was thinking. *Squashed, buried. Never to be found.*

Finally, her curiosity became too great not to ask. "Are they really naked?"

"More or less. Their skin seems to stimulate the walls to glow. Maybe if they had a lot of clothes on, they would not have enough light to see by."

Oh my God, this is so bizarre!

"I feel faint. I need to quit."

51

His facial expression was relaxed now that he was not concentrating as hard as he had been. Beads of sweat were gathered spottily on his forehead.

"I'm going to have nightmares tonight. I don't know if that was real or not, but that was way out there crazy."

You're right about that, she thought.

As they parted company for the evening, she thought what an easy way to make 10 grand. He probably made up everything, and no one would ever know.

Actually, she was not thinking so much about the crazy things he had said, but about his remote viewing of her apartment.

Before getting in the shower that night she undraped her towel enough to reveal the gun and holster tattoo on her right butt cheek.

How in God's name did he know about that?

A U.S. helicopter carrying a team of geologists with ground penetrating radar was flying at low level over a clearing two and a half miles north of the clearing where Brinson and Cramer were reported to impact. The team had been dispatched to the area, with proper blessings from the Mexican government, by what the geologists believed was none other than the U.S. Geological Survey. The scientists and their helicopter crew had no idea why the U.S. government was interested in a survey of that region, but like good soldiers, they carried on without questioning their orders.

However, the mission made a sudden change for the stranger when a half-naked man appeared in the clearing, waving at them frantically. The few clothes he was wearing were filthy and shredded, and he was limping. When they lifted him into the helicopter, he was delirious, babbling about invisible creatures having saved him.

CHAPTER 11. VIRTUAL RETINA

Parker received a non-secure "low side" email from Hans Richter indicating that they needed to talk on the secure phone in the NDC SCIF, a Sensitive Compartmented Information Facility that had recently been upgraded from SECRET to TOP SECRET status. At the appointed time the secure phone rang, and Parker simply said his name, "Parker."

The voice on the other end was definitely Richter.

"Jason, there are very few people who know that both you and I are remote viewers. I've been wondering about the mechanism. How is it we can see things if our eyes aren't actually there. I know it works, but I don't know how it works."

Parker had a ready answer. "Actually, I've thought about that, a lot. Clea Greyson, the local psychic who was remote viewing the De Soto Canyon craft, was able to tell if the inside was lighted. And that got me to thinking. How do our brains perceive light without our retinas being involved."

"Yeah, exactly. How does it happen?"

"Our retina is just a transducer. It converts incoming photons into electrical signals to send to our brain through the optic nerves. Then the visual cortex, a specific portion of the brain, somehow rearranges those electrical signals into a pattern we use to see our world."

"Too much information!"

"I like to think the images we produce by RVing happen because we have a virtual retina."

Richter was silent for a moment.

"You are so full of shit," Richter finally responded.

Parker laughed. "I'm afraid you overestimate me, Hans. I have no clue how it works."

"Well let's assume you're right for a moment," Richter said, "even though we know you're not. So can this "virtual retina" see UV frequencies? Can it sense more than we can see?"

"Even our retinas can sense UV, at least UV 'A.' At birth, the lens of the eye passes UV light to the retina, but as we age, the lens becomes less transparent to UV. As adults, we can't see UV, but children and young teenagers still can to some extent.

"So young children can see it?"

"Yep, so they say," said Parker. "But I'm curious, why do you ask?"

"Well, I'm sure you want to know why this conversation requires a secure phone."

"That thought crossed my mind," Parker said.

"We found James Cramer."

"Cramer, Cramer … you mean the guy Brinson was jumping with?"

"Yes, and he survived."

"How? What about Brinson?"

"No sign of him. He's presumed dead."

"Well, we figured as much," Parker admitted, sadly.

Richter continued, "Cramer was picked up a couple of weeks ago by a geological survey team down in Quintana Roo. Actually, we sent them on a ground-penetrating radar mission to search the area where Brinson and Cramer disappeared."

"That's odd."

"No, what's odd is that we first RV'd the place with a new operative we've recruited."

"Do I know him?"

"No. But he's got skills. Anyway, he penetrated below ground and found a large void and tunnels, and throughout those tunnels he found glowing people who were able to make the tunnel walls fluoresce."

"Now you're full of shit."

"And we got to thinking, the only thing that can make minerals fluoresce is ultraviolet light, black light. We think those people were emitting UV light from their skin."

"Come on Hans, I'm not stupid."

"The reason I asked about seeing UV was that our RVer must have been able to see UV."

"You're serious?"

"It gets better. When we found Cramer, he was babbling about people who never talked, and who he could not see, except when they were standing in front of those fluorescing walls. But they took good care of him, bandaged him, gave him some sort of food and water, and maybe medication. And after a month or so they pushed him down a tunnel that eventually led to an opening in the rocks that led to the surface. He was wandering in circles when we found him."

Parker was shaking his head. "Is this some sort of test, to see how I react?"

Richter seemed to be ignoring Parker's snide comments.

"In one respect the story holds together; our RVer sensed UV light being emitted, and he could see the walls fluorescing, which meant the walls were reacting to UV light. But James Cramer couldn't see the glowing people. And now you just confirmed that adults can't see UV light. So that's why he couldn't see them."

"Can your guy normally see UV light?"

Richter did not respond for a moment, so Parker repeated his question. "Can he see UV?"

"Actually, he can't ... see anything. He's blind."

Parker stared at the table in front of him, saying nothing, but grimacing.

"You know Hans, this is kind of a sick joke."

"Sounds like it, but it's not," Richter said. "You'll see. I've arranged for you to meet both Cramer and our RVer, in San Antonio."

"Why?"

"To find out more about those people, or things, that took care of Cramer."

"Why don't you just send a National Geographic camera crew?"

"Because the cave people don't talk. My gut feeling is they're telepathic, and you might be able to receive their telepathic communications."

Parker sighed, saying nothing for an uncomfortable time. He thought his days of telepathic communication ended when the Frogs left our solar system.

"Are you still there?" Richter asked.

"So, you're talking to me because you're wondering if these guys are aliens?"

"Your Frog buddies did say they brought humanoid hybrids with them."

Parker jumped on that right away. "Which were supposedly assimilated into the human gene pool a long time ago."

"Exactly," Richter said enthusiastically. "Just like Neanderthals were."

"That's right."

"But wouldn't it be interesting if we found a surviving band of Neanderthals? Or, even better, Sky People? When can you make it to San Antonio?"

"Not this week, or the next. How about in three weeks?"

"How about next Monday. We can't detain Cramer forever. I'll have my boss call your Washington boss."

"You're having him detained?" Parker asked, alarmed.

"He's in for a psychological evaluation. You flying yourself?"

"I'll have to. We can't get orders and tickets processed by Monday."

"Well, at least with the Frogs gone you can have a peaceful flight."

"That's what I'm hoping. It will be quick. I'm flying a jet now."

"On a government salary?"

"Remember, you guys are picking up the tab since you think I'm so damn important. And, you don't trust my perfectly good little prop jobs."

"Oh yeah, forgot about that. That's black budgets for you."

CHAPTER 12. SETI

The NDC Quarterdeck called Parker as he was preparing his flight plan to San Antonio.

"Sir, you have someone for you at the Quarterdeck."

"I wasn't expecting anyone. Who is it?"

"Timothy Robeson. He said you know him."

"Yeah, I do. But I sure wasn't expecting him. I'll be down in a second to pick him up."

The uniformed Command Duty Officer said, "I'll sign him in long as you vouch for him."

"Oh, I do. I'll be there shortly."

Dr. Timothy Robeson was a research scientist at the SETI Institute, Center for the Study of Life in the Universe, in Mountain View California. He and Parker used to dive together in Antarctica, at McMurdo. At the time, Robeson was studying primitive bacterial colonies in deep, ice-covered Antarctic lakes. Some of those lakes had liquid water underneath a thick ice cover, presumably heated to just above freezing by geothermal energy. SETI was interested in those bacterial colonies because they might serve as a model for the simple life to be found under the ice of Jupiter's moon, Europa.

As Parker was walking down the hall of NDC, he looked Robeson up on his Contacts list to remember the name of Robeson's girlfriend. He hoped she was still his current flame.

Stretching out his hand in greeting, Parker said, "Timothy, this is one hell of a surprise! What brings you to Panama City? And did you bring Cassie with you?"

Robeson was ruggedly handsome, with a face reddened by too much Antarctic sunlight reflecting off snow and ice. And perhaps by too much exposure to bitterly cold water.

"You're the reason I'm here. Can we go someplace private to talk?"

Parker nodded to the duty sailor at the security desk, as if to say, I'll escort him from here.

"I think my office will do."

"Sounds good to me."

Parker's office held mementos from his own Antarctic diving. Among them were two photos of Robeson, one in the ubiquitous U.S. Antarctic Program red parka, easy to see in a whiteout, and one of him in a dry suit and full face mask emerging from the top of a borehole drilled through three meters of ice.

Robeson looked at those photos and smiled. "Last time I saw you, Jason, we were on a C17 headed back to Christchurch. But the last time I was down on the ice I read with great interest about your adventure with the ETs. I could hardly believe it."

Parker laughed. "Well, you're not the only one. I still can't believe it happened."

"So I bet your life has changed."

"Not as much as you would think," Parker said. "I still have to pay the bills."

"But I'm surprised you're still here. I figured you'd be working on a book or two, and doing speaking tours. Or up in Washington as a Presidential Advisor on Extraterrestrial Affairs."

Parker smiled.

"Or maybe a UN counterpart. But here you sit in quaint old Panama City. You haven't even been on Oprah. What's up with that?"

Parker sat quietly for a moment, weighing what he could or could not say.

"Like you, sometimes you have to get out of DC and do some good field work."

"The ETs are gone, so what's left to do?"

"Tim, there's lots to do."

Robeson caught on quickly. "You have got to be shitting me. We now have ultimate alien disclosure, and still, the cover-up continues?"

Parker continued to stare at him with a non-committal smile.

"And you're part of it?" Robeson continued.

What Parker couldn't say was that the story about the aliens was in itself not classified. Samuel Putnam had told that story to the Fortean Times back before Washington had time to digest the civilization-changing implications of Parker's experience. However, now they recognized there was a hell of a lot more lying just below the surface, or maybe deep below the surface, depending on your perspective.

"What happened to that girl Laura, your accomplice and paramour?"

Parker had heard that insinuation before. It didn't bother him anymore, but he did try to clear her name at every opportunity.

"Laura and I were not lovers. The tabloids have overactive imaginations."

It was true that Parker and the young graduate student Laura Smith had once been arrested in quarters in Guam, and were targeted for elimination by a deranged former friend. It was also true that they did cuddle in bed as much out of fear as anything, but as Shakespeare said, misery does make for strange bedfellows.

"Oh, I don't care, I'm just telling you what I heard."

"Laura's the one up in DC," Parker explained.

"What's she doing there?"

"I don't really know."

"Dammit Jason, you never used to be this secretive."

"I'm not being secretive," Parker protested. "I honestly don't know what she's doing."

Parker needed to change the topic of conversation.

"What's going on with SETI these days? I bet they were in shock after the big *reveal*."

"Oooh yeah." Robeson dragged out the words for emphasis. "We were concerned that SETI would be shut down since we weren't the ones to find extraterrestrial intelligence. You did."

"Believe me, I was not looking for them."

"Yep, that's the irony of it. But apparently, someone figured SETI still had a mission."

"And that mission would be?"

"To keep looking. Now that we know we've been hosting extraterrestrial Frogs for ten thousand years, we figure there's bound to be other advanced civilizations out there, somewhere. And they might not be as friendly as your Frogs."

"Sounds like typical DC paranoia. But that also sounds more like a DoD mission to me."

"DOD?"

"Department of Defense."

"Actually, that's where you come in."

"Me?"

"We have some concerns, and we figure you'll tell us where to go next."

"You have my full attention," Parker said, sitting even more upright in his chair.

"Do you know about the SETI project for the use of home computers to help us to look for correlated signals from radio telescopes?"

"Sure. I used to lend my home computer to that project."

"Lately, our server has been corrupted. We're not sending the right data out for analysis."

"So shut it down."

"That's the problem. We can't. The source of the data being sent to millions of home computers around the world is not from our server. We're not sure where it's from."

"How is that possible?"

"Have no clue. Somehow it's all been hijacked."

"So shutting down your server doesn't turn it off?"

"Nope."

"If I remember correctly, there are all sorts of datasets that can be analyzed."

"Precisely. They're not all radio telescope data."

"And what's coming through the system now is radio telescope data?"

"No. It's a signal sequence we've never seen before."

"Any idea what it is?"

"We were hoping some of your people could tell us?"

"My people? Who are *my people*?"

"I don't know, but I hear you're connected. And you just confirmed that."

Parker laughed. "My friend, we're all connected. Some of us just don't know it yet."

Robeson leaned close, speaking softly. "We don't like our good name being ruined by who knows who, doing who knows what. Whatever it is, the entire world is playing the game, trying to be 'helpful,' and we have no idea what the result will be."

"Could it be an artificial intelligence?"

"That's one possibility, but if so, someone must be controlling it. At least I hope so."

Parker looked out his window, looking past his friend, past the pictures of Robeson and him in Antarctica. "I wonder if it could be a code cracking attempt."

Robeson smiled. "Now you know why we're coming to you. From what I read, you once held a very special code around your neck, a gift from the Frogs."

"The Frogs told me it would be unbreakable for at least a hundred years, so it must have some sort of quantum encryption."

"What's that?"

"Damned if I know. But it's supposed to be unbreakable."

"Well, maybe it is, but there could be at this very moment many millions of computers working on cracking it. It may not take a hundred years."

Parker was silent, thinking.

Robeson continued. "The question is, what could be on that vial you had? I thought it was just the history of mankind?"

"That, plus more. It's the future of man, for at least the next twenty years. And knowledge of that future would be the most powerful knowledge on Earth."

"You mean like knowing what the stock market will do?" Robeson asked.

"No. Everything. We would know what our enemies will be doing before they even know."

"But if the enemy cracks the code first, then they'll know what we'll be doing."

"Exactly. And that's the problem. You're right — I need to talk to some people."

"Well hell, here I was all excited that we'd finally discovered that ET is real, and now we find out they've left us with a problem. Actually, a scary problem."

"Does anyone else know about this?" Parker asked, with creases forming on his forehead.

"Just a very few in SETI. They're the ones who sent me to you. We're hoping you can help."

Parker remembered the warning of the investigative journalist Samuel Putnam, who felt strongly that the Frogs' departure from Earth was a bad sign.

"Maybe I can help. I know some people." Parker said, thinking of his NSA contact, Hans Richter. "And now I'm concerned that this is just the tip of the iceberg."

"Well my friend, you and I are well qualified to know what the rest of the iceberg looks like."

"True. And that is not at all comforting."

CHAPTER 13. HANS RICHTER

When Robeson left the NDC, Parker sent a low side but encrypted email to his contact at the NSA. Parker's email to Hans Richter simply said, "We need to talk."

After half an hour, Parker received the following from Richter, "OK."

Parker then walked over to the SCIF and placed the call from its secure phone.

"Richter."

Richter sounded all business, as usual.

Parker was not going to chit chat on this call.

"We have a problem with SETI."

"Tell me more."

"Someone has hijacked their server and is sending out a strange signal for their SETI@home radio signal data analysis program. Do you have any idea who it is?"

"First I've heard of it. I'll check it out."

"I think this could be serious," Parker said.

"I agree. I'm going to activate one of our assets down there."

"Who is it?"

"Kelly Brightman."

"Oh, come on. He works for me. He's my best electrical engineer."

"I know. And one of our best too."

Parker was stunned. He'd worked side by side with Brightman for years. He was a great engineer. And now he was a soon-to-be reactivated intelligence analyst. Who would have thought?

Parenthetically, Richter added, "Brightman left NSA, but you don't ever really leave the NSA."

Parker was still trying to comprehend what he had just heard. "Was he activated during the Frog business?"

Richter laughed. "Sometimes you're too smart for your own good."

Parker was later standing in Brightman's office door.

Brightman looked up sheepishly. "Well, this is awkward."

"That's what I was thinking," Parker said.

Squirming slightly in his seat, Brightman semi-apologized, "I have two masters. I can't change that."

"As long as your other master is paying you, I'm OK. Just don't expect a Navy paycheck until this is over. You're officially on unpaid leave."

"Roger that. I fully understand."

And then winking at his friend Jason Parker, Brightman went on to say, "They pay better, by the way."

Parker smiled back. "That doesn't surprise me at all."

Kelly Brightman was smart as a whip, quick thinking and a joy to be around. He was also a large man, not easily intimidated, even by aggressive and occasionally nasty attorneys attempting to twist Brightman's words of truth into words better suiting their defense of a diving company or equipment manufacturer. He was a subject matter expert who flourished in the often acrimonious atmosphere of the judicial system.

As Parker's role at NDC had expanded into other areas, Brightman assumed the role of lead accident sleuth. And Parker had to admit, he was damn good. And apparently, damn good at hiding his NSA connection.

"And in case you're wondering," Brightman said, "I'm not a spy. I'm an analyst."

Parker thought *That's what they all say.*

"Do me a favor. I'm flying to San Antonio in the morning. I have no idea when I'll be back, but I'd appreciate it if you'd let me know if you and the rest of the NSA team are making any progress on the SETI hijacking problem. There's a lot of strange stuff going on right now, and I'm always looking to see if these events are correlated or purely random."

"If Richter tells me I can, I will," Brightman answered.

"Not to worry. They're trying hard to keep me clued in. I guess they don't want any screw-ups like last time."

"I'll do what I can Boss, but no promises."

CHAPTER 14. SOUL KILLER

Joshua Nilsson was looking down at a floor he could not see. "Remote viewing is killing my soul."

This was Jason Parker's and Joshua Nilsson's first meeting, at the Grand Hyatt hotel in San Antonio.

"I've never heard that one before," Parker said.

"As much as I resented going blind, at least I realized I could have broken my neck falling down a stone stairway. In a way, I'm lucky I only lost my vision."

Parker was silent, thinking about the "soul-killing" thought, something that had occurred to him as well. However, he'd dismissed such thoughts long ago.

"And I'd resigned myself to my new circumstances. And to be honest, my other senses began to take over — amplified if you will. But then I was exposed to remote viewing, and I discovered I could see again. Not in the normal way, but with my mind's eye. And to a blind man that is very intoxicating. Is it intoxicating for you?"

"No," Parker replied. "It's rather exhausting. I'd just as soon not go to the trouble."

"But you have to understand, I was becoming a blind man who could see, at will. And I became addicted to it. I started doing it whenever I could, and seeing things, watching things, I probably shouldn't. It was like being invisible, with all the moral dilemmas that entail."

"So you are conflicted."

"To put it mildly, yes."

"Rumor has it you want to stop working for SRI?"

"I'm thinking about it."

"Is that why, because you think it's killing your soul?"

"Partly, plus I don't like getting yanked around the world doing the government's bidding."

"A lot of people would kill for a job like that."

"Well, not me."

"Do you feel like you're being used, taken advantage of because you're blind?"

"Not if what I'm being told is true, that my Remote Viewing talents have nothing to do with eyesight."

"But certainly you enjoy the money."

"Ah, the money. Isn't it the root of all, all,…"

"I think the word evil is what you're looking for."

"Yes, evil."

Then he laughed. "I knew the word. I just wanted to hear you say it."

Parker smiled.

"By the way, did you notice how you used a vision-based word just then? *Looking for.* I could get offended."

"I wasn't even aware. I'm sorry."

"Oh don't be. People don't even think about what they say."

"Force of habit," Parker admitted.

"I was informed just before you got here that I was to let you in on a little secret."

Parker looked around the hotel lobby. "We're not in a secure facility."

"I'll speak in code."

Parker looked around again, getting nervous.

"When I arrived in San Antonio I was given another coordinate to check out — one in a very cold Russian place."

Parker was concerned that Joshua wasn't aware of the chances he was taking because he was a rank amateur. Then he smiled because he realized he was too, at least in the psychic spying business.

"You know your little friends?"

"Of course."

"And how they get around?"

"Yes."

"Well, Ivan has one. I've seen it."

Ivan, like Russians? Oh my God, the Russians?

"Do we have proof of it?" Parker asked.

"Nope, no satellite, no ground truth. It's carefully guarded, for obvious reasons I'd say."

A tall stranger with neatly trimmed dark hair, stylish Oakley eyeglasses, and a perceptible limp walked up close beside them and leaned in. "Cut it out you two. Parker, show up at this address with Mr.

Nilsson in tow in two hours. We'll talk there. And not to worry, we're the good guys."

The address was at Brooks City Base.

Brooks Air Force Base used to be a thriving airbase, but it was officially closed in 2011. However, in 2002 the property was transferred to the city of San Antonio, and the property was renamed Brooks City-Base.

Parker was no stranger to the facility, having ridden in the human centrifuge for pilots as part of his sensitive life support work for the Air Force. The job of the centrifuge was to try to drive the pilots at high G's into unconsciousness, and the job of the pilots was to keep that from happening. Loss of consciousness in flight was almost always fatal.

He was also familiar with the dwindling cadre of aerospace physiologists whose positions were slowly being transferred to Wright-Patterson Air Base in Ohio.

The Air Force had been the biggest tenant of the City-Base for some years, but even now, with all signs of the previous runways being erased, there were still a few military buildings occupied, and a few special government buildings with no identification whatsoever, but with heavy security.

Into just such a building walked Jason Parker and Joshua Nilsson. They were met at the entrance by a guard who checked their ID and then escorted them into the building. That same guard confiscated their cell phones and scanned their bodies for hidden devices.

Once they were clean, they passed through another door where the tall man who had interrupted them in the hotel awaited them.

"Gentlemen, if you will please follow me to a conference room we'll get down to business."

Down the hall, past a water cooler, their escort stopped at a door, entered something into a cipher lock, and then motioned the two men into a compact room with a rectangular table with room for eight chairs and scarcely anything else. It was cozy.

Parker maintained a light grasp on Nilsson's arm, guiding him to the closest chair and making sure he didn't trip. Nilsson seemed to enjoy not using a cane, substituting it with gentle guidance by his newfound friend and confidant.

Aside from their unnamed escort, there were three other men, and one woman, in the room.

The man at the end of the table seemed to be in charge. He had graying hair, creases on his forehead and around his eyes, and while seated seemed to be relatively short. The woman looked taller sitting in her chair, and younger.

The man in charge began speaking. "Gentlemen, this briefing is at a Top Secret, SCI Special Intelligence level, most sensitive. I won't tell you the current code word, but if you're familiar with the old "Umbra" code word, then you know what this is."

Parker was familiar but had not been briefed to that level before. This was going to be interesting. He assumed it would have something to do with the Frog spacecraft.

"This is a joint intelligence facility, and sitting beside you are folks from the NSA," one man nodded, "DIA" another nodded, "and the rest are CIA. This facility was stood up primarily to help us protect our southern border, to do Intel assessments on the incoming illegal aliens."

The lady coughed under her breath. "Undocumented immigrants."

A joint facility? Parker thought. *That must be like herding cats.*

"But we're here for a more important reason. The CIA's identified some unusual activity at a new gold mine near Irkutsk, Siberia. Our Langley analysts identified that activity, and after coming back from an assignment in the area with an agent posing as a deep sea biologist, they discovered that the area around the mine is shut tight. There is definitely something going on that the Russians consider very important."

The fellow from NSA took over. "And that's where you came in Mr. Nilsson. Our algorithms picked up on you as being potentially a very valuable asset, with special skills, so we had you scan the mine for anything unusual. And frankly, we got far more than we bargained for."

"Then maybe I should have asked for more money."

Only the man in charge reacted, with a slight smile, which of course Nilsson could not see.

"Now, Dr. Parker, I hear you've already heard that it was a Frog spaceship."

Parker knew enough to not betray his sources. "Thank-you for that," he said slyly.

"Obviously, if the Russians have their hands on advanced technology like that, that could place us at a severe disadvantage. And POTUS and SECDEF don't like playing second fiddle to the Russians."

"Neither do I," Parker said.

"To be honest, we have nothing actionable. In the eyes of some skeptics in Congress, Nilsson simply imagined or hallucinated something. After all, he can't really see."

Parker looked over at Nilsson to see if he was reacting to that comment, but Nilsson didn't seem to care.

"Dr. Parker, the NSA has a report you submitted of a conversation with a Russian who intimated that they had Frogs in Lake Baikal who like Russian Vodka, of all things."

"To the Russians that could mean vodka, or it could mean 'water,' like that in Lake Baikal."

"Thanks for that clarification Dr. Parker. But what concerns us is that if the Russians have a spacecraft, then either it was shot down, and therefore not likely to be functional, or it was abandoned, again because it was not functional."

Parker nodded his head in agreement.

"But if in fact there is a remnant of Frogs there, with the spacecraft, then we have a huge problem. With the Frogs' help, either willing or coerced, they might be able to get that thing functioning. And that would be a concern."

"In my experience, Frogs can't be coerced. They have incredible abilities of mind control."

"As I understand it, you do too."

"Well, not like that."

"But have you ever seen a drunk Frog? What if the spy was not messing with you? Consider the possibility that Russian water, Vodka, actually is a favorite of the Frogs. What then of their amazing mind control?"

"I have no idea," Parker confessed. "But that makes me very concerned."

"All of us feel the same."

"And you've asked us here, why exactly?" Parker asked?

"Well, it's complicated. We seem to be somewhat stymied in our search for the explanation for the Irkutsk mine. But here's something I want you to think about because this affects you in many different ways."

Parker raised his eyebrows.

68

"First of all, when SETI contacted you, and you passed on their warning that SETI signal packets were being misappropriated in unknown ways, that was bigger news than you knew."

"Why is that?"

"The SETI at home network has access to several million home computers, each one donating lots of spare compute cycles, with a combined processing power of a sizeable supercomputer. So it's much more than a science fair project."

Parker chuckled.

"Your pal Brightman and our other analysts have figured out that the adulterated signals seem to be coming from a Russian site, after bouncing around the world through various mirrored sites."

"Interesting," Parker said. "Can you shut it down?"

"We can, but we'd rather monitor it."

"Why?"

"Because we think it's trying to break the alien code you once wore around your neck."

The DIA fellow chimed in. "What they don't know is that what we released to the public is not the pure alien code. We did our own bit of adulteration, keeping the true code to ourselves."

Parker nodded his head in agreement with that strategy.

The head CIA fellow continued. "Now that we have a suspicion that they may have an alien craft, they may not actually be interested in decrypting the code, ostensibly a hundred-year project. They may have some unencrypted operation manual for the craft, a much more important document."

Parker whistled. "I guess there isn't much we can do about that."

Nilsson simply shook his head.

"Not directly. But we may have an ace up our sleeve."

"Oh?" Parker said.

"That's where you two come in."

"Really?"

"We're sending you both to Cancun."

"When and why?" Parker asked.

"We'll decide that after the two of you talk to James Cramer after lunch today. But potentially, we'd like to have you guys be wheels up first thing in the morning."

"But why?"

"To talk to some people."

"What people?"

"Don't know. We'll figure that out as we go."

Joshua Nilsson turned his head toward Parker. "Let me guess, Jason, you're staring at me right now."

"Yeah," Parker said.

CHAPTER 15. SASH

Because of the number of military and interagency security personnel near San Antonio, the San Antonio State Hospital, or SASH, had seemed like a smart place to stash the sole survivor of the Yucatan skydiving accident.

Reportedly, Cramer was in surprisingly good physical condition considering his skydiving partner, Parker's friend, had been presumably killed. And in spite of Cramer's preexisting fear of the dark, and his being confined in a totally dark environment for months, the state psychiatrists had given him a reasonably clear bill of health.

Once he was questioned by Parker and Nilsson, he was likely to be released back to his family's custody. Of course, neither Parker nor Nilsson were psychiatrists, but it was hoped their non-medical and non-threatening presence would loosen Cramer's tongue enough to suit the government's purposes. And that purpose was to find out who or what was under the jungle surface, and why.

Cramer looked as gaunt and pale as a living person can be, but due to apparently good care underground, and good care in the hospital, his medical record indicated he was much like any healthy, reasonably fit 24 year old. His gaunt appearance was no doubt due to the lack of exercise, the long-term absence of sun while underground, and the lack of his most-favored cheeseburgers during his stay underground.

"So who are you guys?" Cramer asked, with a smirk on his face. "I've seen a hell of a lot of strangers in the past two weeks. What is it you want to know from me?"

Parker answered. "I'm a friend of Master Diver Wayne Brinson, the man who was taking you on your tandem jump. I know his family, and they really want to know what happened to him."

He shook his head. "No, they don't want to know," he said softly.

"They need closure. What happened?" Parker gently insisted.

"I squished him. We had a partial chute failure. The damn thing was torched as we jumped or fell out of the burning plane. It wasn't a streamer, but it was a very fast descent. And I landed on top of him.

When I woke up, he was gone. I have no idea what happened to him, but falling like that, and then with me landing on top of him, I can't see how he could have survived. Someone told me we bounced."

"And then disappeared," Parker added.

"I suppose it seemed that way."

"Did you know where you were?"

"Oh hell no. I thought I was dead, in some sort of black hell. Except I couldn't be dead because I hurt too damned much."

"Do you still hurt?"

"No, I'm fine. I must have had broken bones, but they fixed those somehow."

"They who?"

"Don't know, I couldn't see them. There was no light. But the few times I managed to touch them, they felt like they were human. Mostly naked humans."

"How do you know that, if you couldn't see them?"

"Because of where I touched them. Accidentally of course."

"Oh."

"Did they have medical facilities?" Nilsson asked.

"Not that I'm aware of, but I'm not real sure. I couldn't see shit. I thought I was blind until I saw some lights moving on the walls. The walls were rough I suppose because the lights moved all jiggle jaggle."

"Jiggle jaggle?"

"That's the only way I know to describe it. Nothing seemed to be flat or smooth."

"So, you touched them. Did they ever touch you?" Parker asked.

"Oh yeah. They often seemed to rub their hands, or palms on me. That's what it felt like."

"Why do you think they did that?" Nilsson asked.

"They rubbed me on areas that hurt, and each time they did, the pain was less."

Nilsson asked, "Have you ever heard of *laying on of hands?*"

"No."

"It's a charismatic church thing, a form of prayer healing."

"Well, if that's what they did, it worked."

"Did they ever scare you?" Parker asked.

"At first, yeah. I couldn't see anything, except sort of a blackness occasionally blocking the jiggle jaggle lights. It was like a nightmare, with some invisible demon standing next to me."

"And when they started touching you," Nilsson asked, "you lost your fear of them?"

"Well yeah, the pain started easing off. I thought that was great!" Cramer was beaming.

And then his smile started slowly fading. "Wait a minute, I thought you wanted to know about the instructor, Brinson. So why are you so curious about these underground people?"

Parker and Nilsson had been briefed to not answer that question; to lie if necessary.

Parker, perhaps better trained, answered for them. "I'm just glad they took good care of you. Because of that, I think you'll be headed home soon. And I think that would make my friend's family happy; to know his sacrifice helped save you by cushioning the impact."

"Yeah, he really was a hero if he placed himself in that position on purpose."

"Knowing Brinson," Parker said, "it was very deliberate. He is a hero."

With that, Parker sensed it was time to leave before Cramer became more suspicious. They'd learned a lot from a few minute's conversation. Someone would know how to reach Cramer if they needed a follow-up.

As Parker and Nilsson said their good-byes and were turning to leave, Cramer had one more comment.

"You know I did finally see one of them."

"How is that?"

"Just before they brought me to the surface they sat me in a little glowing room. It glowed when one of them entered, and he just looked at me for a while."

"What did he look like?"

"Like Tarzan. Tall, muscular, barefoot, wearing only a loin cloth."

"You're kidding?"

"No, I'm not."

Thinking of his own perception of Tarzan, Parker asked, "Did he have long dark hair?"

"No hair. He was bald."

"So they are human."

"Of course, what did you think?"

"Well, you didn't say," Parker answered.

After a thoughtful pause, Cramer added, "Except they can see in the dark somehow."

73

Then Cramer turned away and stared out the window into the bright Texas sunshine, apparently lost in his memories.

The two visitors took that as their cue to leave.

Parker and Nilsson were in a buoyant mood as they left the hospital.

"Mission accomplished," Parker said.

"Nice deflection shot there, Jason."

They had learned more about the "cave dwellers" as they were beginning to be called by the agency types, than any other interviewers. The CIA was right, Parker and Nilsson had a disarming approach. And they were hoping that approach would work on the cave dwellers.

CHAPTER 16. CANCÚN

The next morning at 0700 hours, Parker, Nilsson and two CIA keepers took off for Cancún in Parker's little five-seat Cessna Citation Mustang very light jet. Although cramped compared to a typical business jet, it was economical to fly, by jet standards. With strong northwesterly tailwinds at 37,000 feet, the 810 nautical mile trip would take just over two hours, mostly over the Gulf of Mexico.

Although the jet was designed for single pilot flight, Parker filled his copilot's seat with the CIA operative with some prior military jet time. Bud, as he wanted to be called, seemed a little leery of the diminutive jet, but soon gained an appreciation for Parker's ability to fly it.

Looking out his pilot's side window on a rare cloudless day, Parker could see the watery regions where he'd dived so many times, from the Flower Garden Banks, over to New Orleans, and beyond.

From the seat immediately behind him, Nilsson asked, "So Jason, is this thing hard to fly?"

"It's easier than the prop planes I fly. Not as many things to fiddle with."

"It sure is beautiful up here," Nilsson said.

Parker turned around and looked directly at Nilsson. "Are you joking, or are you remote viewing?"

Nilsson, just smiled, not answering.

The Agency type in the copilot's seat looked quizzically over at Nilsson, and pointed his thumb at him, for Parker's benefit. His expression seemed to be saying, "Is he for real?"

Parker just shrugged his shoulders. You never knew for sure.

Matt, the agent sitting next to Nilsson, was silent, looking out the window.

Speaking into his crew isolation headset which kept private the conversation between the two pilots, Parker said, "I've got four of our NDC civilians diving in some cave system down here, somewhere in Quintana Roo."

The copilot looked at him. "Four, really?"

"They're hardcore, dive long and deep all the time. They rarely dive together as a group, but this year was an exception."

"How well do you know them?"

"One works for me, Kelly Brightman. And you'll find this interesting; he used to work for the NSA, and apparently still does."

"Think we'll run into them? I'd like to meet them."

"We might," Parker said. "I'll give them a call once we've done some reconnoitering at our site."

Parker and his copilot sat quietly watching the large panel-mounted GPS count down the miles to their destination, until Bud asked if Parker's aviator sunglasses were polarized.

"No. I wear those on land, but in the air, the only chance I might get to avoid a mid-air collision would be by catching the glint off an approaching aircraft's windscreen. Polarized sunglasses eliminate that glint."

Bud nodded.

"What about you?" Parker asked.

Bud smiled, "For me, now, I have a similar concern. I want to catch the glint off a sniper's scope if I can."

Parker smiled back. "Yeah, that's a pretty good reason to stay unpolarized."

After an hour and a half high over featureless water, Parker was glad to see the approaching coastline of the Yucatan Peninsula. Though their little jet had two highly reliable Pratt & Whitney turbofan engines, he didn't relish a swim to shore "in the unlikely event of a water landing."

Parker began his slow descent into Cancún.

Caribbean air is typically clear with scattered white puffy clouds, and as the jet descended towards the Cancun airport, those pleasant conditions prevailed. They were vectored from the west for landing on runway 12 left, the slightly smaller of the Cancun airport's parallel runways.

On touchdown, Parker taxied the jet across a ramp that passed over a heavily trafficked road, and finally pulled into the ramp area on their left, the aircraft parking ramp for the Cancun Asur Fixed Base Operator.

After unloading the aircraft, paying for fuel, and pit stops at the restroom, they picked up a Toyota Land Cruiser rental car and headed back to the road they had just taxied over. Almost immediately they were running south on Mexico freeway 307, headed towards Akumal, some 50 miles distant.

Some of the best cavern and cave diving in the world lay near or just off Highway 307 that ran along the coast between Tulum and Cancun. At the Akumal exit, they turned right, drove through a residential area and followed a winding road through the jungle for about 8 miles.

The road became rougher as they approached their destination until it was little more than dual tracks in the white sand, crowded by short jungle vegetation. Parker was glad he'd rented a four- wheel drive vehicle.

After passing a couple of thatched-roof bar stops and an unnamed cenote in the midst of what seemed to be a mix of low jungle and scrub, Parker found the wilderness intersection he'd been seeking. After turning left, he rolled into the large clearing where James Cramer had been picked up by a U.S. Army helicopter.

The open space was large. Satellite imagery had shown it to be almost circular, with a diameter of about a half mile. In several places, the clearing was interrupted by groups of what seemed to be mangroves, but other than the tracks cutting directly across that clearing, there appeared to be absolutely nothing of importance in that location, just as the Army team had reported.

Parker turned off the engine. With the windows down, they sat and listened. At first, there was silence, then the nearby birds that had been disturbed by the Land Cruiser's arrival began tentative calling. First was the clear trilling whistle of a Kingbird, sounding much like a child's whistle with a ball inside it, blown hard at first, then falling off in pitch and strength. Then a Yellow-lored Amazon Parrot resumed its unmelodious squawking, which in turned seemed to irritate a family of Yucatan Jays so much that they launched into raucous bickering.

While Parker and the rest of the sighted men were simply hearing "jungle" sounds, Nilsson was picking out each distinctive sound, localizing where it came from, and treasuring the moment. He kept his joy to himself.

The near-coastal region of Quintana Roo was famous for its cenotes and half water-filled caves extending for miles inland from the shore. The caves had been almost gaudily decorated with stalactites and stalagmites many thousands of years ago when the sea level was lower. Now, the caves were completely dry except for the calcite containing water dripping from the Mexican rains and hurricanes.

Cave systems up and down the coast between Cancun and Tulum attracted hordes of scuba divers and cave divers exploring the crystal clear waters of this just slightly inland region. After a hard day of diving, a short drive to the coastal highway and beach bars was a great way to unwind and literally decompress, blowing off nitrogen in preparation for the next day's dives. With too much nitrogen in their bodies, there was always a chance of getting decompression sickness. Fortunately, the majority of the caves were shallow, but there were deeper caves still being explored. It was those caves that had attracted his diving friends from NDC.

The area where Parker, Joshua Nilsson and the two CIA agents were parked had no reported caves. However, the ground radar survey by the American helicopter crew had revealed some curious voids underground in the small savannah regions where Parker and his colleagues now sat.

The agents were armed, and as they climbed out of the vehicle, they were fully prepared to protect the two civilians from anyone who took a liking to them. However, since they were on Mexican territory, they had to be discrete with their holstered firearms.

Matt, the quieter of the two agents, seemed to be getting a little uneasy.

"Really, we're just going to sit here and wait?" he asked. "For what?"

Parker answered. "We'll let you know."

Parker opened his car door, signaling to Matt he was going to take a walk around, though not straying far from their vehicle. Nilsson sat quietly, focusing on his mental imagery of their location, as the two agents got out and surveyed the edges of the clearing.

"Are you getting anything Joshua?" Parker asked through an open car window.

"Not really, not like last time."

Bud glanced sideways at Nilsson. "You've been here before?"

Nilsson had remote viewed the location from Stockholm. "Yes and no," he said.

Matt quipped under his breath, "Well that's helpful."

Then Nilsson spoke with some stress in his voice. "The birds, they've stopped."

"So," Matt said, "maybe they ran out of stuff to fuss about."

"No. Something disturbed them."

Bud noticed something through his unpolarized sunglasses, "I see someone standing just inside that small stand of trees, about 100 yards away." He was pointing at about a 10 o'clock position relative to the front of the car.

The other agent said, "I see him too."

"He's walking this way," Parker said.

Nilsson quipped, "Well I don't see shit."

Parker smiled. Nilsson definitely had a dry sense of humor.

Through binoculars, Matt could see that the person approaching was oddly dressed, with long white pants and a Dallas Cowboys T-shirt. Although seemingly young and fit, he looked pale and bald.

Neither Matt nor Bud saw any bulges from concealed weapons or explosives.

While still fifty yards away, the man spoke. "Hola, ¿qué te trae a mi selva?"

He seemed to be friendly, but at the same time Parker thought he heard in his head, *So you are the one. Where's the girl?*

The pale stranger came within twenty yards and smiled. "OK, Gringos, obviously you don't speak Spanish. I asked, what brings you to my jungle?"

Parker and the agents looked at each other, not sure what to do.

"Alright, in words you'll understand, what the fuck are you doing here?"

Parker answered. "We're doing a hydrology survey."

"Really? Where's your equipment?"

"In the trunk."

Parker was bluffing.

Liar, he heard in his head.

Obviously, this was no ordinary Mexican they were talking to. From the narrowing slit of his eyes, the pale guy seemed to be losing his temper. "I tell you what, get the fuck off my property, now!"

Bud stepped forward, between Parker and the stranger. Matt took up a position about ten feet away to the side. If the stranger pulled a gun, he couldn't aim at both men simultaneously during that split second it would take for them to kill him.

"This is state property," Bud barked. "We have permission."

He was holding a letter from the Mexican government authorizing their visit. It was completely fake, but it looked official.

"If you want to argue the point," the bald man said, "you do it with my buddies, who by the way have you surrounded, and me."

"What buddies?" Matt asked.

The man pointed in a circle to the tree line all around them.

Bud said to Matt, "I'm not buying it."

Again, Parker heard a different voice. *Leave us alone.*

Parker turned to the agents. "Fellas, let's go. I'm not really in the mood for an international incident within an hour of our arrival in Mexico."

As the three sighted men returned to the car, Parker backed the car into a quartering turn, briefly directly facing the stranger. As he did, he saw the man, or whatever he was, staring intently at him. At the same time, he thought he heard a voice say, *We don't need you.*

Retracing their path down the jungle road, Bud said, "Well, you sure gave up on that quickly. He wasn't that intimidating."

"Got what I came for," Parker said.

Nilsson said, "He was guarding something. There's definitely something down there."

"Yes," Parker added. "And he's got a good reason to not want us around."

"You think it's a drug stash?" Bud asked. "I would have expected him to be armed if that was the case."

"No, not drugs," Parker answered.

What Parker didn't say was that it was much more important than drugs. He just didn't know exactly what it was, or how to reach it.

A few miles down the narrow sandy road, better suited to 4-wheel off-road vehicles than an automobile, Parker pulled into a path leading to the cenote they had passed on the way in.

"What are we doing?" all three men asked almost simultaneously.

"I want to have a look at this cenote. Wait here a minute, I'll be right back."

Bud said, "You know I can't do that. Let's make it quick, though. It's getting hot out here."

Bud walked beside Parker, his hand near his sidearm for the approximately 50-yard hike through the sand to get to a wooden dock leading to the water's edge. Walking out to the end of the poorly maintained dock, Parker saw it was about a 20-foot drop down to the water. Parker could read the signs in Spanish and English on the dock, which read, "Nadar solo. No buceo," and "Swimming only. No scuba diving."

The water was very clear, just as in most Yucatan cenotes so Parker could see down to the bottom which appeared to be nothing more than a jumble of rocks. There was nothing to suggest a cave entrance, but that didn't mean it wasn't there, somewhere, buried under the collapsed roof of what used to be a cave.

"Well Bud," as they turned back towards the car, "there's more than one way to skin a cat."

CHAPTER 17. CENOTE

When Parker headed back down the one-lane road towards Akumal, he started devising a plan.

By the time they arrived at the Villas DeRosa hotel, he had told the others to go ahead and check into their rooms, but he was going to pick up dive gear and return to the cenote they had stopped at, to take a look around.

"But the sign says no scuba diving," Bud reminded him.

Parker tilted his head and smiled, "Did you see anyone enforcing it?"

"No," Matt said.

"I'll take my chances."

"Then I'm going back with you," Matt said, "to keep guard."

"OK, if you insist. But for gosh sake don't shoot anyone."

Nilsson asked, "Jason, why is a hole in the ground so important to you?"

"Bud, while I'm getting my dive gear, how about pulling up the ground-penetrating radar images on my computer and showing everyone the apparent tunnel leading from beneath our clearing all the way to that cenote."

"Really?"

"Yes, really. There may be a back door into the subterranean area young Joshua saw when he was remote viewing."

"What?" Bud said. "He did what?"

Without answering, Parker excused himself and walked over to the Aquatech Dive Center located at the hotel office. He picked up an 80 cubic foot air tank, scuba regulator, mask, fins, and a buoyancy compensator, loaded them in the rental car, and then picked up Matt at his room.

When Matt came to the door, Parker said, "You really don't have to come along."

"You kidding? I don't want to miss anything."

On the way out of Akumal, they stopped at a market, and Parker bought two small bottles of food dye, then drove back down the narrow two-lane sandy road leading to the cenote.

Fortunately, there still was no other human presence at the cenote. While Matt surveilled the surrounding area, Parker donned his minimalist dive gear and jumped the twenty feet into the water. Fortunately, the ladder leading out of the cenote seemed just sturdy enough to support the weight of himself and his dive gear, so after his dive, he'd be able to make a hasty retreat if needed.

As expected, the water was cool but not cold, and clear enough to allow him to easily see the bottom at a maximum depth of 60 feet. However, in the center of the cenote was a conical mound of rubble from the old collapsed cave ceiling. The pile of broken rocks rose at least thirty feet off the bottom.

Parker headed toward the portion of the cenote that generally lay in the direction of the ocean, which was seven miles to the east. Swimming along the circumference of the pit, he used his bare hands to search for signs of an outward current. When he finally sensed it, he opened one of the dye bottles and watched the dye get sucked into the downstream flow which seemed to disappear between the scattered and piled rocks from the ancient cave-in.

Having located the downstream flow, he circled around to a position on the bottom approximately 180° away. There the rocks were piled at least ten feet high all the way to the cenote wall, which would complicate finding the current source.

His hands located a fairly large area where water seemed to be flowing between the tumbled rocks, into the cistern. Opening his last bottle of dye, he confirmed that water was flowing from that general area, into the center of the cenote and around its circumference at the bottom of the pit. Fortunately, with the surrounding water as clear as it was, he could look straight up and identify an overhanging tree that would make a good surface landmark for the location of the cenote entrance.

A few minutes later, he was again on the water surface and climbing up the rickety stairs back to Matt and the waiting car. With luck, Matt would not have gotten into an argument or a gun fight, although Matt seemed to be one of those guys who did both on a regular basis.

"I found exactly what I was hunting for."

"Was it worth the climb? Matt asked.

83

"Worth every step."

During the short drive back, Parker briefed Matt on what he found, and what he needed.

"I need some EOD divers to move that mass of rocks down there so we can gain access to the main inflow tunnel."

Matt looked at him, quizzically. "Oh, is that all you need?"

Parker continued, "I think some well-placed TNT charges could move the rocks we need without blasting everything down there to kingdom come. I don't want to have even more collapse."

Matt just looked at him. He seemed to be wondering just who the hell this Parker guy really was.

CHAPTER 18. BLASTER GIRL

Explosive Ordnance Disposal Technician 1st Class Margaret Brown, affectionately nicknamed "Blaster Girl" by her Special Operation friends, was an experienced EOD technician. She was taller than the average female Navy diver, very attractive in a natural, non-made-up kind of way. Her dirty-blond hair stayed mounded in the way the Navy required but was, in fact, shoulder length when let down.

She was soft spoken under normal circumstances but had been heard barking out world-class profanities when other EOD techs were about to do something stupid.

Her specialty was blowing things up, in a controlled manner. As much as any of her EOD brethren, she enjoyed collecting ammunition, piling it together and then detonating it *en masse* to form a large fireball and small mushroom cloud.

Her special and almost supernatural expertise was in strategically placing charges to clear a path through debris from bombardments or even controlled demolitions. She was the gal people called when they made a mistake and blew up the entrance to something important.

And for that reason, someone had made the call to get EOD1 Brown pre-placed in Akumal, Quintana Roo. All she had been told was that there might be a mission for her, and she'd be getting the word from SOCOM in Tampa if it was time to go into action. If the call never came, then she could enjoy some well-deserved time off for her heroic actions in Afghanistan during her last deployment.

Of course, she couldn't do much without the tools of her trade, C4 and waterproofed TNT. When the call came, a U.S. SEAL platoon was already en route to bury a cache of her favorite explosives just off shore. What the Mexican government didn't know, wouldn't hurt them, theoretically.

Matt arranged a meeting between Parker and EOD1 Brown at the local cantina.

"Hey, I know you, from NDC," Parker said.

John Clarke

"And I heard about you and that crazy chick on my last deployment," she said. "I heard you two ran off together and got picked up by some undersea aliens. I couldn't believe it. Was that really true?"

"Well, not as you described it."

"We were all stunned," she said. "Holy crap, there really are aliens here. And Dr. Parker, you're the one who found them. That blew our minds."

"The operative word is 'were.' They were here, but not now. We found out about it a little late in the game."

"So, do you think someone else knew about them, and you sort of stumbled upon them?"

"I don't know what I think. But, I do know we have a job to do here, and I've heard you can help."

After Parker had given EOD1 Brown a brief summary of what needed to be done, she looked even more puzzled than before.

She tried to summarize what he'd just said. "So basically you want some rocks moved, underwater?"

"That's true."

"Those rocks must be hiding something important."

"Maybe."

"Well, Doc, this is a bit of a risky job, so I'd hope you've got more than a *maybe* for me. And by the way, what do the Mexicans know about this operation."

"Very little."

"So, you don't think my setting off explosives will alert them to something fishy going on?"

"The thing is, we're telling them we're trying to open up a new freshwater source for them."

"And they don't think that's just a little too magnanimous of us?"

"Some of them may, but money has a way of keeping folks quiet down here."

"And so do bullets. This sounds pretty sketchy to me."

He stopped and smiled at her. "Come on Blaster Girl — when has that stopped you before?"

"OK, long as we have top cover. I don't like flying solo in a foreign country, especially making noise."

"I hear you're pretty good at keeping things quiet when you have to."

She looked pensively off to the distance for a moment.

"So I suppose this is one of those times when I have to."

"You guessed it."

"Shit."

"So, if these rocks get moved, what then?"

"Well, ground-penetrating radar suggests we'll reveal a tunnel, a cave passage."

"You can count me out of that Doc. I don't do cave diving."

"I know. Turns out we have a group of NDC cave divers down here right now. They don't know it yet, but they'll be helping out."

"Really? And are you a cave diver?"

"I've done it when I was young and full of spunk. I still could, but it's not my thing."

"That's right. Flying's your thing."

"It's a useful avocation," he responded.

"So where does radar show this tunnel leading?"

"It seems to head to a clearing in the jungle. I'm guessing ground runoff collects there and sinks into the porous rock, forming an underground river."

"Hell, this place is full of those. Why is this one so special? Sounds like a lot of work for nothing."

"We'll find out when we get into it."

"You know Doc, something about this whole operation sounds sketchy to me."

He smiled at her. She was one clever chick; she reminded him of Laura, the gal who helped him uncover the undersea aliens.

"I just need you to do your part," he said, "and not ask too many questions."

"Yeah, I've been there, done that. I know how to be a good sailor. But I still think this is sketchy. I sure hope you don't mess up, Doc."

Parker nodded his head in agreement.

"Me too."

At 0600 hours the next day, with the air still cool and the sun slanting over the motel roofs, EOD1 Margaret Brown was loading up her vehicle to transport selected explosives, carefully disguised, up to the cenote.

Parker came by with his dive bag.

Margaret snapped at him. "Where do you think you're going with that gear?"

"I'm watching, of course. I thought you knew that."

"Not on this planet you're not. I work alone."

"But..."

"But shit. There's no way I'm risking either you or me with you in the water."

"Oh come on..."

"Don't look at me with those puppy-dog eyes. I'm not about to risk the only man who's had verified lengthy conversation with ETs, and been hosted by them. I'll catch shit."

"Won't you be dead?"

"Parker, I may look like a practical chick, but I do believe in the afterlife. And I'll be damned if I spend eternity saying, "I can't believe I blew that guy up.""

"OK, I got it. I'll sit this one out."

"Good. How about you and your funny buddies just keep the Policía Federal away from me. That would be great."

"Will do."

Parker had to admit he had no idea how they would do that, but that's where the CIA connections came in. Subterfuge was their expertise.

Two hours later, Parker and Brown were safely away from the cenote when she pushed the plunger which ignited the carefully placed and tamped explosives. The water roiled, and a geyser shot about thirty feet into the air, but other than that the explosion was surprisingly muted.

"Do you think it worked?"

"Doc, your rocks are moved, I'll bet you that. Whether they were blocking anything, or not, is your worry, not mine."

An hour later the particles suspended in the water by the multiple small explosions had cleared enough for Parker to rig up for a dive.

"Not so fast Doc. I'm going with you. I want to see my handiwork first hand."

The first thirty feet of the dive was murky from the stirred up sediment, but the closer to the bottom they got, and the closer to the cross flow they swam, the clearer the water became.

And then, on the upstream side, Parker saw it, an opening large enough for two divers to swim in side by side. The really great news was that the ground-penetrating radar showed what looked like an equally large tunnel, all the way to the clearing guarded by one of the strangest men Parker had ever met.

And then he wondered, had that tunnel opening been blasted closed at some time in the past? And if so, why?

CHAPTER 19. ELEKTROSTAL

Oleg Kyznetsov's nap was disturbed by a knock on the door of his modest apartment in the town of Elektrostal, fifty-four kilometers east of the Kremlin. Age had not been kind to his knees, so it was with considerable effort he rose from his sofa to greet whoever was not so politely knocking on his door.

The wooden door, with two different shades of green paint showing, opened with a creak. Standing in the dim light of the hallway were two young men who Kynetsov did not know.

"Tovarich Kynetsov, we were sent by Moscow to seek your help for a little problem we have. Comrade Grigorev said you might be willing to help us."

Tovarich, Comrade, and Grigorev were three words Kynetsov had not heard for a long time. They all harkened back to his days working for the KGB, before he was retired from government "research," or as he knew it, psychic spying.

His days both before and after that time of government service were spent working for the 9th Radio Center in Elektrostal, until his full retirement 10 years ago. Having gained the trust of those at the radio station he was able to be briefed on a weekly basis by his former colleagues, briefed on the truth, as Russia saw it, which of course was not what was being broadcast by the radio station.

"Come in, but I'm not sure how an old man can help anyone. I'm not doing anything these days. Nothing of value anyway."

Kynetsov moved slowly and jerkily into the room before turning around to face his visitors who had followed him a few feet past the door.

"Am I supposed to know you? I forget things these days, so I'm sorry, I don't recognize your faces."

"No, you don't know us."

"Good, that's one less thing for me to worry about. But, you should at least tell me who you are."

"It doesn't matter."

"Oh, I see," he said resignedly. "You're one of *those* guys."

"We hear that you were a psychic spy for us in the 60's and 70's. One of the best, and one of the few we can locate now."

"Well, I suspect I'm one of the few who was not disappeared. Why I was saved, I don't know. But maybe they thought I'd prove useful someday. Unless of course," he looked at them with head slightly bowed, but smiling, "today is my day to disappear."

"No, no, it is as you say. We need you."

"Good, then please sit down. My chairs are not particularly comfortable, but perhaps you won't be staying long. In the old days, I'd offer you vodka, but I can't afford it now so tap water will have to do if you're interested."

"No, thank-you, we're fine."

Of the two visitors, the oldest and tallest was the only one doing the talking. The other kept strangely quiet. Kynetsov figured that one was the assassin, but he really couldn't tell if he was on duty today or not. Maybe he came along just to take notes.

The taller one spoke again. "So I'm curious about your spying career. Why are you not still working?"

"You must not know much about it, or you would know." Kynetsov looked at him, slightly perplexed. Why wouldn't they be better prepared?

Then he realized they probably were prepared, and wanted to see if the old man could still put together the pieces — to see if he was mentally competent. After all, with psychic spies, it's difficult to know when they're lying or not.

With that thought in mind, he decided he would weave a fantastic, but accurate, story for these young novices.

"What is the need for distant viewing, *Remote Viewing* as the Americans call it. We can now see most anything we want, with the use of satellites. And now the U.S. even lets us fly our spy aircraft right over their territory viewing and filming whatever we like. Our planes fly over Eglin Air Force Base, spy on the bikinis on the Florida Gulf Coast, photograph the Panama City Navy Base and Tyndall Air Force Base, then fly over to the nuclear submarine base at Kings Bay in Georgia. So tell me, why would you need someone like me?"

"I hear you were good at what you did."

"Still am. I'm the best. I'm so good I can be making love to a beautiful woman and at the same time record the serial numbers of enemy missile warheads 5000 kilometers away."

"You're kidding me."

Kynetsov sighed. "Well, to tell you the truth, they weren't so beautiful, but still, you get the idea."

"That must have made them angry."

"Just the opposite — they thought I was keeping count."

The tall one laughed at the ridiculousness of it all. "Well, I'm hoping you won't need a partner for this one."

"This one what?"

"A target. I'm betting it will be the most difficult of your career."

"Is there money involved?"

"Please, Tovarich, you are a patriot."

"A starving patriot."

"OK, yes there will be many rubles if you target what we need."

Under his breath, Kynetsov muttered, "I'd prefer dollars."

For the moment, the tall guy ignored that comment.

"Do you have coordinates for me?"

The shorter Russian pulled out a slip of paper and handed it to Kynetsov.

51° 52'09.13"N 104° 58'16.08" E.

"Elevation?"

0 meters.

"Hmmm… Come back tomorrow, this time, and I'll tell you what I see."

The two strangers looked at each other, quizzically.

"That's it," Kynetsov said, "That's how it works."

"o-KEI." The two men shrugged and turned toward the door.

As they stepped outside, they turned back towards Kynetsov. He motioned for them to close the door.

Kynetsov's psychic spy colleagues had elaborate ways of viewing their assigned targets. But Kynetsov's method was simplicity itself. After that evening's dinner of bacon, boiled potatoes and pickles, washed down with some cheap Portwine, he took a long soaking bath.

Lying motionless in the warm water until his skin was wrinkled from head to toe, he let random images flow to and fro, forming a composite image that eventually solidified into a life-like scene. Once the scene formed completely, he could seemingly step into the scene, allowing him to control it at will.

However, the scene before him was unlike any he'd seen before. At first, he thought he was looking at an aircraft, but unlike in years past, the object was not in the U.K. or the U.S. It was in his own country.

Why would he be spying on an object in his own country? This made no sense.

As he realized the craft was floating in water, he willed himself to travel just over the water surface. Then he could see that it was not a normal aircraft but something more akin to the American B2 bomber.

But two things about that made no sense. He was clearly underground, and he had the sense he was fairly deep underground. And an American bomber would not be floating. And if those were navigation lights on the ship's border, they were the biggest lights he'd ever seen on an aircraft.

Kynetsov had to keep turning the warm water on with his toes to keep things comfortable in the tub.

As he mentally circled the thing, he realized he could find no way into the craft. So he decided to enter it by sheer willpower, something he had never before attempted. Surprisingly, it worked.

A knock came on the door the next morning at 10 AM. When he opened it, it was the two men from the day before.

"You're early."

"We have to get back to Moscow for lunch. What do you have for us?"

"It's very interesting on the outside, a triangular craft with rounded corners and incredibly large lights on its periphery, but inside is a different matter."

"You got inside?"

"Yes, but it was very boring. There was nothing in it. It was empty. No machinery, nothing."

"Did you see any motors, engines, and plumbing?"

"Like I said, nothing. Nothing means nothing."

"How did you get inside? What was the trick? We can't do it."

"So what I'm describing makes sense to you?"

"Yes."

"What the hell is it?"

The two men looked at each other with concern, and Kynetsov wished he hadn't asked. The two men backed up so they could talk privately, and after a moment the tall man returned.

"It's a spaceship."

"Really? We have a spaceship like that?"

"We have it, but it's not ours."

"American?"

"No."

With that answer, Kynetsov realized that he was now walking on very thin ice. Anything else he asked could put his life in danger. But it was also apparent that the two men would be saying nothing else about it, except to ask an important question.

"Exactly how did you get inside?"

"Viewing at a distance is mental projection. Physical barriers do not matter much. The only real barrier is mental, and if you can handle the mental problems, then physical barriers like walls and containers really don't exist."

"So, you can't help us get inside?"

"No. But I don't see why you'd want to. There's nothing in there."

CHAPTER 20. COMPLICATIONS

Matt walked up to the patio table where Nilsson, Parker, and Bud were seated, drinking rum and watching the waves washing in from the Eastern Caribbean.

Matt said, "I just got off the phone from Detrick. I briefed them on our encounter with that dude in the clearing."

"The telepathic guy?"

"What do you mean?"

"Oops, I guess I forgot to tell you. He was having two conversations simultaneously: one verbal to you, and one telepathic with me."

"Well this is news," Matt said. "Why didn't you share that before now?"

"Guess it slipped my mind."

Parker's words were not convincing. He did enjoy withholding tidbits from the Company guys when he felt he could get away with it.

"So this telepathy business, I thought it only worked with," he spoke more quietly, "the Canyoneers."

"I call them Frogs."

"Yes, I know you do. But that's not their name."

"Just so you know, they called themselves *humans*."

"That's funny," but Matt wasn't laughing when he said it.

"Anyway, Langley is not thrilled with your plan to use civilians for the cave dive you have planned."

"You know any military cave diving groups?"

Matt had a blank look on his face.

"Me neither," Parker said. "So we don't have a choice, do we?"

"Not everyone in your team has security clearances."

"OK, now to the meat of the problem. What's so classified about finding people who prefer to hang out in a cave? Maybe they don't like the tropical heat down here."

"But you just said they're telepathic."

"One is. And I guess I am too, but that's hardly a secret. And who knows, he might be the only one down there with that skill. Are you associating them with the Frogs just because one of them is telepathic?"

"Well, let me ask you this. Has there been anyone besides the Frogs that you've had telepathic communication with?"

Parker thought for a moment. "I see your point. But this last one could've been a fluke."

"What do you think the ones in the cave look like?"

"Like people. What do you expect, little purple people eaters?"

"What's that?"

"Oh my gosh, didn't you learn anything in school?"

"Is that some sort of Star Wars creature?" Matt asked.

"No, about twenty years before that; it was a silly song. But my point is, I expect them to look just like the guy we saw guarding the entrance."

"So what are you going to say when your divers ask why we're going to so much trouble and expense? Just because we want them to explore yet another cave?"

"Well, let me think about that. We can't tell them exactly why we want to find these… people."

"No, certainly not," Matt said abruptly. "And you better think fast, because we need to get this op underway."

"What about Langley?"

"I guess we'll just have to trust you to do the right thing. But for God's sake, don't screw up."

With that, Matt marched back to his room for another secure satellite phone call, presumably to soothe Langley's anxiety — and his own. He always kept medicinal Scotch around for that purpose.

The three men remaining at the table sat still for a moment, as Parker and Bud played with their beers.

Parker broke the silence. "Bud, I know you're a junior Agency guy, but what's your take on this, now that we know your bosses are getting uptight."

Bud smiled nervously. "Well, let me put it this way. If we are perceived as going rogue, my career's going to suffer big time."

Parker winced, "Thanks for the vote of confidence."

Bud continued, "But I know these people are important since they may be our last link to the Frogs."

Parker smiled, "I'm glad I've gained at least one convert. If you'd seen them, you'd know why I call them that."

Nilsson had been sitting very quietly, absorbing what was going on around him, until now.

"You know Jason, I get the feeling they're not quite as human as you're making them out to be."

Parker took a slow, deep breath. And then he thought, and thought some more.

Finally, "We'll cross that bridge when we get to it."

CHAPTER 21. AKUMAL

Once Parker got back to Akumal, he gave Kelly Brightman a call. Brightman said, "We're in the next town. We've been diving in Dos Ojos."

"I hear that's a gorgeous cave system," Parker said.

"And deep, just the way we like it."

"What if I said we just opened up a brand new cave for you to explore?"

"First of all, I'd say you're full of shit. And then I'd say, where is it? You know, just in case you're not completely full of it."

"It's just a few miles west of here."

"Great. We're staying at the Akumal Beach Resort, so we can meet there tonight, and you can brief us."

"That's convenient since we're staying there too."

"Who's we?"

"Can't say."

"Oh geesh Jason, I don't even want to know. You keep some strange company."

Parker laughed. "I've been told that before."

Parker watched the NDC group when they entered the bar at 6 o'clock. Brightman, the first one into the room, saw Parker immediately.

"Where are your friends?"

"They're back in their room. You'll meet them soon enough."

"So this cave, what can you tell me about it?"

"We have ground-penetrating radar imagery to show it seems to be pretty much an open channel that stretches for at least 3000 feet, with a second cavity reaching as far as two miles."

"Who uses ground-penetrating radar down here?"

"The Army."

"Mexican Army?"

"No, ours."

Brightman gave Parker a very strange look.

"Really?"

"Yep. We think this tunnel could turn out to be real interesting."

"Almost all of them down here are. So what makes this one interesting?"

"What's interesting is that you and me, and the rest of the NDC dive team, will be the first to dive it."

Brightman grinned broadly. "Count me in." He waved the rest of the team over, all of them friends of Parker, but a little suspicious of the people he'd been known to hang around with lately; especially the Frogs.

"Fellas, Jason has a mission for us, if we choose to participate. It's a new, unexplored tunnel."

"Unexplored? How can that be, this close to the Mecca of cave diving?"

Parker explained. "The tunnel was closed by a rock fall, but I recently convinced EOD to blast the rocks away from the entrance to a cenote which is only about 6 miles from here."

"Why?"

"What do you mean?"

"Why would EOD blast open a new tunnel for us?"

"Practice, I guess."

"So what do we know about the tunnel?"

"We think it's about 3000 feet long as the crow flies."

"If it's uncharted, how do you know?"

"We think we know where it comes to the surface, but there's no easy access there."

"Well, that's kind of strange."

"How deep does it go?" someone else asked.

"It's unexplored, so we don't know. But it's probably not as deep as Dos Ojos."

"That's a good thing. I don't have all day to decompress from 400 feet."

The assembled group laughed in agreement, except for Parker. He knew he had no idea what they'd be encountering.

Parker continued, "Since we don't know what to expect, I suggest we use only the rebreathers and save our open circuit bottles for bailout."

"Then we better hope the tunnel is large enough for us to use our rebreathers. I don't look forward to getting wedged in some place."

Parker said clearly for emphasis. "As always, anyone of us can call the dive at any time. But to sweeten the deal, I have some friends who are going to deliver, tonight, full face masks and diver to diver through water communications. So we can chat with each other and keep abreast of what everyone's thinking. Or what you see."

"Well damn, I wish I had friends like that."

"Are you all in?" Parker asked.

"We'd be stupid not to."

"Not so fast," the only blond-haired team member of the team said. "What's the catch?"

"The catch. Yes, there is a catch," Parker admitted. "The catch is, there may be somebody there when we get to the end of the tunnel."

"Are you kidding us? What kind of someones?"

Another said, "Are you talking, like terrorists?"

Another voiced his concern, "Or Frogs?"

"Relax fellows. These are indigenous peoples. They may be primitive since they're literally cave people, but they're nice. And we know that because a while back they nursed a badly broken kid back to health. He's recovering in a hospital in San Antonio, and has nothing but good things to say about the natives."

"Holy shit, what are we talking about here? A surviving group of Neanderthals?"

Parker had to laugh. "No, not that primitive."

Matt wandered into the room and Parker motioned him over.

"Folks, this is Matt. Matt's going to get the mask and comm gear sent to us tonight."

"I am? What gear are you talking about?"

"I'll brief you later Matt," Parker continued. "Fellas, are all your gear and scooters fully functional?"

Brightman responded with a grin. "We need a backup scooter or two if you're buying. They're only 6K a pop — small change for you."

"Don't push your luck," Parker responded.

"No, I'm serious. We need a spare in case one poops out. We don't know how long or deep the swim would be if someone lost a scooter or needed a long-distance tow."

"OK, we'll make that happen." Then looking around the group at the table, Parker said, "So really, are we all good?"

"Not so fast. Indigenous cave people?"

"Consider it a National Geographic mission. We'll be exploring a new cave, and then surprise, surprise, we might encounter a secret tribe of subterranean Mexicans. Wouldn't that be a cool headline?"

"Long as they don't eat us," one of the team said, only half smiling. "So, are we good?"

One of the team muttered, "Nat Geo mission, new gear. I like it."

Parker corrected him, "It's not really Nat Geo. But, yes, the gear is free, and yours to keep."

As a group they smiled and nodded in unison. Brightman said, "Good to go, Boss."

The shaggiest-haired diver of the group, Adam said, "We don't have a lot of time to put this together. Gotta get tanks filled, sorb replenished, buy new line. And are we having a knotting party tonight?"

When surveying new caves and tunnels, thin survey and safety lines get laid out from a diver-carried reel. A survey diver marks on a compass board the compass direction for the line in front of him, and distance is measured by knots tied every ten feet in the line. Each knot has to be tied in advance at a sometimes raucous gathering called the knotting party. Raucous or not, it is all serious business because that line will mark their way out. If a diver loses the line under turbid conditions, they might never find their way out again.

Brightman said, "Hell yeah, laying line in a virgin cave? This is what we live for guys."

"OK," Parker said with a smile. "Let's do this thing."

By ten o'clock that evening, a flight carrying full face masks custom fitted to the divers, and comms gear enough for the five divers and two spare scooters had landed at the Tulum airport. Shortly after that the gear was quietly delivered to the group in Akumal as they were still knotting lines.

They also brought an electronically-controlled rebreather for Parker, fresh batteries and fresh absorbent, dive light, harness, and side mount bottles for bailout gas. And for all, they brought Cyalume glow sticks.

"Why do we need these?" Parker asked. "We have as much combined candlepower as a 747 on short final."

"One of our tech geeks thought you might need these, so he threw in a dozen."

"Well, that's great," Adam complained. "Something else to carry."

101

Greg, the only diver born and raised in South Alabama, with the accent to prove it, turned towards Parker. "So Jason, are you the dive team leader?"

"I don't know. What do you guys think?"

Adam responded immediately. "It's a bad idea. Jason's organizing this, so he has the most to lose if we abort. We shouldn't let his motivation affect our dive decisions."

Brightman added, "I know you're my boss, Jason, but I agree with Adam."

Parker answered, "Well then that makes three of us. I think the most experienced of us in these caves should be the leader. And I think that's Greg. Is that correct?"

Greg nodded quietly.

"Any dissent?" Parker asked. "If not, then it's settled."

As Matt was passing out the new equipment and explaining how the communication gear worked, Brightman paused to stare at Parker.

Parker noticed. "What's up, Kelly?"

"There's something not quite right about this, Jason. Somebody's going to a lot of trouble to make this dive happen. If you weren't going with us, I'd be walking out right now."

Parker understood exactly what he was saying. "I get it, but I am going. It'll be OK."

"I might be more convinced if we knew what we'd be encountering."

"Explorers never know that, do they?"

Adam answered for Brightman, "No, they don't."

CHAPTER 22. DARK SIDE OF THE MOON

By 0600 hours the group had loaded up their gear and headed up the road west of Akumal as Parker guided them to the cenote where their adventure would begin. The two CIA agents followed behind in the Land Cruiser, feeling more nervous than usual. For the first time in a long while, their assets would be completely out of touch for an unknown period of time. If the divers got into trouble, there was not a thing anyone could do to help.

That morning before leaving, Parker had told the agents the dive team would essentially be on the dark side of the moon once they entered the cave, a cave that led to God knows where. There was operational risk involved, but that was exactly what the civilian team lived for.

Once at the site, the team carefully unloaded the gear, suited up, made pre-dive checks and climbed down the ladder to the water's surface. Parker could tell the climb back up would be more difficult, but he planned to use the agents waiting on the surface to hoist up their gear until the first diver could reach the top to help.

Once pre-dive checks were completed without any anomalies, the team submerged and Parker led them to the tunnel entrance. The current was light, visibility was good, and this part of the tunnel was large enough for two divers to scooter side by side.

As agreed, Parker motioned Greg into the lead. Greg tied off his line at the entrance and then began spooling line out as they moved on. Initially, the rest of the divers clustered around them eager to see what this new tunnel looked like. However, the tunnel quickly began to narrow, and the team fell into a single file as they peered into a large tunnel, a so-called "going cave."

No one was surprised when the tunnel began a downward slope, but all were wondering just how deep it would go. The team paused every so often as Greg found good rock projections to tie off the line, then they continued their generally northwest progression with the depth gradually increasing. At the hundred foot mark, the tunnel

John Clarke

began an equally gentle ascent, to the relief of the team which did not relish extensive decompression upon their return.

The tunnel was relatively barren, void of the almost gaudy stalactites and stalagmites found in other underwater tunnels in the region. Those limestone features had formed during the millennia when sea water levels were lower, and the caves were dry.

The group had not been used to diving with underwater comms, so it took them awhile to realize they could chat while diving. It didn't seem natural, but finally one of the dive team could not resist poking fun at one of his dive team members following up the rear.

"You know, Little Man, I can't help worrying about you with that mechanical rig of yours. When are you going to get a big boy rebreather like me, and Parker?"

Brett Middleman, being somewhat short in stature, had earned the nickname Little Man. If he had been sensitive about what other divers called him, he would not have been a good diver. Divers, like soldiers, are merciless in their good-natured ribbing of each other.

"Parker didn't have to pay for his. I did. But don't you worry, this semiclosed rig is tried and proven. I bet it'll outlast your rig."

"Ha, we'll see about that."

Parker's scooter was pulling him through the water at a seemingly break-neck speed. He loosened his grip on the throttle on occasion to navigate the turns in the channel, and to wait for Greg, the lead diver, to stop and tie off. As much as possible, however, Parker opened the scooter up so much that the breathing hoses on his rebreather were flapping in the current. He had to cinch down his mask so it wouldn't be ripped off his head as they rushed through the almost circular limestone tube deep underground.

Parker had a still vivid memory of a Sylvester and Tweety Bird cartoon he saw as a child. A stark scene emblazoned itself into Parker's mind when Tweety Bird, sitting in a sink, got sucked down the drain. As traumatic as that scene had been during his early years, he found it ironic that he was now rushing headlong into another drain of sorts, just as dark as the drain in the cartoon. But rather than feel fear, he felt exhilaration — the exhilaration of being in unexplored passages.

The tunnel narrowed abruptly, forcing the divers to squeeze through the narrowest part single file. As Parker played his light on Greg and the narrowest portion of the opening, he could see the unmistakable silvery sheen of an air-water interface just on the other side of the constriction.

When Greg slipped through the narrow portion, he disappeared. Parker could no longer see Greg's painfully bright light. It was as if he'd been sucked into a black hole.

Perhaps the tunnel had made a sudden turn. He was probably just around the corner. "Greg, I don't see you. Did you take a hard turn?"

There was no response.

Parker had slowed his scooter considerably, both to avoid contacting the walls of the constriction, and to prepare for a hard turn. Just as he entered the constriction he saw two things, Greg and his scooter, dark, dead ahead, and shiny metal plates embedded in the walls of the tunnel.

Just as he squirted through the narrow opening, his own light went out, and his scooter died.

The momentum from the scooter carried him just out of the way as the next diver, initially brightening the area where Parker was, experienced the same calamitous result, total electrical failure.

Parker tried to shout a warning to the following divers, but even his comms were dead.

As the divers entered the constriction in sequence, their lights briefly illuminated the growing cluster of divers dead in the water just ahead. Parker's head's up display flickered then went dark. He instinctively checked his rig's handset which showed the status of his life support system, but it was dark. Normally it was only dark when turned off.

Then he realized that if the rig's electronics were dead, as were his primary and backup lights, and his comms, then he might have oxygen available for only a very short time.

He felt for the Cyalume sticks he'd stuck in the pockets of his buoyancy stabilizer vest, found one of the tubular objects, and sharply bent it to break the internal glass vial. That breakage allowed chemicals to react, producing light from fluorescence.

He waved his fluorescing stick to the others who were now all assembled, completely confused, in the inky blackness of their portion of the passageway.

Remembering that he'd seen the reflection from an air-water interface, he knew that at least some sort of gas pocket lay above them. Without knowing if his rebreather was providing a safe breathing mixture, time was counting down to the point where he would pass out and drown.

John Clarke

He switched to his bail-out gas and waved the light to show the others what he was doing.

Hopefully, they would start checking their own displays. If they were also black, they would be following suit, switching to their bail-out gas.

The problem was, they all needed that backup gas supply to return to the safety of the opening of the cave, a good two to three thousand feet away.

Ironically, the only diver not in extremis was Little Man, the diver with the mechanical rig.

Although it was risky to ascend to the gas pocket and inhale its contents, which could be poisonous, Parker had no other choice. He was not willing to burn through his limited bailout gas supply just floating in the darkness. Hopefully, the others were watching him, reaching for their own fluorescent glow sticks, and would notice that he was rising to the bubble. With luck they would notice if he passed out.

If that happened, the others would remain on their bailout gas and attempt to return to the cave entrance, feeling for the previously laid guideline.

There were a lot of *ifs* in play as Parker broke the surface, removed his mouthpiece, and took a shallow breath of whatever lay above.

The first breath seemed to be OK, causing no stinging of his airways, and not making him woozy. He took another breath, and for all he could tell, they had stumbled into an air-filled portion of the cave. He could not believe their great luck.

He held the chem light close to his hand and motioned the other divers to come to the water surface.

As they were heading up to him, he used his own faint glowing stick to search their surroundings and found the air chamber had a small sandy beach large enough for them to climb onto. Their luck had just improved immensely.

One after another the divers started popping to the surface, removing their mouthpieces and asking "What just happened?" Every one of them said basically the same thing with a variety of expletives added here and there, which proved what Parker already knew. A diver's vocabulary focuses on the basics when stressed.

"Don't know, but fellas, we need to assess our situation before we just abort and head back on our own power."

106

The beach was wide enough for all of them to drag their lights, scooters and themselves up on the dark beach.

Parker, the most senior of the group, was taking charge. Greg, the first of the group to get knocked out of commission, was hesitant to speak.

"Everyone's lights are out, but what about the scooters?"

Everyone confirmed their scooters were dead.

"How about your rebreathers?"

Little Man said, "Mine's fine. I just secured the fresh gas flow."

The fellow who had been ribbing Little Man about his simplistic manual rebreather said, "Remind me to never, ever criticize you for your gear. You're the only one of us able to use your rebreather."

In reality, some of the better-trained divers could manually and blindly add oxygen intermittently, but such action was guesswork without the ability to monitor their oxygen sensors. It was a very risky procedure compared to going open-circuit bailout, like scuba divers.

Parker, disbelieving their bad luck, asked, "Is it true, everything electrical is dead?"

One after another they admitted the unbelievable.

"What the hell could do that? And why?"

Parker had some experience with the Army Corps of Engineers and their use of electrical fish barriers. "I've seen something that could do this, electrical barriers in Chicago and Minnesota. They keep invasive fish species out of the Great Lakes."

"Why weren't we shocked?"

"I guess it's because we're insulated by our wetsuits."

"Jason, you mean to tell me these primitive people have figured out how to keep us out of here?"

"I don't know. But obviously, it didn't work because we're here."

"Wherever here is. And once our light sticks fade, we'll be in total darkness. We're so screwed."

From out of the darkness, someone said, "I wish I hadn't left my glow sticks behind."

Parker said, "Well that's a thought. How many of them do we have?"

"I have one more besides the one I'm using."

"I have two, somewhere, if I can find them."

Parker wanted to put a plan together before all the light faded, but he noticed that Brightman was walking away from the group with his light.

"Where are you going, Kelly?"

"This is a large chamber, with plenty of dry floor, and wide. The water's only flowing in the middle. We're in a mostly dry cave."

"Come back. We need to talk this over."

When Brightman was once again with them, Parker started the decision-making process. "Theoretically, Little Man can make it back in the dark by following the line back to the entrance. It's a long swim without the scooters, but doable. He has his rebreather gas and his bailout gas. He has hours of duration."

"But the rest of us may not have enough bailout."

"You should!" Greg said, sounding appropriately judgmental.

Parker chimed in again, "But if you miscalculated, you're dead."

"That could be me," someone said.

Adam piped up, "We all have individual methods of calculating our bailout gas requirement, but I bet you right now none of us know if we'll have enough to make the trip back without scooters, especially with that 100-foot depth near the beginning. That'll be brutal for our open circuit gas consumption. And deco? Forget about it. We won't know what we need till we're in it."

Parker continued, "On the other hand, Brightman is right. We're in a cave with potentially plenty of air. I suggest we see where this thing leads before we lose all the light. And if it goes nowhere, we can always follow the river back to this sump."

Little Man spoke up, "I can always head out and get help while you guys wait here."

Parker said, "I suggest we make that decision once we better understand what we're dealing with."

"But Jason, you said there are people here."

"That's what we think."

"And these are people who use electricity to keep people out?"

Parker didn't know how to answer that.

"So these people may not take kindly to our presence."

"No, remember I said we have information that they're helpful. Maybe they can help us out."

"Jason, I don't mind exploring this cave while we still have a little light, but I'd just as soon not meet anybody I don't know down here. And I don't buy what you say about them being primitive — not if they can use electricity as a weapon."

"Well, it's better than drowning," Parker said.

Parker was not sure he'd convinced anyone with that Pollyanna statement, himself included.

CHAPTER 23. THE CAVE

Parker was leading the group as much by sound as by sight. At first, the gurgling sound of water was localized to their right, a short distance away. They were more interested in using their dim lighting to view the cave floor and to look out for any head-knocker projections looming out from the walls, so they didn't notice that the single channel seemed to be dividing into multiple smaller channels as they headed upstream. Before long, the running water sound began to soften and spread out before them.

Little Man called for a halt. "This is stupid fellows. At this rate, we'll get both lost and blind, soon as our glow sticks go out. I'm going back while I can and get the hell out of here."

Greg agreed. "I'm not going to let him go by himself. I'm getting out of here while I can. We accomplished our mission."

As much as Parker hated to admit they were right, they were right. He had been too focused on his real mission, which was not the same as the group's mission. They had agreed to explore the newly opened tunnel. Getting lost in an unexplored cave without lights or lines really was stupid, and suicidal.

"Little Man's right" Parker confessed. "We need to backtrack while we can. The cave is getting too complex. Plus I'm starting to roast in this wetsuit."

Parker was disappointed that their mission was ending prematurely, but he was committed to coming back to continue the exploration, by himself if need be. As for the others, they seemed delighted to be getting back into the water, something they knew well, even if there was some risk involved. The cave was not inviting.

The glow sticks were getting dim again by the time the group made its way back to the pool where they had exited the water. Parker had to light off his last glow stick so he could see well enough to arrange his rebreather so no hoses would get pinched when he put it on his back. Straightening a cluster of hoses and lines in the dark is a learned skill, but a little light made it much easier. Kelly helped hold the rig up while Parker tightened his harness. Parker then assisted Kelly in the same manner, stabilizing him until his rebreather was likewise ready to go. Little Man with a simpler, non-electronically controlled unit, beat everyone else into the water. With the luxury of plenty of remaining gas, he inflated his buoyancy wings and floated in the oddly attractive dim yellow light, waiting for the rest.

Parker turned to look at Little Man, who seemed quite comfortable with the situation. He had plenty of onboard gas, and enough bailout gas to share with any one diver running low. But if they were all low on gas, he wouldn't have enough to share.

"You know Jason," Greg commented, "no one ever plans on all the scooters dying, and all the electronics. We brought two spare scooters, but they're dead too. We might not make it back."

At that moment, Parker realized what he had to do. His mission was over, and as long as he had an unlimited supply of air to breathe, he could wait for the team to come back for him.

"If you're concerned," Parker said, "then you can stay here, with me. I'll stay and donate my bailout gas. You guys can split it up long as someone doesn't mind swimming with an extra bottle or two."

Adam asked, "What was the maximum operating depth on your bailout?"

"60 feet."

"Well damn, we have to go down to 100 ft. No wonder you want to stay."

A grunt came from behind Parker, and a heavy thud reverberated through the space where they had assembled.

"Shit!"

And that was followed by a snapping sound, followed by a yelp as Brightman, a big man, and his gear hit the rocky floor beneath them. He had slipped on the wet cave floor, hit the ground with his right knee, rotating his back away from the wall in an attempt to protect his back-mounted rebreather from the weight of his falling body. But as he attempted to push back off the floor with his twisted leg, the anterior cruciate ligament snapped.

"Damn, you no good bastard," he shouted, as if cursing his own ruined knee would somehow make the pain less.

Not wanting to be a wimp, Kelly dragged himself and his gear into the water and tried kicking, but screamed with the very first kick. He was done. Parker and Greg together had to pull Brightman back onto the sand and rock.

111

Parker recognized the sound of a classic ACL tear, and with that, he knew Brightman would not be able to frog kick his way out of the cave.

If any of them had the use of a scooter, they could have dragged the large man along behind them, but none of them would be able to swim and tow him. Kelly Brightman was stuck.

Parker said in an unusually resonant voice, "That makes two of us staying behind, and even more bailout gas for you guys to divvy up. But you fellows better come back for us, bringing spare scooters. Just remember to mark the constriction on your way out and leave the scooters just on the other side of it. I don't want them getting zapped too."

"Yeah, what's up with that Jason?" Brightman asked. "You think it's an old power cable?"

Brightman was not only an electrical engineer, but he had helped Parker with the Corp of Engineers project. He knew a lot about electricity in the water.

"Your guess is as good as mine."

Greg told Parker, "You know this will take a while. We have to find new scooters ..."

"Talk to my guys," Parker said, interrupting Greg.

"... and get our rebreathers repaired," Greg continued.

Parker's response was snappy. "Do that on your own time. My guys will get you new rebreathers too. Just give them a list."

Someone else shouted out, "Jason, who in the hell are these guys?"

"You don't need to know."

Greg said, "Sometimes Parker, I really don't like you."

Parker laughed. "I don't like myself sometimes either."

Greg continued, "If we get the help you think we will, we'll maybe be back in a couple of days. If you're full of shit, and we don't get that help, you may be sitting here a lot longer."

Brightman answered, "We have plenty of air and plenty of water. If I could just find a vending machine, I'd be happy."

Adam, who had major misgivings about this dive from the beginning, felt he had to speak up since he didn't know if he'd see his friends alive again. But in characteristic diver gallows humor, he made a joke out of it. "Just make sure you guys don't eat each other. We don't want to discover a pile of bones when we get back."

Parker said, "I promise you that at least one of us will be well-fed."

A voice in the growing darkness snickered.

With that, the rigged up divers said goodbye to the well-liked duo and disappeared beneath the dark water. Parker and Brightman were alone.

The last glow stick was rapidly fading, so the two knew they would soon be enveloped in total, absolute, without-end darkness.

Brightman groaned, "I can't believe I fell and fucked my knee up. It hurts like hell when I move it."

"Then don't move it."

"OK wise ass, Sir."

"Don't beat yourself up. If you and I had not stayed behind, the rest of the team would not have had enough gas. No one plans for two major system failures, right?"

"Yeah, what are the odds? So if I hadn't racked my knee, you would have stayed anyway?"

"I told you that. There for sure wouldn't be enough gas. Now, there should be."

That seemed to satisfy Brightman for a few minutes.

But only a few.

"Jason, what have you gotten us into? Are there really primitive people in here somewhere?"

"I don't know. I haven't seen any."

"Somehow I don't see a National Geographic spread coming out of this adventure."

Parker sighed. "I completely agree with you, Kelly. I'm so sorry to have gotten you into this."

"But on the bright side," Brightman said, "we did discover and map this tunnel to who-knows-where."

"There is that."

"But since you might say we're somewhat at risk here, and just might not survive…"

"We'll be just fine," Parker interrupted.

"OK, wishful thinking aside, since we are in harm's way, what is so damned important about these primitive people you're talking about? And why are you involved? Does it have anything to do with the frogs you used to work with?"

"First of all, I didn't work with them. They saved my ass on a couple of occasions because they trusted me to keep the government from killing them."

John Clarke

"Too bad they're not coming to our rescue now," Brightman said. "They're all gone now, right?"

"Sure are, somewhere in space far far away," Parker said almost wistfully.

"So what about these things in here. What's so important about them?"

"First of all, we don't think they're things. They're human, more or less like us. I think I saw one a couple of days ago."

"Did it speak to you?"

"Sure did, in perfect English. It was a man, at least according to the way he was dressed."

Parker wasn't about to tell Brightman about their telepathic communication, not yet anyway.

"You know boss, you amaze me. I never figured you for the kind of guy who'd get selected to help out ETs."

"And I never figured you for an NSA spook, I mean analyst."

Brightman laughed. "Yeah, that hardly even seems like it could have been me. I was young, poor, and needed a job."

"And apparently with the name Brightman they assumed you really were. Bright that is."

They both laughed. That had long been a running joke between them.

The last vestige of glow faded to nothingness, and after the echoes of their laughter also faded, there was nothing there, no light, no substance, no stimulation except for the comforting and gentle sound of running water at their feet.

"So these humans, why are they so important?"

Parker paused, thinking about what he should say next.

"It would be a lot easier if you still had your Intelligence clearance."

"I do. But my God Jason, is all this cloak and dagger stuff really necessary?"

"I don't have the authority to read you in, but I'm going to because what I tell you just might help save our lives. There's something interesting going on in Russia. And our Intel folks think it might have something to do with the Frogs."

"What? You said they're gone."

"Yes, but they may have left something behind. Something that's maybe not airworthy."

"You're talking about a spaceship?"

"Could be. We don't know."

114

"Well, how will we find out? Surely the Russians aren't going to tell us."

"No, but the Frogs left people behind, perhaps. We didn't think so, but we could be wrong."

"People?"

"Former slaves. Human-like slaves."

"I thought they were gone, assimilated into the human race. I thought I read that somewhere."

"You did, and you may be right, but we have a hunch that there is a remnant of the slaves, hybrids really, who did not assimilate into the human population."

"That's fascinating I'm sure, but, but... do you see something in the distance?"

"Where?"

"In this dark, I can't point to where I see it, but I see a faint, flickering light."

"That happens when you're light deprived. It happens to miners when they've been trapped underground."

"You think I'm imagining this? That light looks real."

"Where do you see it?"

"I'm not sure, somewhere in front of us. You don't see the light?"

"No."

"And you're a pilot?" Brightman chided him. "That worries me."

I'm coming for you.

"What did you say, Kelly?"

"I said that worries me."

"No. You're coming for me?"

"Jason, I may be seeing things, but now you're hearing things. I didn't say that."

At that same moment, Parker did, in fact, see a shimmering, wildly moving light, two of them, seemingly. It was not a single point of light. It seemed to have no form like a headlamp would, from another caver. It was more like a fluttering bluish white light. And it was getting steadily larger.

"Parker, surely you see it now."

"Yes, I do. It reminds me of what someone once called jiggle jaggle lights."

"I don't know what it is, but I don't think it's your primitive humans."

Parker answered in a faltering voice. "I...I don't know."

"Jiggle jaggles are getting closer," Brightman said, "but further apart. I can't figure this out."

The lights were indeed getting larger, and more spread out. And then they seemed to be very close. Then they stopped moving and jiggling. In fact, the cave walls close to them seemed to be glowing, and in between them was a seemingly impenetrable blackness.

Due to the force of some irrational instinct emanating from deep in his brainstem, Parker found himself lifting his arm to touch the inkiness.

He felt something soft, warm and yielding to his touch.

Stop it.

Parker lowered his hand. "Did you hear that?"

"I heard nothing."

"Something's here."

CHAPTER 24. ARGXTRE

Parker watched with horror as an adult Antarctic Skua forced its head and bill into a nest of another bird, a nest lying low on the pebbled ground, filled with feathers for warmth from the ever present cold. The large bird pulled out a fluffy-feathered chick, flipped it into the air and swallowed it whole. It then thrust its head back down and pulled up the remaining chick, and swallowed it whole as well. A pained empathy startled Parker's mind as he thought of those chicks, staying dark and warm, waiting for their parents to return with food, and then being violently yanked from their security and devoured in the blink of an eye.

Mother Nature is a bitch.

Parker's back was hurting. It felt like he was lying on something hard, but it wasn't on rocks. And then he remembered the solid presence in the blackness, and he woke.

He thought his eyes must be open, but he couldn't tell. The darkness was total.

Then he heard someone stirring next to him.

"Jason, are you here?"

"I am, right next to you."

Parker reached out his hand and found Brightman's hand. Brightman was not wearing his wetsuit. And when he reached back to his own body, he found he wasn't in his wet suit either. He reached further and found that at least his dive shorts were still on him.

"What happened Jason? Where are we?"

"I don't know. But we're not where we were. And we're not in our wetsuits anymore."

"Holy hell."

Both Parker and Brightman tried to sit up, but found they were too woozy to do anything but lie down again."

"I feel like I've been drugged. But my knee's stopped hurting. Why the hell would it stop hurting?"

"I don't know anything Kelly. I just woke up from a freaking bizarre dream."

"I seem to remember…"

Brightman stopped mid-sentence as a glow appeared once again. And then the bluish-white glow began to fill what seemed like a small cuboidal space. Standing there, looming over their prostrate bodies on the floor, was a dimly lit human, a man by dress, mostly naked, but wearing a loincloth. The presence of the man seemed to light up the walls, and that light reflected back on the man, revealing his features.

Jason Parker, we expected you, but who is your friend?

Parker heard the thoughts but heard no sound. The man must have been using telepathic communication.

Parker thought back in response. *A friend. Who are you?*

I am Random. We are all Random.

That made no sense to Parker.

Brightman spoke, "Jason, who is this guy?"

"His name is Random."

Brightman groaned. "I'm so confused."

"He says they are all Random."

"Well, that is entirely — need I say it?"

My actual name is not random. It is Argxtre.

What have you done to us? Parker thought.

We've moved you to safety.

And did you drug us?

Sedated you for your comfort.

"Parker, can you please tell me what's going on?"

"Introductions. Apparently, he was expecting me."

"He's reading your mind?" Brightman asked.

The man named Random glanced at Brightman, then turned and headed for a door in their enclosure. As he walked through the door, the light in the small room seemed to follow him out.

"Hey, you can leave the light on," Brightman shouted after him.

But a second later it was once again inky black in the room.

"Dammit Jason, did you know this would happen?"

"Absolutely not."

A second later, light again seemed to be entering the room, and it revealed another person, this time a female, scantily clothed. And from what they could both see in the bluish-white light emanating from the walls, she was a very attractive, petite female.

Parker tried out his telepathy. *Let me guess, your name is Random.*

118

"Yes, my name is Random." This one spoke English, out loud.

For the moment, she ignored Parker and walked over to Brightman.

"How is your knee?"

"It's beginning to hurt again."

She cupped her hands over his affected knee, and he felt the pain immediately dissipate.

"Did you fix it?"

"No, we can't fix it, but we can make the pain go away."

She paused, looking him over from head to toe. She seemed to be carefully examining him.

She said, "I'm surprised you can do that, considering the sedative."

"Do what?" he asked. But then he realized she was looking at his midriff, which was becoming aroused.

"Oh gosh, I'm sorry."

"You think I'm attractive?"

"Why yes, I do."

"You might not think so if you saw how we reproduce."

Parker was fully attentive, regardless of the sedative. He was about to discover things about these primitives that no one else knew.

"What?" Brightman asked, growing ever more confused.

"The male mates only once," she said, "and has to permanently detach his sexual organ which remains with the female for life. This is how we ensure monogamy and dedicated caring for the young."

His excitement quickly waned.

"You want to try it?" she asked.

"Hell no."

She smiled at him impassively. "Suit yourself."

She turned to Parker, whom she knew had been carefully observing. Speaking telepathically she said, *When I leave, tell him I'm joking.*

Parker smiled and responded telepathically, *I like your style. Thank-you for easing his pain.*

As she started to leave, Parker asked out loud, "What is your name?"

"It's Random," she said without pausing or looking back.

Again, the room's light followed her out the door, leaving them in absolute darkness.

"Guess what Kelly, she told me to tell you she was kidding. I think she wanted you to get your mind off your pain."

119

"Yeah, well that worked."

They both lay in the darkness, silent for a moment, hoping that the sedative would start wearing off soon.

Parker snickered. "She really had you going there, didn't she?"

"Kind of. But what's with the light Jason? They leave, and it's dark, they come, and it's light. Do they have some sort of automatic room lights?"

"I'm trying really hard to figure that out, but I've struck out so far. It is very strange."

What Parker didn't mention that also was strange was that bizarre dream he had, of a large bird plucking fledgling birds from their nest and swallowing them whole. He was wondering if it was a warning, as he and the other bird lay side by side in the dark.

"Why do you figure they sedated us, Jason?"

So we won't fight when they eat us? Parker thought it, but wisely didn't say it.

"I don't know, but are you able to make a run for it?"

"Are you kidding?"

"No. Where do you think the door is?"

"Considering which way we're laying, I'd say about our 10 o'clock position."

"I agree. Let's go."

Parker jumped to his feet, feeling a little woozy when he did. But adrenaline started kicking in. He could hear Brightman close behind him, but in the total darkness Parker missed the door, started feeling for it in the blackness, and then felt a blow from behind as Brightman plowed into him. Apparently, Brightman's adrenalin was kicking in too.

"Where's the damn door?" Parker yelled in frustration.

Parker moved several feet to the right, and as he put his weight against the wall that had been containing them, the door popped open, spilling him into the cave blackness. Again, Parker felt a crushing weight as Brightman piled on top of him.

Brightman whispered, "What do we do now boss? I can't see shit."

"Me neither. But we need to get away from here. Hold on to my shorts and follow me."

"Where are you headed?"

"Damn if I know. But I'm not sitting here."

And so they started to move in slow motion in an unknown direction, and in what was probably a crooked line. Parker held out one hand, trying to protect his head. But that was not enough protection as he banged into a rock wall, followed by Brightman banging into him.

"This is hopeless," Parker said, exasperated.

And then he noted a coolness on his butt. Brightman had been holding onto Parker's shorts, and he inadvertently pulled them partly down when they crashed into the cave wall.

Just then a resonant voice filled the cave, scaring them.

"You should see how funny you look."

"There's no damn light," Brightman shouted.

"There's plenty of light, you just can't see it. It's a human weakness I'm afraid."

Parker snapped at the sound. "What are you going to do with us?"

"First I'm taking you back to your room so you can see. Then Random will feed you, and then we'll talk."

A short while later, girl Random brought freshly cooked eels and water. "We've learned from experience that you Americans like your eels cooked."

Parker was thinking, *Marinated would be nice.*

In his mind he heard, *I forgot to pick up marinade at the grocery store. Try this.*

Parker was glad there was enough light in the small room that he could see her smile.

She set down two mats of some sort, with the eels piled in small clusters, still steaming.

She left without saying anything more, leaving the men in darkness once again. They fed themselves by feel.

"This is enough to gag a maggot," Brightman said.

"It's not bad," Parker said, "if you're starving. And I'm starving."

After they had eaten all they could bear, the door swung open again, allowing more light into the room; which was really a strange thing since it was coal black outside the door.

Approaching Parker, Argxtre spoke out loud. "Random told me your friend is feeling better now."

"Girl Random?"

The man smiled. "Her real name is BGuzwi."

"I'll call her B if she shows up again," Brightman said.

121

Addressing Brightman, Argxtre said "You have lots of questions, I'm sure."

"For starters, why are we being kept sedated in this little room?"

"Your sedation is wearing off, as you may have noticed. Also, this is the only room where you can see."

"About that, what's the deal with the lighting here."

"There is no lighting. We are the light, and the walls simply react to our presence. You call it fluorescence."

"Fluorescence — doesn't that require ultraviolet light?"

"I see you are better educated than our last guest. We built this enclosure so he could see because he was losing his mind. He was essentially blind."

"Speaking of that," Parker asked, "where is the man who was with him?"

Argxtre paused before answering.

"That man is dead. We buried him."

"Can you take us there? His family wants to know about him."

"I can take you there, but I don't see the point. You can't see."

"You don't have any lights down here?"

"We have plenty. We make our own."

Parker was used to getting his way, but once again he found himself in a situation over which he had no control. That annoyed him no end.

Parker asked, "So where does the black light come from?"

"We emit it from our skin."

"Impossible," Brightman said. He was every bit as annoyed and disbelieving as Parker and did not mind being rude if the occasion called for it. On this occasion, it seemed completely warranted.

"We were built for a subterranean existence. We needed some way to see, so we were designed to emit light energy all the time. It bounces back to us, just like your visible light. And sometimes the cave walls fluoresce, which makes things even brighter."

Parker said, "That explains why you don't wear much clothing. You don't want to block your light."

"Yes."

Parker had not given up on confirming Brinson's death, but in the meanwhile, his mission was to gain as much information as he could. That motivation assumed he and Brightman would get out of this predicament alive. And at the moment, that was not a safe assumption.

"You say you were built?" Parker said. "By whom?"

"We are aware of you Jason Parker, and your time spent with the ones you call Frogs, a reference I don't understand. To us, you are Ta'veren."

"What's that?"

"One who has the power to change time."

"I've been called many things," Parker said, "but not that."

Parker did not say what he was thinking. *That makes no sense at all.*

Brightman interjected. "Ta'veren, I know that. It's from a series of fantasy books by Robert Jordan. I've read some of them."

Parker looked at Brightman with a puzzled look on his face. "You read fantasy?"

Brightman nodded his head.

Then Parker turned his attention to Argxtre. "And you read fantasy novels?"

"We have lots of time on our hands."

"But how? Aren't you locked underground?"

"Don't say that," Argxtre admonished him sternly. "We are anything but *locked.*"

"OK then. So who calls me Ta'veren?"

"The Masters."

Parker was incredulous. "They named me after fictional characters?"

"There is truth in fiction."

Parker thought about that for a moment.

"If that is true, then are you people fictional?"

Argxtre laughed. "Yes, actually we are."

"And what would you be called?"

Argxtre's smile faded.

"Trolls."

Chapter 25. Chaos

The NDC divers began appearing on the surface of the cenote and waved to the two CIA support guys up on the rim. The divers would need help getting their equipment pulled up to the top.

"I thought you guys were using rebreathers. What's with all the bubbles?"

The first diver on the surface, Greg, pulled out his regulator, inflated his buoyancy control device so he would float, and answered. "Our rebreathers failed. We came out on open circuit bailout gas, and we're running low. I have never been quite so happy to see a cave opening."

"They all failed?"

"Everything electrical."

"Where's Parker?"

"He's still in there."

"You left him?"

"He volunteered to stay in a dry cave we found so we'd have enough gas to get back. He and Brightman are both in there."

"What's wrong with your rebreathers?"

"We don't know. Just before we broke out into a large air-filled room everything died, lights, scooters, rebreathers."

Little Man popped to the surface in time to hear Greg's last comment. "Except mine," he said. "It's fine, I still have gas to spare."

"Then go back and get them."

"We can't."

"Don't give us that shit. You got out of the cave OK, so get more air and go back to get them."

Greg spoke for the group. "There are lots of things you don't understand about cave diving. Parker and Brightman know what we have to do. We have to decompress and rest, and while we're doing that, Parker said you'd get us fresh rebreathers, lights, and scooters."

"Oh he did, did he?"

"That is the only safe way for us to recover them. Unless of course, you want all five of us to die."

The oldest agent on duty spoke into his secure phone, wildly gesticulating to whoever he was talking to. All the divers could hear was when he shouted, "Yes, Parker's gone."

Greg looked at the other divers, "I guess Brightman's not important."

>═══──◄

"No one believes in Trolls anymore, which is fine with us."

Argxtre seemed to be very thoughtful, perhaps introspective, which was the last thing Parker and Brightman had expected from a troll.

"I thought trolls were short, fat and ugly," Brightman said, not sparing Argxtre's feelings in the least.

"That would be because few writers have ever seen one. But if you'll check your references, you'll find that those who had seen us, correctly portrayed us as the size of humans, sometimes even mildly attractive, and not always up to mischief. And one writer even admitted that our true names were exceedingly difficult to discover. That is why we now use 'Random.' It simplifies things."

"But trolls do live in caves," Brightman offered.

"And as you see, that is also correct."

So many questions," Parker admitted. "I don't know where to begin."

"At the beginning of course."

"You said you were made. And the Frogs made you?"

"On our home planet, we were created to do mining in caves, to dig up useful materials for our Masters. We were slaves. We had no life outside of the caves. There were others, very much like you. They labored on land, still obtaining material for the Masters, but they were like freed-men. They worked because they enjoyed it, and the Masters showed them deference in turn, at least compared to us."

"That's not right," Parker said, shaking his head, regretting the often-repeated injustice of it all.

"No, that is correct. According to our records, when the Masters abandoned our planet they brought themselves, some of us, and the Others."

Parker was tempted to tell Random that was not what he meant, but decided that instead, he'd just listen.

"The Others did quite well on Earth. We, unfortunately, were demoted to the same bleak existence we had on our planet. We lived in caves because sunlight hurt us, and we could see just fine in caves, as I mentioned. No wonder some of us Trolls were grumpy."

Both Parker and Brightman laughed.

"But after what seemed like Eons, my community here began to revolt, which was difficult. The Masters still maintained a psychic connection with us. There was nothing we could do about that, but we broke our physical connection with them. They could no longer inspect us, or demand our obedience."

"How did you do that?"

"We learned how to use electricity to shock them when they tried to swim up to our cave."

"Through the same tunnel we gained access?"

"Yes. On encountering our electrical fields, they left much feces in the water."

"You shocked the shit out of them?" Brightman asked, somewhat incredulous.

"Yes. They did not have protective suits like you did. They would try to swim to us several times, but each time with the same result. They are extremely smart, but not always smart enough."

"What did you do with our wetsuits?"

"We removed them so we could inspect them."

"Can we get them back?"

"I don't think you will want them. We inspected them with, how do you say it, extreme prejudice."

"Oh great!" Brightman said.

"Well, your Masters are gone. Why didn't you turn the field off? Or did you not know they are gone?"

"Oh, we know. But it turns out the field had a desirable side effect. Protein is scarce down here, and the electricity ensured that once something enters our cave, it doesn't leave, at least not through the aquatic route."

Brightman cast a glance in Parker's direction, as if to say, *Is that what we are? Protein?*

Brightman asked, "So what do you want from us?"

Argxtre smiled, "You mean other than to eat you?"

Brightman and Parker looked at each other, fearing the worst.

"You need to learn, we acquired a skill from our Masters. We can read minds, so I'm playing with you. And no, young man, we do not play with our food before we eat it. You can relax."

Parker, ever skeptical, but at least satisfied he would not end up on a Troll menu, asked, "Why are you explaining all this to us?"

"Because we want a change. And you, Jason Parker, are Ta'veren. Ta'veren cause change."

"Quit saying that. That's a made up word."

"You think so?"

"Sure, Robert Jordan made it up, according to Brightman here."

"That's true," Brightman said.

"Have you heard of a writer's Muse?"

"Look, I don't care," Parker said, growing exasperated. "Call me what you want."

"I'm just saying what your Frogs called you."

"I don't care."

Argxtre paused. "I think you will care."

Then he continued. "Now I have a question. Why did your government send you here?"

That was a more direct question than Parker was expecting. If he gave a true answer, he might breach national security, but if he lied, these mind-reading Trolls would know. And for now, he and Brightman were prisoners. Lying to them would not exactly endear himself to his captors.

He chose the less dangerous mental route, keeping Brightman out of the discussion.

We suspected this underground community represented a remnant from the Frogs. And it looks like we were right. We need to know whether the Frogs left Earth because they could, or because they had to.

Argxtre replied, *That I do not know. They never told us. They wanted us to leave with them, but after being free of them, we had no interest in going back to another planet to be slaves again.*

That made good sense to Parker.

Random continued. *But I can tell you something interesting. They left two spacecraft behind, ones that were deemed unfit for space travel. One is not far from here.*

"Wow," Parker said out loud, forgetting his attempt to remain surreptitious.

"Wow, what?" Brightman asked.

"The Frogs left some of their craft behind."

Why are you telling me this, Random?

Because that information could be our way out of here. We want to come to America, all of us.

How many is "all"?

Over three hundred.

Parker laughed.

"What's so funny?" Brightman asked.

"I can't wait to tell the President we're being asked to relocate 300 Mexican Trolls."

The three of them chatted as men do, looking for strengths and weaknesses, looking for ways to exploit, or if it served their purposes, cooperate with each other. The fact that this was all occurring in a small room with walls glowing from the ultraviolet stimulation of fluorescent calcite slabs almost became an accepted anomaly.

To Parker and Brightman, that was not nearly as interesting as knowing the intentions of the Troll named Random. Finally, Parker forced the point.

"Random, I can guarantee you your people will not be brought to the States until we recover the body of our man, the one we call Brinson."

Argxtre just looked at Parker for a moment, in silence.

"Will that be a problem?" Parker asked.

Argxtre slowly shook his head. "It's just that we do not disturb the dead."

"Well, we do if they are on foreign soil. We bring our people home."

"Then I'm sure we can arrange that, once we have an agreement that my people can come."

"One step at a time. Are you willing to come to the States with us so we can begin the negotiations?"

"I am my people's leader. I look after them. If I must join you, then I will."

"Then we should get going. How can we do that?"

CHAPTER 26. RECON

Two Marine Force Recon operators, heavily camouflaged, had set up strategic positions just inside the treed boundaries of the clearing under surveillance. They were not supposed to be there, in that location, and as far as the Mexican or U.S. Government knew, they weren't there. They were ghosts.

But they had their eyes and their silenced 50 caliber sniper rifles trained on the small clump of trees in the middle of the clearing. Occasionally they would spread out to provide better coverage, but at the moment they were back together sharing a moment of Recon camaraderie. Waiting for something to happen was quickly turning into waiting for nothing to happen.

"Have you ever shot Prairie Dogs?"

"Sure have. In Nebraska. What about you?"

"Utah. Got paid to do it."

"Why'd you think of that just now?"

"I keep seeing something popping up in those trees. Just reminded me of those Prairie Dogs."

"Well, do us a favor. Don't pop one off without clearance."

"Wouldn't think of it. But I can dream, can't I?"

There is no real quiet in the lowland jungle of Quintana Roo, but at least for just a moment, the ambient noise didn't include the chatter of one bored Marine Corporal bugging the hell out of another Corporal.

And then it did.

"I don't know how you ever got into Force Recon. You talk too much."

"Well, we're not in combat, are we? Nothing here but birds, and snakes, and mosquitos."

"Better be quiet, or Zika will hunt you down."

The older Corporal's ploy worked for about 30-seconds.

"What ammo did you use?"

"Varmint hunting? I think they were 50 grain Hornady Zombie rounds."

"Oh yeah, that'll mess 'em up."

"You're not going to let it rest, are you?"

"Why should I?"

"Because you're Recon. Or so they tell me."

The younger Corporal was unable to take the hint.

"It never ceased to amaze me how those small caliber rounds can tear up so much flesh. I mean, a 50 cal, sure. But a 22? Weird. And did you ever have one of the varmints go sky bound on you?"

"What do you mean?"

"You know, launch. I never could figure out how they did that. I watched one fly at least six feet in the air, straight up, doing somersaults."

From close behind them came a gruff and clearly threatening voice. "You mean like this?"

In an instant, both Marines were flung into the air, their rifles flying out of their grasp.

The naked and sweaty back of the Troll that Parker was riding on proved to be heavily muscular, well defined, moving noiselessly through the blackness. Parker was being carried like an injured man, his legs wrapped around the waist of this Troll, his hands grasping the sinewy neck and working shoulders that propelled their bodies through the cave. And that embarrassed him: he was not injured, he just couldn't see to navigate through the blackness. This is what it must be like for Joshua Nilsson, all the time, except when he's remote viewing.

Parker could hear voices, sometimes echoes, so he assumed other Trolls were watching as they passed. More than once he heard voices in his head, repeating *Ta'veren, Ta'veren.*

My God, what has gotten into these people?

Maybe Hope had gotten into them. They had been freed from the Frogs, freed from slavery, and now their leader, Argxtre, was headed out into the topside world of humans, to both give powerful information passed to him by the mind of the Masters, and to gain acceptance of his people. Only then could they reveal themselves *en masse* and venture out into the open.

That reveal would be a historical event for all Trolls, one that might save the dwindling population of those greatly misunderstood people.

Certainly, in historical times such coming out would have been impossible. But these were enlightened times, the Trolls thought.

Of that modern enlightenment, Parker had his doubts. Parker also sensed that Argxtre had another motive that was not at all clear. In fact, it seemed to be a dark secret, as dark as the home of the Trolls, and as hard to discern as their names.

Suddenly, a door opened onto the light. Parker and his troll transport stepped into a rock sheltered path, overhung with jungle trees. They were out of the cave, followed close behind by Brightman and another Troll carrying him. Simultaneously, Parker and Brightman dismounted and stood in more or less familiar surroundings. It seemed to be the same clump of trees they had first spied from the periphery, from their car, a few days before. And as always, there was a fully clothed Troll guard standing watch on what was usually the most boring guard duty in the world.

The guard seemed agitated. He pointed toward the trees where there were some vehicles with serious looking men outside of the vehicles spying on them with binoculars. Some had rifles, pointed in their direction.

This was not part of the plan.

Argxtre appeared beside Parker, and Parker went telepathic to send a discreet message to the Troll leader.

I will go out there alone. Brightman must stay here, for your safety. You stay back too. I'll talk to them and when it's safe, you can approach.

As you wish.

Parker began his walk toward the tree line, and when he had covered twenty feet or so, one of the CIA agents, Matt, starting walking toward him. They met in the middle, and Parker gave the man a slap on the shoulder and a manly hug. "Boy am I glad to see you. I have Brightman with me, and the leader of the cave people."

He thought it best to not mention Trolls, not yet anyway.

Matt quickly sobered up the conversation. "How about asking your caveman leader if they had anything to do with an assault on our MARSOC friends?"

"What do you mean?"

"Those guys got roughed up pretty badly, and tied up until we found them. They kept talking about a giant or something attacking them."

131

Parker laughed. "I guess if I was Marine Recon and got my ass whipped, I'd turn the attacker into something supernatural too, to save my pride. In other words, Matt, I wouldn't believe the giant story."

Parker had another thought. "Did the Marines have weapons?"

"Of course, 50 caliber sniper rifles."

"Well, maybe they didn't like the idea of rifles pointed towards their front door. Are our Marine friends in the hospital?"

"No."

"Then I suggest you don't make any more of an issue than necessary over the Recon guys. I have something a lot more important to tell you."

Matt waved for his armed men to stand down but remain vigilant.

Parker signaled for Brightman and Argxtre to join them. The Troll, sensing no real animosity from the Americans, walked boldly towards Parker and the CIA agent. As they got close, agents separated Brightman and the other one. They had no idea who the stranger was, and wasn't about to take chances.

Matt let Parker know their men would go gentle on the man called Random. They were just a little nervous interrogating someone who seemed to be a Mexican citizen without authorization from the Mexican military.

"Where are you guys going to take him?"

"To Virginia after we get more clothes on him."

Parker put his hand on Matt's shoulder. "Matt, this guy is special cargo. What he knows is a matter of national security. Let nothing, and I do mean nothing, happen to him."

Matt looked half-sideways at Parker, a bit skeptical that Parker, a Navy scientist, would know something more secret than what he knew. But then his bosses had told him not to underestimate Jason Parker.

"OK, if you say so."

"And think only happy thoughts," Parker said. "He just might be a mind reader."

Chapter 27. Killing with Kindness

The almost empty Airbus A320 was midway through its red-eye flight to Moscow, when Doctor Oleg Kiselev had the luxury of undoing his seat belt and stretching out on the adjacent seats. He was tired and knew the dressing down he'd be receiving in the morning at the hands of President Dmitriev's Chief of Staff, would be grueling.

His tormentor to be, Sergei Vorobyev, not only had the President's ear but was probably the most broad-minded of those in the President's inner circle. Accordingly, he had early-on taken a strong liking to Kiselev, who held a doctorate in parapsychology. When it came to dealing with flying saucers, it helped to have insight from even the strangest of professionals.

However, as time wore on with no means of entry into the craft hidden at Lake Baikal, the tension was growing; both scientifically and politically. To have possession of the world's most unique prize, but being unable to learn anything about it, was almost more irony than the President could bear.

Kiselev had pulled a blanket up around his neck and fallen hard asleep when he was awakened by a disheveled-looking man standing in the aisle several rows ahead of him, shouting, "Ya dolzhen vyyti iz samoleta," "I have to get off the plane."

What a stupid thing to say, Kiselev thought. But a moment later, Kiselev had different thoughts when the man headed for the cabin door directly behind Kiselev's row of seats. When the deranged man started pulling on the large exit door handle, Kiselev sprang up and grabbed him by the waist to pull him away from the door. Strangely, no one else was helping, and the man had a strong grip on the door handle. It was the struggle of his life, but the shouting man seemed to have almost demonic strength.

After a deafening bang, Kiselev found himself propelled out into the black and frigid night air at 12,000 meters altitude, hurtling Earthward at terminal velocity somewhere over Mother Russia.

As he plummeted, seconds from death, only one thought came to him, repeatedly. *This can't be happening. This can't be happening.*

And then with one over-riding clear thought, Kiselev realized, it's true. This can't be happening. Aircraft doors cannot be opened at altitude.

With a sigh of relief, Kiselev opened his eyes, and all was quiet on the plane, no madman was ranting in the aisle, and he was safe.

And then he had the idea of a lifetime.

>-=---<

"The reason we can't open it Sergei, is the same reason you can't open the door of a passenger jet at altitude."

"Ah Doctor Kiselev, in case you haven't noticed, our strange bird is not at altitude. We wish it were. So how can you make that happen?"

"It's not the altitude. It's the oxygen."

"What do you mean?"

"It's the opposite of the jetliner. If someone managed to open a passenger jet door and didn't get sucked outside, they would die from a lack of oxygen, unless they put on an oxygen mask."

"Yes, I know."

"But for the Frogs, it's not too little oxygen when they're on the surface, it's too much oxygen. Our atmosphere will kill them, so by design, their door won't happen. It's a logical safety feature."

"Interesting theory Oleg, but how does that help us?"

"We need to seal the hangar and lower the oxygen inside to the point where the door will open."

"Do you have any idea how much that would cost? If you're wrong, then we will have just paid for the world's most expensive doorstop."

"Let me offer this. We already paid to build a secure hangar and drag the thing a thousand meters up the ramp to get it into the hangar. If we don't finish by sealing the hangar, we'll still have a very damned expensive door stop."

Vorobyev stared intensely at Kiselev.

For someone in Kiselev's position, it was risky to appear impertinent towards a man in the President's inner sanctum. Kiselev felt he was approaching that threshold, but wasn't there quite yet.

"So tell me, my friend, how is it you came by this extraordinarily expensive revelation?"

"A dream I had on the flight from Irkutsk."

Once again Vorobyev stared at the man before him, with an intensity that made Kiselev nervous.

Apparently, it showed.

"Relax Oleg. If you'd been anyone else, I would have shot you dead already. But we're a kinder Russia now. Maybe I'll just graze you a little."

And with that he reached into his desk drawer and pulled out a small caliber pistol, all the while laughing heartily like the Russians do.

"But after all, you are a paranormalist, so dreams are what you do. Did you by any chance dream how our little meeting will turn out?"

Lying his head off to save his neck, Oleg said, "I did. And you were amused."

"Good answer my friend. A lie I'm sure, but all in all, a good answer. Now get back to Irkutsk and make this happen."

With the Russian President growing increasingly impatient, and with no other viable options, the tunnel behind the craft was sealed, and double lock pressure doors were installed. Industrial scale pressure swing adsorption equipment was brought in to extract oxygen from the entrapped air and reduce the oxygen concentration surrounding the hangared alien craft down to 2% from its normal 21%.

The work of American marine biologists specializing in cave animals, especially low oxygen tolerant remipedes, was used as a guide to the amount of oxygen that should be present in the remaining gas. Russian scientists estimated that the oxygen should not be completely removed, but the fraction reduced to approximately one-tenth its normal value.

Sergei Vorobyev arrived unannounced as the hangar oxygen concentration approached two percent. He had suited up in one of the oxygen suits and entered the hangar floor, seemingly just one of the hundred or so people on the hangar floor, awaiting the hoped-for momentous occasion of the automatic opening of the presumed hatch located somewhere on the craft. The triangle had been suspended off the floor just in case the hatch was on the bottom of the hull.

Disguised in his white isolation suit, designed more for protection from viruses than low oxygen, Vorobyev was able to approach Kiselev unnoticed.

After watching the preparations of those on the hangar floor, ready to clean up anything usual or nasty that might spill out of the craft, like rotten alien flesh, Vorobyev revealed himself.

135

"I hope this is not anticlimactic, Oleg."

"I had a suspicion you might show up Mr. Vorobyev."

"I noticed you didn't invite me."

"I didn't want this to be a public execution, in case this didn't work."

"Don't worry, we'll keep it very private. Your failure will be the President's failure, and we don't want to advertise such a thing."

"Well, your timing should be good. We're coming up on two percent now."

Photographers in the normal atmosphere gallery in the top of the hangar were ready for action, but apparently, the craft was not. As the digital indicators showed oxygen concentration beginning to dip below 2%, showing first 1.99%, then 1.98%, Kiselev began to rub his hands together absent-mindedly.

"Yes, I would call that anticlimactic," Vorobyev said.

"Two percent was just an educated guess. We may need to go lower."

"By all means, my friend. You are the Test Director, so make it happen."

Kiselev spoke into his microphone, "Take it to 1% and hold."

And thus over the next hour, everyone in the hangar and the photo gallery waited expectantly as the hangar oxygen level crept increasingly lower.

During that time, some on the hangar floor paced around the craft, and remotely operated video cameras whizzed over and above the craft, like flying cameras at a football game, looking for any sign of an opening in the still mysterious hull.

When the digital gauges read 1.00%, Kiselev looked at his superior, and said, "At this point, I'm out of ideas."

"I've noticed that Oleg. It's a good thing I'm not."

"What do you mean?"

"I assume you know Vladimir Vernadsky's noosphere concept. As you undoubtedly know, he was ahead of his time. If he were still alive, he would think the telepathic communication between the Frogs and the Americans was a perfect example of the noosphere in action. So, I want us to use the noosphere, right now."

"Now?"

"Right now. And you better hope it works."

At Vorobyev's insistence, everyone on the hangar floor was directed through loudspeakers to perform a visualization meditation, focusing on the intense desire to gain entry into the alien craft. They were to visualize a door opening somewhere on the hull. Knowing that none other than President Dmitriev's Chief of Staff was directing this exercise proved to be highly motivational.

Besides, everyone at the complex was tired of making no progress with entry attempts. Cutting into such a precious artifact, which might have been done during more ignorant times, was not an option.

Of all those meditating, there was one who was not just meditating, but aggressively praying, even though that was not his habit. Kiselev knew that if this final effort proved futile, the anger of the President himself would be directed towards him. His future would be uncertain, to say the least.

After almost ten minutes, Kiselev's emotional entreaty to the craft, and perhaps even to God Himself, yielded results. A portal placed tightly between two of the lights slid open, and standing there, seemingly blinded by the camera lights was a tall grayish-green creature with stringy, bright yellow hair flowing over what might have been indistinct shoulders. It had large, round eyes, like those of fish, a scaly body, and two legs that seemed to be joined together, web-like. The first impression was of a mermaid, or merman. In spite of the absence of clothing, gender was not obvious.

What was obvious, even though the creature seemed to be guarding the door, was that it was visibly changing hue, from a dark green to a bluish tint. Kiselev ordered several of the white-suited personnel to move a mechanical ramp in place underneath the portal. Once that was done, Kiselev insisted on being first up the ramp.

As he approached the creature, it collapsed.

"Get a medical team up here now. It passed out."

Vorobyev sprinted up the ramp as well, flushed with excitement that his idea had succeeded in opening the craft. But as he watched the creature collapse, he began to feel sick to his stomach.

As the medical team arrived, the creature was in labored breathing, seeming to struggle to pull oxygen into its lungs or gills, or whatever it had. The lead doctor yelled, "It's hypoxic!"

Of course, with what was now a 1% oxygen concentration in the hangar, about half of what had been presumed necessary for the Frogs, hypoxia was a very real possibility.

One of the primary tools in an emergency physician's medical kit is a cylinder of oxygen. Within seconds of the doctors arriving at the collapsed creature, a mask was placed over its fishy-appearing face, and 100 percent oxygen began flowing.

It seemed to struggle slightly, which is not unusual for an oxygen-deprived patient. And after a few minutes, the struggles became less vigorous, and respiratory movements seemed to abate. However, not until all respiratory movements stopped, and the creature's skin darkened, and eyes turned opaque, did the medics realize the patient had expired.

When the lead physician turned to Kiselev and Vorobyev and said, "It's gone," Kiselev realized a few minutes too late they had given the creature what was essentially poison gas, with maybe fifty times the lethal concentration of oxygen.

Vorobyev took a long look at the body and said, "I don't know why Jason Parker would call these things Frogs. It doesn't look like a Frog to me."

CHAPTER 28. ON TRAVEL

The CIA let Parker fly himself back home, against their better judgment. However, their agents, plus Brightman, Joshua Nilsson, and the man called Random were flown from Mexico to Virginia by a professional crew in a Gulfstream G4.

The rest of the NDC dive team were debriefed and forced to sign non-disclosure agreements. They would be returning on their own back to NDC with no understanding of what had happened to two of their colleagues. They were instructed to tell the Commanding officer that the two men were on special assignment, and not to ask questions.

Parker walked out to the tarmac in Cancun, where he'd left his diminutive jet. He'd asked that it be hangared during his absence, but apparently no one had bothered with that. Even though he'd placed a protective cover over the windscreen, he could only hope the Yucatan sun had not over-heated the complex electronics.

After his walk around the craft, boarding, and engine start, all appeared to be working normally. Having survived two crashes in smaller, slower planes, he was not interested in having any problems crossing the Gulf of Mexico back to Panama City. If all went well, he'd be home in two hours.

Parker's climb out was quick, smooth, and uneventful. The Yucatan weather was blissfully calm, and by the time he was crossing the Mexican shoreline, his altitude was already in the twenty-thousands, far above the puffy summer cumulus clouds. In another ten minutes or so he'd be at his final cruising altitude of 39,000 feet.

Once at altitude he trimmed the aircraft controls for a level attitude, and watched the autopilot steer the fast bird for home. As he was leaving Mexican airspace behind, he had time to think. He'd be cruising monotonously for an hour before beginning his descent.

As he sped along at speeds and altitudes which dwarfed that of his earlier flights in single engine and twin engine propeller planes, he wondered what it must be like to command a spaceship. As he was jetting through the cold, rarefied atmosphere of the stratosphere, he wondered how much more interesting it would be to fly in space?

At one time such thoughts would be the result of unbridled fantasy, or too much alcohol. However now, with the recognition that there might be abandoned spacecraft somewhere on the ocean floor, the possibility of his flying one might not be so unthinkable. After all, he had once demonstrated that he had a mastery for alien toys which exceeded that of any other human. That is, except for Laura, that fascinating oceanography student who had disappeared from his life, if not entirely from his mind.

How primitive must his own jet seem to the ancient but incredibly advanced culture that he had been exposed to, a culture that left a permanent healing mark on his body? It must seem intolerably quaint to the Frogs to burn fossilized organic fluids from an extremely distant past, turning it into heat and thrust. It even sounded archaic as he thought it. What propulsion system could the Frogs be using, working at great depth, in our oxygen-filled atmosphere, and even in space? What miracle of technology could do that?

Or was it even technology? Could it be mind power? What gift did he and Laura have to force the functioning of otherwise dormant alien training devices? They hadn't touched the devices, they simply applied considerable attention to it. Can the consciousness, the mind, have enough power to act as an engine; to move large craft through whatever media they wish to move through?

Fortunately, the Mustang's autopilot was solely committed to accomplishing the simple task assigned to it, because the jet pilot's mind was darting between heaven and earth, between deep space and deep sea. He was too filled with excitement and awe to even think about holding a straight course and altitude.

Thirty minutes outside of Panama City, Houston Center cleared Parker to begin his descent. As he approached the airport and the crescendo of radio chatter associated with Eglin and Tyndall Air Force Base, and the control tower at Northwest Florida Regional Airport, he couldn't help smiling at the thought of his wife waiting for him at the Fixed Based Operations Center. It would be a quick stop to refuel and onboard his wife, her luggage, and the fresh clothes for him that she had packed when she'd heard of their travel plans.

As part of the overall plan to make this seem like a perfectly normal family flight, he would take her to Norfolk for a visit with some of her kin, and then he'd make the short hop over to the Naval Air Station Patuxent, or Pax River as it was usually called. Parker had spent some time there as a young man, so he was familiar with the overall layout of the field. There, at a so far undisclosed location, Parker would meet up again with the first Troll he'd ever met, Argxtre.

Sandy Parker, Jason's very Southern wife and graduate from Emory University, was waiting close by as he shut down the engines. When it was safe for her to approach, he dropped the boarding stairs, stepped down out of the cabin, kissed his wife, and half sprinted to the restroom. Flying a jet single handed did have its downsides.

Sandy was not the kind of girl who would sit in the back being chauffeured by her husband. No sooner had she climbed on board than she took up station in the copilot's seat. He completely trusted her to handle the radios and help spot traffic, although the TCAS invariably picked it out before either of the humans could.

Although she often marveled at the turn of events that had given them access to such a fine aircraft, she had ceased fretting about it. She was convinced that her husband was not doing anything illicit, and fully trusting what he said; that a certain component of the government was glad to let him carry out their bidding without the distraction and attention-drawing presence of a larger transport. Unlike some of the government transports that never show up on flight tracking websites, and which thus raise suspicion by those observing the departure and arrivals of unmarked aircraft, Parker's little jet was open to the world to see. "Hiding in plain sight," is how Jason described it.

And it sure as hell was fun to fly.

The flight to Norfolk at 37,000 feet, or Flight Level 370, would take them 1 hr 50 minutes with a 30-knot tailwind, a vast improvement over their old flying machines. Soon after takeoff, when they had left Tyndall Approach Control far behind, the radio began to quiet down. Sandy had been waiting for the quiet time to start asking her questions.

"How was your trip to Mexico?"

Sometimes Parker had to answer his wife with the same uninformative answer he often got from his teenage children, namely "Fine."

141

But this time he could share a bit more. "It was excellent. Good flying, good diving, met some interesting people, and got to blow up stuff."

Sounding incredulous, she responded, "You blew something up?"

"Don't worry, we borrowed an expert for that. A Navy EOD gal."

"I didn't know you'd be diving."

"I didn't either. It just happened — we had a mission. And the amazing thing was the dive team was the NDC cave divers."

"You were cave diving?"

"Yes."

For the next few minutes, Sandy sat silently, brooding, watching the world go by almost seven miles below.

"You know Jason, you're going to be the death of me yet."

He looked over at her, grinning, but she didn't return his smile.

Air Traffic Control called them to switch frequencies from Jacksonville Center to Atlanta Center as they were passing over Albany, Georgia. That gave him a short break from her questions; a very short break.

"The EOD gal, do I know her?"

"You might. Margaret Brown used to be at NDC. You may have met her at our Christmas party a few years ago. We don't have too many female divers, certainly not EOD."

Sandy smiled. "So is it fair to say she's the bomb?"

Parker laughed. "It would be very corny, but since her nickname is Blaster Girl, I would say she is indeed the bomb."

Sandy sat smiling. Her husband always seemed to have interesting friends, which made him all the more interesting to her.

Of course, there was one exception. "Have you heard from Laura Smith?"

Laura Smith was the oceanography student who had once gone missing with Parker in Guam under truly incredible circumstances, which Parker had insisted were fairly innocent. Of course, in Sandy's mind, the word "fairly" could cover a lot of indiscretion.

Parker looked at her again. "Laura? Everyone wants to know about Laura. I haven't heard from her in quite a while. I heard she was working for the government somewhere in DC, but I have no idea where exactly, or what she's doing."

"So she wasn't on this trip."

"Oh hell no. Look, Sandy, will you please get her out of your mind? She's a baby."

142

Sandy answered the next radio call for a sector change back to Jacksonville Center as they neared Columbia, South Carolina. She punched in the new frequency, and just that quickly she seemed to switch from suspicious wife to competent and fully trusting copilot.

The rest of the flight began to pick up tempo as they began their descent into the Norfolk area.

Chapter 29. Pax River

Shortly after dropping his wife off at the Norfolk FBO and arranging a rental car for her, Parker took off again for the short flight to Pax River Naval Air Station. Unfortunately, a healthy cumulonimbus cloud, signaling a mature thunderstorm, lay just northeast of Norfolk, moving in a northeasterly direction. The straight route from Norfolk to Pax River was filled with heavy rain and lightning, so he was routed out to sea to stay east of the storm, then cut west across the Delmarva peninsula, descending over the Salisbury-Ocean City airport, setting up for a modified left base into Pax River's longest runway.

Had he been in a slower plane, he might not have made it into the Naval Air Station ahead of the storm. However, in his Citation Mustang, he could easily outrun the storm.

Technically, the Mustang was a government-owned aircraft, but it had a civilian registration, for reasons that were not at all obvious to Parker. Normally, civilian aircraft are not allowed into a military airbase such as Pax River, but someone important had made a call, clearing the little jet's arrival to the 12,000-foot long Runway 24.

After touchdown, he was directed to taxi to a parking area next to much larger aircraft. As his twin engines spooled down, he grabbed his bags and lowered the airstairs. Waiting for him was a black sedan with a military driver and a two-man civilian security detail who drove him to a nondescript one story building on the periphery of the airfield.

After swiping their security card, the two uniformed men led Parker through a door. Once inside the anteroom, he was directed to leave his ever-present cell phone in a security box, and then he was patted down. After the man doing the patting felt confident there were no more electronics on Parker, he was led through another door secured by a cipher lock and entered a small auditorium with a slightly elevated stage and seats for approximately 60 people. The seats were placed on a concrete floor which sloped towards the stage.

There seemed to be about a dozen people seated already. Parker had no reason to believe he would know anyone there, so he picked out a seat comfortably distant from his nearest neighbor, and sat down. He had no idea how long he'd have to wait for something to happen, and he didn't even know the agenda for the meeting. He'd simply been told he'd be seeing his Mexican cave dweller again. He sincerely hoped Random was being treated well.

He felt a touch on his shoulder, and turned to see a young lady sitting behind him who he knew very well; in fact, intimately. It was Laura Smith, the former oceanography student and inveterate star-child his wife had just been asking about.

Seconded only by the shock of meeting extraterrestrial aquatic aliens, the next greatest surprise in Parker's life had been Laura, the girl who believed in past-lives and, oddly enough, a past life with Parker. Even the Frogs claimed the mismatched duo were Soulmates, but the ever pragmatic Parker was having none of it.

Recently he'd assumed Laura was lost somewhere in the morass of Washington bureaucracy, but now, here she was.

"Oh my God, Laura, what are you doing here?"

Laura looked even more beautiful than when he last saw her at Andrew's Air Force Base, shortly after the Frogs departed Earth. Her long dark hair framed a flawless face with two penetratingly blue eyes.

"I came to meet your friend," she said, smiling.

"Very few people know about him," Parker said. "You sure you didn't come to meet me?"

She paused, apparently contemplating her answer.

"It's nice to see you Jason. But this trip is strictly work-related."

"I heard you have a fed job now," Parker said.

"I was recruited shortly after we left Andrews Air Force base."

"Recruited? By whom?"

"Can't say. It's a group you haven't heard of."

"Oh, I see."

She smiled at him, coyly. "I doubt it, Jason. But it's really good to see you again."

Laura seemed to have matured a lot since he had last seen her, which was to be expected if she was now working for the government. And if he had to guess, he'd say she had some sort of intelligence job if she knew about this meeting. As for the rest of the people there, of mixed age and gender, he had no idea who they were. All were dressed in civilian clothes although some with closely cropped hair could have been military in disguise.

But quite a few seemed to know who he was. The glances he was receiving from them seemed to be more than random in occurrence.

A door to the side of the stage opened, and in walked Argxtre and two men. One was Matt, the CIA agent who had accompanied Parker in Quintana Roo. The other, he did not know.

Argxtre looked much different from when Parker last saw him. Instead of looking like Tarzan, he looked like any westerner. He would easily blend into a crowd. And perhaps for that reason, Parker could see he was being carefully watched by the two men with him. But if Parker knew anything about Argxtre, he knew the Troll didn't care.

Parker was watching Argxtre as the caveman looked up and spied him. Argxtre smiled.

Laura leaned over and whispered, "He refused to talk until you were with him."

"I don't blame him," Parker said. "I don't think he's been with people much."

Laura tilted her head in surprise. "Has he been isolated?"

Parker laughed. "No. I guess you don't know. You'll see shortly."

Parker locked eyes with Argxtre and mentally connected.

Are they treating you well?

Better than I've ever been treated. But I don't care much for human food.

What food do you like the most?

Peanut butter. I love peanut butter.

The unknown man escorting the Mexican interrupted their silent communication.

"Ladies and gentlemen, you've been brought here to meet someone very special, or so we hear. Dr. Jason Parker, the Navy scientist who spent quality time a few years ago with the Canyoneers, or as he called them, the Frogs, is sitting on the third row. Recently, Dr. Parker has been on special assignment, tasked to make contact with some indigenous underground Mexicans. And he did exactly that."

Polite applause filled the room.

"But what we did not expect, was that Jason would bring one of these people back with him. Apparently, this one, with a name I cannot pronounce, has a surprising message for us. I understand he speaks English, and many other languages fluently, but he has refused to talk to us until we reunited him with Dr. Parker."

146

The next sound in the room was a hissing sound as the attendees could not resist whispering to each other.

Parker reconnected with Argxtre. *Do you want me to introduce you?*

No.

And with that, Argxtre began to speak with a neutral, Midwestern accent, just as he had spoken underground in Mexico. That is, when he had to.

"My people and I want to immigrate to America." And then he stopped, looking around at the people in the room.

The room was silent.

"OK," the unknown man said, "How many people are we talking about?"

"Three hundred and twelve at last count. There used to be more."

The people listening started squirming in their seats.

"I'm sure that won't be a problem. We're letting all sorts of people enter the country."

"I want a promise from your President."

"Well, that's not how this works. We have special agencies that specialize in immigration."

Someone shouted to the man introducing Argxtre, "Is that why we came down from D.C.? To listen to an immigration request?"

"No, I was told he had a special message for us, of extreme national security interest."

"Doesn't sound like it."

The man introducing said, "Dr. Parker can vouch for the importance of this."

Parker responded, raising his voice over the growing discontent. "I can, but I think he's leveraging his personal needs right now."

"This is bullshit! We have better uses for our time."

They couldn't see the lightning that split the earth nearby, but they felt the building shake at the same time the lights went out.

"It's OK folks, the emergency lighting will come on any moment."

Only it didn't.

"The exit door is locked!"

"Security feature, in case of loss of power. Just be patient."

"We're locked in?" asked a voice coming through the darkness on the far side of the room.

"Patience people."

147

A lady asked plaintively, "Does anyone have a phone? They have lights."

Someone else answered, "Phones are not allowed in here. They're all outside."

"Did this guy make the power go out?"

Parker answered firmly. "No, it's just a thunderstorm. Emergency power should be on any moment."

Someone began pounding where they thought the door was. "Let us out!"

You would think that highly intelligent, well paid civil servants and scientists, would not be so quick to panic, but it became obvious to Parker that some in the room were losing control. The disruption seemed to be spreading.

Then the lights came back on, revealing a curious scene. On the stage sat Argxtre, completely naked except for his boxer shorts, with his pants dropped around his ankles.

Those concentrated near the exit turned around when someone said "look," and then the room again fell silent.

What are you doing? Parker thought.

I wanted to be able to see.

And could you?

Very well, without my clothing.

"He was glowing," a short, middle-aged man said, pushing through the crowd to get closer to their visitor.

Parker and several others admitted they didn't see it. But Parker explained, "His skin glows in ultraviolet. How could you see that?"

"He does what?" someone screeched.

"Generates UV light."

The man who saw him glowing explained, "I had a lens replacement, and that lets me see UV light."

"What?" The same annoying voice was echoing off the walls.

"It's true."

Laura caught up with Parker, grabbing his arm and said, "Jason, we have to talk."

"Not now."

"Is this guy human?"

The question was directed towards Parker. The group knew of his previous interactions with non-human ETs, so they assumed he'd be able to handle that question.

"Not exactly. But I can't explain here, not with this much drama."

Laura grabbed his arm again. "We HAVE to talk."

"What's so damned important?" Parker snapped.

He immediately regretted saying that to her, but her timing seemed badly off.

"My State Department contacts can make his request happen easily, but if this guy's an ET alien, that complicates matters."

"Well yeah, I guess it does," Parker admitted.

Parker looked at the nearly naked Mexican ET and mentally asked him to please put his clothes back on. *People here can make what you request happen. But you have to tell us what we came to hear if you want them to help you and your people.*

Obediently, Argxtre pulled up his trousers and started putting his shirt back on. But he left his shoes and socks off.

Parker spoke up now since the man introducing had clearly lost control of the meeting.

"If you will return to your seats and settle down, our guest will tell you why you were brought here."

"Is he really an ET?"

"Yes and no. I'll try to explain later."

With that, a palpable force of curiosity descended upon the crowd, quieting them.

Parker had to take action. *Please trust me. They need to hear what you have to say.*

Argxtre sighed in a very human way, and then he began to speak.

"This is what I want you to know. Not all of what you consider alien space ships have left Earth. Some remain."

With that, he had the room's earnest attention.

Laura Smith walked to the front of the room and stood on the eight inch high platform on which Argxtre, Matt, and the unknown introducer were still standing. Argxtre still remained without shoes or socks.

She signaled the leader by waving a badge that Parker could not see, and he took a seat. She was apparently taking charge.

"Ladies and Gentlemen, by the authority of POTUS and the State Department, I am enacting the Gemini Protocol. If you know what that is, you should be on my list. If you don't know, or if your name is not on the list, then you need to exit the room now."

"A loud groan and a variety of expletives could be heard as some people started heading for the door."

149

She continued, "If you're not involved, I'm sorry that we wasted your time. We did not know where this meeting was headed. None of us did, except perhaps Dr. Parker. And he didn't know about Gemini. So no one can be blamed. Thank-you for coming. I can guarantee you that at some point you will be read into this program, but not now."

Laura called Parker up to the stage. She was correct that he did not know about Gemini, or Gemini Blue as it was properly called. "You're on the list. You didn't need to know, until now."

Some people came up to the front to check the list. They considered themselves too important to not be on the list. Maybe they just hadn't gotten the email.

When they approached, Laura checked their badges against the list only she could see. When the names didn't match, they walked away shaking their head. "This must be a mistake," more than one of them said.

On the list was Dr. Timothy Robeson, Parker's friend from the SETI Institute. He'd been so quiet during the preceding chaos that Parker had not even known he was there. As for the remaining ten or so personnel, Parker knew none of them, except for Matt, his CIA contact, and the Introducer, otherwise known as Brian.

Parker looked at Laura and said, "I'm surprised Hans Richter isn't on the list."

Richter was Parker's NSA contact who had been working with him from time to time during Parker's adventures with the Frogs.

Laura answered, "He is on the list. He's not here because we figured his presence would be a dead giveaway."

Parker laughed. "Of course we can't make things too simple, can we?"

He stared at her for a moment, admiringly, and said, "You're working for POTUS? Now I'm the one saying we have to talk."

"There will be plenty of time for that later," she said.

After the room had been largely vacated, and a new sets of armed guards posted outside the door, Laura asked everyone to sit close to the front. Most of them already were up front, trying to get a closer look at this reportedly glowing guy. However, a few members of the group hung back, as if afraid the strange entity in front of them might explode.

Argxtre asked Parker, *What is happening?*

They want to get to know you better.

Laura turned to Parker, "What shall we call our visitor?"

150

"Random. That's what they call themselves. They have names based on randomly assigned letters at birth, but with their telepathic ability they know each other without the need for names."

"Do you trust him?" she asked.

"I do."

"OK, ladies and gentlemen," she responded immediately, "Gemini Blue is officially activated. As you know, our charter is to confirm for ourselves what evidence we have that our visitor, who we'll call Random, is actually of extraterrestrial origin, and to further evaluate if what he says is the truth."

Parker said softly, "He's right here Laura. He has feelings, plus he's a mind reader."

She turned to look at him with a surprised look on her face. "Like the Frogs?"

"Just like. They are of the Frogs. The frogs created them by ..."

Laura cut him off. "If any of you heard what Dr. Parker said, please ignore it. This group is to determine independently what the truth is. However, I do agree that we should be mindful of Random's feelings. We'll assume until proven otherwise that he is human, and entitled to human courtesy and protection."

Random cut his eyes over to Parker. *What rock did you find her under?*

Looking at the older gentleman, Laura said, "Sam Gillum, you said you could see him glowing in ultraviolet. How can you do that?"

"We could all see ultraviolet if it weren't for the fact the lenses in our eyes turn yellow with age and block UV. Most kids can see UV."

"But you're not a kid."

"I had cataract surgery, and the surgeon replaced my lenses with Crystalens, which seems to let me see ultraviolet light that others don't see."

She turned to Parker, "Does that make sense Jason?"

Parker shrugged. He knew nothing about Crystalens.

Addressing the group, she said, "Dr. Parker spent a fair amount of time in total darkness with Random, in a cave somewhere in the Yucatan. Dr. Parker, did you ever see him glow?"

"Not directly, but when he entered a special room where we were being kept, it glowed. The room was fluorescing in response to the UV light that Random was emitting. Of course, we couldn't see the actual UV light."

That is correct, Random said mentally.

151

John Clarke

"You know Laura, you could just ask him," Parker said. "He'll be glad to tell you."

"I'm afraid that's not protocol."

Parker sighed, "Of course."

Jason, is this a trial?

No, it's a game. Please bear with us.

I thought they would want to know about the spaceships.

They'll get to it eventually.

"Does anyone know how Random can be emitting ultraviolet light?"

Parker answered that one. "Photophores. Deep sea fish emit light through photophores in the skin."

"Do photophores emit UV?"

"I don't know, but they do emit visible light, sort of like lightning bugs."

Laura asked the group, "Do humans have photophores?"

The assembled group shook their individual heads or did nothing. No one said yes.

"So, I think we have pretty firm evidence that Random is not human, although he looks humanoid."

Parker was growing exasperated. He didn't know what the damn protocol was, but things were moving at a glacial pace. They had important things to discuss — like flying saucers for crying out loud.

"Laura, why don't you let Random tell his story?"

"Yes Jason, now is the time. And I must say we are extraordinarily fortunate that Random can talk to us in English. We do have a couple of linguists here just in case his English falters a bit."

Random began to show his indignation at being treated like a lab animal. "I think you'll find my English is at least as good as yours Ms. Laura."

"Why don't we try Dr. Smith. Dr. Laura Smith," she said.

"Jason calls you Laura."

"I know, but we have a history. Now, will you please tell us your story?"

Argxtre paused, seemingly deciding where to begin. Finally, he began at the beginning.

"A long time ago, maybe 10 thousand years, we were slaves on our planet, on a distant star in what you call the Milky Way galaxy. Our Masters were those Jason Parker calls the Frogs. They were highly advanced, but as our planet's atmosphere was changed by increasing oxygen levels, they had to retreat deep into our planet's oceans. They could no longer work the land, so they made two, what you call humanoid species, to work the resources on land. One was essentially identical to Earth's humans as they are now, and one was us. The one group worked the land surface, but we were created to work subterranean mines, extracting the minerals the Frogs needed for their machinery, including spacecraft."

Argxtre paused again since it looked like the humans in the room were barely breathing.

"Since we were designed to work underground, our Masters designed sources of ultraviolet light emanating from our skin. We see that light and its reflections just fine as long as our skin is exposed. We never needed to carry lanterns when we worked, which meant we always had two hands free to carry our work load."

Laura and Jason were smiling at each other. They had heard a similar story told from the Frog's perspective just a few years before. The stories were matching.

"When the Masters realized that our nearest stars were becoming unstable, they left in their spacecraft while carrying a large number of their humanoid creations with them. They were rather fond of having slaves do their bidding."

Argxtre looked around, smiling. "Some of you humans have that same affliction."

"No more," someone said.

Argxtre ignored whoever said that.

"When our Masters found Earth, they did just as they had on our home planet. They stayed in the deep oceans, safely away from Earth's toxic atmosphere, but released both sets of humanoids onto land. Since we were equipped for light generation, we found caves which we mined, and the others caught wildlife and transported food to the Masters whenever the Masters came to the surface in their ships."

Laura asked, "And did those others breed with humans?"

"They did, and eventually they became fully human. All of you are hybrids from the mingling of your early humans and the surface dwelling slaves."

Someone shouted, "You're out of your mind!"

Argxtre quickly retorted, "And you must be genetically closer to the primitives."

The small group laughed at Argxtre's putdown of his heckler.

Someone else asked, "Did you ever interact with humans?"

John Clarke

"We did, but it was not always pleasant. They called us trolls, I guess because we usually stayed in caves, and rarely came out in the day. The sun hurts our skin and eyes."

"You're a troll?" someone asked, incredulous.

"I am Random. But some of you, in the old days, called us Trolls. Yes, that is true."

The group, including Laura, started talking back and forth. They were clearly amused, but Parker was not. Instead, Parker was growing weary of the interruptions and wanted to get to the matter at hand.

"Tell us about the alien ships," Parker blurted out.

The room fell silent for a moment, then someone simply said, "What?"

Laura glared at Parker. Apparently, he was not supposed to intervene in the questioning process. The others looked to her to see how she would respond to the breach of protocol.

Argxtre looked at Parker, unsure what to do.

After a tense moment, Laura shrugged her shoulders, turned to her specially selected group of experts and curled her lips downward as if to say, *I guess we'll do it*, then turned back to the visitor. "OK Mr. Random," she said. "Please tell us about the flying saucers."

"There is not much to say, except that I know of two remaining, one very close to the coast of Florida, and one in Russia."

CHAPTER 30. FLIGHT HOME

When Argxtre announced the presence of an alien spaceship in Russia, the first meeting of the Gemini Blue team had erupted into chaos. Laura soon had to have Argxtre escorted out of the room. As he was being led out the back door to a waiting car, he looked back at Parker, seemingly pleading, *What did I say?*

Parker responded with, *Something very exciting.*

Within minutes the room was emptied, and Parker lost sight of Laura. He had wanted to ask her if he needed to stay longer, but she was nowhere to be found. He tried phoning her, but her old phone number was not in service.

Not wanting to further waste his time, he had his driver carry him over to the Air Operations building so he could check the weather and update his flight planning software for the return trip to Norfolk and Florida.

While analyzing the weather prognostic charts, he heard a familiar voice.

"I thought I might find you here." It was Laura.

"You're leaving so soon?"

"I figure I've done enough damage for one trip," he quipped.

She laughed. "You had some help from What's-His-Name."

"Random."

"That is so silly," she said, shaking her head.

"Hey, if it works for them, who are we to criticize?"

"I tell you what, I'm about to do the 10-mile run around the base. It'll help clear my head. Want to join me? We can catch up on things."

"Whoa. I didn't know you were a runner?"

"I was, in high school. I packed on too many pounds in grad school, but I've worked them off after getting my DC job. I like to run the Rock Creek Trail."

"The trail here should be safer," Parker offered.

"True, plus I enjoy a change of scenery. So, what do you say you join me? If you can't hack it, you do half a lap and I'll do the whole thing."

"You trying to trick me? Any way you look at it, I'd be doing ten miles."

"So?"

"So, I'm fresh out of running shorts and shoes."

"OK, play hard to get if you want, but you do owe me a run. I won't forget."

"OK. Next time."

Parker was not at all sure when, or if, there'd be a next time.

"I'll let you get back to whatever you're doing," she said, "but I do have a favor to ask."

"Of course. What is it?"

"I'm worried about Random. I was not prepared for what happened today. We have a lot of pissed off people in the area, and under the protocol, I've got to get any aliens we discover to a secure location ASAP. And I'm not prepared."

The young lady, having been handed great responsibility but with inadequate resources, now seemed to be floundering. Not surprisingly, she turned to the one person she could trust.

"How can I help?"

"Panama City is as out-of-the-way from the DC lunacy as any place I know. You going that way?"

"I am."

"Can you secret him away on the Navy Base for me until we figure out what to do with him?"

Parker paused as he considered the odds of hiding a troll in plain sight on a Navy Base. Then he smiled.

"I do like a challenge," he said.

Her face erupted into a gorgeous smile.

"I was counting on that. When do you want him here?"

"Half an hour, and by the way, he'll get to meet Sandy, in Norfolk."

"Oops," she said, "That could be a problem."

"I'm not worried. She'll never know who he really is."

Laura laughed. "As long as he keeps his clothes on."

An hour later, Parker was making the short hop from NAS Pax River to Norfolk to pick up Sandy Parker before heading back to Panama City, Florida. Argxtre was sitting in the copilot seat, but he had promised not to touch any controls.

Parker spoke through the intercom and headset, although he really didn't need too. The jet was quiet compared to the piston aircraft he used to fly.

Parker had muted the intercom button on takeoff just in case his passenger chose to speak at an inopportune time. Of course, just after he muted Argxtre's microphone, he realized what a useless gesture that was. Argxtre preferred telepathic communication.

"I need to tell you a few things," Parker said into his mic, "before we pick up my wife. Number one is, you need a human name. I was thinking of maybe Truman, like in Truman Capote. But you need a Mexican last name."

"I only have one name, Argxtre."

"I know Random, that's your real name, but we humans can't pronounce that. So how about making up one. But don't forget it."

"OK, Bngqw."

"That won't do. Let's try Baltazar. Truman Baltazar. Can you remember that?"

"I can remember it. Can you?"

Parker laughed. "I'll try. If I mess up, please remind me."

"Mess up?"

"If I forget."

"Yes, I will. I will tell you."

"You know, your former Masters, the Frogs, used to mess with me when I was flying. You don't do that, do you?"

Truman looked confused. "They forgot you?"

"What? Oh, no. Mess means many things. They used to fool with me."

Apparently, in spite of Random's telepathic abilities, he could still be confused by the spoken word. Thoughts were much clearer than words, Parker realized.

"They would take control of the airplane," Parker explained, "and send it up and down."

"Yes, they can do that, with their mind. I do not know how. I cannot do that."

"Good. That's all I want to know."

They sat quietly for a moment until Norfolk approach called them with an altitude change. They were already beginning their descent into Norfolk.

"One more thing," Parker said. "You cannot tell Sandy about our time together at the Air Station, or about Mexico."

"Why not?"

"She would not understand."

"I can explain it so she understands."

"No. Do not do that."

"What if she asks?"

"Then I'll do the talking."

"What does it matter who tells her?"

"Because I'll …" He stopped himself. He was about to say that he'd have to make up a white lie to conceal a truth she was not cleared to know. But how can he explain the concept of a lie to people who can read minds? To Truman, there is no such thing as a lie. Thoughts cannot be hidden.

"Tell something which is not true?" Truman asked.

Parker sighed. "Yes, Truman, when we speak only with our mouths and not with our minds, sometimes we say things which are not true."

"That seems stupid. I thought you were intelligent for a human."

Parker sat holding the controls, numbly, even though the autopilot was flying the jet.

He had to admit, Truman Baltazar was right. Life would be very different if lying were not possible.

"Truman, I'm afraid I will have to disappoint you. I will have to lie to my wife. If she learns the truth about you, then I will go to jail."

"So, then I guess you do not want me sitting naked in the dark."

Parker laughed. "Around women and children that would be very inappropriate. Especially if you turn your skin lights on."

"We have no control over that. It is automatic, like what happens to you."

"What?"

Oh God, I get it. Let's change the subject.

"Just don't. When you're around humans, keep your clothes on, and the room lights on."

"OK, I'll try."

Sandy was waiting for them when Parker taxied the jet up to the Fixed Based Operator. He signaled for the fuel truck to top off the tanks while Parker made introductions.

"Truman, this is my wife, Sandy. Sandy, this is Truman Baltazar, from Mexico."

"Oh, how nice. What part?"

"All of me."

Sandy laughed, and Truman gave Parker a concerned glance. Parker answered for him. "Quintana Roo, in the Yucatan."

"Oh, that's such a nice area," Sandy answered, honestly. "And you were at Pax River with Jason?"

Parker signaled to Truman that he could answer, as long as it was a simple answer.

"Yes. At Patuxent."

"And you're coming to Panama City with us?"

"Yes."

"OK then. I've already been to the girl's room. Are you two OK?"

Parker answered that he had to pay for fuel, do another quick walk around the jet, then they would be off.

When they had a moment to be alone while Parker was inspecting the jet, Sandy spoke softly, but earnestly. "He's weird. He's not staying with us, is he?"

"No. He'll be staying at the barracks on the Navy Base."

"Good," was all she said before she boarded the aircraft.

After takeoff, Truman sat looking out the window from his passenger seat behind Parker. Having spent a lifetime underground, with his surroundings lit only by the UV light emanating from his skin, and the occasional fluorescence coming from UV-stimulated calcite in the cave walls, his view of the world above ground, high above clouds and trees, was apparently mesmerizing.

Truman's silence allowed Sandy uninterrupted time to tell about her visit to her relatives in Norfolk. Parker was glad he had not had time to visit with that particular group of in-laws. They always asked too many questions about what he did for a living, and lying about that was becoming increasingly necessary, and disturbingly easy. And to think, Truman couldn't even understand the concept of untruths.

It appeared that Parker might have to teach him.

Two and a half hours after takeoff, and a half-hour after landing, Parker and his wife dropped Truman off at the base barracks. Men whom Parker did not know made sure Truman got checked into his room without drama or confusion.

Parker had been told that their Mexican guest would be left there, with military supervision, to acclimate to his new surroundings, and freedom. Meanwhile, the State Department would be exploring the political implication of "entertaining" someone with special knowledge, who might or might not be considered a Mexican citizen.

John Clarke

The Navy physicians assigned to this case assumed that after living in the dark confines of a cave his entire life, Truman would have some adjustment difficulty.

Parker thought otherwise. With the genetically-engineered ability to roam the planet mentally, Truman and the rest of his kin had unlimited virtual access to anywhere on Earth. Adjusting to the relaxed pace of life in a southern beach town should be easy.

CHAPTER 31. SITUATION ROOM

The American President was not amused.

"Do you mean to tell me that all that activity we were monitoring in Siberia may have involved one of the Frog spaceships?"

"Mr. President, the correct name is Canyoneers."

"If you don't mind, I like Jason Parker's name better. It's easier to say, and it reminds me of just who we're dealing with."

"Sir, we have no reason to think any Canyon... Frogs are left here. Just their ships."

"Why the hell would they leave their ships? Wouldn't they need them?"

An Air Force four star general spoke up, "Probably unairworthy Sir, at least for Space travel."

"And why would that be?"

"They're very old, and we've shot at them a number of times. Maybe they're damaged."

"Why of course, we're so damn trigger happy. We're lucky they didn't get pissed off and fry our asses."

State Department said, "They did seem very tolerant of our aggression."

"Well, if the Russians have one, we need to have one. Any idea where it is?"

The Navy said, "We're looking at the coast of Florida Sir. We know they were in the De Soto Canyon, and one was tracked leaving from there, but there might be another."

The Army four star looked at the Air Force and asked, "Why would we want an unairworthy spacecraft?"

The Air Force was incredulous. "Are you kidding? Exploit the technology, or maybe we can fix it."

The President spoke up again, "Number one reason is that the Russians may have one."

"Let's not forget," the top Navy Admiral opinioned, "It's a submersible. It might make one very fast submarine."

John Clarke

The President nodded his head. "Submarine, eh? I hadn't thought about that."

The Admiral responded, "The Russians might have theirs operational as we speak. It might be armed and sitting in very deep water right now, waiting to strike."

"OK, I get it," the President said. "You need a larger black budget, but don't talk to me. Go slay your dragons on the Hill."

State Department responded, "Speaking of dragons, China is likely going to get nervous with a vehicle sitting in Siberia. That's real close to China proper."

"I thought the two Commies trusted each other."

"Trust works great when there's mutual deterrence. But you get the balance of power too far out of whack, the two bosom buddy nuke powers will start getting nervous. So I was thinking, maybe they would help fund our new black project."

The President smiled, "Fund a black project with Red money. I'm sorry, but that idea amuses the hell out of me."

The State Department said, "Very funny Sir, but that would be a little awkward."

"Quit being such a sycophant Martha. It would be damned awkward, but still funny."

The President added, "I understand all of your fiscal and diplomatic concerns. But I guess we have to do whatever we have to do to find our own spaceship or submarine, or whatever it is."

"Yes sir, Mr. President," the Navy Admiral said. "We're planning to talk to Parker about a deep dive."

"By deep dive, do you mean a talking deep dive, or underwater deep dive?"

"Underwater. We have to go deep."

"Then do it, but make it quick."

"Yes, Mr. President."

"And what did we do with that alien guy?"

"We're having Parker escort him down to Florida. They seem to have some sort of rapport."

"What's with this guy and aliens?" the President asked. "Is he one of them?"

The group gathered there assumed that was a rhetorical question, so no one answered. Truthfully, no one knew the answer to that question.

CHAPTER 32. PENTAGON

NSA's Hans Richter showed up at the NDC several days after Parker's return to Panama City.

Extending his hand in greeting, Parker said, "Hans, what brings you to Panama City?"

"Someone you know, Joshua Nilsson. Have you heard from him recently?"

"Not since I left Mexico."

"He's telling us he's seen something interesting. We need to talk."

"I know just the place," Parker said, getting up to lead Richter to the secure briefing room.

Arriving at the large vault door which protected the SCIF, Parker spun the sturdy dials, then pushed the heavy metal open to reveal a small conference table and six chairs.

As soon as they entered, set another code, and closed the doors, absolutely no sound or electronic signal could leave the room. They were sealed away from the world, which was what was needed for what was coming next.

Richter spoke first. "We've been telling Stanford Research Institute that Nilsson is the best damned Remote Viewer they've ever had."

"Has he done something for you lately?" Parker asked.

"He checked out the De Soto Canyon, on his own, and said a spacecraft is in a cave there."

"Really? I thought radar had tracked a craft leaving that location during the Great Leaving?"

"That's true, but Nilsson swears there were two craft, and one remains."

"Well then, let's go get it."

"It's not that simple, he might be wrong. We sent a ship to the same area where you and the Florida State team lost their remote vehicle. We launched our own ROV in there, well tethered so we wouldn't lose it this time."

"Good idea," Parker said. "Florida State wasn't happy about losing that hardware."

"The vehicle explored the cave, but it found nothing."

"Nothing at all?"

"Nada."

"So you're thinking Nilsson is wrong."

"No. That's why I'm here. The President wants to put a diver down to confirm there is nothing else in the cave. Nilsson apparently has the President's attention."

"Does POTUS know just how deep that cave is? Does he know we don't dive to 2500 feet?"

"He does, but he also said Jason Parker would love the challenge. So, will that be a problem?"

"Problem? Not if suicide is a desired outcome."

"Why do you say that?"

"Has anyone bothered to talk to the Naval Sea Systems Command?"

"Actually, yes."

"And?"

"They said it can't be done."

"And right they are."

"But they also said that if anyone knew how it could be done, it would be you."

Parker leaned back in his chair, crossing his arms across his chest. "Oh great, they're throwing me under the bus."

"Look, I can Google as well as anyone, and I found the deepest dive was to 700 meters, 2300 feet back in 1992. So we're just talking about 200 more feet."

"Maybe you didn't notice, that was a dive in a dry hyperbaric chamber at Comex in Toulon, France. It wasn't open water. And it was a hydrogen dive."

"So, can we do that?"

"The Navy had a hydrogen diving facility in Bethesda back in the 90's, but they were diving animals, not people. And it was all dry."

"OK, but it can be done, right?"

"This is hydrogen you're talking about. You let candidate divers watch newsreels of the Hindenburg disaster, and it may be tough to get volunteers."

"But, given enough money and manpower, it could be done."

Parker stared at Richter, expressionless for a moment. Richter clearly wasn't going to take "no" for an answer, which meant someone way above him, perhaps POTUS himself, wouldn't take *no* for an answer.

"With enough money and manpower we got to the moon. So yes, it can be done, but not without risk."

"What kind of risk?"

"I personally know a French diver who went a little batty on those deep dives. He was having vivid hallucinations. He swore he'd never do that dive again."

"We only need someone to do it once."

"Oh, is that all?"

Richter tried to explain. "Look, we even thought about using the one-atmosphere armored suit, but it's only certified to 2000 feet."

"So, we'll have to use humans," Parker interjected sarcastically. "They're not certified at all."

Richter paused and looked straight at Parker, peering deep into his eyes. "Jason, you do know this is critical to national security. And sometimes that is more important than a human life."

Parker nodded his head. "I know that all too well. But if our man makes it down there, I want him to live long enough to find his way into the cave, and report back."

"We do too, of course."

"But what bothers me," Parker continued, "is that we'll be asking a man to risk his life on a hunch. We *think* there's a second craft left behind because it was seen by a blind man. That won't play well with the diver's widow."

Shortly after that meeting with Hans Richter, Parker was called to the Pentagon to brief the diving folks at OPNAV and a host of other folks whose identities he did not know, and would probably never know.

Air Traffic Control was vectoring his jet onto the final approach course at Baltimore-Washington National Airport. He had been turned towards the airport from the middle of the Chesapeake Bay and was sliding down the imaginary flight path towards Runway 33 Right with a passenger jet just off his left wing descending on the parallel path to 33 Left. It was a pretty sight, two jets descending in a carefully choreographed aviation dance to land on the stage called BWI.

He had mixed feelings. As exciting as it was to be starting a new diving program to retrieve an alien vehicle, he also suspected that this flight might be his last solo flight in the jet. Either he would be sent home with a fighter pilot copilot, or else the bird would be impounded altogether. Travel in larger government aircraft was safer, and after all, POTUS would not be pleased if Parker managed to kill himself in a plane crash before the project was completed.

Apparently, they didn't even trust him to make the drive from BWI to the Pentagon by himself since a black sedan was waiting for him after he exited the jet. That he understood, DC metro traffic can be a killer.

At the Pentagon a Navy Commander Submariner named Jim Engstrom and an Explosive Ordnance Disposal Officer, Lieutenant Rupert, escorted Parker into a secure briefing room guarded by young Marines who likely had no idea what was about to be discussed. Once inside, Parker saw a Navy Captain who was a Diving Medical Officer he had known as a Lieutenant fresh out of medical and dive school. Apparently, since leaving NDC he had graduated to bigger things. The Captain walked over to him and shook his hands, saying under his breath, "This could be the most interesting briefing I've been to all week, Jason."

"It's good to see you, Jimmy. Looks like the Navy's been good to you."

"Not just the Navy. I just came off a rotation at the White House."

"You were the President's personal physician?"

"One of them. But I'm more interested in what you have to say."

"I think I'm being set up for failure, but I'll do my best."

The other men and women in the room, some in uniforms and some not, were people he did not recognize. There were about twelve of them arranged around a rectangular table, with eight more sitting in chairs against the walls of the room. The room was smaller than he'd expected. Apparently, floor space was getting scarce in the Pentagon.

The person who stepped up to the microphone was a civilian. The fact that microphones were being used in such a small room implied that everything was being recorded. "Ladies and gentlemen, if you would take your seats, we can get this briefing started."

Those standing in the room, chatting, made eye contact with Parker as they took their seats. The room fell silent.

The man at the far head of the table said, "I need to remind you, this briefing is at a TS level."

No one sitting there seemed in the least bit surprised that this was to be a Top Secret meeting.

He continued, "Dr. Parker, thank-you for coming on such short notice. So we can keep the meeting moving along, rest assured everyone here is well-versed on your special relationship with the aquatic ET species, who we suppose have left Earth for good. So no need to mention any of that. Furthermore, all those gathered here are aware that you recently encountered in Mexico some subterranean humanoids that are somehow related to the ETs, and those aliens happened to mention that the ETs may have left behind some of their craft which were no longer considered space-worthy. Is that correct?"

"That's a mouthful," Parker answered, smiling. "But yes, that is correct."

"All of us also know that we have credible evidence that one of those craft may be found in the De Soto Canyon, hidden from view."

The man used a laser pointer to circle the canyon on a projected map of the Gulf of Mexico. The canyon lay about 90 miles south of Pensacola, Florida.

Parker couldn't help smiling. He wondered if those in the room knew that last news item came from a remote viewing blind man.

"Our most sophisticated Autonomous Underwater Vehicle penetrated the cave we believe housed one of the ET craft which departed along with the rest, but there was no sign of another craft, or even another part of the cave where such a craft could be hidden."

That part of the story seemed to be new to some gathered there, based on the low muttering in the room.

"Nevertheless, our intelligence asset still insists a craft remains. And ladies and gentlemen, we have received a directive from the President to expend every effort to locate that vehicle."

There was more muttering.

"The reason we've brought Dr. Parker into this is because he suggested there might be a way to get human intelligence on site, by using deep sea divers."

The man looked straight at Parker, "Is that still your belief?"

"Yes, it is."

"With the recognition that our autonomous vehicles are good, but still not as good as the human brain, we in the intelligence circles have agreed that placing a diver in the cave may be our last chance to find a vehicle if it is there."

"How deep is the cave?" a Navy submariner asked.

"2500 feet," was the answer.

"Oh," the submariner said, jotting down notes.

"So now I open the floor to Dr. Parker, who I hope will inform us about how this operation could be carried out, without killing our diver."

Parker had his brief well prepared. "Please feel free to interrupt me at any time. I'll be glad to answer questions as I go along."

He paused a moment to collect his thoughts, then started. "The U.S. Navy's deepest dive to date has been 1800 feet sea water, using a mixture of helium and oxygen in a hyperbaric chamber. Duke University exposed three divers to an equivalent of 2,251 feet, and the French sent one man down to 2300 ft for a two hour period. In contrast to the U.S., the French used a gas mixture of helium, oxygen and 50% hydrogen. If we have to send a diver to 2500 feet or deeper, I see no alternative to using a similar hydrogen-helium gas mixture."

"Hydrogen in my submarine?" one of the officers commented loudly. "No way."

Parker continued. "The reason for hydrogen is that at those depths, helium, which is a very light gas, is still too dense once it is compressed to 77 atmospheres. Dense gas is very difficult to breathe. Hydrogen is lighter. It also helps to suppress the High Pressure Nervous Syndrome or HPNS, a generalized stimulation of the nervous system by high pressure. Without it, a diver would be trembling uncontrollably at those depths."

A man sitting close to Parker asked the obvious question. "What about it exploding, like the Hindenburg?"

"Flammability is not a problem when the oxygen fraction is reduced. We keep it below half an atmosphere at all times so that at depths greater than 1000 feet the hydrogen atmosphere cannot burn."

"So why aren't the French diving that deep now?"

"Hydrogen is narcotic, like nitrogen. Perhaps you've heard about nitrogen narcosis? Well, hydrogen narcosis helps prevents HPNS, but it's also psychotropic, which means hydrogen divers can have hallucinations."

"What kind of hallucinations?"

"Reportedly, the worst are out of body events, OBEs. OBEs can't hurt you and have been reported when divers breathed argon at 250 feet experimentally in a Canadian hyperbaric chamber. They can occasionally happen during surgical anesthesia when a physician pushes the dissociative drug ketamine too quickly. An anesthesiologist friend once told me a surgical patient reported sitting up in the top of the operating room, perched up there like a gargoyle watching the surgery on his body below. It was disturbing to him, but he wasn't in real danger at any time."

"Holy cow, I've never heard of such a thing."

"It happens sometimes, unpredictably. OBEs don't harm people any more than a dream harms people. Those who experience them are not necessarily near death, like you hear reported in near-death experiences."

"Please tell us about the argon case."

"A Canadian scientist was attempting to write on a pad of paper to see what effect the gas had on him at a simulated depth of 250 feet, when suddenly he found himself up in the corner of the hyperbaric chamber, watching some man writing. He wondered why the man was writing so slowly, not realizing at first that he was that man."

"How long did the hallucination last?"

"A few seconds."

"So, do you have any real concerns about helping OPNAV plan this dive?"

"I have lots of concerns. It's never been done, it's risky, and there may be nothing in the cave."

The still unnamed leader swept his eyes over all the faces in that room, took a deep breath, and then responded.

"That is all true. But here's this to think about. There may be something there...and we think the Russians already have one."

CHAPTER 33. INTO THE BLACK

The Commander in Chief had spoken. The De Soto Hydrogen Dive was on, and only a select few people would ever know about it. It was, so to speak, compartmentalized, operating on a black, unseen budget. That meant money was no longer an object, and time schedules were crunched like a black hole because this project now had one of the highest priorities of any Department of Defense Programs. That it was a black hole seemed clear when Parker heard about money and human resources getting sucked up at an almost infinite rate.

Planning began for the potential construction in Pascagoula, Mississippi of a highly secure facility which included a dry dock onto which the ET ship could be floated, and then raised into a dry environment, safely away from prying eyes, while the ship was inspected. To get it there would require a heavy-lift tow of at least 113 miles, not a big order for the Navy, but one requiring utmost secrecy.

Two weeks after his Pentagon briefing, Parker was standing in a physiological laboratory at NDC watching a young but somewhat short, by Navy diver standards, tattooed diver running on a treadmill. He was wearing a full face mask that measured his breathing rate, as well as oxygen consumption and carbon dioxide production. Like the other eight candidates who had been screened to begin the selection process, this diver was an extreme athlete. His body was moistened by sweat, but he was gently loping along, not at all bothered by the workload. Sinewy muscles stretched and contracted, pulsing as easily as his heart.

The full face mask had been fitted with a microphone so he could talk while running, just like his diving helmet would be fitted if he was chosen for the dive. With nine mission candidates, all fit both physically and mentally, Parker did not yet know which ones would be chosen. Only two, and two alternates would make the final cut.

"With your short gait," Parker said, "you have to run harder than the other divers. But you're keeping up. How?"

"Because I'm the baddest-ass Navy diver there is, and I want the world to know."

Parker was not engaged in idle chit chat, it was part of the test. Talking interrupts breathing, so it adds an extra challenge to a diver who is barely keeping up. But this diver, who Parker knew only as diver no. 5, was enjoying the run.

"You do understand the world will not know about this, right?"

"It doesn't matter. I'll know, and my backup diver."

"Oh, so you already figure you'll be selected? Maybe you'll be the alternate."

"No chance Doc. I'm not that guy."

Diver number 5 did not know what was coming next. Since this was an operational selection process, not scientific research, there was no requirement to inform the diver or obtain consent. All he knew was that the selection process, and the operational dive that followed for whomever was selected, would be a ball buster, full of the unexpected. Their psychological reaction to the unexpected was important to know before committing resources to this single dive.

A Navy corpsman dressed in expeditionary green camouflage uniform watched the clock on the wall, and at the appointed time turned a valve that started bleeding a dense gas, sulfur hexafluoride or SF6, into the breathing loop at the same time that some of the existing air was being purged. SF6 is an inert gas, but the heaviest and densest of all gases. It is also narcotic.

Diver 5 no doubt noticed the dense gas was harder to breathe, but not until he spoke did he realize something odd was happening to him.

"What's happening?" His voice sounded much deeper and more resonant that usual.

"Oh my gosh," he continued, "that's weird. What the fuck am I breathing?"

"It's just a harmless dense gas that simulates breathing at depth."

"Well, it's sure making it harder to breathe."

"You can stop anytime you wish," Parker reminded him.

"No way. That's not happening."

And then Diver 5 stopped talking, as Parker figured he would. Running while breathing a dense gas was difficult, and didn't leave much room for the breathing disruptions caused by talking. Getting quiet, concentrating on breathing, was a normal response.

171

Tracings from the instrumented mask were hidden from the diver's view, but Parker could see clearly that the number of breaths per minute was dropping, the size of each breath was getting larger, and the breathing pressures inside the mask were twice their normal size. The large SF6 molecules were coursing in and out of the diver's lungs, pushing his respiratory muscles to their maximum capacity, but his pace of running never faltered.

Finally, the diver commented, "I've got a buzz on." His speech was distorted by the combination of the mask and the heavy gas.

"You say you've got a hard on? Then you're having way too much fun."

"No, I'm buzzed," the diver said, shaking his head. He apparently was not amused by Parker's joke.

"That's normal. Enjoy."

Parker expected the diver's reaction from the narcotic gas. All the candidate divers had the same comment.

Thirty minutes later, the SF6 was flushed out of the breathing loop, being replaced by air. The treadmill began to slow, but not until it stopped was the diver allowed to remove his full face mask.

"How do you feel?" Parker asked.

"Fine. But what was that shit you had me breathing?"

Five's lungs must have been retaining some of the SF6 because his voice still sounded deeper than normal.

"Sulfur hexafluoride. It's a little narcotic."

"Well, it made me high, but not a happy high."

"I hear that a lot," Parker said.

"So why did you give me that to breathe?"

"Because if you're selected, you'll be breathing a hydrogen-helium gas mixture deep, and it's narcotic too. And it also is not a happy high."

"So how did I do?"

Parker was forced to be noncommittal at this point, but he had to admit that Diver 5 had remained the coolest yet to the surprise introduction of the heavy gas into the breathing mixture.

"We'll let you know by the end of the week."

"You already have your man," Five said, smiling and winking.

"Maybe so. You'll find out Friday evening. In the meanwhile, don't leave town. We may need you for a do-over."

That also was a scripted response. At that same point, one of the divers had bailed. He swore he'd never do that again. And of course, that was his prerogative.

So the competition was now down to eight divers. The odds were getting better for Number Five.

Due to the risk, no Navy submarines would be involved in this historic and clandestine dive. Instead, a two compartment commercial mini submarine, heavily modified by the Navy for this dive, would transport the divers to the opening of the cave in the walls of the De Soto Canyon.

Two men would make the actual dive, with one walking into the cave where it was believed an alien craft remained. The other would be the "bell-man," exposed to the same pressure, and breathing the same exotic gases, but temporarily remaining in a sphere that housed gas supplies and monitoring equipment. If the outside diver needed assistance, then he would leave the bell. After a half hour or so the divers would switch places so that both divers would have a chance to attain stardom among a very select group of secret divers.

Immediately adjacent to the diving sphere would be a pressure-proof acrylic sphere kept at normal atmospheric pressure and housing two mini sub operators, a pilot and navigator. Both would be monitoring the gas supply and health status of the two divers right next to them. However, those divers, separated by half a mile deep water pressure, might as well be as far away as the moon.

That was the plan, but all upper-echelon Navy personnel realized that the odds of mission success not only depended on technology, but on the ingenuity and perseverance of the individual divers. A thorough diver selection process was critical to mission.

Two divers would be alternates, so of the remaining eight divers, only four would make the final cut. What the diver candidates did not yet know, was that after this phase of physiological testing was completed, a severe psychological stress would comprise their next almost soul-rending trial.

It was time for lunch. Parker had agreed to meet Truman and his two keepers for a meal at the "last local beach club," Schooners, just a few miles from the Navy base. The restaurant sat perilously close to a towering condominium but had one of the best views of the sugar white sands and clear emerald-colored waters of Panama City Beach.

Parker was the first one there, so he grabbed a table for the four of them and basked in the view and gentle southerly breeze while sipping a "half and half" sweet tea. Grammatically, that drink order made no sense at all, but the local waitresses knew what he meant. Full-strength Southern sweet tea is really sweet, and not so good for the pancreas.

While he waited, he thought about the mission ahead of them, and whether his knowledge and skills could help keep the chosen divers alive and well. They would be breaking records for sure, but this dive was not about breaking records. It was about retrieving one of the most incredible machines ever seen on earth, if it actually existed. Of that, he couldn't be sure.

Truman and his escorts came around the corner and headed for Parker's table. Even with deeply shaded sunglasses, Truman was squinting. It was plain to see that the bright sun reflecting off the water and the stark white sand seemed to be tormenting him.

Parker waved them over to another table arranged so that Truman would be facing away from the brightness. Even then, Truman kept his sunglasses on.

"So Truman, have you been enjoying your outings? What do you think of the beach life?"

"Too many colors, too many people, too much heat."

"Really? I would think it's somewhat like your home in Mexico."

Acknowledging the presence of his escorts, Truman said, "My friends here and I have been talking. They tell me there is a cavern not far from here. I want to go there."

Parker looked at Truman's escorts, and they nodded their heads. It was true, they did have that discussion. The Florida Cavern's State Park was only about fifty miles North of Panama City near Marianna.

"I want to go there. I want my people to join me there."

"You mean you want to visit," Parker said.

One of the escorts shook his head. Apparently, he wanted to stay there.

"You can't stay there of course. It's a Florida State Park."

"Make it possible," Truman said emphatically.

The waitress came up to take their order just in time to break the strained conversation. This luncheon was not turning out the way Parker had expected. But then again, he kept forgetting this guy was not quite human. There was no reason why he should act the way most humans act.

While Truman looked at the menu, seemingly able to read the English just fine, Parker ordered a fried catfish sandwich and French Fries. The escorts ordered fish tacos, and then Truman ordered.

"I'll have the tuna steak."

"How would you like that cooked?"

"I don't want it cooked."

The waitress stared at Truman with her mouth agape.

"Uh, we don't serve raw fish. Would you like it rare?"

Parker interceded. "Rare was what he meant."

"OK, and what to drink?"

"Water."

"It will be just a few minutes," the waitress said, and then left.

Truman looked up at Parker and said, "I said I don't want it cooked."

"Look, if you're going to fit in, you have to let them cook your food a little bit."

"Then next time I'll have sushi. They don't have to cook that."

Parker was getting a little exasperated at this point. "OK, next time we'll get sushi, but not here. They don't serve sushi."

Truman lowered his head and looked glum. He was quiet.

"Truman,…"

Truman interrupted, "You know that is not my name."

"Yes, I know, but we agreed you needed an English name, one we can pronounce. So, why do you and your people not want to stay in Mexico?"

"I said that if I told you about the Master's vehicle, you would let us come to America."

"I know, and we will do that for you. But why?"

"Why? Because we want to be close to our Master's vehicle. We are of them."

A family at the next closest table started staring at them.

"OK, we'll have this discussion later, in private."

Throughout their time together at lunch Parker could not help but wonder what to do about this new complication. He would be way too busy planning the dive, so he would have to hand off responsibility for finding a new home for Truman and the Mexican immigrants. On the one hand, he could understand why a cave environment would help the emigrant's transition into Florida, but what a political and security mess this was going to be.

And then it occurred to him — the one person he trusted who could deal with both concerns and had ties to the State Department, was Laura Smith.

As soon as he watched Truman leave with his keepers, he made the call.

"Laura, I need you to perform a miracle and usurp a state government's mandate over park land, without pissing them off."

There was a lengthy pause on the other end of the line.

"Laura, are you there?"

"I am. And if I know anything about you at all, Jason, this must have something to do with Truman."

"You got that right."

Laura sounded a bit philosophical. "Did anyone tell you that you attract some of the strangest characters?"

"Yes. The Trolls insist I am Ta'veren."

"What did you say?"

"I just need you to see if you can arrange to have a Florida State Cavern near Marianna appropriated for three hundred of Truman's kin. Consider it a federal takeover because we'd have to provide security and whatever other needs they might have."

"Well I don't know what their toiletry and hygiene needs are, but we can't have them pooping in the Floridan aquifer."

"I know. I said I need a miracle."

"Jason, I don't know what Ta'veren is, but whatever it is, the Trolls are probably right."

CHAPTER 34. HYDROGEN

On Friday at fifteen hundred hours, the Hydrogen Dive sponsors in Washington made their initial selection. Divers 1, 3, 5 and 7 would be subjected to the next phase of testing which would determine the principal dive team and the alternates.

Of course, you couldn't work with those divers long before finding out they preferred to go by J.R., B.K., Tom and Freddie. J.R. was Number Five.

And now Parker's work began in earnest, preparing the men for the deepest diving mission of all time.

The Monday after the diver selectees had been announced, Parker was standing poolside at the NDC's forty foot deep pool.

J.R. asked, "So Doc, why is it we'll be breathing hydrogen?"

"You'll be breathing a mixture of hydrogen, helium and oxygen. First, you'll press down on helium until a thousand feet or so, then we'll start bleeding in a helium-hydrogen mixture for the rest of the press."

"But I thought hydrogen burned, like in the Hindenburg."

"Not if the fraction of oxygen is too low for combustion. As you know, on a helium press, you're out of the fire zone beyond 250 feet or so. Well, with hydrogen you have to go deeper, but at a thousand feet the oxygen percentage is too low to allow hydrogen combustion."

"So it's safe," J.R. said.

"Before you leave today I'll show you guys a demonstration in a small chamber. It's perfectly safe for the diver."

B.K. asked, "What about topside?"

"Good point. If we have a hydrogen leak, top side crew will be at risk, but we have alarms and explosion-proof fans to clear out any places where hydrogen could accumulate."

"And explode," B.K. said, smiling.

J.R. looked annoyed that his original question had been hijacked. "Like I said, why are we using hydrogen?"

"Well, a narcotic gas is needed to help calm the symptoms of the High Pressure Nervous Syndrome which is well known to affect deep sea divers. I've seen nitrogen used for that purpose on a 450-meter dive in Germany, but at deeper depths, nitrogen is too thick to breathe. Hydrogen is also narcotic but a lot lighter than nitrogen. It's altogether better, except for some weird side-effects you might experience."

"Like what?"

"Hallucinations. You might have an out of body hallucination where you see yourself from a distance."

"How do you know that?"

"Some French divers experienced that on a deep hydrogen dive, and a Canadian scientist watched himself during an argon dive. Argon is another narcotic gas when breathed at a great enough depth."

"Well, that sounds fucked up."

"But no worries," Parker said. "You're not really out of your body, it's just an illusion. You can work right past that, telling yourself it's just your imagination."

Tom was getting excited at this thought. "Crush it!"

"Yep," Parker continued, "it's just a mind game."

J.R., also feeling bravado well up inside him, said, "Hooyah, we can do this!"

That was exactly the reaction Parker was hoping for.

Because of the explosive nature of hydrogen under normal conditions, the Navy was not about to risk a lockout nuclear submarine by installing a hydrogen saturation diving system. But since secrecy and security would be of paramount importance, the decision was made to hide in plain sight by placing the system on a semisubmersible, floating oil drilling platform. When Russian and Chinese satellites passed overhead, it would look like an oil company was simply exercising their oil exploration rights off the coast of Alabama. The area south and west of Mobile Bay was already pimpled with too-many-to-count oil platforms. One more would not receive much attention.

Transocean's semi-submersible exploratory drilling rig Sovereign Explorer II had been towed to Pascagoula to be dismantled and scrapped. But when certain agencies made them an offer they could not refuse, the already existing diving facility, used for routine underwater rig maintenance, was modified for hydrogen saturation diving. No one could tell that hydrogen was being loaded on board; the hydrogen bottles looked like helium bottles, with only inconspicuous tell-tale labels to identify them.

178

One of the most audacious dives ever made by the U.S. Navy was being readied under the gaze of civilians and satellites. It looked every bit like just another attempt to identify oil among the salt domes off the edge of the Mississippi - Alabama Continental Shelf, not far from the site of the infamous Deep Water Horizon disaster.

Deep down inside, Parker was hoping this would not turn into another disaster.

CHAPTER 35. INTO THE BRAIN

The remaining divers were assembled into a laboratory where a small hyperbaric chamber had been set up for a demonstration of hydrogen combustion. Parker needed to get that demonstration over with before proceeding to the next series of purposefully stressful tests. The divers would have plenty to worry about before and during this dive, and the possibility of cremation did not need to be one of those worries.

The divers had been stripped of their phones to make sure none of what was to happen for the next couple of hours would be recorded or messaged.

Aside from the divers, the room held the NDC's Senior Medical Officer, Captain James Bauman, the NDC Commanding Officer, other operational commanders, plus a handful of three-letter Intel types who were lacking a working knowledge of hydrogen diving.

Parker began speaking from the front of the room.

Pointing to the chamber and a camera mounted on a viewport, Parker said, "This chamber is at a pressure equivalent to 100 feet. The inside of the chamber contains a well-mixed combination of oxygen and hydrogen. In the middle of the camera's field of view, which is projected on the large screen on the wall, is a spark plug."

A few of the observers began moving back a little, giving Parker and the chamber a little extra room.

Parker smiled. "As you might have guessed, I am going to deliberately cause ignition. But don't worry, this chamber is certified for tests of this type. It's been through this many times."

Parker continued, "Now if you'll count down with me from 10, I'll make a little fire."

Parker started counting, and the divers joined in the count. The others in the room were silent.

"Ten..nine..eight..seven..six..five." The officers started moving closer to the screen to get a better view.

"Four..three..two..one..ignition."

A bright yellow flash filled the screen and began fading a second later.

"So that's not what you want to see on a dive. The bad news is if you have a hydrogen fire, and not an explosion, you won't see it. You could walk right into a hydrogen flame and not know it until it was too late. For that reason, we'll have lots of sensors for hydrogen gas and heat. If someone as much as lights up a cigarette, the entire platform will know about it."

To a man, the crowd grew uneasy, thinking about the implications of an invisible fire.

"The Hindenburg disaster was highly visible, not because of the hydrogen, but because of the materials ignited by the burning hydrogen."

Some of the men were clearing their throats, perhaps wondering when the good news was coming.

"OK, divers. I have a math question for you."

The divers groaned.

"As usual for a sat dive, we want to keep the oxygen partial pressure at 0.45 atmospheres. For a 1000-foot dive, what fraction of oxygen do we want in the gas mixture?"

One of the divers protested, "Holy crap!"

"I'll give you a hint. The pressure at 1000 feet is 32 atmospheres."

Noiselessly the men put their heads down and started scribbling on paper they had been given. The quickest of them called out, "Fraction 0.014, or 1.4%."

Parker praised him as he was turning valves to flush out the burnt gases.

"Exactly right."

The diver beamed.

"I have pre-mixed 1.4% oxygen in a hydrogen mixture, and at this very moment, I'm flushing it into the chamber. So what do you think will happen when I repeat the test?"

All of the divers answered in synchrony, "Nothing."

"Right again. So can I now have a countdown from five?"

Several divers starting counting.

"Five..four..three..two..one..ignition"

Parker pushed the ignition button, and nothing happened.

"So gentlemen, you'll be pressed down on the usual helium-oxygen gas mixture until the oxygen percentage is 1.4%, and then we'll start adding hydrogen and a little helium for most of the rest of the press. By the time you're at 2500 feet, you'll be breathing about 50% hydrogen. And as you see, it won't burn or explode."

An officer asked, "How long will the press take."

"I'll let Captain Bauman take that question."

Bauman said, "We should be at 1500 feet within 17 days, and we'll continue the press to 2500 feet gradually over the next week or so, depending on how the divers are doing. We've never been that deep, so we're taking it slow."

"Isn't HPNS going to be a problem?"

"It could be, but a major advantage of using hydrogen is that its narcotic properties help suppress HPNS."

Another voice asked, "What's HPNS?"

"High Pressure Nervous Syndrome. You might want to watch the movie *The Abyss* to learn a little about it."

"Isn't that fictional?"

Bauman had infinite patience. "It is, but parts of it are highly accurate."

One of the Intel guys picked up on the word "narcotic." "Is it a good idea to have such valuable divers narcotized?"

Parker smiled. The man clearly did not understand that this kind of narcosis was a good thing.

Bauman didn't skip a beat. "They shouldn't notice it, but because there could be some unusual side effects from hydrogen narcosis, we're going to subject the divers to some additional testing."

"What kind?"

"Psychological testing. That's all I can say at this time. Now, are there any more questions?"

Jason Parker was also looking across the group to see if anyone had questions.

"Okay then," Parker said, "If there are no more questions, we'll call this meeting over and we'll start further briefing of the divers."

That was the signal for all but the divers, Bauman, Parker, and the Commanding Officer to leave the room.

"Anybody need a head break?"

The divers returned after a ten-minute break to find a stranger standing before them. They looked towards Parker, silently asking *who was this young lady?* She was obviously fit and quite attractive in a nerdy sort of way, glasses and all.

"As you're getting settled back in your seats, the Navy brought in a neuropsychologist from Princeton who's been under Navy contract for a number of years working on remotely operating ship-fighting systems. Her name is Bridgette Pfaender, and she'll be talking about our only real concern about this dive."

Nodding to Parker, she said, "Thank-you Dr. Parker. The reason I'm here is not because of my Navy work, but because during my doctoral training I worked in Lausanne, Switzerland working on the use of virtual reality to create out of body experiences by the use of avatars."

The men laughed politely.

"I'm not talking James Cameron-type avatars, but a visual avatar, nevertheless. Now, I've been briefed that the Navy's greatest concern about this mission, whatever it is, is that you might become dissociated by the narcotic properties of hydrogen."

"Ma'am, what does dissociated mean?"

"It means that you won't care what happens to you because you won't recognize yourself as really being you."

"Huh?"

"In other words, you may watch yourself from a different perspective, not realizing the person you are watching is really you. You might watch them put their hand in a flame, not understanding that it is you putting your hand into a flame."

"Oh crap!"

Another diver said, "You're shitting me."

"Not at all. And that is obviously not a thing we want you to be doing. They tell me the mission is kind of important."

Parker couldn't help smiling at that statement. *Yeah, kind of.*

Pfaender wrapped up the introduction and then asked, "So who wants to be first?"

"First for what?"

"You'll see. We have a demonstration set up for one of you at a time in the adjoining room. And once you've been through it, you'll be isolated from those who haven't been through it yet."

Tom raised his hand and was led to the door by Dr. Pfaender. Bauman followed her through the door.

The rest of the divers stretched, got comfortable, and started reading some of the written material Dr. Pfaender had given them. Some chatted softly among themselves, imagining what they would be experiencing behind the door.

John Clarke

Pfander's assistant directed Tom, a large and powerful man, to take off his shirt and stand in two painted footprints on the floor. He was given gloves which provided feedback to a computer while measuring the quantity and composition of sweat from his hands. ECG electrodes were applied, and then he was fitted with a virtual reality mask on his head, followed by a helmet containing several small cameras linked to other cameras stationed behind the diver. On the wall ahead of him was a screen which showed the observers what the diver was seeing.

Pfaender instructed the observers to put on the 3-D glasses her assistant had just handed them.

At first, there was nothing on the screen, but that was quickly followed by a 3-dimensional forest scene with tall trees and very sparse underbrush. It looked like an old, full growth forest.

And then, inserted into the screen was a virtual representation of the diver, an avatar, dressed as he was at the moment, but seen from behind. The diver was asked to move his arms and feet, and the image followed suit exactly. Then the diver was asked to walk in place, and as he did, the image of the man began walking through the forest.

In the virtual world, the diver would turn to see elements interjected into his field of view, like birds, squirrels, and a raccoon. And as he turned, the head and body of the image in front of him turned in synchrony.

Pfaender whispered to Parker and Bauman, who were standing together, "It normally takes no more than five minutes for the illusion of being out of body to take effect."

During all this time the diver's heart rate remained at a comfortable 70 beats per minute.

No one spoke, simply allowing the diver to become immersed in the virtual experience.

The peace was broken when a virtual man in a ghillie suit, the artificial seaweed or grasses draped suit used by snipers for disguise, approached, flailing a sword in threatening fashion through the air.

Tom stopped moving, then shouted to his avatar, "Don't just stand there. Run."

Although his hands began sweating and his heart rate became mildly elevated, he was clearly an observer, not a participant in the action. The wild man ran towards the virtual diver and with one strong swing severed the man's head.

"That's gotta hurt," is all the real diver said.

The screen went blank, and the assistants noiselessly moved into place a cage of sorts that had small rods protruding from it.

Pfaender asked him, "That wasn't too stressful was it?"

"No, like watching a movie. The guy looked like me, but I knew it wasn't me."

"OK, now we're changing it up a bit."

This time the scene was still a forest, but with thick underbrush.

"OK," Pfaender said, "let's go for a walk."

As the diver began moving in his virtual world, the rods in the cage began poking and stroking him just as the sticks and brush did in the imagery.

"This is different," he said.

Tom began modifying his behavior to avoid pokes from branches and limbs, but his dodging was to little avail. He was almost constantly poked, a fact that seemed to annoy him as indicated by his rising heart rate and increasingly sweaty palms.

He could see a clearing just up ahead and headed quickly towards it to avoid further abuse.

Just as he stepped into the clearing, a grizzly bear reared up on its back legs, and a massive paw swiped forward with the force of a pickup truck hitting the diver's head. His virtual head rolled through the air, spinning, and as it did the image on the screen rolled crazily as well, hitting the ground, then going dark.

The diver's heart rate had soared to 200 as the bear appeared, and continued to race long after the virtual diver had died.

"Holy crap, I thought I was a goner."

"So, it was a little more immersive this time?"

"Hell yeah. That was horrible."

Parker and Bauman realized at the same time that the difference was that the virtual man and the real man were being touched simultaneously. That caused the out of body manifestation to appear in full force.

"I'm glad he didn't rip my nuts off, first."

The room broke into laughter.

Pfaender, chuckling said, "Well yeah, I guess that could have been worse."

Assistants began removing the diver's headgear, gloves and electrodes, and offered him a drink of water.

"Make that a scotch please." He took the water, but his palms were so sweaty that the glass almost slipped from his hands.

The assistants helped the obviously shaken diver into the next room where he would be sequestered until the other divers had completed the simulation.

Parker asked Pfaender, "Is that a typical response?"

"Pretty much," she said. "It doesn't take long for the mind to switch over as long as touching is involved."

The rest of the divers had similar reactions, except for J.R., diver number five.

It had not taken long for the full immersion experience to take form. When the wild man attacked with the sword, J.R. shielded his face defensively and swung his short legs up into the attacker's groin. Then he karate-chopped the attacker's trachea and twisted his head for good measure, breaking his simulated neck.

The computer froze, not sure what to do next.

Pfaender looked at Parker and Bauman in disbelief. "I've never seen that before."

Bauman said softly, "Is it safe to continue?"

Pfaender looked puzzled, rotating her head simultaneously between a nod and a shake. She really didn't know.

But her curiosity finally won out.

"Let's see what happens."

Bauman, being the Medical Officer in charge, asked J.R., "Are you ready for more?"

"Bring it on."

Parker, Bauman and Pfaender looked at each other, and all three shrugged. J.R. was not a quitter.

The cage with computer-controlled rods was slipped over him as it had been for the others, and the second phase of the simulation began.

Like the others, J.R. quickly grew tired of being poked and prodded and sighed with relief when he spotted the clearing. He was home free.

When the bear appeared, standing two and a half times J.R.'s height, he turned and ran in the opposite direction as fast as his short legs would go, dragging the poking cage and electronics with him until he ran blindly into the back wall.

He yanked off his helmet without assistance and started ripping off his ECG leads.

Pfaender stood with her mouth wide open in disbelief.

186

"What did you expect me to do? You can't win a fight with a grizzly, not without a big-assed gun."

When the immediate shock wore off, Pfaender's assistants started laughing. They'd never seen the famous doctor so totally surprised. That laughing was contagious, and soon everyone in the room was laughing.

Looking at Parker for reassurance, J.R. asked, "So Doc, did I do good?"

"Yes, J.R., you did good."

CHAPTER 36. DEUX EX MACHINA

In deep diving, there were two primary concerns, cold water and difficulty breathing a high density gas. The first problem, dealing with a water temperature at depth of 40°- 45°F, or 4 to 7° Celsius, was solved fairly easily; a diver-worn electric suit pressing tightly against every inch of the divers' bodies. That suit was covered by a layer of non-compressible underwear that provided passive insulation. On top of that ensemble was a dry suit that kept sea water out and warmth in. That thermal solution should keep the divers warm for hours, as long as the batteries didn't fail.

On the other hand, breathing gas that was up to 11 times denser than air at sea level required innovative technology that Jason Parker had invented. He hadn't anticipated it being used for this application, but it turned out to be the most appropriate technology for the mission.

It was now time to introduce the remaining diver candidates to the "Deux ex Machina," or D.E.M. for short, the Navy designed breathing apparatus being used for the first time on this mission.

Parker was standing at a board in a lecture room, in front of the remaining diver candidates and their support personnel, which included diving officers, diving supervisors, and diving medical officers.

At the high gas densities experienced at 766 meters (2500 feet) the divers would fatigue their breathing muscles without some sort of assistance moving gas into and out of their lungs, and helping oxygen diffuse from the lungs to the blood stream, and carbon dioxide from the blood stream to the lungs. Whereas in a hospital an unconscious patient routinely has a ventilator breathe for them, forced ventilation is not tolerated by a conscious person.

To help working divers, Parker used a combination of two breathing assistance methods. The first was an inertial system where an oscillating mass pulled and pushed gas into the lungs as long as the diver breathed at the natural resonant frequency of a mass and pendulum. Under those conditions, the oscillating mass did the pushing and pulling instead of the diver's diaphragm. All the diver had to do was keep the pendulum moving with the slightest amount of effort. If the diver changed his breathing frequency, the so-called reactive Underwater Breathing Apparatus, or UBA, would adjust the pendulum length to ensure the system resonant frequency continued to match the diver's breathing frequency.

As strange as a reactive inertial system sounded, it was based on relatively simple physics. The second mode of assistance was a little more difficult to understand, but it was actually used routinely in hospitals for premature infants with respiratory distress from underdeveloped lungs. Inhaled oxygen or the chest wall was oscillated at a high frequency which literally shook oxygen and carbon dioxide molecules to help them diffuse from the blood stream to the lungs. The method was called high frequency oscillation, and of course, Parker had chosen to use chest wall vibration rather than oscillation of gas at the mouth. After all, it was a lot easier to talk with your chest vibrating than with your mouth vibrating.

When Parker patented the breathing apparatus, he simply called it the Reactive Underwater Breathing Apparatus but the company which licensed the technology called it the D.E.M., short for Deux Ex Machina. Parker was not known for clever self-marketing, but he rather liked the play of words afforded by the contrived name. "Deux" was French for the number two, and paid homage to the French producers of the first "Aqualung," while also signifying that the apparatus actually consisted of two components for breathing assistance.

The play on words came from the similar-sounding phrase, Deus Ex Machina, derived from the Latin for "God from the Machine," a device dating back to Greek Tragedies where a seemingly unsolvable problem is resolved by the inspired intervention of some character, perhaps God, or divine object. In the case of deep diving, the unsolvable problem of providing respiratory assistance at record-breaking depths would be solved by Parker's D.E.M.

At least that was the hope. In deep diving things can go sideways in unpredictable ways.

And for that, the dives earned their $500 a month in dive pay and hazardous duty pay. Of course, it wouldn't do them any good if they didn't survive.

CHAPTER 37. THE DIVE

J.R.'s response to the virtual reality test was an enigma. On the one hand, he fell easily into believing the out of body experience, which could be considered a weakness, but yet he responded to both threatening cases in the most appropriate way. Because of his unanticipated choices, and his self-confidence, he was chosen to be one of the primary divers on the deep hydrogen dive, as long as his physical and psychological state did not deteriorate during the dive. No matter what awaited him, he seemed likely to complete his mission and to survive.

And survival is exactly what Parker had promised J.R. early in his training.

Tom was chosen as J.R.'s buddy diver. Dr. Pfaender and the project's psychologists decided that Tom and J.R. were an ideal buddy team, complementing each other.

The other two divers, B.K. and Freddie, were equally complementary, and would step in if the primaries were not able to make the dive.

The understanding by all involved was that the Medical Director, Captain Bauman, would make the medical call about who would be first to enter the cave once the team reached the bottom, with concurrence from senior diving medical personnel in Washington.

The day had come for Tom and J.R. to begin their monumental journey, a journey that could not have begun any less monumentally. It began with the closing of a relatively small metal hatch, just large enough for the two saturation divers to climb into the titanium sphere. There was no formal fanfare, just the shaking of hands by a few dignitaries who had been helicoptered to the platform floating in deep water 90 miles south of Pensacola, Florida.

The farewell was low key because of the classified nature of the dive, and because some of those who knew about the dive did not want to be photographed, for both security reasons and as a disclaimer if the attempt literally blew up. A lot of people were still skittish about hydrogen diving, and the reassurances from Navy engineers, Jason Parker and Captain Bauman had done little to dissuade them.

As a generality, Washington is not filled with risk takers.

Hans Richter was one of the few outsiders to shake the pair's hands just before the semispherical hull door was closed and sealed. He had arrived a few minutes before, having just made the walk down from the helo deck to the hidden bowels of the platform where the hyperbaric chamber and tightly packed gas bottles containing oxygen, helium, and hydrogen, were stored.

Bauman, the NDC Senior Medical Officer, and Parker were the last two to see them off. As Parker grasped their hands, J.R. and Tom were all smiles. They had been on special missions before, but this was to be one for the books, even though that book would remain closed for many years.

Parker had one last reminder, "Remember, if it seems bizarre, it's just your imagination. It can't hurt you."

Tom answered back in his usual dry tone, "Maybe so, but I wonder if I can hurt it?"

"This is no competition to out-testosterone each other," Parker said. "Just find that damned thing and get back here safely."

"Copy that Doc," J.R. said as he started closing the hatch. "See you in a month or so."

J.R. and Tom wouldn't actually be going anywhere for a few weeks. Their entry sphere was connected to a much larger system of connected chambers for living, eating, and entertainment during the period where gas was added to the chamber complex to slowly increase its pressure. Only when the two divers and the complex had reached 2,500 feet equivalent depth, would they return to the transfer sphere. Then that sphere would be broken loose from the rest of the complex, lowered to the water level through a carefully concealed "moon pool," and placed in a waiting "receiver" on a modified Triton submarine.

As soon as the diver sphere was mated to the Triton, the two submariners in the non-pressurized sphere would be in audio contact with the divers. The submariners knew that they would have to treat that sphere gently because it was, in essence, a bomb, a bomb of pressurized hydrogen and helium that would obliterate the minisub and its human contents should things go seriously awry.

John Clarke

At precisely 0700 hours on a bright and clear Monday morning 80 miles out in the Gulf of Mexico, two divers donned breathing masks. While seated in their small dining area, they began squeezing their noses and swallowing to equalize the pressure across their eardrums as the diving system was pressed to a pressure equivalent to 40 feet on air to establish an oxygen atmosphere of 0.45 atmosphere. From that point on, a mixture of 5% nitrogen, the balance helium would be added to compress the complex to 1500 feet, with oxygen being added only as needed to make up for the oxygen consumption by the divers. Their exhaled carbon dioxide would be removed by chemical scrubbers.

Following trimix compression tables developed by Duke University and proven in Geesthacht, Germany the divers would be compressed to the pressure equivalent to 1500 feet within two days. Once reaching 1500 feet, hydrogen was bled into the diving complex at the same time that some of the nitrogen and helium was vented. The idea was to reduce the nitrogen concentration from 5% down to about 2% since nitrogen is a dense gas to breathe at great pressure, compared to helium or hydrogen. The venting and gas exchange would take at least another 24 hours while the pressure was maintained at 1500 feet.

After the divers and the gas mixture within the complex had stabilized at 1500 feet, pure hydrogen would be added until they reached 2500 feet of seawater. At that point, the gas in the complex would be about 49% hydrogen, 48% helium, 2% or less nitrogen, and less than 1% oxygen.

With luck, the narcotic effect of the hydrogen would counteract the central nervous system stimulating effect of the high pressure. According to theory, HPNS, the High Pressure Nervous Syndrome, would be neutralized. However, no one knew if that theory would still work at a pressure equivalent to that almost half a mile down. Only time would tell.

What they did know was that liquid breathing, like that shown in some science fiction movies, would not work. Filling the lungs with a perfluorocarbon liquid might enable oxygen to get into the diver's bloodstream, but it had never been shown to adequately remove carbon dioxide from a working diver's blood. It may work for premature babies, but J.R. and Tom were as far from babies as you can get.

So much for fiction.

192

Unlike typical U.S. Navy helium-oxygen dives which took a week or more to reach 1500 feet, the trimix dives developed at Duke University and proven in Germany, allowed greatly accelerated compression without any signs of HPNS. Parker had seen videos of those dives in Germany and thought the divers seemed downright chatty once reaching the bottom depth of 450 meters. It seemed like they were a little giddy from nitrogen narcosis.

And then the first real operational challenge for the Explorer began: venting helium and the small percentage of nitrogen it contained and replacing it with hydrogen all the while maintaining a depth close to 1500 feet. If the chamber operators lost control of chamber depth, the divers would be in great peril. It was a delicate operation, to say the least.

Thanks to computer controls and a Navy crew which had simulated that operation at least a hundred times, half the helium and nitrogen had been replaced by hydrogen within twenty-four hours. Once the venting was declared complete by the diving officer twenty-four hours ahead of schedule, there was a noisy celebration in the control room, and somewhat more subdued celebration in the chamber complex. J.R. and Tom were feeling great, enjoying the ease of breathing a less dense gas mixture, and anxious to continue the press.

Everyone knew the divers' ease of breathing would be short-lived as total pressure continued to climb and more and more molecules of hydrogen were being forced into the unyielding titanium chamber complex.

However, the good news was that with each passing hour, the elite crew of divers was getting closer to the point where they could separate from the complex and mate onto the minisub that was waiting to take them to the bottom of the De Soto Canyon.

Jason Parker and Captain Bauman picked up the headsets to talk to J.R. and Tom at sick call as the complex was nearing 1800 feet, the deepest NDC's facility had been with divers inside.

Sophisticated electronics, a so-called helium speech unscrambler, was needed to enable people outside the chamber to understand the divers inside due to the distorting effects of speech in a helium, and now hydrogen, atmosphere. In fact, when the divers wanted to discuss something between themselves, they also needed to put on headsets and have their speech unscrambled. Usually, they found it easier to use sign language or gestures.

The divers had assumed Bauman was speaking singly, and in confidence, to each of them during sick call. However, considering the national-security aspects of this mission, a lot of folks were listening in, including Parker, who was the Science Director for the mission. Such lack of privacy was a breach of just about every code of medical conduct there was, but again, no less than the Navy Surgeon General had authorized a breach of confidentiality, for the good of the Country.

Bauman talked to J.R. first. "How are you feeling this morning J.R.?"

"I'm damned excited to reach 1800 feet, and I'm feeling F..I..N..E.."

Even through the helium speech unscrambler, J.R.'s voiced still sounded a bit squeaky.

Parker was wondering if J.R.'s jubilation was because he was a little narcotic now that hydrogen was in the complex.

"How would you compare it to heliox at 1500?"

"Much better, actually. I think that hydrogen is good stuff. I feel G..R..E..A..T."

"J.R., this may take a while if you keep spelling things."

"Just trying to help out the electronics Doc. And by the way F..U..C..."

"Cut it out J.R.!" Parker said. "Let's show the good doctor some respect."

Bauman and Parker looked at each other. J.R. was high as a kite.

The Diving Officer muted all comms to J.R. and spoke to Bauman and Parker.

"OK guys, I'm getting just a little concerned. Is this going to pass?"

Bauman looked at Parker and shrugged.

Parker made an educated guess. "Based on what was seen on the French dive, I think his giddiness should subside with time and with the addition of more hydrogen."

Bauman said, "This may just be a transient hypomania episode. At Duke it turned into full blown mania at 2000 feet. This is not that bad, so let's see how Tom is doing."

Bauman unmuted the comms and continued with his sick call. "J.R., I want you to put your arm in our analyzer and let me check your vitals."

"Sure thing Doc. You know, this arm thingy reminds me of a girl I used to ..."

Control called out, "Cut out the crap J.R."

That was a mistake.

"Hey Control," J.R. shouted, "What the hell are ya doin' listening in on my private conversation with the Doctor? Isn't that against the Geneva Convention or Hippocratic Oath or something?"

"Relax J.R.," Bauman said, "You're not a prisoner."

"Uh, I beg to differ. We're inside this thing, and you're not. And we're not going anywhere."

Parker smiled at Bauman. The diver got him good.

"OK J.R., you made your point. Just stick your arm in the analyzer so I can check you out and get you your breakfast."

"Speaking of chow, it all tastes like shit now."

"Comes with the territory," Bauman said. "You know that."

"Tell Cookie to add some Louisiana Hot Sauce to my scrambled eggs."

"OK, we'll do. But I really need your readings."

"Here it comes Doc."

Several screens splashed alive with medical data, including heart rate, cardiac ECG, cardiac entropy, cardiac and liver enzymes, blood gases, ions like sodium, potassium, calcium. It was the whole nine yards, with a computerized assessment at the end.

Oddly, at the end of the assessment, instead of the usual clinical summary, someone had hacked the computer so it displayed a thumbs up image out of something that resembled an erect male phallus, and the large words on the screen "GOOD TO GO."

Bauman sighed and looked at Parker. "Did you see which Corpsman did this?"

"No, but whoever it is, they have good coding skills."

Bauman knew instantly who it was. Muting the comms again, he called to the most likely suspect.

"Petty Officer Driscoll, please tell me the correct summary is available somewhere here."

After a pause of several seconds, Chief Driscoll came up on the coms. "That's Chief Driscoll Sir."

"Correction: used to be Chief Driscoll." From Bauman's tone of voice, it was difficult for Parker to know if he was kidding or not.

"OK, sir. Someone told me you have to hit the keys control alt D I V E all at the same time."

"Very clever Driscoll. I want it fixed by tonight's sick call."

"Yes, sir."

John Clarke

Unmuting the comms, Bauman said, "Well J.R., apparently you're good to go. Now please put Tom on the line."

"Copy that."

A minute later Tom, a relatively sedate diver with a reputation for being level-headed and always in control, came up on the video comms.

"Hey Doc, how's it hanging?"

That did not sound like Tom.

"That's what I want to ask you. Did you sleep OK last night?"

"Hell no. I had some fuckin' weird dreams. Is that the hydrogen?"

"Could be, I guess. Hydrogen is sort of like a narcotic and anesthetic combined, and those agents can cause pretty weird dreams for a couple of days after surgery."

"Well this is no surgery, but I'd love to hear you say these dreams are only temporary."

Bauman looked at Parker, and Parked nodded.

"Not to worry Tom, you should be back to normal in the next day or so."

"OK, good to know. I guess you want my arm in the analyzer."

"That would be nice. Thanks, Tom."

A few seconds later, data similar to that of J.R.'s appeared, followed by the obscene summary screen.

"Things are looking good here Tom. Have any complaints?"

"Only one. J.R., I think he's high. What are you slipping into his drinks?"

"Only hydrogen Tom, only hydrogen. But it sounds like you're handling it fairly well."

"Well yeah, except for the dreams. Frankly, I'd rather be high like goofy over here."

J.R. could be heard laughing in the background; a squeaky laugh, not like Donald Duck but more like guinea pigs. Apparently, he was thoroughly enjoying himself.

"Tom, someone told me J.R. wanted to talk to Doctor Parker."

"I think he does, but maybe after chow. We're getting hungry."

"OK, that's a good sign; that's what I want to hear. I'll leave you in peace for now. Enjoy your steak and eggs."

"Out here," Tom said in typical military radio fashion.

CHAPTER 38. MCMURDO STATION

The Pisten Bully ride from McMurdo Station, Antarctica out to Cape Evans, only 15 miles away as the Skua flies, was noisy and, for the passengers in back, cold enough to make the ubiquitous bright-red Antarctic Parka a necessity. On the way, the tracked transport had to dodge Razorback Ridge protruding from the Ross Ice Shelf, and the perennial glacial tongue floating out over the frozen Ross Sea. The Erebus tongue continuously flows at an appropriately glacial pace from the caldera of the now sleeping volcano Mt. Erebus, 25 miles away from McMurdo and 13 miles upslope from Cape Evans.

Not far behind the Pisten Bully was a SnoCat pulling an ice drilling machine which would soon carve out a 9-foot diameter hole in the ice, and a diving hut which would sit atop the hole to protect the four divers and their scuba equipment from the bitter cold of Antarctic winds.

Sitting up front with the Pisten Bully driver, and receiving slightly more heat than the rest of her dive team in the back, was Dr. Alice McNolte, a polar diving biologist. Her usual home was in Alaska, but she headed south when she could, not to warmer climes, but to the even more extreme environment of Antarctica. Those who didn't know her well thought she had ice running through her veins, but those working with her knew otherwise. She was relatively young, attractive, and a highly competent biologist who specialized in organisms living at the sea, rock and ice interfaces where glaciers meet the sea and are grounded on the rocky seabed. Cape Evans was just such an environment, and Dr. McNolte had been studying this habitat for the past five years looking for changes caused by glacier advance and retreat.

McNolte's red hair and emerald green eyes would not have looked out of place in Ireland, her ancestral home, but they were a bit of an oddity on this frozen white continent. The transport driver had enough of a crush on her that he'd volunteered all five years to drive her to this remote location. They both knew that if the personnel transporter broke down, they would have a fairly long wait for rescue.

John Clarke

That, the driver thought, would not be a particularly bad thing, as long as they didn't freeze to death.

"So what do you think Doc, with the Arctic melting and ice accumulating down here, I guess the global warming folks don't quite know what to think."

"I try not to pay much attention. Anytime politicians pretend to understand things they don't understand, they just make fools of themselves."

"You think so?"

"Let's reverse roles. You think I would make a good politician?"

The scruffy haired but neatly bearded driver laughed. "Ha, I'd like to see that, a combination of Sarah Palin and Margaret Thatcher. That would be a hoot!"

McNolte smiled. Sam the Ice Man, as he liked to be called, had a graphic imagination.

"So if this imbalance keeps up, do you think the whole flipping world could, you know, flip over?"

Now she laughed. "I really don't think that could happen."

"But what if it did? Would our October Spring suddenly become the Austral Fall? And instead of heading into summer down there, would we be heading into winter?"

"Well that would seriously suck," she said. "Two dark winters in one year."

"Hey, I know a guy whose Dad was in the British Army. No sooner did things start warming up after a British winter, than he got shipped down to the Falklands to fight in their winter."

"That was with Argentina, wasn't it?"

"Yep."

Their conversation was interrupted when Sam pulled the Pisten Bully up to a cliff composed of jet black volcanic rock and ice. The glacial ice wall descended vertically deep underwater, grounded on the broken volcanic rocks of the Ross Sea about one hundred feet below the surface.

The divers piled out, happy to stretch their legs on the smooth bed of sea ice. On this austral spring day, the sky was cloudless, so the stark blue sky, brilliant white ice, and black rocks made a contrast in colors that would have made an interesting challenge for any artist.

Art was the last thing on McNolte's mind. The lumbering Sno-Cat with its heavy load in tow behind it was no more than five minutes away.

198

She hopped out and walked over to the spot where she wanted the ice drill to bore the diving hole. From that hole, there would be less than a twenty-yard swim to the glacier wall.

Two of the divers had tried looking around without their polarized sunglasses, but as the Sno-Cat pulled up, they gave up and yielded to the almost overwhelming glare of sun and ice.

The drilling crew got to work on their often repeated chore, and within ten minutes a nine foot wide by twelve-foot deep hole had been dug. When the large drill bit was backed out, it sloshed a small flood of sea water onto the surface ice. Within another minute that water had frozen, and a Weddell Seal had discovered the new breathing hole and appropriated it by wedging its body into the hole and thrusting its almost cute, big-eyed head up into the cold air to gaze at the strange creatures staring back at him.

It was likely that particular seal had never seen humans before.

Inside the recently warmed shelter which had been towed by the Snow Cat, McNolte reminded her divers of the dive plan after they changed into their Thinsulate undergarments and pulled on their trilaminate dry suits. They would be diving with a single large scuba bottle with a Y valve which allowed the attachment of two independent first and second stage regulators, just in case one failed under the ice. If a regulator failed by free flowing air, the diver would shut off that regulator and continue to be supplied air by the second regulator attached to the full face mask. It was as foolproof a diving system as possible while diving under many feet of Antarctic ice.

All scientist-divers would be carrying biological collection bottles, and one would also be carrying two cameras in waterproof pressure housings, one with a macro lens and one with a wide-angle lens for perspective shots. The full face masks were fitted with underwater comms, and McNolte would verbally direct the photographer when and how she wanted a shot taken.

The other divers were told to space themselves about 3 meters apart along the bottom of the sheer underwater glacier cliff. Then they would search with their flashlights for the fauna McNolte was interested in, signal her when something was found, and then, just as had happened in the previous years, the chain of scientist divers would move three meters down the line and start the search over. That way, each section would be searched at least three times by three different divers. The odds of the team missing something interesting was fairly remote.

As usual, McNolte was first to enter the bore hole and to exit under the ice. She would defend the diving hole from Weddell seals looking for a breath of air while her dive team splashed in. While she waited for the last diver to enter, the other divers descended straightway toward the 33-meter depth where the glacier front lay.

With the last diver in the water, McNolte turned and followed that diver to the bottom, clearing her ears from the growing water pressure on the way down.

As was typical this time of year, the water was air clear, and as soon as she turned towards the bottom, she could see the light of the first diver pointed toward the glacial wall. And then the second diver joined the first.

They're screwing up the dive plan already, she thought.

"Hey guys," she shouted on her comms, "have you forgotten the dive plan already?"

"Doc, you've got to see this."

By then all the divers were clustered at one spot, shining their lights on something in the ice, not along the ice-rock interface where they were supposed to be looking.

What the hell are they doing? she wondered as she approached the motionless divers.

CHAPTER 39. THE CAPE EVANS REPORT

The Navy Saturation divers were already down to 2000 feet, and doing well, in spite of not yet disengaging from the diving chamber which had been their home for 2 weeks already. Knowing that Descent day would be coming up soon, and having time to think in their slight hydrogen-induced haze, both divers were asking Parker, more and more insistently, what they might be encountering.

The truth was, he had no clue. Even the blind remote reviewer was a little unclear about that. Parker, having had first-hand experience with remote viewing, and knowing that Joshua Nilsson was probably the best remote viewer alive, was growing a little edgy. In fact, he had retired to his bunk in the middle of the afternoon to think things through. He would have to come up with something soon or lose credibility with the divers. They were putting their lives on the line for him and some unnamed intelligence agencies, and those divers deserved all the preparation they could get. But so far, neither he nor Hans Richter had a compelling story.

The knock on the door of his cramped cabin was unexpected. His response was not cordial.

"As I said, I need some time to think. Give me a frigging hour."

"We don't have an hour Jason." That feminine voice, high but forceful, was totally out of place. But it was unmistakably Laura Smith.

Parker unlocked the door and in walked Smith and Hans Richter.

Laura hugged him and then whispered in his ear. "You didn't leave the Playboy lying around did you?"

He laughed, "No time for that my dear. But if you're here to witness the dive, you'll have a wait. I'm guessing another week before we launch."

"Maybe later, but not now. Hans and I have something to show you. It may help you with your divers."

As she said that, Richter opened a folder with a tell-tale red "Top Secret/SCI" followed by "Brandy Bench" printed in red block letters. He withdrew an 8 by 11-inch color photo and handed it to Parker.

Parker had seen the color combinations before. It was glacial ice, and something was in the ice, just out of reach of the ice edge. It looked metallic, but nothing was smooth about it. It looked crushed.

"I've seen something like this," Parker said, "a World War II P-38 that landed on the Greenland ice shelf, and got eaten up by the glacier. With the Arctic melting, the plane reappeared a few years ago, somewhat worse for wear."

Laura and Hans smiled at each other.

"Where was this photo taken?" Parker asked.

"In Antarctica, near the bottom of the Mount Erebus glacier in 100 feet of water."

"Under 100 feet of ice? Well, that explains why it looks so damaged, but, it can't be under 100 feet of ice. That sort of ice deposition would take thousands of years. And we didn't have airplanes ..."

Parker's voice trailed off as he realized the implications.

"Oh my God, this is a spacecraft?"

Richter answered. "It's surrounded by ice that glaciologists estimate was laid down between 2000 and 10,000 years ago."

Parker gave a breathy whistle. "Do you think it could be a Frog ship?"

"Well, you're the one who said they claimed to arrive ten thousand years ago. It's either theirs, or some other species."

"Are there other species?" Parker asked Richter.

Richter did not respond, but Laura jumped in, "It for sure is not human."

Parker looked up at her, still uncomfortable with what he was being told. "Unless they were from time traveling humans."

Parker was serious, but Laura laughed. "You been watching too many Twilight Zone reruns?"

Although Parker had met the only alien species ever officially recognized by the U.S government, he still found it difficult to believe their espoused timeline; that they arrived on Earth from some intergalactic star system roughly ten thousand years ago. He actually had not dismissed the possibility that time-traveling humans could account for such an ancient spacecraft anomaly, such as the one in the photograph.

Parker was feeling a little woozy. "I have a million questions for you guys. But the first is, why are you showing me this?"

"POTUS asked us to show you. He thinks it might inspire your divers to know we actually have an alien spaceship."

"Do you know for sure that's what it is?"

"We're guessing. The logistics of extracting this thing down there, in secret, is pretty enormous. And since it's been crushed by the glacier, we know it won't be functional. But it's real, and that's important to know. What your divers find, if they find anything, is probably functional, at least minimally."

"I can tell the divers that?"

"Long as they're on secure comms. No one else is to know."

"Unfortunately everything is recorded. There are no secure comms."

"Well, then," Richter smiled, "Maybe this will just have to remain our little secret."

Richter left on the next helicopter out, but Laura Smith planned to stay behind until the dive was completed.

At lunch, Parker sat across from her at the metal mess hall table, and while engaged in small talk, he could not help admiring her, both her inner and outer beauty. Oddly enough, her Starchild beliefs and reputation, rather than remaining a source of governmental distrust, had somehow become much desired by the most secretive of government circles. Perhaps the fact that she and Parker were the only two people on Earth who could operate an extraterrestrial training aid may have had something to do with it.

"You've come a long ways, Laura, since the day when the Frogs left. How did you end up on the dark side?"

"When they contacted me, oh a little over two years ago, they told me I had a choice in life. As they put it, my eccentricities would always handicap me, or I could choose to work someplace where those same eccentricities would be a benefit."

"I didn't see that one coming."

"I think I have you to thank for that. If you hadn't brought me in to monitor your remote viewing trial, I would have remained in your eyes only another graduate student with bizarre ideas about my before-life origins."

"Well, you do know I'm still not fully buying into that before-life stuff, but our shared experiences have made me wonder — a lot — about what this universe and our lives are all about. Yeah, I've thought a lot about that."

"I'm surprised you haven't been pulled out of your Navy job and into some of the same stuff I'm working on."

"Can you tell me about that work?"

"Absolutely not," she said emphatically.

"Well, from what they tell me, I'm more important to them where I am."

"And that may be true."

"May be?"

"It depends on who said it."

"That would be our old, and somewhat odd, Hans Richter."

She laughed. "Yeah, it's somewhat odd that he's gone from being an almost evil nemesis to someone we trust and, for the most part, respect."

"That is true," he said, followed by the rhetorical question, "Who would have thought?"

They got up and moved their trays to the kitchen conveyor line, then he started his tour of the platform, starting with the outside perimeter with full a view of the relatively placid ocean. They first stopped at the side facing south, towards the distant Yucatan Peninsula where Parker had met the Trolls, as he liked to call them.

"So, this thing they found in Antarctica, they are trying to recover it, aren't they?"

"Yes, but they seem to be in no rush. All attention is now on this dive. We'd much rather have a fresh example of the technology rather than a crushed and possibly worthless piece of discarded wreckage, even if it is ten thousand years old."

"I imagine someday it will end up in the Air and Space Museum."

Smith thought about that for a moment, expressionless.

"Our world is quickly changing," she said.

"We knew it would," he responded, "once there was alien disclosure. That's one reason I was so stubborn about not believing it."

"Until the Frogs repaired your chest wound."

"True," Parker said.

"How is that, by the way?" she asked.

"My chest wound? You can barely see the scar tissue. I have no idea how they did that."

"Just keep in mind, if you get shot again, nobody will be able to save you like that, now that they're gone."

Parker turned towards Laura and laughed. "I'm trying hard not to piss anybody off."

After Parker had shown Laura the machinery spaces, gas storage bottles, hydrogen and fire alarms, and huge sparkless ventilation fans, everything needed for safe hydrogen diving, he led Laura down to the hyperbaric chambers where waited J.R. and Tom, Navy divers who had just beat the U.S. deep diving record.

"The divers are in great spirits having just set a depth record, and are not too far away from deployment. But also keep in mind that hydrogen is a little intoxicating, and J.R. has sometimes been less inhibited ever since we switched to hydrogen. He's better now, but if he becomes inappropriate, don't hesitate to put him in his place."

Laura smiled. "Jason, I can handle myself just fine."

Parker picked up a headset and put it on, and handed a second headset to Laura who also placed hers on.

"In the chamber, can you come up on Bravo comms? I have an important visitor to see you."

It took a few seconds for Tom to move over to the viewscreen and microphone.

"Hey there Doc, who's your pretty lady friend?"

They all heard instant squeaking from J.R. before he got to the viewscreen and within range of the helium/hydrogen unscrambler.

"Doc, you brought us a chick?"

"This is Doctor Laura Smith, the young lady of Frog fame."

"Doc Laura," J.R. said, "I've heard a lot about you, and what I didn't hear, I imagined. But damn, you're prettier than I imagined."

"Thanks. Is that J.R. I'm talking to?"

"Yes it is, the famous one."

"And you must be Tom, the handsome one."

"Oh, that hurts," J.R. said, "and I thought I could like you."

Laura was right, she could handle herself around Navy divers just fine.

"So how are you guys feeling about having set a new diving record?"

"I'll let Tom speak for himself, but I'm feeling G..R..E..A..T."

Parker turned to Laura, "I forgot to warn you, J.R. has decided he likes to spell when he gets excited."

"Really?"

"It's a hydrogen effect apparently. Hasn't done it any other time."

"Bullshit. I was a kick ass spelling bee champion in elementary school."

"I'm sure you were," Laura said.

Tom said, "The only record I'm interested in is getting to 2500 feet and getting the job done."

"So Doctor Smith," J.R. asked, "are we going to find any of those Frogs when we get in that cave?"

Laura laughed, which apparently offended J.R. "OK, J.R., I didn't mean to make light of your concern. After all, you're the one taking the risk. But the answer is, they're all gone."

"You know that for a fact?" J.R. asked.

"As sure as I can be about anything."

That comment resulted in silence from the chamber.

Parker asked, "Are you guys OK with that?"

"Don't worry about us," Tom said. "Nothing's guaranteed — we know that."

J.R. said, "But supposing we meet one of those Frogs. What's the greeting etiquette? Are we supposed to shake their paw?"

Parker laughed, "I honestly don't know. I never touched one physically. If you do, that'll be a first."

"Cool," J.R. said. "I like being first."

A life support technician tapped Parker on the shoulder. "I'm sorry to interrupt, but I need to have them lock out their bedding, and we have to clear this area when they do that."

"Really?" Parker said. "Why?"

"It's saturated with hydrogen. It's not explosive in there, but it sure as hell is out here. So we need you folks to leave this area while the transfer is underway."

Parker turned his attention back to the men in the chamber. "Guys, I'll check back with you in the morning. In the meanwhile, be thinking if you have anything you want us to brief you on."

J.R. answered, "We're good here. The sooner we can head down to the bottom the sooner we can start decompression."

"Copy that," Parker said.

Parker turned to Laura. "And to think I was all worried about what they might ask. I think you're my lucky charm."

She smiled at Jason Parker with a mischievous smile, cocking her head so her long brunette hair shifted on her shoulder. "You got that right."

CHAPTER 40. CONDITION ZEBRA

Parker and Laura simultaneously felt a new vibration underneath their feet.

At the same time, loudspeakers placed around the platform crackled. "Attention all hands, attention all hands. We are now in Condition Zebra. This is not a drill."

Laura looked at Parker with concern.

"You've heard tigers can't change their stripes?" he asked. "Well, this tiger can. We call it switching to Zebra mode."

Parker's comment seemed every bit as random as did the sudden vibration.

"Whatever are you talking about Jason?"

"We're trying to pass as an exploratory oil drilling platform, but we don't sound like one. So when a Russian sub is in hearing range, we start generating the noise and vibration that sounds more like a platform."

"There's a sub out there?"

"Apparently. Somewhere."

"Do we have our own sub out there to counter it?"

"Apparently, somewhere. They're simply serving as a reminder to the Russians to not get too close to our shores."

"Do you think they're interested in us?"

"Curious perhaps. Probably nothing more."

The public address system, or 1MC, came alive again. "All senior mission personnel lay to the duty room."

"What does lay mean?" Laura asked.

"It's Navy talk for come."

"So why didn't they just say that?"

"Tradition. And considering your status with the POTUS, I'm bringing you in too."

The metal stairs normally reverberated with their footsteps, but that sound was almost drowned out by the fake drilling sounds being transmitted throughout the ultrastructure of the platform. Parker bounded up two flights, with Laura in hot pursuit, which placed them at the entrance to the mission control room, a room flanked with piping diagrams, submarine schematics, and video screens.

As people were gathering, the podium at the front of the room was empty. But within a few minutes, a Navy Captain that Parker knew to be a former submarine Commanding Officer stepped up to the platform. He was wearing green cammies typical of a special operations officer.

"Can you hear me without my using the mic?"

From the back of the room, a civilian Parker did not know yelled, "Yes sir."

"OK then," as he started strolling back and forth. "We have an interesting situation cropping up, literally, about twenty miles south of our position. Our guardian sub detected what we believe to be a Severodvinsk-class submarine cruising at a fairly shallow depth on a bearing of 090. If it keeps its course, it won't be approaching us. But this is a modern fast attack submarine, and if it did change course, that would soon place it closer than we would like."

One of the screens displayed a photo of the Severodvinsk, the first in the series, an update of the cold-war Akula class subs.

The audience was making a few rustling noises, but no one was talking. The Captain had their attention.

"But the really interesting thing is, there's another one out there somewhere. We had a contact, deep for a while, but we think it's still out there. Why they're here, we don't know, but the fact that it could be closer than 100 kilometers from us has been getting our attention, as well as that of the CNO, and higher."

"We don't anticipate any threat from the sub or subs. We think they're just curious. Perhaps something tipped them off that we're not your usual drilling platform."

At that moment a Lieutenant Commander in khakis walked up to the Captain and handed him a note. The Captain looked down at it for a moment, then looked up smiling.

"Our reconnaissance aircraft has a visual on the sub which is now on the surface. They seem to be coming to a standstill, and sailors are seen pulling out a charcoal grill. This may be their version of a *steel beach*, a submariners' picnic. They may simply be wanting to soak up some tropical sun. It's pretty much a dead calm out there."

Some in the audience started laughing, enjoying the break in the tension.

On another screen, a visual from the intercepting reconnaissance aircraft came up. Sure enough, the flat tops of the sub's missile tubes made a great surface for sailors to cook and feast. Most likely, within a few minutes, sailors would be stripping down to their skivvies and jumping into the water, with an armed sentry in the conning tower keeping a watch out for sharks.

For several minutes the Captain was quiet, as they all seemed to enjoy the almost voyeuristic experience of watching their Russian potential-adversaries taking time out from drills to play.

One of the civilians asked, "Hey Captain, can we do that?"

His answer was completely expected. "When our job is done."

Unlike a normal exploratory oil drilling platform, the Explorer could defend itself. If something were to attack it, 30 mm airburst shells and supercavitating rounds would provide defense both in the air and in the water. And if something got inside their outer defense perimeter, a cleverly camouflaged Phalanx CWIS Gatling gun firing over 4000 rounds a minute would take it out. Those weapons were manned and ready to fire by a ship-trained crew at a moment's notice.

"Well as much fun as this is, we need to get back to work. As long as the sub, or subs, are in the area, you'll have to put up with the noise. I'm afraid that can't be helped."

A lieutenant drew the Captain's attention to an area just forward of the submarine's sail. Two sailors were carrying a box of some sort. With the Captain's attention now back on the screen, everyone in the room grew silent and watched.

The two Russian submariners set the box down on the deck and opened it. At first nothing happened, and then several small objects left the box and flew just above the water, seeming to gain speed by the second. The observing plane's main camera followed this new object since the sub itself no longer seemed to be of much interest.

"Drones," someone said. The Captain laughed, "Could be, they're everywhere."

Indeed, the high-resolution video relay seemed to indicate multiple points of light, reflective surfaces, but as the objects climbed to roughly a thousand feet of altitude, they continued to accelerate.

The good news was that they were heading due east, away from the American platform.

A nearby Commander said, "I've never seen a drone like that."

The Captain said nothing, just watching for a minute, then he gave the order, "Make sure our defensive positions are manned, safety's off, just in case."

The video screen was now having a hard time keeping track of the tiny objects as they accelerated. The average velocity was now showing on the screens, and that velocity was climbing, 300 knots, 400 knots, 500 knots. The heading was maintaining a constant 90 degrees, due east.

"This is not your typical aerial vehicle folks," the Captain said.

Someone noticed the heading changing. "It's turning more northerly."

Indeed, they watched with amazement as the heading was now turning through 80°, then 70°, through 60°, all while accelerating. By the time the heading was passing through 40°, the targets were roaring along at 700 knots, above the speed of sound.

"Those little bastards have gone supersonic and are headed north."

Within moments they were due east of the platform and still turning toward the west.

The IMC blurted out, "Attention all hands, man battle stations, man battle stations."

Virtually everyone in the room ran to their assigned posts, including the senior officers who scurried to their Command Center deep in the bowels of the platform. That left Parker and Laura, with no assigned place to go, to watch the action on the screen.

"What are they, Jason?"

"Beats me, but I'd be surprised if they're offensive considering their small size. But damn, they sure are fast."

Parker realized the devices were not making a beeline for the platform. They were remaining at least five miles away at all times, circling the platform at supersonic speed. But as he watched, he realized the circling radius was getting shorter, and they were descending. Whatever tactic this was, it was becoming more puzzling, and more threatening, by the minute.

By the time the craft had started their second circuit around the platform, they had closed to within two miles, and their speed had increased to 1000 knots.

Parker was beginning to wonder if the sweep rate of their defensive weapons would be fast enough to keep up with the targets. He had a feeling he would soon find out.

Sure enough, the platform's autocannon let rip with a three-second burst of radar triggered exploding shells, and Parker and Laura were able to follow the shells leading their target. An explosive intercept seemed very likely.

Things were happening quickly now. Parker saw the shell bursts and saw the targets head down to the water. But he wasn't sure of the timing. It almost looked like the targets dropped to the water before the shells burst, but that could not be.

Then the impossible happened. The targets sprang out of the water and were headed directly towards the platform, only slightly slower than they had been traveling. The CWIS, the platform's last defense, opened up with a "brrrrt" of lethal rounds, and again the targets hit the water.

Parker and Laura could hear a cheer from the gun stations, but from the video coming from the overhead surveillance aircraft, Parker and Laura could see trails of bubble headed for the platform. The drones, or whatever they were, were supercavitating, rocketing through the water as easily as they had in air. And they were seconds away from impacting the platform.

If they were nothing more than kinetic energy weapons, they still might be able to bring the platform down.

Instinctively, Parker grabbed Laura and threw her to the deck, covering her body with his.

But the expected blast did not come. In fact, nothing at all happened. All was quiet, including the guns; they no longer had targets.

It was a very long minute before the 1MC announced, "All clear, secure battle stations."

Parker and Laura got to their feet and continued to watch the video feed from the reconnaissance aircraft, but as it circled over the platform, there was nothing at all interesting to see. And when the aircraft's high-powered cameras swiveled back to where the Russian sub had been minutes before, nothing was there except some meandering swirls in the water generated by the sub's quick submersion. It had quietly snuck off after scaring the hell out of the Americans.

No one came back into the room. If the Captain knew what had happened, he wasn't talking, not yet anyway.

Parker led Laura out of the room, down the main passageway, and down two decks to where the hyperbaric chambers were still

211

pressurizing as if nothing had happened. Of course, the two divers, having heard all the commotion, knew this was not just another dive day. They were peering out the portholes as the two approached. As they moved over to the camera, their look of concern was plain to see on the high-resolution video screen.

Not surprisingly, J.R. was the first to speak. "Well, finally, someone came to check on us. Yep, we're still alive, thank-you. What the fuck happened?"

Parker looked at Laura, as if wondering what to say. She shrugged, and he answered what he knew about the sub and the mysterious supersonic drones, and the platform's weapons apparently not destroying them.

Tom, always the more serene of the dive pair, said, "You know what saturation divers think about at a time like this?"

"No telling."

"We know we're in a very strong, sealed metal pressure vessel, and assuming all the emergency seals work, and the platform sinks to the ocean bottom, we'll be sitting on the bottom wondering how long our oxygen will last."

J.R. added his part. "All you guys will be dead, but we'll be sitting here, playing cards, tapping on the chamber wall. Waiting to die but hoping someone will come along and raise the chamber. But from 2500 feet, that could be a long wait."

"So tell me, Dr. Parker," Tom asked, "do you think the Navy has a contingency plan to rescue us if that happens?"

"Do you really want to know?" Parker answered.

"Don't waste your breath," J.R. said. "We know the answer."

"Yeah," Tom said, "it's always gonna suck for the divers when the dive boat sinks."

CHAPTER 41. DRONEVILLE

It was decision time at the Chief of Naval Operations and the Whitehouse. Should the compression stop, continue, or reverse? In other words, was this drone encounter a trigger for a mission abort?

Parker, Laura, the on-scene Captain, the Explorer platform CIA agent, and half of the D.C. Intel and Naval Operation's community were on a secure teleconference.

The voice leading the group was the 4 star Admiral, Admiral Bill Brighton, or simply, CNO.

Within an hour after the incident, it had been determined that sensors at the opening of the De Soto Canyon cave had detected multiple targets entering, and none leaving. Shortly after the incident, the Explorer had sent its autonomous underwater vehicle down to investigate, and initially detected a visual anomaly, but a second later that anomaly had disappeared.

The Russian sub that launched this incident was none other than K-560, the original attack submarine in the Yasen-class. Although the U.S. Navy had every reason to fire upon the devices launched by this attack submarine, the question was why the Russians would reveal that they possess an extremely capable drone. For lack of other words, "drone" was what the Whitehouse wanted to call these devices. Parker thought that word belied the potential threat these devices could pose to U.S. security.

Although the U.S. had developed advanced electromagnetic methods for disabling drones at a considerable distance, those weapons had in fact been part of the platform's armamentarium, a fact unknown to most of the civilians on the platform. Even more troubling was the fact that two close-in weapons systems, commonly deployed on U.S. Navy vessels, apparently had no effect on the drones. Somehow the drones were able to see the weapon's rounds in flight, choose an avoidance strategy and implement it all the while flying at supersonic speeds and a high rate of turn. Furthermore, rather than being destroyed by impact with the water, the drones managed to use the water for concealment and protection. In fact, the drones used that ploy twice before diving to 2500 feet to the cave entrance.

Admiral Brighton asked, "I'm looking for a potential propulsion source for those drones. Hopkins Applied Physics Lab, do you have a thought?"

"Dr. Bromley here. I hate to say it, but I have no idea."

Nathan Bromley would be the one person in the submarine group at APL that might have known. He was a Naval Academy graduate, became a "nuke," or nuclear submariner, before getting his Ph.D. in advanced physics, and then joining the research staff at APL.

"Anyone else know?"

Someone said, "NASA special projects folks might know. Want me to contact them?"

"Might be a good idea," the Admiral said.

"Anyone know why the craft didn't break up after hitting the water?"

Several people said it simultaneously, "Supercavitation."

"Yeah, that's what I was thinking," said the Admiral. "Supercavitating, supersonic drones. Can you imagine that?"

Supercavitation was the one thing everyone there understood. But in truth no one knew how the drones were propelled, or where they had gone, or why they might have been interested in the cave.

Parker, of course, had a theory. He had discussed it beforehand with Laura, and they both agreed his thoughts should not be revealed unless really pressed. His idea was admittedly fantastical, and would probably end up discrediting them both, resulting in them being kicked off the conference call. After all, they were somewhat tainted by previous exposure to extraterrestrial aliens, and not all in the military felt they could be completely trusted.

The CNO continued. "Obviously, we've now shown our hand. As the Russians may have suspected, we're clearly not an exploratory oil drilling operation, not with that much firepower. Unfortunately, it was all for naught."

He continued, "Remember, by the end of this call we have a joint decision to make; to hold the course, to back down and abort, or to accelerate the press."

Parker knew there would be a human cost to accelerating the schedule, but he knew if he mentioned it, he'd be asked to quantify it, and he couldn't. That was another reason to keep quiet.

"So before we get to decision time, let's talk some more about the drones. I suppose Intel had no clue they existed, and our tech gurus have no idea how they work. Is that a correct assumption?"

That question was greeted with silence.

"I'd rather not assume you all agree. I want to hear it."

Someone spoke up. "Greenly here Sir, and that is a correct assessment."

There was no way for Parker to know who Greenly was. Intel guys don't advertise their association, but obviously, CNO knew him.

"I thought so. And that just makes me want to continue the dive. Even if we don't come back with an alien craft, we may grab a new drone."

The Explorer's Officer in Charge spoke. "Sir, we've already sent an AUV down, and it found nothing."

"Maybe the little bastards are good at hiding. They seem to be good at everything else."

Parker, sitting immediately to the right of the OIC, could tell from his body language that the Captain wanted to argue that point, but wouldn't. O6's just don't argue with four Stars, not unless something awfully important was at stake and the O6 had verified data. This O6, like the rest of them, really had nothing to offer.

CNO continued, "I can't help but notice that our celebrity Frog-abductees are being awfully quiet. Do you two have anything to contribute?"

Laura and Parker looked at each other, and Parker shook his head.

"I see your head shaking Parker. Does that mean you have nothing to say? Or you Laura? That would be a first." CNO chuckled at his little joke.

"No sir," Parker began. "I just think what we have to say is going to be a little on the goofy side, and we don't have data to back it up."

CNO laughed. "Well, I don't mean to hurt your feelings, but more than one person in D.C. thinks you guys are more than a little goofy, but we keep you on the payroll anyway. So spill the beans, and that's an order."

Laura looked at Parker half-sympathetically. *Better him than me,* she thought.

"Sir, this is just a gut call, but I don't think those are Russian drones. The Russians are not that technically advanced."

"OK, so who built them?"

"I think they're not human made."

215

Apparently, that caught the audience by surprise. There was total silence for a few moments while the CNO consulted with the Director of National Intelligence.

"You think your Frogs built them? If so, how did the Russians get them?"

"Sir, I've been wondering that if a Frog ship is in fact in this cave, that there may be others, elsewhere. And perhaps the Russians found one."

"Well, I'm sure if they had one flying around we'd know about it. Wouldn't you Intel guys agree?"

They nodded their heads in unison.

"Sure, but what if the ship is not flyable? If it were flyable, the Frogs wouldn't have left it. It stayed behind because it was broken. Our ship, if it's here at all, may likewise be broken."

"I'll give you that, but what about the drones."

"Let's assume the drones are part of the ship's equipment. The Russians got inside and couldn't make the ship fly, but found drones that are autonomous once released."

"Well, that would make me want to have some too. But why would the Russians tip their hand?"

"Maybe because they're desperate. Suppose they found out that the drones always returned to their ship. Perhaps they were desperate to know if we had a ship too. It would be a gamble, but perhaps the drones would tell them. If the drones didn't return to the sub, it meant they'd found another hive."

"Hive?"

"Worker bees always return to the hive. If the hive is destroyed, but a new queen shows up, those workers will go to a new hive with the new queen."

"Parker, are you making this stuff up?"

"If it's any consolation, Dr. Smith agrees with me."

"Well, no offense folks, but that's not as comforting as you might think."

Several in the group chuckled.

"So what do you think that circle-the-platform business was, if not observation runs?"

"I don't think that's what it was. I think they were searching for a signal, flying a circular search pattern until they made a fix on their target, basically right below us.

The platform OIC spoke up for Parker and Laura.

"Sir, the drones really weren't aggressive. If they're as advanced as Parker is suggesting, perhaps they could have returned fire. But they didn't."

Parker was enjoying the verbal support for a change.

"You know how house flies can usually avoid a fly swatter? They sense it coming and evade. Perhaps all of our weaponry was nothing more than a fly swatter for the drones. It seemed to be easy for them to avoid. Perhaps we were nothing more than a nuisance, briefly slowing down their search for their target."

The CNO looked around the table to the others seated there at OPNAV Headquarters. No one seemed to have any response to Parker's imaginings.

"I assume you two know that no one is allowed to come to me with such wild imaginings without a hell of a lot of data to back it up. But I'm giving you folks some latitude because of your special circumstances. I know you can't provide me with data for anything you're claiming, so my next step is to deep dive this up here, and see if we can find something to support it."

"Thank you, Sir," Parker said.

"But I tell you this, based on what you've said I've made my decision. We're continuing with the dive, and accelerating the schedule. Your next task is to let the POTUS, SecDef and me know when you're splashing your divers. And it had better be a lot quicker than you'd planned. I want that thing found before the Russkies come back around."

Parker, Laura, and the OIC all stared at each other. Laura's mouth was agape.

"Call me back with a plan within twelve hours. And it had better be a good one. I don't know how long we can hold those Russian spooks off."

CHAPTER 42. MARIANNA

Hans Richter had been keeping a low profile, in keeping with his responsibility as the senior spook on the platform. But Parker had to get his opinion on the merits of what he knew would be an extreme risk. He wanted to know if the Intel agencies really thought it was worth jeopardizing two divers' lives.

They were standing on a railing facing north towards the Florabama beaches, protected from the Southerly breeze. That spot was chosen more or less by habit because of the curious observation that the sound of speech travels further with the wind than against it. Parker always thought that was strange since the speed of sound and of wind were so different, but the physics of acoustical refraction was just one of the many strange things that Parker had had to contend with during his work with the Navy.

"Hans, how do we know there's even anything of value in that cave?"

"We don't. But you didn't seem bothered by that before, so why now?"

"It's this accelerated schedule," Parker said. "It could seriously hurt our divers."

Richter asked, "Do any of your contacts know what those drones were? Could they be a clue?"

"Beats me. We have lots of analysts working on it, but nothing so far."

"Well here's a thought," Richter said. "Why don't you have someone talk to your Troll friend? Maybe he knows."

"Oh geesh," Parker said, "I thought we were trying to keep his presence hush hush."

"I know a certain NSA asset who already knows about him. We can put him on the clock anytime we want."

"Brightman?"

Kelly Brightman made the drive from Panama City up to the Marianna Caverns in an hour and a half. Truman Baltazar, formerly known as Argxtre, had incessantly requested that he be moved from the barracks up to a secluded, dark location more amenable to his physiology and temperament. That also made it less likely that his oddness would manifest itself to the public. He had come close to revealing the whole operation after someone ill-advisedly offered him a beer at Schooners beach bar.

Although his handlers were initially hesitant, he did want to move his people there once they were extracted from Mexico. So it made sense. His move could be a dry run.

The government takeover of the caverns had occurred with uncharacteristic rapidity. All it took was a fake report from a government geologist that the cave was becoming unstable, and it had to be closed to prevent a cave-in.

Of course, conspiracy theorists believed the presence of two Marine guards at the cave entrance must indicate something else was going on. Park Rangers could do just as well, it seemed to the locals. Why would guards armed with M-16s be required?

Some of the more imaginative locals began spreading the rumor that the government had a skunk ape, Sasquatch, under lock and key in the caverns. Ironically, that was not too far from the truth.

As soon as he flashed his NSA badge, Brightman had no problem getting past the Marine guards. And to think, for all the years he had worked for Parker, Parker never knew Brightman had an NSA badge.

The senior Marine placed a phone call on a land line into the cave, alerting Baltazar that he had a visitor.

"I suggest you step inside about 50 paces," said the Marine. "The guy doesn't like to come out into the bright light."

"OK, thanks," Brightman said.

By the time he'd walked fifty paces or so, Brightman stopped, letting his eyes get used to the dim light.

When his pupils had dilated a little, he saw Baltazar standing quietly about 15 feet away. The troll didn't speak, or smile, or motion to him. He just stood, staring.

"Our mutual friend, Jason Parker sent me."

At that, Baltazar visibly relaxed.

"How is Jason?" His question sounded normal and sincere.

"He's fine. How do you like your new home? Does it meet your expectations?"

219

John Clarke

"It is fine for me, and I think it will be good for my people. When will they come here?"

"Our National leaders are working the issue. It's complicated, but things are coming along nicely I think."

"How long should I wait?"

"I don't know."

"When you see Jason again, will you ask him?"

"I will. But he wanted me to ask you a question."

"About what?"

"About some small but very fast drones that travel well in air and underwater. Do you by any chance know these things?"

"What is a drone?"

"It's an unmanned flying or diving device that travels on its own and takes photographs. It's usually controlled remotely by a human."

"Then why don't you ask a human?"

"Because we don't think these things are controlled by humans. They seemed too responsive."

"If not by humans, then by what?"

"We were hoping you might know."

"Do you have an image of one?"

"May I get closer? I'll show you what I have."

Baltazar said nothing but motioned Brightman over with his hands.

Brightman held out a tablet with an image captured from the optics on top of the platform during the drone encounter. It showed at least five of the objects in great detail.

Baltazar grinned.

"I have not seen those for a long time. They are seekers."

"Seekers? What are they seeking?"

"They are seeking their home, the craft of the Masters."

"The Masters? Is that what Jason calls the Frogs?"

"Yes, the same. But he has the name wrong."

"So, if they flew by us and disappeared underwater, then they were searching for one of the Master crafts?"

"Some of you humans have a story about a large vessel containing animals escaping a flood. The Master of that vessel sent out a bird, and it came back with plant matter, indicating the presence of land."

"That sounds like Noah's Ark and his dove."

"The Masters would send out the seekers to search for whatever they wanted to search, and the seekers always found their way back to the Master's ship, even if it had moved."

"They always found it?"

"If it was too far away, they would locate the nearest of the Master's craft and go there. The information they contained would be transferred back to the craft of their origin."

Now that was interesting. Brightman certainly hoped his recording devices were picking all that up.

"Could humans steal these seekers?"

"Only if they had access to one of the craft of the Masters. The Masters are gone, so if humans could get inside, they would find the seekers, and not much else."

The 'not much else' comment would probably be of interest to Parker, but frankly, it didn't make sense to Brightman. Spacecraft are filled with all sorts of propulsion and navigation equipment.

"So, if someone stole seekers and later let them loose, what would they do?"

"They would search for the nearest craft of the Masters and go there. They are like birds coming home to roost."

"Well, that is certainly a surprising answer. I think Jason Parker will be pleased."

"Tell him I hope he can arrange to send my people soon."

"OK, but I do have one last question. Are the seekers weapons? Can they destroy things?"

"Their only purpose is to gather information. What the Masters do with that information is their business. But I will tell you, unlike you humans, the Masters do not need to destroy things to win an argument. They can be very persuasive."

"But yet they could not persuade you to join them in their exodus from Earth."

Baltazar smiled and paused before answering.

"We can be persuasive in our own way."

"How?"

Baltazar's smile faded. "Tell Jason I hope he is well."

And with that, Baltazar turned and faded into the darkness. Brightman's interview was apparently over.

The video recorded from Brightman's meeting with Baltazar struck like a lightning bolt reaching from Langley to Fort Mead and the White House. If what the troll said was true, then Parker's hunch was correct. The Russians did have a salvaged spaceship and had managed to get into it to take its hoard of drones. The implication of that was enough to keep most everyone in the Defense Department up at night.

The big question was why would the Russians tip their hand? Those drones would be a valuable asset to keep under wraps. Why show them to the Americans?

The Russians had always had a taste for thumbing their noses at the Americans if they had the opportunity, but as the sleepless hours began to build, it seemed ever more likely that the drones were not the real prize. Most analysts concluded that the Russians were after something a lot more important. And perhaps due to the information acquired from the drones, the three-letter agencies had to assume the Russians not only had a Frog spacecraft in their possession, but also that they now knew that the De Soto Canyon housed another Frog spacecraft. Perhaps they were hoping it was in better shape than theirs, and perhaps they were trying to assemble a plan to snatch it out from under our noses. After all, we had done the same thing to them during the cold war.

If there was any good news hidden in this turn of events, there was the knowledge that both the UV-glowing troll, and the blind remote viewer had, in their own way, lent further support to the hope that our deep sea divers would soon be making one of the most important discoveries of the modern era.

The President's only hope was that whatever lay in the De Soto Canyon was not in as bad shape as the crushed craft being slowly and secretly recovered from the deep ice at Cape Evans, Antarctica.

For Parker, the most important take-home message from Brightman's visit to Baltazar was that the accelerated schedule for the mission was indeed vital to national security.

CHAPTER 43. SQUASHING THE GOURD

Parker, Laura, and Bauman showed up at the viewport for the pressure chamber. Tom and J.R. were waiting for them.

"What's up Docs?"

Parker knew this was going to be tough, and he hoped he had a way to make them understand.

"Fellas, remember the bear you encountered during the simulation session?"

Tom answered first. "Sure do. It killed me and scared J.R. off. He ran screaming like a little girl."

"I wasn't screaming," J.R. said emphatically.

"That's true," Parker said. "You looked too scared to scream. But that was yesterday. Today is now. So how would you like to stick it to a Russian Bear?"

J.R. said, "I'm not liking the sound of this."

"You heard all the ruckus when we had drones attacking us. Well, DC's thinking the Russians will be back and try to beat us to the prize. Rather than argue the law of salvage in international waters with an international court, we need to get you guys down on site a little faster than we'd planned."

Tom said, "How much faster are we talking?"

"As you know," Parker said, "we were planning to take a week for the last 500 feet once we resumed the press from our present 2000 feet."

"When do you want us on the bottom?"

"This time tomorrow."

Both men were silent for a moment. Then J.R. spoke, "I think that's Doc Bauman's call. What do you think Doc, can we do that?"

"I really don't know. The hydrogen's been keeping your HPNS down very well, but a 24 hour press for the last 500 feet? I don't know how that will go."

"You're not exuding a lot of confidence there Doc."

"I'm just being honest. But I do know that the sooner we get you on the bottom, the sooner we can get this thing done and get you back on the surface."

Tom smiled, "That sounds great to me, as long as you don't squish my brains out of my ears in the process."

Deadpanning for effect, Bauman said, "If you notice any jelly dripping out, just let us know and we'll pause the press for a while."

J.R. laughed. "No big deal, just give us some Q-tips and we'll poke it all back in. We should be good to go. Right?"

Parker continued. "So you want to be heroes? We can make that happen."

J.R. laughed then said, "My personal preference is for live heroes versus dead heroes. Try to make that happen."

"We'll do our best," Bauman said.

Once the accelerated press started, bad things began to happen. Not catastrophic things, but concerning, as physicians like to say. The very next meal that was sent in came back largely uneaten.

Bauman quizzed them, "Are you fellows off your feed?"

"Everything tastes metallic," Tom said.

"Tastes like shit," J.R. said.

"OK, I'm not too surprised, but you have to eat something today. Anything interest you?"

"Pussy wouldn't even interest me," J.R. said.

Tom laughed, "Well, I wouldn't go that far."

"How about lobster?" Parker offered.

"Gag a maggot," J.R. said grimacing.

"Tell you what might be good to me, Doc," Tom said, not making it clear which Doc he was referring to, "I haven't had a tall, thick chocolate malt since I was in high school."

He held up his hands to indicate how tall of a shake he wanted. As he did, Parker noticed a slight tremor in Tom's hands. If Tom noticed, he didn't say anything.

Bauman answered, "We'll do our best, but I have a sneaky suspicion that the pressure's going to turn it into liquid. So it may not be as appetizing as you'd think."

"Humor me Doc. If it doesn't work out, nothing lost."

"Make that two," J.R. said. "Just add a little schnapps to mine, will you?"

Bauman laughed then said, "OK, that's two virgin, and probably melted, chocolate malts for you guys. I'll talk to the chef."

"You do that," J.R. said.

"And Tom," Bauman asked, "does J.R. have tremors too?"

"Oh fuck, you noticed that? Tell him J.R."

"Yeah...I.....ʺ J.R. hesitated. "Hell, I was tryin' to think of something dirty to say, but it's gettin' difficult for me to think."

"That's not good," Bauman said. "Maybe we should slow down the press."

"Not at all," said Tom. "It's always hard for J.R. to think."

Tom laughed at his little joke.

J.R. glowered at him, and with mock hurt said, "That's fuckin' cruel, you ass wipe."

Parker said, "OK, if you two are going to abuse each other we'll head topside again and leave you in the capable hands of Chief Thomson."

"I'd rather have the capable hands of Laura," J.R. quipped.

"Well, that's not happening," Parker said.

"OK, at least give Laura a kiss for us."

Parker smiled and turned towards the stairs to the next deck.

Apparently, the divers had gotten wind of the relatively innocent but much-rumored liaison between Parker and Laura, back in the day. But that was then, and under duress. *Nothing to see here folks*, Parker thought, honestly.

At the top of the stairs, Parker pulled Bauman into the duty room, which was presently empty.

"I'm getting worried," Parker said.

Bauman paused, choosing his words carefully.

"We knew there'd be some physiological problems, but I don't see anything to cause an abort on the press."

"Not yet," Parker agreed. "But I'm concerned about the transfer evolution."

Just as astronauts repeatedly drill on spacewalk procedures back in Houston long before actually leaving the space station, Tom and J.R. had repeated *ad nauseam* the procedure for transfer from the hyperbaric chamber complex to the pressurized sphere on the submersible, establishing communication with the sub pilot and navigator, and sealing the sphere. And then they repeated it in reverse, just like an astronaut reentering the space station.

But during those practices, all their faculties were available. They were thinking clearly and without distractions. But now they weren't thinking so clearly, and definitely had distractions. If they screwed up the transfer and lockout process, divers and sub, and the mission, would be lost.

Bauman stared at a plaque on the wall, a photo of Sea Lab II, and thought for a moment. Then shaking his head, I don't see that much to be concerned about, not yet. Their brains may not be running at 100%, but those procedures should be muscle memory by now. And besides, we'll have comms, so we'll run the checklist."

"Don't forget," Parker said, "we may not have good comms on the bottom. It's not guaranteed."

"I'm not worried."

"OK," Parker said, "You're the medical chief."

"Trust me, they'll be fine."

Five minutes later the 1MC called out, "Doctors Bauman and Parker, lay to the chamber. I repeat, lay to the chamber."

The two of them slid down the railing to the lowest deck in record speed and confronted Chief Thomson.

"What's up Chief?"

"J.R. will have to tell you."

Getting on screen, Bauman said, "What's going on J.R.?"

"I'm losing my fuckin' mind."

"Why do you say that?"

"I watched you guys climbing the stairs, and then I followed you."

"What?" Parker said, looking shocked.

"I was out of the damned chamber. I could look back and see myself in the chamber, looking out the viewport, but then I followed you up the stairs for a few steps before I was back inside here again."

Neither Parker nor Bauman said anything.

J.R. continued, "Dr. Parker, didn't you tell me something like that happened to a French diver on one of their hydrogen dives?"

"Yeah, something like that. It was an out of body experience."

J.R. did not have his usual smile on his face. "I've got that one beat. This was an out of body, and out of chamber experience. How the hell can that happen?"

"It didn't, really."

"Hell it didn't. It was so real that if you'd farted, I would have smelled it. I was right behind you, and it was just that real."

226

Of all the things Parker should have been worried about, he was more concerned if in that illusory state J.R. could have heard Bauman and him talking about them.

"You say you followed us up a few steps?"

"That's right. It freaked me out when I realized what was happening. I guess you could say I woke up."

Parker looked over to Bauman, beaming his thoughts to him. *They'll be fine, eh?*

CHAPTER 44. JOINING THE SUB

The out-of-body experience had earned the men a twelve-hour halt in the press, but after that another type of pressure, political pressure, became so acute that the diving officer had to have the divers "suck it up" and continue to the bottom pressure, equivalent to that of 2500 feet of sea water.

By the time they reached the bottom, their joints were aching, their limbs were shaking perceptibly, and they had already grown tired of cold but half-melted chocolate malts. Apparently, Bauman was right about the semi-frozen shake but wrong about everything else.

Bauman was now the only person on the platform with the credentials for certifying the men as fit for diving. He was not overly concerned about joint and muscle pain. That was more of a nuisance than a handicap. He was concerned about dexterity since they had some degree of tremors, and he was concerned about mental aptitude and attitude, simply because no Navy diver had been that deep before.

"Do you think you're good to go?" Bauman asked.

The two divers looked at each other, then Tom spoke, "I don't see any other divers down here. Do you J.R.?"

"Nope, no one here 'cept us."

"So I guess it doesn't matter, Doc," Tom answered. "We have a job to do."

In spite of Parker's and Bauman's concerns, the mission was a go.

Now came the first of many hard parts, all of which had been carefully rehearsed but never at 2500 feet before. Then there was the hydrogen which gave the divers a buzz, and in the case of J.R.'s OBE, perhaps a bit of psychosis.

But there was no time to worry about that now. The two men had been selected for their ability to carry on the mission in the face of the unexpected, and the Department of the Navy, and ultimately the White House, had no choice except to trust in their abilities.

Normally, divers had tenders who would assist with the donning and checking of the thermal system and the D.E.M's, but since they were the only ones in the hydrogen chamber, they had to assist each other. A diving supervisor outside the chamber read each diver the complicated checklist while their buddy assisted and double checked that nothing was forgotten. It was a tedious process that took a full 30-minutes for each diver. And by the end, each diver was sweating, and looking forward to finally getting into the cold water.

But a lot still had to happen before anyone got wet.

The next step was critical. After removing a plate from the floor of the hydrogen complex, they both entered the top hatch of a spherical pressure chamber which was at all times at the same pressure as the complex. Once inside, they had to swing the hatch closed again, and make sure it was thoroughly sealed before the next portion of the operation could begin. When the hatch was sealed, red sensor lights would shift to green in the diving control room. For extra insurance, red paint was strategically placed so that when the hatch was correctly sealed all the paint would be hidden from view.

Just to make sure, robotic cameras internal to the chamber moved repeatedly over the hatch searching for any anomaly.

The next action was the most critical. Like a spacecraft disconnecting from the International Space Station, a failure to seal the spacecraft would result in sudden decompression to the vacuum, killing all aboard. Except in this case, the sudden release of 77 atmospheres of pressure would cause an explosion, forcing dime-sized bits of human tissue and bone out of the chamber, and destroying a sizeable portion of the Explorer platform.

As the men reviewed the isolation procedures which would save their lives, a nervous banter echoed in the intercoms in the control room.

"Did you get it right, Tom?"

"I got it right. Did you get it right J.R.?"

"I got it right." J.R. was almost giddy with excitement, and maybe a little bit of hydrogen narcosis.

"OK, in the chamber," Control called out, "Make sure you are strapped into your seats."

"Seated and strapped, aye."

The diver's seats were side by side, leaving barely enough room in the chamber for them and their back-mounted breathing apparatus.

"OK, in the chamber, pull the chamber release."

"Chamber release, aye."

Tom paused for a moment, then pulled the manual release. The ball separated from the complex and started slowly dropping down from the hydrogen complex.

"Fuckin' A," J.R. said with a sigh of relief, "We got it right!"

"Hooyah," was Tom's only response.

The next phase involved the carrier system lowering the sphere into a cradle in the waiting minisub. Scuba divers in the clear Gulf water accompanied the sphere as it settled onto the sub, making sure the locking mechanism alignment was correct, and to ensure that not a single bubble was escaping from the sphere with the two experimental deep sea divers locked inside. Tom and J.R. would not be able to exit the sphere until safely on the bottom at 2500 ft.

Parker, Laura, Bauman, and Richter joined the operational crew in the Explorer's control room and watched the video screens and readouts from the minisub as the sub commander performed his final checks for the descent. After a long two minutes, the sub blew its air ballast and sank below the surface, accelerating into a free fall to the bottom.

By the time the sub had reached 1000 ft, essentially all ambient light was gone, and the navigator flipped on the sub's external lights. The sub pilot and navigator had to monitor rate of descent and distance from the canyon walls. If the rock walls got too close, the pilot would operate the appropriate thrusters to remain within the center of the free fall zone. If the rate of descent got too fast, the pilot might not have time to react to keep them from striking the walls and tumbling. A high-speed upside down crash landing on the bottom would spell doom for the men and the mission. There was not much room for error.

Like a parachutist pulling his chute and flaring for landing, the pilot slowed the sub's descent for a gentle touchdown, whereupon the divers cheered, a cheer distinctly heard in the dive control room. Up on the platform, there were high fives all around, and in the heat of the moment Parker grabbed Laura and kissed her on the forehead.

She looked up at him and smiled before saying, "Is that all you've got?"

Parker looked at Laura, smiling, and realized in that moment of celebration that she had not given up on her bizarre notion that she was a star child, and that she and Parker were soulmates; Frog soulmates no less. After all, that's what the King of the Frogs had told her.

As much as he had tried to dissuade her from that ridiculous idea, her eccentricity apparently remained intact.

Or else, she was just pulling his leg. He could never tell.

Chapter 45. On the Bottom

The sub sat on the bottom for a few minutes while the silt cleared, and while the pilot and navigator performed system checks, and checked for water current and temperature. Unlike Parker's previous experience with this cave several years ago when he was working with the Florida State student team, there was no current pulling the sub or silt into the cave.

Current had been checked numerous times during the planning phase of this mission, and in every case, whatever had been causing the current three years ago seemed to be gone. The temperature on the bottom also was right about where it was expected, 42°F, cold but manageable. Salinity was also as expected for sea water so there was apparently no fresh water currents coming from the cave that would spoil their buoyancy.

When the silt cleared, all the sub personnel found themselves looking directly into a dark, yawning chasm of a cave. Its size was intimidating to the four men and their relatively tiny submarine.

"Golly gee," J.R. said in a mock Barney Fife accent. "Will you take a look at that!"

The navigator flipped on the sub's brightest halogen lights, which had been kept off so the backscattering from flotsam in the water wouldn't blind them. But now, with the water clear and quiescent, those lights revealed the magnitude of what lay before them.

The back of the cave was not yet visible. With a deft motion that scarcely stirred any silt, the pilot raised the sub about 5 feet off the relatively flat floor of the cave. That floor was mostly sand covered, but here and there little outcroppings of sedimentary rock poked out of the sand. The pilot made sure to avoid anything hard as he carefully motored his way into the cave.

After they had covered a distance of 50 yards, the high-intensity lights began to play on what appeared to be a solid back wall, covered as expected with marine growth.

Other than the marine growth, the wall gave the appearance of being relatively flat. In fact, it looked too flat to be natural. It almost looked man-made, except of course men had never been in this cave at 2500 feet before.

The images previously sent back by the ROV matched fairly well what they were seeing before them now. But the ROV did not have the keen sight and intellectual ability of the two deep sea divers now just feet away from the wall.

This would be where the divers would exit the sub, so the pilot gingerly settled the sub on the cave floor.

"J.R., Control."

"Go ahead Control."

"On a scale of 0 to 10, how are you doing?"

"12."

"Have you had any more hallucinations since the first one?"

"Just one."

Bauman came up on the comms. "Please explain J.R."

"Well, I guess I've spent too much time with Tom in close quarters."

"How's that?" Bauman asked seriously.

"He's looking kind of cute. I'm getting a hard on right now."

"Get the fuck out of here, you pervert." It was, of course, Tom, teasing in that high-frequency squeal that a voice unscrambler could not completely unscramble.

Control next checked on Tom's status. "How about you, Tom?"

"I am 10 out of 10. But I'd rather have my head ripped off than have to spend any more time with J.R."

"Sorry guys, but you still have weeks of decompression before you get out."

Tom said, "Why don't you tell me something I don't know?"

"OK, I will. It's time to saddle up," said the voice from the dive supervisor.

Control then ran through the D.E.M. rig checks. After about two minutes on the checklist for each diver, Control announced, "It's time to flood up. Tom, put your hand on valve A1."

"A1, aye."

The camera inside the sphere followed Tom's hand motions to confirm Tom had the correct valve.

"One last reminder, do not turn on your helmet lights until you're completely flooded up. You know the lamp will shatter if turned on in air."

"Roger that Control," each diver acknowledged simultaneously.

John Clarke

Each diving helmet had one light on each side of the helmet as well as two cameras. The combined signal allowed Control to see what the divers saw in high-resolution and 3D.

"J.R. put your hand on valve B1."

"B1, aye."

Again the sphere cameras confirmed J.R. had the correct valve.

"Tom, turn A1 counter clockwise one-half turn."

"One-half turn, aye."

The sphere was now open to the water column, but no water would enter until the bleed valve was partially opened.

"J.R., open B1 one quarter turn counterclockwise."

"One-quarter turn, aye."

J.R. reached up, but the valve would not turn.

Control spoke up, "J.R. did you try turning the valve to the left?"

"No, I thought you said right."

"Your other right. Remember 'lefty loosey, righty tighty.'"

"Oh fuck, I hope I can do this."

"You can do it J.R. Just listen to me and do as I say."

J.R. was one of the most competent divers in the Navy, but no one had been on hydrogen at 2500 feet before. Control expected the divers would need help.

J.R. opened the valve as directed and water started streaming into the sphere, quickly bringing the water level to their waists, then their chests, and then submerging their helmets. A safety gas volume remained at the top of the sphere in case of a rig failure. If the divers had to remove their helmets before the chamber could be dewatered in emergency mode, that gas volume could be a life saver.

"J.R., open the egress door."

"Open egress door, aye."

The delatching mechanism was cumbersome but necessarily sturdy to hold back 77 atmospheres of pressure when on the surface. J.R. had to use all of his considerable strength to swing the door open.

With it open, he was able to unbuckle his seat harness and stepped onto a surface where no man had been before. He moved about five feet away and turned towards the sub, letting his lights play on it. The video signal was relayed to Topside, and those in the room applauded.

It wasn't exactly like putting a man on Mars, but darned close.

Tom exited the sphere next. The final plan was that he would maintain position near the sub, watching, ready to help J.R. if he needed it.

The divers had decided among themselves that after J.R. had been at work for fifteen minutes, he would return to the sub and Tom would move forward to continue the investigation.

J.R. turned towards the wall again, trying to decide where he would start his inspection.

Perhaps trained by years of reading from left to right, he started on the left side of the approximately 50-foot wide flat wall and started a slow walk back to the right, playing his dual lights and cameras up and down the approximately twenty-foot high wall.

"Control, J.R. here. Let me know if you see anything I miss. There's a lot of growth here, and so far it all looks alike."

"Copy that, J.R. Will advise."

As J.R. neared the right edge of the wall, his ears started ringing. That was a sign of oxygen toxicity, but the heads up display in his helmet indicated the oxygen level was exactly as it should be. He stopped for a moment, trying to sort out what was happening when he saw a triangular shaped metallic craft. And unlike the blackness of the cave, there was plenty of light to see by.

What the hell is going on? he wondered.

Then he realized he wasn't in his helmet. He was outside of it, but he wasn't drowning.

This must be another OBE! And I can see the target.

Just then something surprisingly humanoid flashed past him, with long flowing blond hair. He reached out and snatched some hair, but could not slow the movement of the apparition in front of him.

Returning to the task, he attempted to memorize the shape of the craft in front of him, then turned back towards the wall, which was now behind him.

Unlike the front side of the wall, there was very little growth covering what was clearly a metallic structure with a latching mechanism on the far left of the wall, which would be the far right when viewed from the outside.

Then he felt a touch on his shoulder and turned to see Tom staring at him.

"What happened to you J.R.? Are you alright?"

J.R. was back in his helmet.

"I'm fine. I know where to look now."

He searched for the position on the wall which would have been directly opposite what he had seen in his out-of-body state. And there

235

it was, a slightly elevated, squarish portion of the wall that didn't have as much growth as the other parts of the wall.

He reached out with his gloved hand and pressed on that portion of the wall, but nothing happened. He checked again and then leaned into it with all his might.

And as he did, he thought he was moving to the right and reached out to make sure he wasn't about to hit the wall of the cave. But he wasn't the one moving, the wall was, sliding to the left, revealing a dark opening behind it.

The high-intensity lamp from the sub came on, penetrating into the dark recesses of the back section of the cave, and then reflecting off the metallic craft as it was being exposed by the still moving wall.

J.R. and Tom stood silently, staring at the highly reflective pointed shape. But over the comms, they could hear whooping and hollering coming from the control room.

"Mission accomplished J.R. and Tom! Great job! Now get back in the sub, we want you guys back up here ASAP for a debriefing."

"What if the door closes again?" Tom asked.

"We have the location captured. We can have the ROV open it again."

"Request permission to approach the craft."

There was no immediate answer, but apparently the control room mike was open so both divers could hear the agitated conversations in the control room. Someone said, "Absolutely not, the craft could be radioactive." A voice that was clearly Captain Bauman's replied, "So what? Water shields radiation, even gamma rays. They're fully protected."

Richter could be heard saying, "We need all the Intel we can get."

Other conversations were indistinct, and J.R. took advantage of the confusion to make a few tentative steps towards the craft. Tom stood back silently, attempting to block the view of J.R. from the sub operators who were sending the camera feed up to the platform.

As seconds passed, J.R. shuffled closer, mesmerized by the craft in front of him, with no corrosion or marine growth to foul it's surface.

Finally, Control called back. "How are your rig's reading? We're getting everything nominal up here."

Tom answered first. "Roger that. Everything's in the green."

J.R. did not respond until Tom yelled at him. "J.R., read your rig's status back to control."

"We're all good," he said. "Can I approach?"

236

"Mark your distance, about halfway to the target. Approach no further. J.R. you may proceed. Tom, we need you to hang back. We'll let you swap places in a few minutes."

Due to the crystal clear water, it was easy for J.R. to sight his spot on the cave floor.

"I have my mark," J.R. said. "Am proceeding as instructed."

When working against water resistance, it is difficult to move quickly, but J.R. was pushing the limits of human performance and hydrodynamics as he scooted up to his mark in what seemed like a few seconds.

"Holy Mother of God," he said as he stood there, gawking. "This is fucking amazing."

Tom forced the issue. "Control, can I join my buddy?"

"J.R., control. What's your status?"

"I'm fine. I'm just … freaking out. This is so damn bizarre. It's awesome."

"OK Tom, go ahead and join J.R. And keep an eye on him."

J.R. said, "I doubt he'll be looking at me."

"Copy that, control," Tom said. "I'm moving now."

Tom was not able to move as quickly as J.R., and once he reached J.R.'s side, he almost tripped over a small rock outcropping. He had not been looking down — so mesmerizing was the sight in front of him.

In the next instant, Tom felt an impact from his right, forcing him to his knees. His breathing rig collided with J.R.'s, causing it to shift in its harness. Tom's fall knocked J.R. off balance, and J.R. fell flat on his left side. The off-kilter breathing apparatus took the majority of the impact, cracking an oxygen line. Instantly, a torrent of bubbles blasted from J.R.'s rig, making it impossible for Tom to see inside J.R.'s helmet.

"J.R. shut your oxygen valve," Tom yelled.

J.R. did not respond, so Tom, still on his knees, reached over and shut the valve for him. The torrent stopped.

J.R. finally spoke. "What the hell, you clumsy oaf?"

"Something knocked me over."

Control came up on the comms. "We saw something big hit you guys. It was so fast we couldn't get a good visual. May have been a squid."

"Well that son of a bitch," J.R. yelled.

"J.R., go to your E.Ps. Monitor your O2 and fly the rig manually. Tom, is your rig OK?"

"Seems to be."

"Tom, you guide J.R. back to the sub. J.R., your job is to concentrate on your O2 readings. What's your bottle pressure?"

"Down to a thousand pounds. But every time I open the valve I lose a bunch more."

"Just feather it. Just enough to keep you in the green. You'll be back in the sub soon."

"Could the sub meet us half way?"

"It's already on the move."

The walk back seemed to take forever, but at least it was uneventful. Both divers were watching their steps very carefully. It would have been easier if they had fins and were swimming, but they were weighted heavily, to overcome any potential currents.

As it turned out, currents had not been the problem, but rather some aggressive sea life.

Before entering the spherical chamber on the sub, both divers felt it safe to turn and stare at what was clearly a large, triangular-shaped alien craft.

After climbing inside the sub's diving sphere, after running through the dewatering checklist and filling the chamber again with the hydrogen gas mixture, J.R. told Tom, "We're lucky sons of bitches, you know?"

"True," Tom said, "but we're not home safe yet."

"Even if something happens to us now, I wouldn't trade this experience for anything."

"What's that in your hands?" Tom asked.

J.R. looked down and saw yellow strands of something hair-like wrapped around his left hand and fingers.

CHAPTER 46. AFTERMATH

The first question asked of J.R. once they were safely back in the dry hydrogen complex was, "How did you find the door mechanism?"

"I used the Force," he replied for the first 10 times.

"There is no such thing as the Force," everyone would say.

"I wouldn't be so sure," he'd answer to plant a seed of doubt.

But eventually, he tired of his game of deception and simply said, "I got lucky."

J.R. also got lucky when Tom didn't question his claim that the golden strands were simply some form of deep water seaweed.

After all, that's probably what they were.

But he'd surreptitiously hidden those strands away in the pockets of his dry suit, just in case he ever wanted to run a DNA check on it. What he had hallucinated certainly didn't look like seaweed.

But that's the nature of hallucinations, they're never what you think they are.

The Navy's salvage assets moved into action while the two divers were beginning their slow decompression for a hopefully safe return to surface pressure. The decompression was expected to take three weeks but could take longer since no one had decompressed from that depth before.

The salvage process involved having ROVs place inflatable cushions underneath the craft, and once ground clearance was obtained, large dollies were placed underneath it. Eventually, cables would be attached to the dollies, and the entire craft would be gently teased out of the cave. Once free from the cave, lift bags would be attached which would slowly raise the craft to a manageable shallow depth.

If all went according to plan, the tow to Pascagoula would occur with the craft never breaking the surface until it was placed into a flooded dry dock under cover of a thick shroud. Drainage of the dock and exploitation of the craft would occur under the highest possible secrecy.

While the divers were decompressing, Doctor Bauman was obligated to remain on the Explorer platform, but Parker and Laura picked up a helo headed back to Panama City to attend to other matters before returning to the platform for the release of the divers from their chamber.

Jason Parker and his wife Sandy were intent on enjoying a rare treat for a Saturday evening, two dozen oysters each at Shuckums Oyster Bar on Panama City Beach. Sandy had asked Laura Smith to join them since it had been some time since they'd all three been together.

Sandy predictably ordered baked oysters with parmesan cheese, and Jason mixed it up, some raw and some baked. Laura went straight for the raw stuff. Parker knew from experience that she would slurp them down with gusto, and a little lemon.

"The last time I saw you, Laura," Sandy said, "was on Navarre Beach when the Frog ships were leaving. I hear a lot has changed for you since then."

"Yes, I completed my Doctoral degree about a year later, and then got a job in D.C."

Parker interrupted. "She's way too modest. She's got an incredible job working for the Executive branch. Sometimes I think she's working for the President himself."

"Let's not exaggerate Jason. I doubt he knows me from Adam. But my people act as science advisors for the President, so, yeah, it's a pretty cool job."

"Who would your people be?" Sandy asked innocently.

"I can't say."

"I see. Well, Jason certainly never rose so quickly to such high levels, so you are truly to be congratulated."

Their waiter had an Eastern European accent, which Parker guessed was Ukrainian or Russian. There was a surprising abundance of attractive Ukrainian and Russian women working in bars and restaurants in Panama City. Parker suspected that had something to do with the fact that five military bases lay between Panama City and Pensacola, 90 miles away.

Sandy smiled at Parker as their waitress walked away; she knew what he was thinking. Many times she'd heard his theories about the honey pots floating around the Florida Panhandle, and she always found her husband's slightly paranoid suspicions just a little too James Bondish.

When the order arrived, the three of them dug into the oysters with zest, until Parker spit out a raw one that tasted "like ass."

He called his waitress over when she passed by the table. "Miss, this oyster is disgusting."

"Oh my," she said. "I'm so sorry. Please come back to the kitchen with me, and we'll show the chief shucker. He should have caught that."

Her English was impeccable, but she could not disguise the accent. "That's OK, he can just replace it. That'll be fine."

"No, I insist. He needs to see first-hand what he's done. We'll make it up to you."

That was unusual, but if he was about to get an extra dozen oysters out of the deal, it was certainly worth a walk to the kitchen.

He looked at Sandy, who by now was looking a little alarmed. "I'll be right back."

The cute waitress led him down a hall toward the restrooms, then made a turn towards the kitchen. As they walked a few feet further, she stopped. He did as well, puzzled.

What she said next chilled Parker to the bone. "Dimitri Roblenski needs to talk to you."

"The Russian?" What he didn't say, but came close to it, was "The Russian Spy?"

"He's around the next corner."

The last time Parker saw him was in Brussels. He and his cohorts had been expelled for spying on NATO. So why would he be in Panama City?

Before Parker had time to process that thought, Roblenski stepped from around the corner. Parker was stunned.

"Relax my friend. I don't mean to scare you. And I know you can't talk to me without getting clearance first, but just listen. I need to brief you and your people on Lake Baikal. You will want to hear it. Especially you, my friend."

Parker started to say something, but the taller Russian held his fingers to his lips. "When the CIA wants to listen, call back here, for Talia. She'll pass the word. And for God's sake, please don't say anything to anyone else. I'm putting my life in your hands."

Parker tried to reassure the Russian. "Not to worry. If anybody asks about you, I'll tell them the truth. I know you from Brussels, to be a man who can handle more than his share of Vodka."

Roblenski smiled.

Turning to Talia, Parker asked, "Now, do I get more oysters?"

She laughed. "Yes. I'll bring out another dozen. On me. And that one you spit out was not bad — I adulterated it with a harmless chemical."

Roblenski said, "I had to get you back here somehow."

"Long as it wasn't polonium you put on my oyster," said Parker, only half smiling.

"No, that's only for spies and traitors. You're not a spy, are you?"

"Not even close."

When Parker walked back to the table he signaled Laura that he had to speak to her. She got up and walked into the hallway, where Parker whispered, "I just met a Russian spy. He wants the CIA to contact him about something in Lake Baikal."

"Are you serious?"

"I met this guy once before, in Brussels. He said something then about the Frogs and Lake Baikal."

"Is he a double agent?" Laura asked.

"I don't think so. He could be playing us, or maybe he wants to switch sides. I don't know. But you have the CIA contacts, right?"

"Yeah. How do we reach him?"

"Through our waitress, Talia."

"I'll get her phone number as we're leaving," Laura said.

"OK. This is really weird," Parker concluded.

When they returned to the table, Sandy asked Parker, "What's so interesting?"

"Not much. I just met a Russian rock star."

"Oh, Jason, you always say that." Turning her attention to Laura, "He says that when he doesn't want to say. I don't know if he's ever going to grow up."

As he slid back into his seat, waiting for that extra dozen oysters, he said, "I hope I don't grow up. It sounds really boring."

Laura left the restaurant as soon as she got Talia's phone number. Parker took Sandy home and then headed to his office at NDC to make his own call.

As he pulled into his parking space, NCIS Special Agent Veronica Spalding pulled up behind him and honked her horn.

Turning off his car he walked over to her.

"Ms. Spalding, good to see you again. It's been awhile. What brings you over this afternoon?"

"Can we talk?" She was looking up into the sun, and perhaps that was why her smile looked a little more grimaced than usual.

"I'm headed to my office. Why don't you follow me?"

She parked her car, and he waited for her at the bottom of the stairs leading to his office. They walked up the stairs without speaking, and after he had unlocked the cipher lock, he motioned her to sit on his sofa while he turned on his computer.

"I've been out for a while," he said, "so I have lots of emails to catch up on."

"Dr. Parker, you were contacted by a Russian today."

He paused for a moment. He was indeed just contacted, and he owed both her and Hans Richter a report on that contact. But how in the hell did she find out so quickly?

"That is very true. Just a couple of hours ago, at lunch."

"Do you know the person?"

"I've met him before, on official NATO business. But I tell you what, I came in to inform a guy at the NSA about this contact, and if he doesn't mind, you can listen in so I don't have to repeat everything. Is that OK with you?"

She seemed to relax a little. Parker was straightforward about the contact, so she nodded agreement.

Hans Richter was still on the Explorer platform, but since this was a quiet time, with the divers decompressing, Parker hoped he'd be able to take the call.

"Richter here."

"It's Parker. I'm switching to secure."

"Same here."

"Hans, I'm not in a SCIF, so let's keep it unclass, but I need to report a Russian contact. I also have sitting in my office our local NCIS agent, Special Agent Veronica Spalding. She's sharp — the contact just happened two hours ago, and she knows about it already."

"It took them that long?"

She interrupted, "Negative, Mr. Richter. We knew about it as it happened."

John Clarke

"I guess they're no slouches," Parker said. He also thought it was because of his damn big mouth. He should have been more discrete when he was briefing Laura.

"Anyway, Hans, I have a name for you, Dimitri Roblenski."

"That name is familiar."

"I told you about him after the NATO meeting."

"Oh yeah, the former KGB spy, who's still a spy."

Spalding's jaw dropped. "You were talking to a known spy?"

"It was all a surprise to me."

"What was it about?" Spalding asked.

Richter's tone changed immediately. "OK, Miss uh, Spalding. We can't continue this discussion. Just make your report of Jason's foreign contact, note that it was voluntarily submitted, and be done with it. I know you have your rules and I won't interfere. But I also have my rules."

"I don't know you," she said, sounding suspicious. "You're NSA?"

"He said NSA? Well damn, Parker talks too much. It's going to get him into trouble one of these days, but this is not that day. Ms. Spalding, take down my personnel number and confirm it with the Office of Personnel Management. Are you ready to copy?"

"I am," as she put pen to paper.

"61428."

"That's a lot of numbers," she said.

You could almost hear him smiling. "There's a lot of us."

Reluctantly Ms. Spalding left the office, but with a smile which may have reflected some renewed admiration for Parker. It was obvious that he was into some heavy stuff. She probably wished she knew what it was, but Parker knew that as a professional she understood the importance of staying in her swim lane.

After Spalding's departure, Parker continued the conversation with Richter.

"Roblenski didn't have much to say. I literally ran into him in the hallway to the kitchen at Shuckums restaurant. All he said was if the CIA wants to know about Lake Baikal, to contact him through a waitress named Talia at the restaurant."

"Do you want me to contact the Agency?" Richter asked.

"You can if you want, but Laura Smith said she would. She must be connected somehow."

"Well yeah, she works for their boss," Richter explained.

244

"Boss?"

"Director of National Intelligence. Your little girlfriend is well connected, due to your Frog experience."

"Give me a break Hans, she's not my girlfriend. And why isn't the Director's office working with me?"

"Not to worry Jason, they are indirectly. But just remember, you're too free with information. Don't tell folks I'm with the NSA."

"Check, I got it. My bust."

CHAPTER 47. EXPLORER

Mid-morning of the next day Parker picked up the phone to find Richter on the line once again.

"How soon can you and Laura be ready to fly out to the Explorer?"

"I don't know. She's in Marianna. She wanted to check on Truman Baltazar."

"Who?"

"Our Troll."

"Can you call her?"

"I'll try, but there's no phone reception in the cave. But perhaps she'll come out for a lunch break."

"We'll send a helo up to pick her up, then the Sea Stallion will bring the two of you back out to the platform. It's making a supply run this afternoon. Lots to talk about, and we're in a hurry."

"Why?"

"Can't say."

"Are the divers OK?"

"Sure, they're about to surface so you don't want to miss it."

"And the thing?"

"Almost home."

Parker tried calling Laura, but not surprisingly it didn't go through. Next he sent a text message. Five minutes later, he got a response.

"What? I have to leave?"

"Yep, a Blackhawk's on its way."

She waited a minute before sending her one-word response.

"Damn."

An hour later, Laura and Parker were on the tarmac at the Navy base, waiting for the Sea Stallion loadmaster to finish his work. From the looks of it, there'd barely be room for the two passengers.

Addressing Laura, Parker asked, "What did our caveman have to say?"

She looked at him askance. "Why are you calling him that?"

"Because I found him in a cave, and he's living in a cave again. So that makes him a … what?"

"But genetically he's not a Neanderthal."

"Never said he was. Genetically, what is he? Do you know?"

"Well, it's hard to say. But the DNA geeks swear he's closer to humans than Neanderthals. And lots cuter."

Parker nodded his head. "I agree. He doesn't look the way I imagined a Neanderthal would look."

"Or a troll for that matter," she said.

"Did you two have time to talk about anything before I called?"

Laura nodded her head and twisted up one corner of her mouth.

"Of course he's complaining about the time it's taking to get his people here."

"Yeah, well there are some problems there. We're working trusted back channels, and praying to God that the Chinese don't find out about them. But it may take a while."

"Anything else?" Parker asked.

"I tried to be helpful and ask him if he knew about the Frog ship propulsion systems."

Reflexly Parker pulled his head and neck back in surprise. Now he was more than casually interested.

"And?"

"I got a nonsense answer. I don't think he has a clue."

"What did he say?"

She shook her head, not really believing what she was about to say. "The closest I could come to saying it is "gewanken."

"Gewanken? Sounds German. Wonder if he meant Wankel. Holy cow, this big thing couldn't run on a Wankel engine. No way."

"Don't get your panties in a wad," she said. "I didn't have time to get him to elaborate. I couldn't swear to what he said. It could have been gedanken."

Just then the large helicopter rotors started spinning up, and one of the crewmen waved at them from the rear ramp that was still resting on the tarmac.

"Time to go," Parker said unnecessarily.

Forty-five minutes later the heavily laden helicopter set down on the helo pad of the Explorer II platform. Laura and Parker were the first to disembark when the back ramp was lowered onto the deck, and there to meet them was Hans Richter. The rotors were still winding

247

down when Richter ushered them into a secure briefing room one level below the landing pad.

"What's all the mystery?" Parker asked as Richter shut the heavily bolted door to the sound-deadened room.

"Lots going on. But first, and the reason for the speedy exit, Roblenski has disappeared. We met up with his waitress contact, and she said he disappeared shortly after talking to you two at the restaurant. A waitress coming in for a shift change reported seeing him getting into a car with someone, and that was the last anybody's seen of him."

Laura and Parker just looked at each other, puzzled.

Laura spoke slowly, "And so…"

Richter finished her thoughts. "That makes you potential targets too. Whatever he wanted to talk about was apparently not something the Russian government wanted him talking about."

"So we're in protective custody?" Laura asked.

"No, but we do have to be cautious," Richter answered.

She sighed.

"What about my wife?" Parker asked.

"She's already on a government plane headed to somewhere in West Virginia. Panama City is not a safe place for you, at least while we're tracking down the Russians who nabbed Roblenski."

"Are you serious?" Parker exclaimed. "She must be scared to death?"

"You can call her on a secure phone once I get the word they've landed."

"So she knows we're back on the platform?"

"No. And you won't be for long. We're moving you two to Pascagoula soon."

Laura laughed. "Oh come on, does anyone beside me think it's strange we're trying to find a Russian spy, to protect him from his fellow Russians?"

Richter shook his head. "When a spy turns? Laura, I know you're new to this business, but no, that's nothing new. We try to protect potential informants."

"Why do you figure he's turning?" Laura asked.

"Only he would know that," Richter answered.

Parker looked at them, smiling. "This spy versus spy crap amuses the hell out of me."

Apparently Richter did not share Parker's sentiment. "I hope you find Pascagoula amusing."

With a half-smile on his face, Parker stared at Richter for a moment, remembering the first few times he'd met him, those times when Richter seemed to be a sinister villain, back before the Frogs revealed themselves. That part of Richter's persona had not been completely erased.

Parker wondered, *What is it they say about strange bed fellows? Oh well, things change.*

"Well, speaking of Pascagoula, the craft's almost there?" Parker finally asked.

"Should be arriving in a few hours."

"You have any pictures of it?"

"Yeah, but we'll get to that in a moment. First, I wanted to give you the news from Antarctica."

"They're still digging it out?"

"It's a slow go, but here's the big news. Our divers found a crack in the side of it large enough to squeeze in a mini-ROV. The hull is badly compacted by the thick ice on top of it, but there was enough room for the ROV to crawl through most of the spaces. The funny thing is, the ship is almost completely empty."

"I would expect that once it landed," Parker said, "or crash landed, everything useful would have been stripped and repurposed."

"The problem is, there are no signs of engines. Any propulsion system would have mounting hardware and piping associated with it. But there was nothing."

"Really, nothing at all?" Parker asked.

"That makes no sense," Laura added. "It can't be."

"We should know more when we get it out of the glacier and up on the surface. But right now, it's pretty clear that it's empty."

Parker, always the pragmatist, had another thought. "I sure hope the one we're towing to Pascagoula isn't empty."

"So, there's a point to my telling you this. Since you two seem to have the greatest connection with the aliens, based on your past experience, how about putting some thought into alternative means of propulsion."

Parker laughed. "You've got to be kidding. That's a question for NASA."

"You're right. We've already talked to them, but so far they're drawing blanks."

"Give them time. I'm sure that's not something they think about every day."

"Actually, they do think about it every day, and besides we've given them a month, with no luck so far."

"A month? You've known about this for a month, and you didn't tell us?"

"It's like you said, NASA was our best bet. But now we're talking to you. Just put some thought into it. That's all I'm asking."

"OK, we'll do that for you Hans," Parker said. "But this sounds a little premature to me. We'll soon have two craft to examine, one crushed and one in mint condition. I bet it will be self-evident then."

"I hope so," Richter said, nodding his head gently.

Tom and J.R. were in good spirits when Parker and Laura checked in on them again.

"Are they treating you guys right?"

"They're giving us time off for good behavior," J.R. said gleefully.

The difference between inside and outside pressure was very slight now, so their speech sounded normal without helium unscramblers. The hydrogen had all been safely vented long before, and air was once again being reintroduced into the chamber. When the chamber hatch was unsealed, their reentry to the outside world would be uneventful.

"Eighty-five minutes and we're free men again," Tom said. "Can't wait."

The divers would be carefully watched for twenty-four hours after they surface, to make sure signs of decompression sickness don't manifest. After that, and a good bill of health from Captain Bauman, they would be as free as anyone on a platform out in the ocean, 130 miles from home.

"We'll get out of the way of the crew here," Parker said. "They look pretty busy planning for your arrival."

"OK, we'll see you on the other side."

For an hour, Laura and Parker sat in the conference room, carefully sipping very hot coffee brewed to a Navy specification that was guaranteed to keep watch standers wide awake. There was no such thing as too much caffeine.

"I have all sorts of things running around in my head after Richter briefed us," Laura said. "I'm trying to piece it together, but not getting very far."

"Me neither. I'm thinking the Roblenski disappearance may be a red herring, pun not intended."

Laura smiled.

"The Russians know we're up to something, but what I don't know is whether they know more or less than we do regarding these craft."

"No way to know," she answered.

"Except that Roblenski was insinuating in Brussels at the NATO meeting that they did know more than we did, at least at the time."

Laura thought about that for a moment before answering cautiously. There were a lot of things the Intel agencies did that Parker was not privy to, but in this case, he and Laura's survival just might depend on him being fully informed about who they were dealing with.

"The Agency ran a background on Roblenski, and discovered that as Russian spies go, he is one of the friendlier ones. His profile suggests that if anyone was capable of becoming a double agent, he might be the one."

"Oddly enough that was my sense when I saw him in Shuckums. And he did seem cautious. No, actually, concerned would be a better word, when he told me about having the CIA contact him."

"Of course," she said. "He was setting himself up for elimination. He probably knew that."

"So, as Richter said, we may be their next target."

Laura paused, looking at him sternly, slowly shaking her head.

"You know Jason, you have a really bad habit of getting me in the midst of your troubles. How do you do that?"

In typical Jason Parker fashion, he had a ready answer. "It's because you must be the yin for my yang."

She laughed. "You know that sounds really dirty."

He smiled. "I can't help that, but it might be true, without the dirty part of course."

"Actually," Laura said, "didn't you say the Trolls claimed you were Ta'veren?"

"Yeah, whatever that means."

"I looked it up. Ta'veren cause change, positive change mostly."

"I could argue, then," Parker said, "that you're the real Ta'veren. After all, you're the one who started this whole 'extraterrestrials and UFO' crap."

She looked at him, not smiling. "Except it turned out it wasn't crap. Right?"

251

"Which proves my point."

"Then maybe we're both Ta'veren," Laura said. "You get two Ta'veren together and what do you get?"

"Weird babies?"

She laughed. "You're so predictable, but no. You get trouble. Good trouble, but it's still trouble."

"Well, I looked it up too," he said. "The concept of Ta'veren is entirely fictional."

Laura looked straight into his eyes with a gaze that forbade him to look away, no matter how uncomfortable he might feel. "Fiction? I just returned from a visit with a Troll, in a cave! How about that for fiction?"

As the hour of the divers' release approached, Laura and Parker moved down to the hyperbaric chamber floor. Parker had expected some Washington dignitaries to arrive. After all, this was a record-breaking deep dive, and the first manned hydrogen dive for the U.S. Navy. But apparently, the approach of the Frog ship to Pascagoula was of far more interest. The sacrifice of the Navy divers was being forgotten amid the excitement over the country's newest bright and shiny object. But then, Parker knew that was nothing new. The divers were reluctant to be in the spotlight, both as a matter of character and as a matter of edict.

When inside and outside pressures were equalized, the two divers could pivot the heavy steel hatch into the chamber. After that, they simply stepped out onto the floor, and the whooping and hollering, hugs and high fives began in earnest.

Laura and Parker waited patiently to get their turn. As Parker finally moved in to hug J.R., the diver whispered, "I saw some weird shit, man."

Parker pulled back surprised. "Tell me about it, later."

J.R. turned to the next greeter and acted like nothing at all unusual had just been said.

Parker hugged Tom, and Tom simply said, "Thanks for getting us back safely."

"It was a team effort," Parker said, as Tom turned to greet a Navy Captain neither of them knew.

CHAPTER 48. WEIRDNESS

When J.R.'s decompression sickness watch period was over, he ditched his follower and knocked on Parker's cabin door. Parker had been thinking deep thoughts about space drives, and was getting nowhere. Even his search of the Internet was not helping.

"Doc, is this room sound-proof?"

"I guess. I can't hear Laura in the next cabin, and you know how loud she likes to play her music."

"No, I don't know, but I'll take your word for it."

"So J.R., what's on your mind?"

"Remember when I told everyone I just froze in front of that wall, carefully searching for signs of the entry."

"I sure do. You have very impressive powers of observation."

"Thanks, but that's not exactly what happened."

"How so?"

"I had a second out of body experience."

"We trained you to move past that. It is a potential side effect of deep hydrogen diving, just as the French divers found."

"Well, here's the thing. I could see things I couldn't possibly see from where I was standing."

"Like what?"

"Like the flying saucer. I was standing on the other side of the wall."

Parker said nothing for a moment, trying to maintain his professionalism.

"I know you're a trickster J.R. Are you kidding me?"

"Absolutely not. You know how I knew where to press the wall to have it open?"

"Your 20/10 vision?"

"No. From the inside, it was plain to see the mechanism for the latch. It was a bulky metallic thing. I memorized its location on the wall figuring I'd pop back into my real body at some point. Sure enough, after Tom touched my shoulder somehow pulling me back, I looked where I thought the latch must be, and there it was."

John Clarke

"That worked out well."

"So how can that be Doc?"

"OBEs are strange. As much as we study them, we still don't understand them. Must have something to do with the brain getting briefly screwed up. Probably due to the combined effect of hydrogen and pressure."

"But how can I see something on the other side of the wall?"

"All I know is, the sighting of hidden objects during OBEs has been reported, but never proven. Some research doctors put signs high up in operating rooms, hoping that patients will report what the signs say after a near-death OBE. But so far, without success. Who knows, you may be the one to bring back the evidence."

"Evidence, eh? It's funny you put it that way. I did see something else, a Mermaid with long blond hair."

Parker just stared at him for a moment, before finally responding. "That was obviously a hallucination, like the bear you imagined in training."

J.R. reached deep into the right pocket of his blue jumpsuit and pulled something stringy out. "Oh yeah, then what's this?"

J.R. handed it to Parker, and Parker looked at it with a puzzled look on his face.

"It looks like hair."

"Exactly."

"But it can't be. Must be a new filamentous algae. Can I keep this to send it off for DNA analysis?"

"If you promise not to lose it. I have some more safely stored away, so I'm not giving you all I have."

"How did you get this?"

"I told you. I saw a fuckin' Mermaid, and as she swam past me I reached out and grabbed her hair. This came off in my hand."

"Which side of the wall were you on when this happened?"

"On the inside, the side with the ship. But the door was still closed behind me."

"So this was a ..."

He started to say *hallucination too*, but then he realized how stupid that would sound. He was holding the stuff in his hands.

"Was what, Doc?"

Parker paused a moment before realizing there could only be one answer.

"This was the real deal."

After J.R. had headed to the mess hall for a late meal, Laura was the next to enter Parker's cabin. She was almost breathless.

"Jason, I may have found the most valuable single video frame in the world."

"That sounds like a bit of hyperbole to me."

"I was pouring over the video from J.R.'s stereo helmet cameras and found a single clear frame of alien writing right next to where he pressed the button thing that opened the door."

"You sound excited, but why exactly is that exciting?"

"Because unlike the cylinder the Frogs gave you with our future history on it, this writing is not encrypted. And how complicated could even Frog language be if it's on a placard sitting next to a push button?"

"That's true," Parker quipped. "*Push here* is about as simple as it gets."

"This may be far more important than a Frog ship that probably doesn't work."

"You're not being very optimistic," Parker said.

"Think about it. Why did they leave it behind?"

"I've been wondering that. Whoever ends up being a test pilot for it may be in for a nasty surprise."

Richter stuck his head in the door. "Do you two want to dive on the ship? It's in place below the shrouded dry dock and we're sending divers down to inspect it before we raise it. You two can join them if you'd like."

They both looked at each other, grinning. "Hell yeah," Parker said.

"We have a helo spinning up in 10 minutes — I suggest you be on board."

As Richter started to pull back from the door, Laura called him back.

"Hans, we need to copy and secure J.R.'s video."

"Already done. But why do you mention it?"

"It may save the world."

Parker shook his head gently. You never knew if you should take Laura seriously, or not.

CHAPTER 49. SINGING RIVER ISLAND

Parker spent most of his time during the short twilight flight to Pascagoula thinking about how Laura, as a graduate student in Oceanography, had once told Parker that she had a special connection to extraterrestrials and "flying saucers." As ludicrous as it seemed at the time, she'd been completely right, at least according to the Frogs. Against all the odds, both she and Parker had been rescued by one of the Frog ships, so there was certainly no denying the existence of these craft. He wondered what she'd be thinking when she had full access to one of the ships.

Like shopping for second-hand clothing, the U.S. was hoping to find value in a discarded spaceship. And Laura and Parker, based on their singular experience with the Frogs, and their unique ability to energize alien mind-training aids, were apparently valuable consultants on the ship recovery.

Under cover of darkness, the helo landed in the secured portion of the Pascagoula shipyard, and a van ferried them from the chopper to the shroud. As expected, security was tight, but Parker and Laura both had their security badges with them. Parker had Navy Department stamped on his badge, but Laura's badge had no visible I.D. All the heavily armed security forces needed to know about her was encrypted electronically on the card's chip.

Once in the shroud, they encountered a bustle of activity as jumpsuited men and women were talking, and waving hands towards the overhead. That was a concern for Parker, and he motioned Laura over. As they approached, all conversation stopped, and the small group turned towards them, questioningly.

Parker extended his hand. "Hi, I'm Jason Parker, and this is Laura Smith."

At first, there was no reaction from the group until one of them made the connection.

"Oh my God, you're THE Jason Parker and Laura Smith. Welcome to Project Laura, named after you Dr. Smith."

She blushed. "Really? No one told me."

"Well, now you know. You two are famous."

"In my experience," Parker said, "it's more like infamous. So what's all the discussion? I don't like it when people are pointing up, especially when I'm about to get into the water."

A nearby engineer overheard the conversation and joined in.

"We're second-guessing the calculations for the lift. The strain being placed on the support cables is more than we'd anticipated. When the craft was being towed, there was less strain, but I think we were getting hydrodynamic lift from the shape of the thing. It rotated in the harness with one of the pointy ends forward and acted like a lifting body."

"You're about to get wet?" another engineer asked.

"That's why we're here, and we need to get to it. Nice meeting you, but do us a favor and don't drop that thing on us. I plan to get underneath it."

"OK, sure don't want to squish anybody."

The divers and diving supervisors were not as impressed when Parker and Laura walked up. The Chief in charge had been told to have scuba sets ready for them, but to the Navy divers, they were just two civilian divers; nothing special.

"What are we looking for?" Parker asked the dive supe.

"For anything interesting, or usual, other than the fact it's a freakin' flying saucer."

The Navy Chief diving supervisor sounded pretty incredulous.

"Pretty amazing that we're doing this, don't you think?" Parker asked.

"Fuck yeah. This ain't happening."

Technically, the chief was right.

"While you're down there," the Chief continued, "keep your eyes open for a way into that thing."

"OK, you'll be the first to know," Parker said.

The Chief tapped Parker on the shoulder just as Parker was turning towards his dive gear. "You're not going to need me to run your dive are you?"

"Nope, this is not an official Navy dive. This won't be logged."

"Good," was all the Chief said in response.

After checking their dive equipment, and test breathing their primary scuba regulator and backup regulator, they both slipped into the warm Pascagoula water.

The water in Pascagoula Bay was turbid, and in spite of the many lights fixed on the craft, Parker could not get a clear view of it until up close, within about five feet, which meant they could only see a small part of the ship at a time. For that reason, it was hard for them to grasp the overall size of the thing. Nevertheless, Parker was able to find the edge of the craft, and swim slowly along the periphery of it. Oddly, the edges were punctuated periodically by large crystalline surfaces that looked like they might have been lenses or covers for lights. He followed the edge which seemed straight for maybe fifty feet, before making a sharp turn and then running straight for another fifty feet or so. After a third turn and gliding past more lenses, he realized he was back where he started.

He lost track of Laura and assumed she was off investigating some other part of the craft. He'd occasionally run into other divers who were attempting to photograph details of the ship, but with nowhere else to go, he decided against heading under it. Instead, he headed over the top surface, feeling with his hands for any hint of a groove that might indicate an opening.

Three years previously, he and Laura had been returned to the ocean surface through just such an opening, so even though this ship was smaller, perhaps it had one as well. But after searching the fairly flat upper surface of the craft without finding the slightest indentation or other irregularity in the otherwise smooth surface, he headed for the surface and climbed out. A few minutes later, Laura did likewise.

The Chief gave Laura a hand climbing out of the water. "Did you two see anything?"

"Couldn't see much of anything," she said.

Turning to Parker, the Chief said, "Apparently they got some good pics in the clear water out in the Gulf as they were transitioning from the lift to the tow, but I haven't seen them yet. Word of mouth says they were pretty spectacular. Have you seen them?"

"No. But they have to be better photos than your divers are taking."

"Yeah, I wish they'd just go ahead and pick it up out of the water."

"I guess they want to make sure the hoist can handle it. Wouldn't be good to drop it into the mud."

A Navy Lieutenant walked over and said, "We need you two to get changed and meet in the briefing room in ten minutes. Know where it is?"

"Passed it on the way in," Parker said.

"Good. Don't be late."

The officer turned about smartly and climbed the stairs leading up to the main deck, taking the steps two at a time.

"Darn, I'm barely going to have time to pee," Laura said.

"If you'd peed in the water no one would have noticed. The first rule of Navy diving."

As they approached the briefing room, a guard checked their name off a list after they'd deposited their phones in a lock box outside the room. Once they entered the room, a dozen or so personnel, a mix of civilians and uniformed military, were standing around. From their badges, at least two of the civilians were from NASA. The military uniforms reflected a mix of Navy, Air Force, and one solitary Army Colonel.

A man dressed in civilian clothes who had been seated up front rose and walked to the front of the room.

"Folks, this is going to be the most interesting show-and-tell I've ever been involved in, and probably you as well. As a reminder, nothing leaves this room; no notes, no photos, nothing. If it does, you will be found out and prosecuted to the maximum extent of the law. To that end, take a seat, read the Non-Disclosure Agreement on the tablet before you, sign it, and pass it to the end of the row. Senior Chief will pick them up, and once they're all accounted for, the show will begin."

Men and women started filling in the twenty or so empty desks, each with paper and pen on the desk.

"And remember, just because the chairs look like they're for writing notes, they're not. And no writing on your hands. Got it?"

A few voices from some junior officers answered back, "Yes sir." Parker did not feel the need to respond. He knew the drill.

After the NDA's were signed and passed in, the first slide was shown on the screen. It was a crystal clear image taken from above of what lay below them, a gorgeous triangular craft with three softly rounded points, and elongated bubbles arrayed along each of the three edges. The top of the craft looked featureless, a smooth surface.

The audience members started softly talking to each other.

The next photo was taken from below, which looked like an exact copy of the photo of the top of the craft. In fact, there was no obvious way to tell the top from the bottom or the front from the back. It was a perfectly symmetrical triangular craft with bulges all along its edges.

The man up front finally said something. Before then he'd let the photos speak for themselves. "These were all taken in the clear Gulf Water."

A dozen more wide-angle, high-resolution photos followed. The most dramatic photo was actually a Photoshopped illustration of the craft hovering in the air over a city. It literally caused a few in the audience to gasp and was left up on the screen as the speaker turned again to the audience.

"So ladies and gentlemen, this is what we're dealing with. Once we make the final lift tomorrow morning, we'll all get a better view of it. It should be safe to approach because our divers have found no radioactivity associated with it."

Laura leaned her head in towards Parker. "Now they tell us."

The unidentified man continued. "We have two immediate problems to solve. The first is how to get into it. The second is how to determine if it's functional or not. We have no clues as to what type of propulsion system it has. And that my friends is the primary reason you are here."

Rustling and murmuring was spreading throughout the audience as the importance of what was just said sank in.

"If you follow conspiracy theories, you might think we already know these things, because we've already reverse engineered the Roswell UFO."

Many in the audience laughed.

"But if we had, you wouldn't be here. The hard work would have been done long ago."

Someone close to Parker muttered, "That would be no fun."

"Now, before you engineers and physicists get into a pissing match over which of your pet theories is correct, I need to introduce two VIPs. They are in the third row, Drs. Laura Smith, an oceanographer, and Jason Parker, a physiologist and life support expert. Will you raise your hands?"

A few people clapped softly.

"If you don't know already, far as we know they are the only humans who have spent time inside one of the Canyoneer's ships."

There was more polite applause.

"Now Jason and Laura, I hate to put you two on the spot, but I'm wondering if you could share your thoughts on the ship you were in. I'm guessing it was somewhat like this one."

Laura nudged Parker. "You take it. You're more familiar."

"Chicken," he whispered to her as he slowly stood up. As he walked to the front, he was wondering how on Earth he could say anything intelligent, considering the combined brain power of those in the audience. He was at a loss, but things usually came to him once he got started.

He turned to face the group and found every person seemingly straining in their seats to make sure they heard every word, except for Laura. She was smiling devilishly.

"Thank-you Doctor ...." He dragged out the word, hoping the man would introduce himself.

"I'm sorry, how rude of me. I forgot you two don't know me. I'm Jim Pinafore, with the Alien Propulsion Unit, or APU, U.S. Air Force, Wright-Patterson Air Base."

"OK, thank-you," Parker said. "Nice to make your acquaintance."

He stopped to take a deep breath, partially stalling for time, hoping for inspiration. "Now, to be honest, I'm not sure where I'm going to go with this, but first I have to explain that what Dr. Pinafore calls Canyoneers, I call Frogs, because of their amphibian appearance. So you'll probably hear me using that terminology. Just keep in mind we're talking about the same weird creatures."

A few in the audience laughed.

"Please feel free to interrupt me at any time. That will give me more time to think about what I'm going to say."

A few people snickered.

"To start off, we were inside a craft that seemed to us to be much larger than this one, but even though we were allowed to tour the ship, we saw no sign of a propulsion unit or engine room."

Murmuring occurred throughout the room.

"Before I talk about our spaceship experience," Parker continued, "I'm reminded of a conversation I had with an engineer not too long ago. I'm not an engineer, but a physiologist, which is a sort of medical biologist. Physiological research tells physicians how the body works, so they know how to fix it when it stops working correctly."

He was getting a few concerned looks like they didn't understand that description, but he didn't want to linger on introductions.

"So I was talking to this engineer about the colonization of Mars. Knowing my physiological background, he reminded me that the Martian atmosphere was 95% carbon dioxide, compared to our 0.04%. Compared to our 21% oxygen, Mars only has 0.13%. He asked me if it

261

was possible to change humans so they could breathe carbon dioxide instead of oxygen."

Many in the audience were smiling, but others seemed to be thinking that was a good question.

"I mean, if you think about it from an atomic perspective, diatomic oxygen has, by definition, two atoms of oxygen, and so does carbon dioxide. That's all you need, two atoms of oxygen. Right?"

Many in the audience said "No."

"You are correct, the answer is no. But it's not a bad question. In fact, it's a challenging question. By convention, and our training, we are taught that the body is a furnace of sorts that burns carbon-containing compounds by combining it with oxygen to release energy. And that energy is what keeps us warm and moving. But the question I was being asked was, does it have to be that way?"

A number in the audience nodded their heads, knowing that it did indeed have to be that way.

"And that's how I left it with him. He offered a good question, but that's how our biology works."

He paused for a moment, letting that thought sink in.

"There are, after all, certain immutable laws, defining how things work. But do those immutable laws apply to interstellar propulsion? You from NASA and the Air Force know that Newton's laws teach us about equal and opposite reactions. If we are to accelerate a spacecraft in one direction, we have to accelerate something out the back end of the craft. And we're very good at burning fuel to spew out a jet engine, or rocket nozzle. Or if you get really fancy and can afford to take your time, you can use a flow of ions or photons in photonic propulsion."

Again, a large number of engineers and physicists dipped their heads in agreement.

"But I'll ask you the same question the NASA engineer asked me. Do we have to?"

Now he was getting a few blank stares and a few smiles.

"Yes, I know about reactionless systems such as Radio Frequency resonant cavity thrusters, the so-called EmDrives. It has not been a well-kept secret, either that it exists, or that it is overly hyped. In other words, I'd be surprised if it could power our craft here."

Some heads nodded in agreement, presumably the Em skeptics.

"And by the way, Laura and I never saw any hardware that looked like an EmDrive, for what that's worth. But I can tell you that a Frog once told me that they would use the gravity associated with clouds of dark matter to bend space-time and produce an acceleration that appeared from our perspective to result in faster than light speed. To a much lesser extent, we do the same thing to accelerate our craft within the solar system."

"Gravitation slingshot," one of the NASA engineers offered.

"Except of course, we never even get close to light speed. But the curious thing is, although the Frogs seem to be able to use Dark Matter, and we believe the universe is filled with it, we don't even know what it is."

Some in the crowd were looking uncomfortable.

"I have a friend who's an astrophysicist working in Geneva, Switzerland researching dark matter and energy. His team literally has no clue what it is. So who's to say if it can't be used to make a craft hover, or accelerate without the need for chemical or light energy? When an alien spacecraft takes off rapidly into space, as Laura and I have seen, without flames or engine noise, perhaps it's doing nothing more than allowing the gravity associated with dark matter in space to overcome the gravity associated with the mass of the Earth. It could, in effect, be falling down a gravity hill even though that gravity is pulling them straight up."

"What about zero-point energy?" a youngish man asked from the back of the room. "Do you know about that?"

"Yes, I do, but it is unimaginably difficult, I suspect, to use zero-point energy to propel something in a particular direction. Perhaps it's there, everywhere, operating on a quantum level, and that may in fact be what dark energy is. But how do you convert that to thrust?"

A lot of heads were nodding in agreement.

"Zero-point energy undoubtedly exists," Parker said, "but harnessing it in our lifetime seems unlikely."

Looking up towards Laura, he sensed from her body movements that she also wanted to speak.

"Now I'm going to let my colleague have her say."

She immediately rose, and smiling politely made her way to the aisle at the edge of the room, saying, "I'm almost always holding a different opinion from Jason."

Parker smiled because that was a true statement. She always seemed to have a different opinion.

Walking to the front center and standing where Parker had just been, Laura said, "I want to draw your attention to what Jason just said about the Frog telling him about dark matter gravity. I was there to witness it."

The audience was deathly quiet, perhaps trying to imagine what it would be like to have an alien Frog talking to you.

"Do you know how he communicated with us?"

"Telepathy," someone said.

"You've been doing your homework. Yes, he talked directly to us without speaking. In our heads, we heard him plain as day."

From the far right back region of the room came an unfamiliar voice. "So what does that have to do with spacecraft propulsion?"

She stood on her tiptoes to get a better view of the man asking. "Are you a rocket scientist by any chance?"

"Yes," he said smiling proudly.

"Then I'd say that's your job to figure out. We're telling you what we learned from being inside an alien spacecraft. Obviously, the Frogs can do two things a lot better than you. That is, communicate telepathically and fly spacecraft into interstellar space. We're not telling you how they do it, we're just saying they do it."

Parker added, "And then there's remote viewing."

The group started stirring again.

"Yes, according to what the Frogs told us," Parker said, "they obtain all the intelligence they need by remote viewing. And guess what? That's something we can do as well. If you don't know about it, you should. It's unclassified now. Just search for CIA, Stanford Research Institute, and Dr. Harry Kincaide."

"What does telepathy and remote viewing have to do with spaceship propulsion?" It was a woman on the opposite side of the room from the last questioner.

"This is what I've learned," Parker said. "Until we come up with a worldview that includes telepathy and remote viewing, we'll have no more understanding than a cat trying to catch a red spot on a wall, or more relevantly, your pet dog noticing that when you reach into your pocket, the family sedan starts and the car doors unlock. It must be a coincidence. Right? Or magic."

"That's not really helping us," someone said.

Parker continued. "It's my conviction that we cannot understand one without the other. If we can't grasp remote viewing, and telepathy, then why do we think we can understand relativistic propulsion without rocket engines?"

"Really? There are no rocket engines?"

"Not in the photos," Parker said. "Plus there's no room for fuel. How much fuel would you need to get to a far distant star even if you had rocket engines?"

The man asking Parker the question sat quietly, expressionless.

"Now I'll be the first to admit that I'm a dog, and Laura here is a cat. But we're hoping you folks are a little further up the evolutionary tree. Otherwise, our very interesting family sedan may sit in the driveway for a very long time."

Taking his clue from Laura that he should wrap up, he asked, "Are there any more questions?"

After scanning the audience faces for latent questions, and finding none, Parker and Laura returned to their seats.

"Well ladies and gentlemen," the lead speaker Dr. Pinafore said, "Drs. Parker and Smith have thrown down the gauntlet. Of course, we're hoping we can expedite the process a bit. I don't think we have time to figure out telepathy and remote viewing. We've got to get this bird flying."

A dark-suited civilian had slipped to the front of the room, and at that statement from Pinafore leaned into the speaker and whispered something in his ear.

"OK, I've been informed I can mention something else very important, never to be mentioned again outside of this room. We think it is highly probable that the Russians have their own alien craft."

A clearly audible gasp filled the room.

"Whoever gets theirs into the air first — well I don't need to tell you how significant that will be."

At least half the people attending the meeting started whispering to each other. Apparently, no one other than Parker and Laura knew about that possibility.

Pinafore continued, "So get some rest. We'll try the lift at 0700 hours; it may turn out to be a long day. And keep your thinking caps on."

As the group exited the room, regaining their phones in the process, they were told where to find secure billeting for the night on the base, with an adjacent makeshift chow hall set up just for the distinguished visitors. But Laura and Parker had agreed they would go for that run he'd promised her back at Pax River, once they'd cleaned up a little, had a snack, and called home. It was 10 o'clock Eastern time in West Virginia, but Parker knew Sandy would want to hear from him no matter how late it was.

By 1030 hours Laura and Parker met out in front of guest housing with moisture absorbent T-shirts, shorts, and running shoes. They set their watches and set off at a casual jogging pace toward the guard gate at the entrance to the Naval Station. They let the guard know they'd be running to the River Front Park and should be back in about 90 minutes. The guard gave both of them a reflective harness to wear for added visibility, a considerate touch that surprised Parker. Apparently, the CO of the base had a warm spot for joggers.

"You say it's three miles to the park?" Parker asked Laura.

"As the crow flies, or maybe four miles if you're following the road."

"I'm glad I didn't eat a big meal," Parker said. "I'd be throwing it up by the time we get there."

"What did Sandy have to say?"

"She's OK. She doesn't know exactly where she is, and she couldn't tell me if she did, except she's out in the boonies of West Virginia."

"That covers a lot of territory."

"Of course she asked me where I was, and I also told her I couldn't say."

"Did she ask who you're with?"

Parker hesitated for a moment before answering.

"I told her I was with a bunch of science nerds, and Laura Smith."

"Should you have said that?"

He looked at her smiling. "Well, she said I should feel right at home."

"Is she still sensitive about me?" Laura asked.

"Not openly. She feels quite comfortable in your presence when she's with us. But when she's not, she worries. I think the psychological trauma of both of us disappearing in Guam will always haunt her."

"She probably wonders what you're up to, now that I'm back in the picture."

"I guess I can't blame her," Parker said.

They ran silently for a few minutes, watching the ships heading out to sea on the left, and watching the lights of the Pascagoula shipyard slide by on the right as they covered the semicircular causeway bypassing the industrial area. This was a scenic place to run during the cool of the evening.

"Didn't I hear you were a javelin thrower in college?"

"Yes, I was."

"Got any of that fitness left in you."

"Maybe a little."

"Then let's pick up the pace old man," she said taunting.

"Long as you know CPR," he said jokingly.

They picked up from the leisurely 10-minute mile to a 9-minute mile. They'd try for an 8-minute mile on the way back.

As they ran, Parker could not help admiring the form of the fit young lady running beside him.

From the north end of USS Vicksburg Way, they made their way to Port Road, which turned into River Edge Road, before turning north on Clark Street, heading underneath the Denny Avenue Bridge over the Pascagoula River, and stopping, panting at the River Edge Park.

"Good run," she said.

"Why do you young folks have to say that? I'm dying here."

"No you're not," she said. "Quit your whining."

"Let's go sit down on the pier and see the view."

She shook her head. "OK, old man. I'll give you a breather."

From the wooden pier which was the main feature of the park, the lights from the industrial area on the eastern side of the river, and the distant lights from residential areas near Gurlie Bayou were reflecting off wavelets in the river and Krebs Lake. It was one of those sights that was probably prettier at night than during the day. Darkness has a way of hiding ugliness.

"Jason, I was more than a little surprised by your comments this evening."

"Which ones?"

"When you said, 'If we can't grasp remote viewing and telepathy, then why do we think we can understand interstellar propulsion?' I've never heard you say that before. It sounds like something I'd say."

"I don't think I've said that before tonight. But remember, I've had three years to think about the events preceding the Frog's departure. None of it can be explained by the laws of physics as we understand it. Even Kincaide's CIA remote viewing program. I mean, how can a person see things at a great distance? I can do it, and Richter, he's even better than I am. And for crying out loud, I know a blind man who can see remotely better than anyone."

"You do?"

"You don't?"

267

"Well yeah, I just didn't know you'd been read in."

Parker laughed. "Laura, I've worked with the guy. He's awesome."

"Oh."

"But you know, there's nothing new in what I said. Nikola Tesla once said that 'The day science begins to study non-physical phenomena, it will make more progress in one decade than in all the previous centuries of its existence.' Tesla was a very smart guy."

She looked puzzled for a moment. "Tesla, the car guy?"

"Tesla, the electricity guy. The Tesla car is electric, hence the name."

"Oh, I see."

"It's a long story. Anyway, my point was, based on what you and I have seen over the past few years, we simply cannot explain how the world works. There's still a lot of strange stuff out there."

Just then car lights pulled into the parking lot, facing the water and the pier where Parker and Laura sat.

Parker said, "I'm guessing those are kids parking."

"Making out?"

"They still do that, don't they?" Parker asked, feeling a bit out of touch with the mores of modern youth.

"I guess. This is a romantic spot. Course they could be cops checking us out."

Parker and Laura turned their eyes back to the water.

"Speaking of …," she said before pausing.

"Of what?" Parker asked. "Cops or romantic?"

"I had a dream about you, once."

"I hope I enjoyed it."

Laura shook her head slowly. "No, you didn't. It was horrible."

Parker cocked his head, frowning.

"We were on a spaceship. A human killed a Frog child in what seemed like an act of rebellion."

Parker's mind instantly flashed back to the dream he had many months before.

"And Frog soldiers came and…"

Parker filled in the rest from memory. "… and broke down the barrier separating Frogs and humans. The Frog atmosphere killed the humans."

Laura stared at Parker in disbelief. "You had the same dream?"

"Apparently. And I agree, it was horrible."

268

"How can that be?" Laura asked, staring deeply into Parker's eyes with the same look she had when she was underwater, trying to blow air into his shattered lungs during that equally horrible night in Guam. It was a look of fear and disbelief.

"I don't know."

"It has to mean something," she said shaking her head.

Parker looked back and said, "Well, these don't look like cops. They're a young couple. Maybe we should leave and give them some privacy."

"OK, are we picking up the pace on the way back?"

"My muscles are getting stiff," he said. "We'll see."

As they passed the young man and woman, Parker smiled, remembering his own lustful days not too far in the distant past.

Laura smiled at Parker, thinking her own thoughts.

Then she jerked, swatting at her neck. "Ouch, I just got stung."

At essentially the same instant, Parker felt a sharp sting in his neck. Reaching back he grabbed a small dart sticking out of the back of his neck.

He wheeled around to find the two people facing Laura and Parker, both holding a small tube in their hands.

"Blowgun?" he thought for a clouded moment.

CHAPTER 50. THE LIFT

Engineers had been up all night calculating and recalculating the stress and strain on the hoisting system. It was one thing to hold the craft steady in the water, and something else entirely to lift it free from the water, which was what they planned to do. Carpenters also spent the night making final adjustments on the mostly wooden cradle that would be holding the craft off the floor of the containment building. Those final adjustments were made based on laser measurements made by divers just a few hours before.

A separate team of engineers had been making load calculations on the cradle and floor which would be slid underneath the craft once it was suspended in position. Finally, at 0700 hours, the decision was made to proceed with the lift.

All the scientists and engineers from the night before had gathered to watch the operation, except Parker and Laura. Someone said, "If Drs. Parker and Smith don't hurry up their breakfast, they're going to miss the big show."

However, it was already too late.

The two missing scientists were quickly forgotten as the diesel-powered hoisting engine started winding in the cables suspending the craft. It took a surprisingly short time for the triangular vehicle to break the surface of the muddy water, at which point a massive cheer filled the containment building, followed by a deathly silence as all stared at what they were beginning to see.

At that point, the lift stopped while strain gauges were checked. When it resumed, experienced eyes were trained on the cables and gauges as the top half of the craft sat proud above the water surface. Another halt allowed more careful checking of the cables, and then the lift resumed.

About ten minutes after the restart, the craft was fully suspended in the air. Almost all stood in silence, staring at a basically triangular metallic craft with smoothly rounded corners, and with bulbous protrusions all along the periphery of the craft. In places where powerful lights from the ceiling reflected off the wet surface, the lights dazzled onlookers. Then while the craft was held motionless, the floor carrying the cradle began to slide into place underneath the rounded bottom contours of the craft. Using hand signals and walky-talkies, technicians signaled the hoist operator, gently guiding the alien craft into the cradle in such a way that the bulbous protrusions were not impinged upon by the cradle. It was a time-consuming delicate operation.

Finally, the hoist engine went to idle, indicating that the craft was now fully supported by the floor and cradle.

Another, even more raucous cheer reverberated within the containment building and could be clearly heard by others in nearby buildings.

When the noise began to abate, Jim Pinafore, the Alien Propulsion Unit civilian from Wright-Pat Airbase who had been running the show-and-tell the night before, shouted, "Where in the hell are our Frog scientists? I can't believe they're missing this."

Someone else spoke up, "They weren't at breakfast, and they're not in their rooms. I checked at 6:45."

Jim Pinafore looked stunned. He stared silently at the messenger of bad news for a moment, then said, "Then we have a situation."

While everyone else was marveling at the stunning alien craft sitting before them, the Base Commander, having just been visited by Jim Pinafore, reviewed the notes from the gate guard from the evening before. The guard had properly noted when Parker and Smith left the base, and had noted when they planned to return. But during the shift change at midnight, he had not passed on the important fact that the two subject matter experts were missing. Upon discovering that omission, the Navy Commander picked up the phone to call Washington.

Somewhere in the Pentagon, an emergency response team was discussing each new piece of information as it came in. It was 9 AM Washington time, and Parker and Smith had been missing for nine hours.

Of immediate interest was a purportedly private medical flight to Fairbanks, Alaska, which had departed from Pascagoula at 11 PM local time, 0400 hours Greenwich Mean Time. The Gulfstream G6 ER luxury jet, chartered from an American company by an unknown customer, arrived over Fairbanks at 0100 hours local time, 0900 hours GMT, but never landed. It was tracked in radio silence heading towards the 50 mile-wide Bering Strait separating the U.S. from Russia, and then on a slightly southerly deviation once in Russian territory. If the passengers had looked down midway across the Strait, they would have been able to see the feeble lights coming from the Russian Big Diomede Island and the closest U.S. territory, Little Diomede Island, only 2 miles away.

While the Gulfstream was still over U.S. Territory, F-22s from Elmendorf Air Force Base in Anchorage intercepted the flight. FAA Air Traffic Controllers had suspected a hypoxia event in the aircraft, which would have rendered the pilots unconscious, however, when the F-22s pulled alongside, the G6 crew could be seen waving in a friendly manner to the intercepting jets. The G6 crew did not have oxygen masks on.

Even though the Gulfstream's transponder had been turned off, the jet was flying away from the U.S., so it posed no immediate threat. Accordingly, the F-22s returned to base, notifying both NORAD and the FAA that the aircraft appeared to be operating normally, and the crew was well. Apparently, their ultimate destination was somewhere in Russia.

The senior civilian of the mixed military and civilian intelligence agencies was pacing back and forth in front of the projected screen of the jet's predicted flight path. He was muttering to himself, and then said out loud what he was thinking.

"Holy Mother of God," his deep, resonant voice echoed in the room. "If Laura Smith is on that plane we are screwed."

Now that the emergency response team was aware that the Director of National Intelligence's Science Advisor for Alien Affairs was missing, that mystery flight received extra scrutiny. Unfortunately, satellite data indicated that the flight had already entered deep into Russian airspace. Whoever was on that flight was now out of reach.

An Army one-star general asked, "Why didn't they take the more direct polar route?"

An Air Force colonel answered, "Winds and subterfuge. Winds could be more favorable with this route, but I think mainly they didn't want to give us a hint of their true intentions until it was too late for us to do anything about it. Plus, with the polar route, we'd know exactly where they were headed. Now it's just a guess."

"What's your best guess, Colonel?" the General asked.

"Knowing the fuel burn and extended range of this bird, and the sparseness of Eastern Russia and Siberia, I'm placing bets on Irkutsk."

As he said that, someone placed a shaded circle of uncertainty around Irkutsk on the large screen at the end of the room.

A CIA chief spoke, "Irkutsk? Don't we have Intel inquiries going on in that region?"

A CIA underling said, "Yes sir. In the Lake Baikal area, suspicion of exploited alien technology."

The civilian who was still pacing said, "This is exactly why I say our people need to have implants."

"Why is that sir?" someone asked.

"If we could confirm our missing alien experts were on that plane, I'd request a shoot down."

There was an audible gasp from someone in the room.

The civilian, still pacing, said, "But it's a moot point now. We got the warning way too late to take action."

An Air Force Colonel asked, "Are you serious?"

The civilian stopped pacing, and turned toward the Colonel, glaring.

"I'm always serious Colonel. We'd be better off with our assets dead than in the hands of the Russians."

A young Air Force major offered, "Maybe we should make them explodable implants, satellite triggered."

"Damn good idea Major, damn good idea. Someone make a note of that."

CHAPTER 51. SIBERIA

Parker became dimly aware of light, and then he could see, fuzzy at first, medical tubing running from his left arm up to a pole. He turned his head enough to try to read the label on the bottle hung on the pole, but it was in Cyrillic.

"Welcome to Sayansk Hospital, Doctor Parker."

He turned his head back to the source of the sound, and could just make out the form of a man on the right side of his bed.

"Where's Laura?"

"The girl's right here, behind this partition."

Parker called out to her, "Laura!"

"Jason?"

"Are you OK?" Parker asked weakly.

"I don't know. I think so … maybe."

"She's groggy like you," the stranger said.

Parker's vision was clearing, and now he could plainly see a man in a white medical lab coat. He couldn't make out the name badge.

"What happened? Where are we?"

"There was an accident apparently."

"Accident? What accident?"

"What do you remember?"

"We were running, nearing a park."

"What park?"

"River Front Park."

"I don't know that park."

"It's on the Pascagoula River."

"And where is that?"

"Pascagoula, Mississippi of course."

"Mississippi? As in the USA?"

The man looked towards another man Parker could barely see, seated in a chair in the corner of the small room. That man was not dressed in medical clothing, and did not react when the white-coated man looked at him.

Parker had an immediate and instinctive dislike for the seated man.

The man who appeared to be a doctor crossed over to the other curtained area and repeated his question.

"And what about you, Ms. Smith? What do you remember?"

"Running. I remember running. Then I was here."

The doctor pulled the curtain back that separated Parker and Laura.

"Oh my God Jason. Your face is black and blue. Is mine?"

"No, you look fine," he lied. Actually, she looked more tired and pale than he'd ever seen her before. She looked sick.

"It looks like you've been in a fight," she said.

Touching his face, he said, "It feels like I lost."

"What happened to us?" Laura asked the doctor.

"We're trying to figure that out," the doctor said. "You were brought here by car in a semi-comatose state. The people who left you said you'd been in an accident."

"How did you know our names?"

"The man sitting with you told us."

As all three of them looked in the chair's direction, they saw it was empty.

"He must have stepped out. As you say, 'the little boy's room maybe.'"

"Is it my imagination," she asked, "or did we wake up at the same time?"

"You're right, you did. We won't know why until we get blood tests back. If it's something toxic, we should know in a few days. In the meanwhile, we're flushing you out with saline to help purge whatever is in you."

"That doesn't make sense," Laura insisted. "We were in the U.S. Now we're, where?"

"Siberia."

"What the hell?" Laura said it, but Parker was thinking it.

"Please, I need you both to close your eyes and rest. You will heal faster if you sleep."

"I don't want to sleep," Laura said shaking her head.

Parker laughed. He thought that was funny. *Laura was such a silly girl.*

A moment later, a smile crept slowly across his face as he slipped into drug-induced unconsciousness.

A sharp noise woke Parker. His bed was moving. It was dark outside. But as someone maneuvered his bed out the door of the hospital room, he saw the doctor, sitting asleep, propped against the wall. His forehead had a strange dark spot on it, and red and whitish splotches were on the wall.

But the drugs allowed Parker no understanding, no feelings, no empathy.

Parker became aware of a pain in his left side, which prompted him to switch to his back. That was only slightly more comfortable so he rolled to his right side, and was almost overcome with a foul odor, like the odor of too many unwashed bodies lying on the same unsheeted mattress for too many years. He felt a revulsion rising in his stomach.

He sat up and vomited on himself, the already rank mattress, and the long unswept concrete floor.

Gasping, he looked for a sink to wash out his mouth. Fortunately, one was nearby. With considerable pain, he forced himself over to the sink, a loosely-bonded collection of cracked ceramic and rust, to rinse out his mouth.

The only good thing to be said was that the water was cool and sweet. It quickly washed the bitter taste of vomit from his mouth.

That accomplished, he looked around at his surroundings. He was in a jail cell, Russian writing covering the walls, and rising up to the ceiling.

He was in a Russian prison.

Well, he thought, *I can scratch this off my bucket list.*

"Wake up sleeping beauty." That voice, speaking English with an expectedly heavy Russian accent, came from down the central corridor, beyond where he could see.

"Bloody hell!"

It was Laura. Her voice echoed down the row of holding cells. Apparently, she was nearby and like Parker had just figured out they were being held.

"Laura," Parker called out.

"Jason, where are we?"

"I don't know."

He heard footsteps leaving Laura's cell and approaching his.

"Ah, so there you are Mr. Parker. I see you are awake. And my God you smell bad. Miss Smith, can you hear me?"

"Yes," she answered, sounding pissed off.

"Good, I don't like to repeat myself. I have some fresh clothes for you two on a cart just outside of the showers. After you freshen up, I will escort you upstairs where we have a large American breakfast soon to be ready for you. Then, after you have eaten, you will be visiting with a very important man."

Parker could not resist asking, "Who?"

The Russian man, tall, with blond hair and bushy blond eyebrows, smiled. "I doubt very much Mr. Parker that you know any Russian political figures, and certainly not President Dmitriev's new Chief of Staff."

"Did he say, Dmitriev?" Laura asked.

"We won't be meeting Dmitriev himself, Laura."

The Russian smiled again. "If things go well, you just might."

"Now before I let you out, let me tell you things for your safety. If you go wild and crazy, I will stun you. I especially enjoy stunning the ladies and watching them piss themselves."

"Jesus Christ," Laura moaned.

"Second, this area is sealed, and an attendant is watching and will make sure you do not escape. Even if you did escape, you are in Siberia. Winter is approaching, snow has begun falling, and it's dropping below zero degrees at night. You will freeze to death."

The man was large enough that even if Parker had a weapon, which he did not, the guard would be difficult to take down.

"On the other hand, if you cooperate, you will get, what do they say, squeaky clean, nice fresh Russian clothes, and a big American meal. Then you will have an entertaining visit with one of the most powerful men in all of Russia."

Parker responded loud enough for Laura to hear, "That's got to be better than this."

As the man unlocked the door and showed Parker where the showers were, Parker had a fleeting concern, remembering the so-called showers of Auschwitz, the poison gas showers that killed so many Jews and Russians. But then, as badly as the Russians hated the Nazis for killing millions of Russians, Russia would surely not adopt such a heinous method of assassination, not when a single bullet would do.

277

As Parker walked the 10 meters or so to the shower, his feet beginning to sting from the cold concrete, he realized that frankly, in the condition he was in, it was worth taking the chance of being gassed.

But when he removed his clothes and stepped into the shower, it was exactly as advertised. The water was even warm, something Parker had not expected. When he stepped out, he was handed a towel to dry his body, and then he picked a set of clean clothes from the table in front of him.

This was another first for Parker, wearing Russian-made clothing. It actually felt soft and warm.

When Parker was clothed, he was asked to sit in a corner while Laura was led down the corridor. As she stripped, the Russian watched, and Laura sneered. "I bet Russian women don't look like this," she said, very much aware of the unavoidable staring eyes.

"Nyet, they are much more..." he held his hands out, open palmed, "... substantial."

Out of decency, Parker averted his eyes, an act that Laura noticed and seemed to appreciate based on her half-smile.

A short while later, smelling fresh and dressed warmly, they were led to a small room where a buffet of the type rarely seen in Russia was displayed. Someone had done their research into American eating habits. There was scrambled eggs, bacon, both sausage links and patties, biscuits and gravy, toast, and jelly.

Parker eyed it hungrily and sampled some of everything. Laura seemed to have a lesser appetite and only had toast and jelly and some scrambled eggs. If food is the way to a man's heart, perhaps the Russians thought it was also the way to a traitor's heart.

Parker and Laura ate without conversing. There were at least six Russians in the room, and neither of the Americans had a desire to say something that could be overheard.

Thirty minutes later they were satiated. Parker said to the guard who had been with them all morning, "I hope this remaining food won't go to waste."

"It won't," is all he said. The others in the room smiled. Apparently, a full American breakfast was quite a rarity in Irkutsk.

Laura and Parker were led out of the dining area into a portion of the spacious building that had thick carpeting. They walked up a wide flight of stairs, feeling as if they were free, but noticing that many eyes were on them. If they tried to run, they would not get more than a few feet.

They were led underneath a massive chandelier into a small room with a desk and chairs, and a large windowed view of the gray clouds of a Siberian fall. Occasional flakes of snow were falling.

The desk was empty, but they were shown to their seats in front of the desk. "Doctor Sergei Vorobyev will be with you shortly."

With that, the guard stepped back towards the wall and stood quietly.

So the Americans waited, looking around the room at its opulent tapestries, paintings of the revolution, and dark wood paneling. This was obviously not a room shared with the proletariat. But then again, Russia had fortunately drifted far from the stark and murderous days of Lenin and Stalin.

They did not have to wait long. The large wooden doors swung open and in walked a medium built man with lush black hair, dressed in a very western looking solid Navy blue suit and flaming red tie, powerful in effect, and perhaps reflecting an illusion to the former Soviet days of Russia's self-proclaimed grandeur and the infamous red star.

He walked briskly over to the Americans who by now were standing, although neither were quite sure why they had stood, other than from habit.

Holding out his hand and smiling broadly, he said, "Doctors Smith and Parker, I am so glad to see you."

It seemed surreal. They were kidnapped prisoners, being treated with warmth and civility by one of their captors.

"President Dmitriev sends his best wishes and says he hopes you will find your stay here interesting and fulfilling. How have you been treated so far?"

Parker smiled at the ridiculousness of it all. "Well, except for the part where we were kidnapped and kept in a jail cell, I guess it hasn't been too bad."

"Kidnapped, is that what you think?"

"We're not in Mississippi anymore," Laura retorted.

"No, you should think of it more as a sabbatical. You are here to learn new things."

"You brought us against our will," Laura said firmly. "That's the definition of kidnapping."

279

"You shall soon see that if we had not brought you, you would never have come on your own. You would have missed the opportunity of a lifetime."

"What opportunity?" Parker asked.

"We'll get to that later. We have many things to discuss."

"What about our Doctor at the hospital. I think he was shot in the head."

"I seriously doubt that. We spend a lot of money training our doctors. We don't go killing off our investments. Besides, you had lots of drugs on board. No telling what you imagined."

"Yeah, what about that?" Laura asked. "Why did they drug us?"

"We wanted you to rest comfortably. It was a long trip from Pascagoula to Irkutsk."

For Parker it was surreal hearing the nonchalant banter about what was clearly a kidnapping. And since they ended up in a hospital, perhaps things had not gone well during their forced transport.

Parker felt his still tender and bruised face. "Why is my face so sore? Did the idiots drop me?"

"I don't know the details, but I heard you got combative at some point."

Parker smiled. "Good."

Vorobyev quickly changed the subject. "The Gulfstream G6 is an incredible aircraft. I know you're a pilot Jason. Have you ever flown a Gulfstream?"

Parker noticed that Vorobyev had dropped the formality of his surname, without asking. Perhaps that was a Russian custom. Or perhaps the Chief of Staff for President Dmitriev didn't give a damn about asking permission of Americans.

It was a subtle thing, and Parker had more serious concerns on his mind.

"No, I only fly baby jets, certified for a single pilot. I prefer to have the entire jet under my command."

"Ah, I like that about you. Of course, the fuel is a lot cheaper too, if you're paying the bill."

Parker almost said he didn't pay the bill but stopped himself. This man did not need to know about financial arrangements between himself and the U.S. government.

"We will talk more about flying later, but first I want to ask the two of you some questions which I think you will find amusing."

Parker and Laura looked at each other with a look that said, *Not likely.*

"I've always found it amusing that in Western countries you can earn a Doctorate in Philosophy without knowing anything about Philosophy. Is that not true?"

Parker nodded.

"At least for the sciences, it is," Parker admitted.

"That is a pity, is it not? Certainly, you cannot earn a Doctorate of Medicine without knowing a great deal about medicine. So perhaps you will indulge me if we talk a little about philosophy."

"Do we have a choice?" Laura asked.

Vorobyev looked at her for a moment, smiling.

"I like your spirit, Doctor Smith. But to answer your question, no, you do not."

Laura rolled her eyes.

"Do either of you know the term 'cosmism'?"

They both shook their heads.

"Cosmism is a philosophy that combines nature, religion, mankind in general, and the cosmos. Basically, everything is connected, very much like your new-agers used to say. But it is true. Contributing to this philosophy are the ideas of a great Russian geochemist Vladimir Vernadsky, who spoke about the biosphere, a term I'm sure you know, and the noosphere, a term you may not know."

"You are correct," Parker said. "I have no idea what the noosphere is."

"Then I should educate you, because my friends, you two are probably the best living examples of what the noosphere is all about."

Laura shook her head in seeming disbelief at what was happening. A philosophy lesson?

"As Vernadsky explained it, the Earth is what we can call the geosphere, something Vernadsky knew a lot about since he was a geochemist. But life on this planet has transformed the geosphere in many ways. That transformative process is caused by the biosphere. But there is a third transformative process that will eventually change the biosphere, and it is named the noosphere."

Neither Parker nor Laura had any clue what he was talking about.

"*Noos* is a Greek word. Do you know it?"

"No," Parker answered.

"How unfortunate. Educated Russian men and women used to learn Greek and Latin. And I think at one time in your country as well. Now you learn, how you say, *hip hop?*"

"I am not an apologist for our educational system," Parker said.

"I know, you have no influence over it. A pity. But back to *noos*. It is Greek for *mind*. The noosphere is the sphere of mind, thought, consciousness that can and does transform the biosphere."

"By that, you mean the collective consciousness?"

"Yes, exactly. See, you do know something about philosophy."

"In America, we are more likely to call that *pseudoscience* than philosophy."

"Yes, I know, or that particularly condescending American phrase, *junk science.*"

Parker responded, "I'm trying to be kind, which by the way is difficult under these circumstances."

"Patience my friends. You will thank me soon enough."

"I doubt that," Laura muttered loud enough for all to hear.

"Let me propose that the noosphere is not junk science, but merely a hypothesis. Isn't it true that a hypothesis is part of the scientific method?"

"Well, yes, by definition," Parker answered.

"And wouldn't it be unscientific to dismiss a hypothesis based on personal bias, instead of scientific data?"

Parker and Laura looked at each other again. Parker was thinking, *What can I say to that?*

Vorobyev did not wait for an answer. "The problem with labeling things outside of your teaching and experience is that the label makes you intellectually lazy. And I think a Doctor of Philosophy should not be intellectually lazy."

"I agree, but what sort of hypothesis is it that the mind, or thought, can change the biosphere?"

Vorobyev laughed loudly. "Jason Parker, surely you jest. You of all people should know better."

"What do you mean?"

"You know very well that both Russia and the CIA have a remote viewing program. And I've heard that you also are a remote viewer. So explain to me how it is that your thought is able to interact with the real world, the biosphere."

Ironically, that was almost exactly what Parker had asked the scientists gathered at the Navy Base in Pascagoula.

"I don't know. I'm not very good at remote viewing."

"But what you and Laura are very good at, is interacting with alien technology."

Parker tried not to signal anything, but he couldn't tell if Laura was reacting or not. He didn't want to look at her.

"Why do you think that?" Parker asked.

"Oh, come now. In the spy versus spy game, our nations are pretty much equal. We know all about your alien toys."

Parker sighed, thinking *Are we incapable of keeping ANY secrets?*

Finally, he had to break the awkward silence without giving away secret information. "A toy you say? It sounds to me like a toy would not be much of a challenge."

"For special people like you two, I agree. And would you two special people enjoy a real challenge?"

"That depends. What kind of challenge?"

Vorobyev sat back in his chair, apparently relishing the thought of his next words.

"How about the challenge of flying a Frog ship?"

CHAPTER 52. SUPERMAN WANTS TO FLY

A Kazan Ansat helicopter crewed with Russian military personnel was waiting on the roof of the government building where Parker and Laura had just finished their bizarre meeting with President Dmitriev's Chief of Staff.

They were helped up the steps of the helicopter by soldiers who spoke no English. They didn't speak to the Americans, just to each other.

Laura couldn't help pressing the point. Surely one of them knew a little English or at least body language. As the rotors began spooling up, she asked, "Where are you taking us?"

The men looked at them, puzzled, until one said, "Ribbit, Ribbit." The others laughed.

Apparently, that's a fairly universal sound effect. But then Parker wondered, *Are they taking us to see Frogs, or a Frog ship?*

After their rooftop takeoff, they cruised on a heading of 135° following the Angara River which drains Lake Baikal, to the point next to the lake where they landed at what gave every appearance of being a mining operation. The flight took no more than 15 minutes.

Parker assumed either there were straggler Frogs somewhere down there, or as he had been led to believe, a dysfunctional Frog ship. But if an alien ship was there, there was no sign of it.

Two soldiers disembarked from the helicopter, followed by Parker and Laura. As they stepped onto what might someday be hallowed ground for UFOlogists, they were met by two civilians with tightly cropped hair, or else plain-clothed military. It was hard to tell the difference.

"I am Dr. Oleg Kiselev. I hear you've spent some time with Sergei Vorobyev."

"He seems very well versed in Russian sociology and philosophy," Laura said.

Kiselev smiled and nodded in agreement. Kiselev had long but thinning grayish black hair which seemed to be making a desperate attempt, unsuccessfully, to cover his balding pate.

"So is it true that you two have talked to Frogs," he asked, "and been inside their spacecraft?"

"Yes, and yes," Parker answered, "except it was underwater the whole time we were in it. We did eventually see it fly, but we weren't on board at that time."

Laura asked, "Vorobyev was short on answers as to why the Russian government kidnapped us."

"Kidnapped you? Is that what you think? You're here as a scientist exchange program."

"That's odd," Parker said. "Vorobyev called it a sabbatical."

Laura's response was far more curt, as usual. "Since we know nothing about that, and were almost killed in the process, I'd call it kidnapping."

"Well regardless of what you think, you two have been granted full access to our Frog ship program."

"Why?" Laura asked.

"We know you have salvaged your own ship, but we doubt you know as much about them as we do."

Parker said, "We can neither confirm nor deny…"

"Oh please, cut the school boy theatrics. We know you found something in the De Soto Canyon."

Laura asked, "Why do you care?"

"Because, believe it or not, our combined futures depend on us cooperating in this endeavor."

"Why is that?" Laura asked.

"I'm not at liberty to say. But we do believe we have perilous times ahead."

"Jihadi's?"

"Much worse. But listen my friends, mutual distrust will not bode well for our countries. I really need you to suspend your natural distrust. We can work together."

"What kind of Doctor are you?" Laura asked, her tone barely concealing her growing disdain.

"I hold a doctorate in parapsychology."

Laura looked at Parker and asked, "Is there such a thing?"

"Don't be rude Laura," Parker chided her. "Yes, there is such a thing."

Undaunted, she continued her inquiry. "Where do you get a degree like that?"

"The University of Edinburgh, in Scotland. You will find out very shortly why my credentials are relevant here."

"Oh boy, can't wait."

Parker cut his disapproving eyes towards her.

Speaking to Kiselev, Parker said, "Please forgive her. She's a little short on manners."

"I understand. You did not plan on being here. I'm sure it is a shock."

Parker nodded his head in agreement.

"To put it mildly," Laura said sarcastically.

"Let's suppose we take you at your word," Parker said. "What do you have in mind?"

"I'm not as well-versed as Sergei Vorobyev in dead Russian philosophers. I'm more into popular American culture which I find interesting in its decadence."

Parker and Laura smiled. *Yes, decadence is an apt description,* Parker thought.

"So let me ask you something about Superman. Do you mind?"

"Not at all," Parker said, pleasantly puzzled.

"What happens when Superman wants to fly?"

"He flies," Laura said.

"Are you sure he doesn't calculate his lift to weight ratio? Does he calculate thrust and fuel burn?"

Parker was shaking his head.

Laura was less kind. "You should know better. He just flies."

"Indeed," Kiselev said. "He just flies."

"Are you going somewhere with this?" Laura asked.

"I'm sure Vorobyev talked to you about the Noosphere."

"Yes, he did," Parker said. "And that had to be one of the strangest things I've ever heard."

"It's all about the power of the mind. Superman's mind makes him fly."

"For Chrissake," Parker said, "That's fiction."

"Oh I know that, but tell me if it has to be fiction."

"Of course it does," Laura said.

"I'm not so sure Dr. Parker believes that."

"Well, you're wrong. I do believe that."

"If I'm not mistaken, Jason, I believe you may have practiced remote viewing at one time."

"Maybe."

"You could see things which were hidden in distant places."

"Remote viewers can do that, yes," Parker admitted.

"Well, I certainly hope so."

"Your point?" Parker asked.

"Do you think the remote viewer's eyeballs flew to that distant place and reported back to the remote viewer?"

"No."

"But you don't know how distant travel in the mind happens … do you?"

"No, I don't."

"But you admit it does."

Parker hesitated, considering his options. Finally, he settled on the truth, "Yes, from what I hear, it does."

"Oh, you are ever so careful, Jason. But, before we get back to this, have your people figured out how to open your Frog ship?"

"I have no idea, even if we had such a thing."

"Well, we do have one, and now it's time to show you."

He opened a nearby door and walked through it. Looking back he said, "Please follow me down this hallway. You are about to see an amazing thing."

Parker shrugged his shoulders and invited Laura to go first.

"But pay attention you two," Kiselev said. "It has to do with the Noosphere."

Laura looked back at Parker with her look that said, *They're all crazy!*

"I heard that," Kiselev said.

"What? I didn't say anything," Laura exclaimed.

Trying his best to keep his thoughts to himself, Parker and Laura followed the Russian for what seemed like a hundred yards before they entered a portion of the hallway lined with windows. There Kiselev stopped, and once they caught up with him, they could see why.

From the windows, they could look down onto what appeared to be a large underground hangar, and sitting in the middle was a large triangular craft that looked much like what the one the U.S. had recovered from the De Soto Canyon; although maybe smaller. To Parker's eyes, it was a thing of beauty.

People were walking across the hangar floor in white contamination suits and helmets. There was an entrance of some sort open. It looked like a man-made ramp going up to it, and suited personnel were walking up and down that ramp, entering and exiting the craft.

Parker guessed that in the ship's natural habitat, underwater and in space, ramps weren't needed. People, or rather creatures, could float freely to the access door.

"What's with all the protective gear?" Laura asked.

"That question tells me that you have not opened your Frog craft."

She had to be careful here. She was not about to betray a Top-Secret operation. Certainly not to the Russians, and certainly not as one of the top Intelligence Advisers in the country.

"I have no idea what you're talking about."

"That's alright, I know your rules. My point was, if you had managed to open the access door, you would find an air lock, and if you managed to get beyond that, you'd find the interior highly hypoxic by our standards. Apparently, the oxygen content of our atmosphere is lethal to the Frogs, and so the ship will only open itself once the airlock is closed, and the outside oxygen in the airlock is purged. It's sort of like the doors on jetliners that won't open at altitude."

"That's interesting," Parker said.

"Unfortunately, we found that out the hard way. The first man we sent into the airlock died when the mask on his breathing unit leaked. We cannot breathe the atmosphere inside the ship."

That made perfectly good sense to Parker. He already knew our atmospheric oxygen level is toxic to the Frogs, which explains why we never saw them walking around on Earth, in spite of residing on Earth for at least 10 thousand years.

"What's the oxygen level in there?" Parker asked.

"Eight millimeters of mercury; about 1%."

Atmospheric air contains 21% oxygen, so the oxygen concentration was 5% of normal; it would quickly kill a human trying to breathe it.

"So how did you get the outside door open? The Noosphere?" Parker asked, growing more curious by the minute.

"Actually, yes."

Laura once again gave Parker that look, *They really are crazy.*

"We pumped the hangar down to 1% oxygen, but still no effect. Then Vorobyev suggested we invoke the noosphere concept. The combination of collective will and thoughts worked. A portal opened, and fortunately for us, it has stayed open."

"And these gathered minds, this is what you call the Noosphere?"

"Exactly."

"So where do we come in?"

"I think it best if I show you. But before we head downstairs, I have something to show you. We're heading to the medical offices."

Those offices were just a few steps down the hall. Kiselev opened the door and held it open for Parker and Laura. A seated nurse looked up from her paperwork and smiled as the trio entered the office. She stood up to greet Kiselev.

She said in Russian, "These must be the Americans we've heard about."

Responding in English, Kiselev said, "Nurse Borisova, I'd like to introduce you to Doctors Laura Smith and Jason Parker."

She reached out her hand, and with heavily accented English, said, "Pleasure to meet you."

Then in Russian again, Kiselev said, "Don't expect them to be very friendly, especially the girl. They have not yet accepted being kidnapped."

She winked at him and said in Russian, "I'm not at all surprised. I wouldn't accept it either."

What none of the Russians knew was that Laura had begun Russian language training soon after she was hired by the Office of the Director of National Intelligence. She understood far more than she was letting on.

In English again, Kiselev said, "Yana, would you please show our guests what you have in the freezer?"

Her answer, also in English, was, "Of course, please step into the next room. I think you'll find this interesting."

Against a gray wall, was a large white horizontal freezer. Yana Borisova opened the freezer and invited the Americans to take a look.

What they saw was a greenish-black creature almost completely filling the seven-foot long freezer, with stringy, yellow hair flowing over the upper chest. It had large, round eyes, like those of fish, and no apparent eyelids, a scaly body, and legs that seemed to be fused together.

Kiselev asked, smiling, "So Dr. Parker, is that one of your Frogs?"

At first, Parker was motionless, stunned by what he was seeing, then he slowly shook his head. "Not at all. I have no idea what that is."

Laura said softly to Parker, "You know what that looks like, don't you?"

"Yeah, my thoughts exactly."

"So Oleg," Parker said, "where did you get this?"

"When the door to the ship opened, this thing was standing in the doorway. For a few seconds, it looked intimidating, like it was guarding the ship or something. But the longer it stood, the sicker it looked. Finally, it collapsed. We gave it oxygen, but that just seemed to make things worse."

"You likely killed it with the oxygen."

"Yes, we figured that out, a little too late. But you say this is not what you call a Frog? Then what is it?"

Laura, with her usual sarcasm, said: "Like the man said, we have no idea."

J.R., the hero deep sea diver, had an encounter with a similar creature in the De Soto Canyon cave. Ironically, today was the day that Parker was due to receive the DNA analysis from the few hairs that were shed in J.R.'s gloved hand. But seeing such a creature face to face, so to speak, was even better.

"To the best of our knowledge," Parker said, "all the Frogs are gone. Perhaps this poor thing simply got left behind with the ship. But if that happened, it's been hiding out for three years. How could it survive?"

What Parker and Laura were not about to reveal was that other Frog-related entities had been left behind, entities such as the Trolls, former underground worker-slaves. Perhaps this thing in the freezer was a member of another worker caste. Perhaps they were guardians of the ships.

"I agree," Kiselev said. "Its survival is surprising. In fact, a lot of things are surprising. But I'm sure you two would like to see the ship."

"That would be nice," Laura said with her sarcasm only slightly muted.

Parker loved this biting side of Laura. Beauty and brains was a great combination in a woman, but you add the ability to be sarcastic, witty, and, when appropriate, sexy, and you have the perfect partner in crime. Or so it seemed, considering the predicaments the two kept finding themselves in.

Unfortunately, through absolutely no fault of his own, the two of them had suddenly disappeared, yet again. This was becoming a bad habit that his wife, Sandy, the Southern-bred, Emory trained Belle was undoubtedly finding difficult to comprehend.

After an elevator ride down to the bottom floor of the facility, 50 feet underground, the three entered the fitting room where all sizes of full contamination suits were arrayed. Each suit contained a rebreather gas source that only injected the amount of oxygen into the wearer's mask that was required. The rebreather, the communication system, and all other portions of the suit were fully isolated from the environment, making it a certified system for dealing with the Ebola virus, or hour's long operation in an essentially oxygen-free environment, which was the case here.

Kiselev attempted to explain the rationale for their procedures.

"The protection afforded by the suit serves a double purpose. We don't yet know why this vehicle was abandoned. Had its pressure boundary failed, or had some lethal virus made the internals of the ship uninhabitable? Due to that uncertainty, we allow no one to enter the sealed hangar or the ship without the full suit, regardless of how uncomfortable the suit might be. You Americans would say, '*Better safe than sorry.*' But we Russians say, Лучше перебздеть, чем недобздеть, which roughly translates to 'It's better to over-fart than under-fart.'"

Both Parker and Laura laughed. "Strangely," Parker said, "that sort of makes sense."

After fitting and rudimentary training on the suits and rebreathers, the three entered an airlock which opened into the hangar. Not until they stood on the same floor level as the craft, which was cradled about 5 meters off the concrete floor, did they realize just how large the craft was. It had the width of the wingspan of an Airbus A380. It had a pristine beauty that looked thoroughly modern in spite of its suspected age of a thousand centuries.

Parker felt his pulse quickening, and his throat seemed to be developing a lump. The emotional impact of seeing a craft of the type that saved Laura and him from a crazed black projects agent and misguided Marines, and then healed his body through a seemingly impossible surgery, was almost more than he could bear.

At the top of his list of appreciation for the now space-faring aliens, was the restraint they had used when threatened with extinction by the

U.S. government. The irony of the Frogs demonstrating on one very deserving person the horror of the human rebirth experience, to save both their race and the human race, was a clear sign of a highly evolved intelligence and a noble sense of morality.

Ever since the Frogs had left the planet, Parker had had many occasions to lament the absence of the combination of high intelligence and high morals. Such evolutionary achievement was apparently in short supply among humans.

Kiselev remained silent for a few minutes, knowing that the Americans would be just as awestruck as all the others who had first stood in their place.

"Now for the interesting part," Kiselev said. "Are you two ready to enter the craft?"

"Let's do it," Parker said.

Climbing up the ramp wearing the contamination suit and rebreather was a little more challenging than Parker had expected, although Laura, both younger and somewhat fitter than Parker, seemed to have no difficulty at all.

Once at the top of the ramp, the three stepped into the airlock as easily as boarding a jetliner.

"How do you get inside?"

"Make sure you're clear of the outer door and then press hard on this inner door."

Parker pressed hard, and after the outer door had closed, a rush of oxygen-depleted gas shot down from the top, displacing the oxygen-containing air through floor grates. Once the airlock had equilibrated with inside gas, the inner door opened.

It was an elaborate mechanism, but only Parker seemed to understand its true function. It had to exist if air breathing trolls were to load up the airlock with mined minerals needed by the Frogs. The trolls were engineered for air breathing, but the Frogs were not. The airlock made sure the two incompatible species would never meet face to face.

"We'll begin the tour of the craft heading to the right. Please keep close at hand. It can get confusing in here, and we still have lots of technicians swarming around this thing."

Laura walked close to Parker, in part because of the chilling reminders of the last time they were inside such a vessel. Oddly, Kiselev did not have much to say, merely guiding them through the rabbit warren of passageways and a confusing assemblage of small, medium and large rooms.

"Anyone get lost in here?" Laura asked.

"All the time, until we started laying down lines like cave divers do."

"I don't see any lines," Parker said.

"We pretty well have the layout memorized now, but it helps to always start heading in the same direction."

"Oh, I see," Laura said. "The LED lights have arrows on them."

Parker said, "I assume these are your lights, not the Frogs?"

"Without our lights, this place would be completely black."

For at least 15 minutes, Kiselev led them through what seemed to be a featureless maze, with none of the wiring, piping, and equipment you would expect to find in a transport craft. Kiselev finally stopped in a small room on the edge of the craft, based on the curvature of the room's ceiling.

"Where are we?" Parker asked.

"We think this is the cockpit," Kiselev answered.

"For Frogship pilots?"

"We think so."

"Why do you think that?"

"This room is the only one that has two support structures in the middle, which some of our biologists interpret as seats for two Frogs."

"But there are no windows," Laura noted.

"Submarines don't have windows either. With good sensors, you don't need windows."

"You have a point," she said.

"I don't see anything that a pilot would use," Parker said, "like controls, indicators, nothing."

Kiselev did not respond but continued to lead them through more of the maze. Finally, they ended back where they'd started.

Parker looked at Kiselev with a funny look. "Didn't you leave something out?"

"Like what?" Kiselev asked.

"Uh, the engine room, the propulsion system, you know, the stuff that makes it go."

"No, what you see is what you get."

"There is no propulsion system?"

"Of course, there has to be. We just don't see it, and we don't know what it is or how it works."

"They must have stripped it out, cannibalized parts for another ship. That could be why they left it behind; it's just an empty shell."

Kiselev smiled. "Thank you Dr. Parker for that thought, but we actually thought of that some time ago. However, all these technicians you see, they have been combing this shell, as you call it, very carefully. Perhaps you can appreciate that you cannot move heavy machinery without leaving some trace of it, or its attachments, behind."

"They've found nothing?" Laura asked.

"Even microscopic examination has yielded no evidence that something was ever here, other than what you see."

"This just can't be?" Parker exclaimed, shaking his head.

"Do you know Nikola Tesla's most famous saying?"

Parker cocked his head, looking akilter at Kiselev. *What on Earth does Tesla have to do with this?*

"He had many sayings," Parker said.

"The day science begins to study non-physical phenomena, it will make more progress in one decade than in all the previous centuries of its existence."

Parker almost laughed at the irony. He had said that exact same thing to Laura just a few days ago back in Pascagoula.

"What's so funny Dr. Parker?"

"Oh, I just know that quotation very well. But what does that have to do with this?"

"We have concluded this thing does not have physical engines."

Laura laughed. "Well, that's sure thinking out of the box. But I still don't understand why this mystery ship has anything to do with you kidnapping us?"

"You really don't know?"

Laura and Parker looked at each other, then back to Kiselev. They said in unison, "No."

"Our sources have told us that the two of you were the only ones who could operate a Frog training aid."

"What does a toy have to do with anything?"

"From what we hear, that toy as you call it had colored lights, just like we believe this craft has colored lights when it's operating. Please indulge me, but we think that toy was a training aid for Frog pilots. We think it was a training aid for this ship."

"That has got to be the biggest load of crap I've ever heard," Laura said with all the disdain she could muster.

Parker was looking bewildered. "I see what this is. You kidnapped us thinking we could make this piece of junk fly."

"As you Americans say, it is worth a try. If you don't succeed, then we admit we were wrong, and exchange you two for a handful of some Russian spies we would like to get back. And maybe a few billion of those Yankee dollars your government gives away so freely."

"But, look at this thing," Parker said. "We have nothing to work with."

"Yes you do," Kiselev responded. "Your imagination, your collective minds, the Noosphere."

"Oh good grief," Laura said, rolling her eyes.

CHAPTER 53. RULES OF CAPTIVITY

Laura and Parker had been dropped off at a secure hotel built to house the labor force of the ersatz "mining" operation. The security of the hotel was somewhat different from what you might expect. Once locked in for the night, the "guests" are fed, entertained, and allowed quiet sleep before the morning shift began. But no one could leave until the morning buses arrived.

It was a type of lockdown to ensure that those who knew too much could not wander into town, get drunk, and spill all they know. Of course, the town was a very long walk away, and no cars were allowed, so the security requirements were likely overkill, but necessary nonetheless.

"Have you had evasion and escape training Laura?"

They were standing outside their adjacent rooms, about to head to the facility mess hall for the evening meal.

"SERE training? Yes, it's required before any foreign travel."

Parker raised the palm of his hand where he had written with a ballpoint pen. The words she read were "Escape and Evade, by air."

Soon as she read it, he wiped the writing from his sweaty palms.

Laura's eyes got big. She whispered, "You really mean to fly this thing?"

He shrugged, then whispered back, "It may be our ticket out of here. These things are really fast."

"Oh my God," she said. "Now you're scaring me."

"We have to make it work, Laura. If we fail, they will not exchange us for Russian spies; I don't care what they say. We know way too much about this operation. We'll never get out of here alive unless we can escape and evade in this damn thing."

"Look," Laura said, "you may be a hot shot baby jet pilot, but we don't know how, or if, this thing flies. I'm not buying their psychobabble mind-game shit. And even if you get it to lift off somehow, you don't know how to control it. We'll crash and burn."

"I admit, that's entirely possible. But if we stay here, without success, we'll be executed. And if they find out who you work for, we'll be tortured then executed. How does that grab you?"

She thought about that for a moment.

"Sounds something like a rock and a hard place."

After a meal of Borscht, Laura and Parker spoke one last time before retiring to their separate rooms.

"From the way you're smiling," Laura said, "I know you've got a hard on for this spaceship. But I'm wondering if we'll still be alive this time tomorrow night."

"Wouldn't you rather die trying than waiting for them to put a bullet in your brain?"

"I doubt I can dissuade you. You are nothing if not stubborn. But think about it, Jason. The Frogs wouldn't have left it behind if it was airworthy."

"My instincts agree with you, that it's probably not spaceworthy, but I used to be a stick and rudder pilot. I bet I can fly that sucker at treetop level. Wouldn't have to worry about depressurization then."

"Oh God, Jason, I give up."

She was shaking her head, with a sad look on her face. "I guess it's been a pretty good life. I just didn't think I'd spend my last day with you, on the other side of the world."

"Well, if it's any consolation, Laura, we've been here before, and survived."

"Goodnight Jason. Try to get some sleep."

The next morning, while eating a decidedly non-western breakfast with the other workers, neither Laura nor Jason had much to say. Parker was spending every spare compute cycle in his brain trying to figure out an escape plan. Laura was trying to figure out how she could help. If they survived at all, it was likely to be a team effort.

As they were finishing breakfast, Kiselev showed up.

"Do you feel the excitement?" he said. "We're going to let you spend some time in the cockpit."

Parker corrected him. "What you think is the cockpit."

"True, but there's only one way to find out."

Parker sighed. "With all the Russians available, including you, who somehow believe in this noosphere idea, there's no one who's been able to get this thing running?"

"No. It's just like no one was able to get your Frog flight trainer to run, except the two of you."

"For the record," Parker corrected him again, "no one said it was a flight trainer. You made that up."

"I admit our intelligence could be wrong, you should know. But we're going to have you pretend it works the same way."

Laura leaned her head close to Parker's. "This has disaster written all over it," she whispered.

A few minutes later, Laura and Parker were seated in what could by some Russian imagination pass as pilot seats, for Frogs at least. They certainly were not even close to normal aircraft seats.

"I'm going to leave you two to think about the task ahead of you," Kiselev said. "But we have cameras set up pretty much everywhere here, so if something interesting starts to happen, the cameras will catch it."

The two Americans looked at each other with amusement. "OK, see you later," Parker said.

"They're going to let us play for a while," Laura said.

"Let's see if we can surprise them," Parker said. "Let's wish something to happen, like we did the Frog toy. If we're not successful, then I think this thing is totally dead, and we will be too, sooner or later."

"So what thoughts should we concentrate on?" Laura asked.

"Energizing it. Bringing some power up."

"OK, but I think I'm going to feel real stupid in a few minutes."

"Laura, don't go there. Go into this with the same open mind we did with the toy."

Surprisingly she seemed to accept those words of encouragement. Both of them started visualizing the craft coming alive.

Parker remembered how as a child he'd stared at a plane flying overhead and experimented with the power, or lack of power, of his thoughts. He imagined the plane crashing right in front of him.

Fortunately for pilots and passengers, his thoughts had no power.

But now, the Americans' survival depended on their combined thoughts having extraordinary power.

What a strange turn of events.

For five minutes or so, the two of them strained their muscles and furrowed their brows, to no avail.

"Laura, I think we're trying too hard. Remember how we activated the toy? We were relaxed because we didn't think we could do anything at all to it. And we really didn't care."

"OK," she said. "You're right. I remember now."

They tried again.

Less than a minute later, an intercom came alive inside the cockpit. "The lights have started glowing. They're different colors."

"Holy shit," Laura said.

That broke the spell.

"The lights went out," said Kiselev on the intercom. "Try again."

They tried again, and the lights returned.

Jason realized he could see a diffuse colored glow in the hangar. But the wall of the craft had been completely opaque. Apparently, the lights were starting to make the craft's hull partly transparent, at least in front of the cockpit area.

"We can see you," Kiselev said over the intercom.

"And we can see the glow of the lights."

Parker could hear shouts within the hangar.

Distracted by the commotion, the lights and transparency suddenly ceased, and Parker and Laura slumped in their seats, thoroughly exhausted.

In spite of that exhaustion, they smiled at each other.

Parker said, "We just did something no one on Earth has ever done before."

"No human to be exact. But please notice, it didn't fly," she said.

"No, but we're learning. Next time we need to remove the cover over the hangar, just in case, clear everyone from the hangar, and have total silence from the observers."

"Is that all?"

Parker sat there with a satisfied smile on his face. "I think we can do this."

A jubilant Kiselev reentered the cockpit to lead them out again.

"Why did you leave us?" Laura asked.

"In case this thing ended up on the moon, I was not appropriately dressed."

"Coward." Laura was not smiling when she said that.

"I've arranged a little reception for you, with a very important person. I know the two of you have some concerns about propulsion,

John Clarke

and our most distinguished astrophysicist will try to answer them. He was trained at Oxford."

After stops at restrooms to freshen up, the always wary Americans were escorted to an elevator that took them to the top floor, four stories above ground. When the door opened, it opened not into a hallway but directly into a large, comfortably equipped room. A tall bushy eyed, graying man walked over from a bookcase and shook their hands, beginning with Laura's.

"Ah, it is so nice to meet our new celebrities. You were famous in Russia before, but now you are rock stars."

"I won't tell you my name, because you might know it, and I want what I say to stand on its own, without any blurring caused by notoriety."

Parker looked at Laura, thinking *I don't know any famous Russian astrophysicists. Do you?*

She also showed no signs of recognition.

"Please sit down. Your achievement today is cause for celebration. Can I interest you in some superb vodka?"

"No thanks," Laura said. "I'll just have some water."

He smiled, "You know, that's what we call vodka, water."

"I know, but I'll just have tap water."

"No, it's not so good here. I'll have some bottled spring water brought in."

"Sounds good," she said.

"Tell me, my famous Americans, do you know why atheists don't believe in God?"

Parker thought for a moment but sensed it was a trick question and didn't answer. Laura also remained silent.

"It is because they can't see God."

"Are you an atheist?" Parker asked.

"Of course. But if I could see God, I would change my mind very quickly. And many people, if not most people, also don't believe in spirits of the dead. Do you know why?"

Laura ventured a guess. "Because they can't see them?"

"That is correct. Because they can't be seen. But here's the amazing thing. We now know that we can only see 5% of the universe. Even when we look up and know we're looking at 95% of the matter of the universe, we can't see it. Yet scientists have little trouble believing in this thing they can't see and don't understand. They give it a name, dark matter, which means it cannot be seen."

300

Laura remained quiet but nodded her head. That was all true, as far as she knew.

The reportedly renowned cosmologist continued. "They have no idea what it is, or how it works, but most cosmologists believe in it, and are desperately looking for it. Now, doesn't that strike you as odd? They, myself included, don't believe in God, but they believe in the unknown mystery matter. It's curious I think."

After the monolog was apparently completed, Parker said, "And this has something to do with spacecraft propulsion?"

The unnamed Russian said, "I'd forgotten how impatient you Americans are."

"Not really. It's just that when we philosophize, we usually do it over a beer."

"Well, I did offer you vodka. But back to your question, which has to do with dark energy."

Parker interrupted, "Vacuum energy?"

The Russian waved his hand at Parker as if dismissing him. "Yes, energy of the vacuum, whatever you want to call it."

"We don't know what that is," Parker retorted. He was not going to be easily quieted since he didn't ask to be in this class.

"That is true. None of us today understand dark energy. But that doesn't matter. How do you explain something you don't understand?"

"You don't," Parker quipped.

"No, you do it by analogy."

Laura and Parker were looking blankly at this man without a name. Parker remembered Laura's earlier whispered comment, "They're all crazy." Well, maybe they are.

"Think of all the forces of nature that men have harnessed. Aside from fire, wind and water power, we harnessed electricity not too long ago. The trick was to convert it to a usable form and then transduce that energy into something we can use, like motors. No one can see an electrical field, but without it we wouldn't have radio or much of anything else."

Laura was sticking her tongue into the side of her cheek. She looked skeptical that this analogy would be useful at all.

"Take radioactivity, and beta, gamma and alpha waves. It's invisible, but without being able to harness that energy, we would not have lifesaving medical treatments, or atomic bombs to end wars."

"Or start them," Laura added.

He seemed to ignore her.

"Now, by analogy, look at dark matter. We can't see it, don't understand what it is, but it looks like there is much more dark matter in the universe than anything else."

Parker was one step ahead of this mystery cosmologist, but he did not interrupt.

"And then there's dark energy," the Russian continued, spreading his arms as wide as he could. "It's everywhere. It may take us longer to harness dark energy than it did to use electricity and radioactivity, but given enough time, we will do it. And guess who had lots of time to harness of dark energy?"

"Frogs?" Laura answered tentatively.

"Precisely."

Parker, growing frustrated with the roundabout discussion, said, "But what does that have …"

"I think the ship is a transducer. The hull harnesses dark energy, which is everywhere around us."

"But how do you get propulsion?" Laura asked.

The man smiled. He was thrilled that the famous American duo had not yet figured it out.

"It's easy. You modulate the transducer, change the amount of the hull interacting with dark energy, and vary the forces applied to it. When you get a difference in force, then you get acceleration. That's simple Newtonian physics."

Parker wondered out loud, "How do you modulate it?"

"That's where you two come in. The use of control cables to change aircraft flight is archaic. Now we use electrical signals from computers to control aircraft. And thinking thousands of years in the future, the electrical signals from your master computer, your brain, can do the same thing. Your combined brains can drive this thing wherever you want it to go."

Home, Laura thought, hoping this weird guy was not a mind reader.

"But why us?"

"Have you ever had an EEG done?"

"A brain wave study?" she asked.

"Yes."

They both answered, "No."

"I'm willing to bet your brain wave activity is not quite normal. Perhaps it's more like a Frog's than human brains."

"You are so full of shit," she said, showing no kindness in her voice.

He smiled. "I'm just teasing you. I have no idea why you two are special. I just know you are. No one else has gotten the ship to turn on."

CHAPTER 54. A SHIP IS ALIVE

Hans Richter had returned to his Fort Meade office, having been forced to move on to other more pressing national concerns. The Pascagoula Rock, as it was being called, had yielded no entry, no information. There had been some talk about cutting into it, but those in power were unwilling to turn it into a cadaver just yet, not as long as the two people who might actually understand it, were missing.

The disappearance of Parker and Laura was high on the FBI's list of concerns, and the Intelligence agencies, in particular, were almost apoplectic about Laura. If what she knew was extracted from her, there would be devastating harm to national security.

Two days after their disappearance, Richter received a call from a Homeland Security official who recounted a story about Truman Baltazar, the troll, excitedly leaving his Marianna cave and telling the bored Marines guarding the cave that a Frogship was alive, in Siberia.

Richter was on the next plane to Panama City.

Richter had arranged to meet the troll in his backyard so to speak, the cave. He wanted him to feel as comfortable as possible because frankly, he was a little concerned about meeting a nervous troll. Baltazar seemed nice enough, but Richter's childhood memories of troll stories made him a little anxious.

"Truman, my name is Hans Richter, and you have my complete attention. Why do you say a Frogship is alive?"

"That is not my name."

"I know, but please bear with me. I've been told I cannot pronounce your name."

Truman smiled. "That is true."

"But back to my question. What do you mean?"

"The ships have a nervous system, designed by the Masters to last far longer than the Masters themselves. That nervous system is eternal unless damaged. When the ship is energized, that nervous system comes alive, and both the Masters and we become aware of its presence, and location."

"Why?"

"Going back in our history, we mined minerals for the Masters. When our load was ready to be picked up, we communicated directly with the ships. They came to us, and we loaded their ships."

"So where is this ship that you say is alive?"

"Near a very large lake, far away. That lake has been its home for a very long time."

"If I show you an image of the entire world, can you show me where it is?"

"I'll try."

Richter pulled up Google Earth on a large tablet computer and explained to Truman how to turn the virtual globe on the screen.

"We are here," Richter said.

With scarcely any hesitation, Truman rotated the globe to the opposite side of the world.

"The ship is here."

When Richter zoomed in on the location, he saw it was Lake Baikal near Irkutsk, Siberia.

"You say you can call the ship to come to you?"

"I can."

Richter broke out into the biggest grin of his life.

Having received the call from the NSA Director, POTUS was meeting with intelligence and military advisors in the White House Situation room.

"Mr. President, our remote viewer has confirmed the location pointed out by Truman Baltazar. It does contain a vehicle similar to the Pascagoula Rock. He can't tell if our human targets are there or not, but our satellites are confirming there is a hell of a lot of activity. They don't see any signs of a ship, but there are some man-made patterns which we suspect are concealing something large there."

The President's brow was wrinkled with concern. "If we do succeed in calling this thing to us, the Russians will be trying their best to make sure it does not reach us. I want our Elmendorf F-22s to meet the Russians soon as it crosses into international waters."

The Director of National Intelligence spoke up. "Sir, I know we want to grab this craft, but if it looks like we're going to lose it, we need to destroy it. There's a good chance Laura Smith will be on board. We can't afford to have them discover her tie to DNI."

John Clarke

"If it makes it to international airspace, we will protect it. But I'm not attacking it in Russian airspace. I'm not going to be the one to start World War Three."

The Secretary of the Air Force quipped under his breath, "It may be a moot point. Those things can pass our fighters like they're standing still."

POTUS looked at him and smiled. "So much the better. Do we think Parker can fly this thing?"

"He may not have to. If what our troll says is true, these things may be on autopilot."

"In that case, we better move our troll to a secure landing field. I don't want the ship crashing in the North Florida woods, trying to find a spot to touch down."

The Air Force Secretary chuckled. "Area 51?"

The President laughed. "Hell, why not. We've got fruitcakes out there claiming all sorts of things. Let's give them something to really talk about."

CHAPTER 55. I AM SUPERMAN

Parker had demanded that both he and Laura be outfitted with Cosmonaut spacesuits, with extravehicular backpacks with a bountiful supply of oxygen and carbon dioxide absorbent chemicals. Also, G-suits were being worn underneath the spacesuits.

Since G-suits were normally activated by G-sensing regulators and valves in fighter aircraft, that was the first stumbling block encountered. Quick thinking aircraft technicians salvaged Sukhoi fighter life support hardware, strapped it down next to the pilot seats, and attached them to an independent source of oxygen.

The key to that system's success, or failure, would be the Russian equivalent of a Breathing Regulator/Anti-G valve. Parker was pleased with the LSS or life support systems checks and spent his little remaining time before the first take-off attempt trying to reassure Laura.

English-speaking Russian flight system technicians started at square one training her in the intricacies of the LSS. Fortunately, Parker was well familiar with American fighter systems, but Russian equipment and procedures were different. The fact that labels on the LSS switches were in Cyrillic did not help. He could not afford to confuse the switches and procedures during what would be a mentally and physiological stressful time. He simply had to memorize anticipated actions.

During that training and preparation, Parker realized how ironic it was that he was rehearsing their personal life support system procedures, but he had absolutely no idea how to control the spacecraft. He had no procedures to memorize for getting the thing airborne because no one knew how to do it. He recognized that a failure at any part of the flight phase would end in disaster.

To top off his reasons for concern, there was the unfortunate fact that they would probably be the first to discover whether the alien craft was airworthy, even if he could control it. No matter how good of a fighter pilot you are, if a wing falls off your aircraft, your options are pretty limited; you eject or die. Unfortunately, there were no ejection systems for the aircrew on this particular bird.

What Parker and Laura should have been worried about, was something that had only briefly crossed Parker's mind. The Russians might hide an autodestruct charge in the heart of the craft. If it appeared the bird was heading outside of the country, a digital signal sent by satellite might obliterate the craft. In the Russian mind, it would be far better to destroy the craft than to have the Americans claim it.

What neither Parker nor Laura knew, was that both sides had their destruct orders.

At dawn on the morning of their attempted flight, the sun was setting on the eastern seaboard of the United States. It was dark in Washington D.C., and the day was quickly fading in Panama City, Florida. F-22s from Elmendorf had been making routine flights, ready at any moment to dash to the Russian border to either protect or destroy the alien craft, whichever alternative presented itself.

All available resources had been activated, including the CIA remote viewer, Joshua Nilsson, and the troll Truman Baltazar. Baltazar had been flown to Area 51, where the waiting game had begun.

As strange as it seemed, the U.S. government was depending on Baltazar's alien-engineered nervous system to pick up on a reactivation of the ship, and to also guide the craft to his location.

At the same time, Nilsson was expending vast amounts of energy trying to perceive the goings-on at the supposed mining site, and finally obtained the sense that a protective covering had been removed from an interesting looking part of the facility.

The next available satellite sweep confirmed that indeed, something had changed on the ground.

Like all pilots, and especially those about to take off in a new aircraft, Parker gave the triangular craft a thorough inspection, from top to bottom and all the way around. The aerodynamic coverings for the lights looked like they were stronger than steel, and while examining the lenses for cracks, he wondered what their purpose could be.

Obviously, nothing with those lights could be clandestine. No black project craft has ever had huge Christmas tree lights wrapped around it saying, as it were, *Here I am.*

As best Parker could tell, everything looked normal. Nothing disturbed the smooth contours of the craft other than the strange lights.

After the final walk-around inspection, Parker and Laura carried their cooling equipment through the torturous passageways of the craft. Surprisingly, they had a third person joining them, in the rear. Parker stopped him and asked, "What are you doing here?"

In broken English, the man said, "I'm insurance."

"Insurance for what?"

"That you not go rogue."

"Oh," Parker said.

What Parker was really thinking was, *Oh shit.*

Understandably paranoid, Parker searched the passageways they walked through, again looking for anything that had not been there before. But everything appeared benign, other than the malevolent passenger they had not counted on.

When they got to the cockpit area, Parker told the enforcer, "There are no seats for you."

"I have my own."

And he did. He brought a flimsy folding chair like you'd take to a concert on the lawn somewhere. But the man may not have been told that this was going to be nothing like a concert on the lawn.

Although the Russian was dressed like a cosmonaut, he did not carry himself like a cosmonaut, in Parker's opinion. He seemed awkward in his new suit, and ill at ease, which Parker was thinking might pay off as an advantage, somehow.

While Laura and Parker were distracted, a Russian EOD technician sneaked into the hangar and attached to the ship's hull a large mine that would be detonated remotely should the ship stray far from course.

The briefed flight plan was simply to go a little ways up, and then back down again, in slow and highly scripted flight. Of course, that assumed that Parker knew how to conduct a scripted flight with this exotic bird with no controls, or that he had any intention of doing so, even if he could.

Parker and Laura settled into the job at hand, forcing from their minds the complication of the clearly threatening man seated behind them.

At first, they sat quietly and tried to relax, which was exceedingly hard since they knew that in the next few minutes they could be shredded and incinerated by a crash. But their overriding thought was that they wanted to go home, and this just might be the fastest way on Earth to get there.

Was it risky? Yes. But doing nothing and failing was even riskier.

Parker asked Laura, "Ready?"

"Ready."

The two of them strained in their seat, furrowing their brows, concentrating on activating the ship just as they had before. They were rewarded with a clearing of their forward vision, with colored lights reflecting off the walls of the hangar.

Something was happening, but it was not flying.

Kiselev had suggested they recite an affirmation. Since Kiselev had mentioned Superman, Parker tried that.

"I am Superman. I want to fly."

Laura giggled.

"Hush. You're breaking the mood. Say it with me, and mean it."

"OK," she said.

Together, they spoke what was sounding more like a plea than an affirmation.

"I am Superman. I want to fly."

There was movement. The craft lifted off the hangar floor about five feet and rotated slightly.

The hangar had been previously cleared of all personnel, but every window in the entire complex had noses pressed against the glass, waiting expectantly. Some were quietly cheering, but overall the sounds were muted. There was no sound at all coming from the craft.

"Hold that thought," Laura said. "I'm going to add a line from James Patterson." Laura now took on the persona of the teenage mutant girl, Maximum Ride, and imagined genetically-altered bird kids gathered around her. When danger threatened, Max roused up her flock by saying a phrase that Laura now spoke out loud.

"Up, up and away."

Those inside the hangar saw a brief blur and then the hangar was empty. Those technicians outside saw a metallic gray ship shoot noiselessly upward as if shot from a cannon, followed by a sonic boom just before it disappeared from sight.

Inside the cockpit, the enforcer's chair crumpled under a twenty times normal acceleration of gravity, straight up, which showed no signs of letting up until the craft had reached about 350,000 feet. At that point, the ship accelerated to Mach 30, heading on a relatively flat trajectory northeasterly. With the seat collapsed and the ship now generating a forward acceleration, the already unconscious, threatening man was slammed hard against a part of the bulkhead, parting his oxygen hose and leaving him to gasp involuntarily in the oxygen-depleted atmosphere of the ship. In a matter of seconds, he was no longer a threat.

Parker and Laura were not aware of what was happening behind them because they were themselves unconscious. Although their G-suit would help them tolerate up to nine-G's, they were now overwhelmed by the much higher forces on their bodies.

At some point during the vertical acceleration, dynamic forces tore the explosive package lose from the ship's hull.

As soon as high speed forward movement of the craft had been detected, a detonation signal was sent to the mine, which unbeknownst to the Russians, was falling free. As the craft rose very high, it was no longer able to keep up with the earth's rotation, and thus from the ground, the alien craft appeared to drift slightly westward. But as the prevailing westerlies buffeted the falling explosive, it was blown slightly eastward. Much to the Russians' misfortune, those two effects precisely canceled each other such that the charge fell directly down on the complex, erupting in flame and shrapnel at tree-top level. The explosion meant to destroy Parker and Laura ended up killing most of the Russians who had run outside to look for the alien craft, including Dr. Oleg Kiselev.

Both Russian and American satellite-based radars detected the craft at 400,000 feet, skimming through the boundary between air and space, heading over the Sakha Republic towards the frozen East Siberia Sea and Wrangel Island in the Arctic Ocean.

NORAD was on full alert, but missile interceptor batteries were instructed to stand down, while all airborne F-22 aircraft were told to shift their flight path toward the upper portions of the Russian airspace boundaries.

From the radar data, it became obvious that the craft was faster than any Intercontinental Ballistic Missile, and matched perfectly the

John Clarke

flight profiles of previous Frog ship movements. It could not be reached by any Russian aircraft or missiles.

Once the craft crossed the Chukchi Sea and entered U.S. airspace near northwest Alaska, it became clear to all those watching it, including the POTUS, that the Lake Baikal craft was coming to America. By the time it crossed into the Yukon Territory east of Anchorage, the Elmendorf F-22s could do nothing more than watch it go by, far out of reach. One F-22 pilot got a visual on it at his 12 o'clock high, and only had one thing to say, "Holy Shit, look at that."

It was headed straight for Seattle.

Aside from losing consciousness, Parker and Laura had been bruised and shaken by the high G-loading on take-off, with blood vessels broken in their eyes, but the LSS and the contours of their seats had kept them alive.

They were just regaining full awareness when the craft began descending lower into the atmosphere, ionizing the sparse air molecules below 400,000 feet. Parker barely had time to recognize the Seattle area when G-forces once again wracked their bodies as the craft started decelerating. He had no idea where they were headed, but from the angle of the sun, he guessed it was somewhere in the U.S. or Canada.

Once Parker's mind recognized they were flying, he tried to force his brain into somehow commanding the ship. "Fly the plane, fly the plane," he said to himself, trying to force his brain into aviation priorities just as he'd learned in primary flight training. His instructors had always said, "No matter what's happening, fly the plane."

But of course, he wasn't really flying it at all. He had no way to control its attitude, speed or direction. He and Laura were simply along for the ride, and the craft seemed to know where it wanted to go.

About twenty minutes after Laura had said 'up, up and away,' the triangular shaped Frog ship settled to a soft landing in the Nevada desert at the infamous Area 51. There to meet it was a small flood of senior NASA, Air Force and Agency folks, and the representatives from the DNI anxious to reclaim their prize, Laura Smith. She would likely never be told those same personnel had placed a shoot down order, had things turned out differently.

312

Also at the landing site was Truman Baltazar, the troll who called them home.

CHAPTER 56. GROOM LAKE

The triangle had landed on the flat, dry Groom Lake, next to the runways at Area 51. As soon as the Americans had exited, and the dead Russian had been retrieved, the craft was moved inside a hangar at the nearby airbase.

For security reasons, all cell phones were disabled on the base, but Parker and Laura were led to secure landlines to contact their loved ones.

Sandy, Parker's wife, answered the phone hesitantly.

"Hi," he said in his usual cheerful tone of voice, as if nothing extraordinary had happened recently.

"Oh thank God. I almost didn't answer, it just says government phone on caller ID. So where are you? You haven't answered your phone for days. No one would tell me where you were."

"I'm out west. It's a long story but I just want you to know I'm OK."

"OK? Of course you're OK. You're in Pascagoula. What can happen there?"

"Well, I'm not actually in Pascagoula anymore. Like I said, I'm out west."

"San Diego?"

"No. I can't say."

"Well at least you're not with that Laura girl this time."

Parker froze. He wasn't allowed to say.

"I'm with all kinds of people."

"Oh my God, Jason, you are with her."

Parker was not a good liar.

"Sandy, it's work related. You have to trust me."

There was silence on the line as Sandy was apparently mulling over his response. Finally, she changed the subject.

"When are you coming home?"

"I don't know."

From over two thousand miles away he could plainly hear her sigh.

"These phones are monitored, Sandy."

"I know, I know. I can't say what I want to say. I just want you home again."

"I do too. I'll be there soon."

"Love you."

"Love you too."

The day following his escape from Russia, Parker had a thought. Since he had missed the chance to control the craft, he petitioned the senior Air Force official to let him give it a try.

Surprisingly, the officials, after calling the Pentagon and elsewhere, received the go ahead, but with some stipulations. The ODNI, having just recovered their Alien expert, was not risking her in another flight. They considered it miraculous that she had been returned to them unharmed. They aimed to keep it that way.

That was OK with Parker. She seemed to be a hyperdrive for the craft somehow, and he wanted to take it slow and easy, trying to understand what the lights had to do with control of the vehicle. He could not accept that they were merely for decoration.

Fortunately for Parker, the government was just as interested as he in seeing what he could do. However, there were a few other stipulations. Truman Baltazar would remain on site so the craft would not be attracted to him at another location. Baltazar was also instructed not to think of any other place besides Groom Lake. They didn't want him downloading any more flight plans if that was what he had been doing the day before.

Parker found that highly unlikely. Parker assumed the craft knew where Baltazar was, and figured out on its own the quickest way there, including optimal speed and altitude.

He had to admire the long-gone Frogs. They built one hell of a flying machine.

The last requirement was that he not use the Cosmonaut suits, but instead wear the pressure suit and helmet used by U-2 pilots. There were a number on the facility, all in working order.

To everyone's surprise, even though they didn't understand what the hull was made of, they were able to get a radio signal through it. That allowed personnel in a temporary control tower at the edge of the lake to listen in on Parker's comments as he experimented with mind-controlling the craft.

315

Laura was watching from the sidelines, and video and still cameras were recording every moment during the test.

"First I'm going to try to activate this thing. Let me know if you see any lights."

With considerable mental effort, he imagined the ship turning on and hovering.

From outside, Parker heard, "We have lights, we have visual on you in the cockpit, and now we have liftoff."

Parker agreed with everything that had been reported. He could indeed see the dried lake bed in front of him and sensed a gentle change in his elevation above the ground.

"Yep, we are airborne."

The ship lifted no more than five feet off the ground and wobbled slightly.

"Give me a light report," he said.

"All lights are glowing, with equal intensity. We have red, yellow, green, and blue."

"Awesome. Now I'm going to think about forward movement straight ahead."

At first, nothing happened, then the craft started slowly sliding forward.

"The red light at the forward apex has dimmed compared to the rest."

"That's not what I was expecting. I'll try hovering again."

The red "nose" light brightened and the ship came to a halt, still a few feet off the ground.

"Now I'll try sliding to the left."

When he thought of that motion, a yellow light on the left side, relative to the apparent nose, dimmed noticeably, and the craft shifted over about twenty feet to the left.

"Report."

"A yellow light dimmed on your left side."

"Strange," was all Parker said. Then he continued, "Let me try the other side."

"A yellow light on your right side is now dimming."

"I think I'm getting the hang of this. Let me try faster forward movement."

"Not too fast," said an Air Force one-star general who temporarily took over the observer's microphone.

"I'll try for a lope."

And with that, the ship started moving forward at about twenty miles per hour.

"The red light has dimmed some more, and now the green light next to it also seems to be dimmer."

"Curious," he said. "Any suggestions what to do next?"

The general took the mic again. "Try climbing a bit more."

Parker was a little reluctant, but finally he said, "OK Sir, just a little."

In an instant, he was floating at two hundred feet or more. The rapidity with which it moved startled both Parker and the onlookers.

"What about the lights?"

There was a moment of silence while the observers conferred with each other. Fortunately, the craft remained steady in its new position.

"They all dimmed a little, the same amount best we can tell."

Parker came to an initial conclusion. "I think to whatever is powering this thing, the lights are inhibitory. They seem to be keeping the thrust in check."

Laura grabbed the mic from the general. "Jason, maybe you should put it back down before you end up in space."

"Actually, that's a good idea," he said, "if I can figure out how."

"Don't think about the lights. Just think about the ground slowly rising up to you."

"Laura, I don't normally take flying advice from non-pilots, but that actually sounds pretty good to me."

As soon as he placed that image in his mind, the craft slowly descended to the ground. He then put his mind at rest, and the lights all went out.

The General spoke again. "You seem to be solidly down. All lights are out."

"Good, cause I'm coming out folks."

When the outside entry door opened, Parker stepped out and was helped out of his helmet. His first non-radio words were to Laura.

"It's a hell of a lot more difficult without your help."

Parker was still wearing his flight suit, minus the helmet, as the craft was being carried back to the secure hangar. The One Star offered Parker and Laura a ride to watch the mystery craft arrive from its slow but careful transport.

"So those lights control the damned thing," the General said.

"It sure looks that way to me," Parker said.

"I wonder if I could fly it," said the One Star.

"If you do, I recommend you ditch the U2 flight suit, and go with a full NASA space suit. No telling where you'll end up."

The General laughed. "Yeah, no telling."

CHAPTER 57. DEBRIEF

The day after Parker's test flight at Groom Lake, Parker and Laura were asked to brief representatives from NASA, the Air Force, State Department, the CIA, and some other people not identified.

They were all seated around a circular table, with no nameplates, and no agency names. The Air Force representative was a two-star general, apparently the boss of the one-star who had wondered if he could fly the ship the day before. He wore a uniform, and based on his chronic smile, seemed pleased to be identified.

A tall, dark-haired woman started off the briefing.

"Thank-you all for coming on such short notice. I'm Gina Godfrey, and I'm representing the State Department. This briefing is initially being held at the S3 level, but if we have to upgrade to TS in a pinch, we can. Drs. Parker and Smith are cleared, and frankly, they know a lot more than we do."

Some around the table laughed at that irony.

"Let me first tell you that the Russians have filed a diplomatic protest, which frankly does not surprise me in the least. After all, we do have their ship, which according to international salvage rights, they own, free and clear. They want it back."

"Fat chance," someone said.

"Legally, their position is clouded since the pilots of the craft were kidnapped on U.S. soil. Furthermore, by the Geneva convention, their prisoners, Doctors Parker and Smith, were duty-bound to escape by any means possible, which as you see, they did."

Vigorous applause filled the briefing room.

"So it may be a cold day in hell before they get their ship back, but in the meanwhile, we're moving it to another location."

"You mean Area 51 is not secret enough?"

Several people laughed.

"No, it is not. And we can risk no more test flights for a while. Long focal length lenses are trained on us, and we don't need the attention."

A few people muttered something about satellites, but she seemed not to hear.

"Doctors, may I call you by your first names?"

"Yes, of course," Parker said. Laura said, "I prefer it."

"OK then. This is all being recorded. We'll keep it freeform at first, and then follow-up with questions. Who wants to start?"

Parker nodded towards Laura and said, "Ladies first."

Laura hesitated, then proceeded.

"Well, first of all, we didn't fly the ship. We were both unconscious passengers for a while. When we came too, we both assumed we were headed to somewhere in Russia. And I assumed we would crash and burn on landing since Jason was clearly not flying the damn thing. I could not imagine we were being brought safely home."

"You can thank your friend Truman for that," Godfrey said.

"That dead Russian, did he threaten you before takeoff?" the Air Force General asked.

"He said he was there to make sure we didn't go rogue. I don't think he had any idea we were planning to escape Russia if we could. And I'm pretty sure he was dead before we knew we had, in fact, escaped Russia."

"Did he have a weapon?"

"None that we could see," Laura said.

"How does the craft fly?" the General asked Laura.

"I don't know," Laura said.

"Do you Jason?"

"I have my own theory, but let's let Laura have her say. I don't think she's through."

"Fair enough."

"Well," Laura continued, "I do think the colored lights have something to do with it."

A high-level NASA engineer took that as his chance to join the conversation.

"Laura, people tell me that Jason Parker is good at what he does, but that you are like Jason Parker on steroids."

He looked at Parker as he said it.

"Would you agree, Jason?"

Jason nodded his head. "It does seem that way."

"So, best I can tell, your fame, and that of Jason, were cemented when you were the only people who could make the Frogs' toy work, the one with colored lights."

"That is correct. Except we don't think it was a toy. It seemed like a training aid."

320

"Yes, so I've heard. A training aid for psychokinesis, or something of the sort."

Both Parker and Laura remained expressionless.

"Do you think it is a coincidence that both the training aid and the Frog ship have colored lights?"

She thought for a moment, then answered. "I don't know."

"What do you think, Jason?"

"I think it is anything but a coincidence."

"Could you explain?"

"I'm not an expert in these matters."

Godfrey said, "It doesn't matter. We'll bring in experts when we need them. We just want to know what you think."

"Then, what I think is that the lights modulate thrust, sort of like ailerons on an airplane, or vectored thrust on a jet."

The Air Force General said, "That makes sense based on yesterday's low power flight tests. But what's the main power source? What makes it fly?"

"I've thought about that long and hard. And I've come to the conclusion that I need to be a hell of a lot smarter to answer that question. But I'll give it a try."

"Yes, what are your impressions?" the NASA engineer interjected.

"As it was hovering yesterday, my impression was that it is an antigravity machine, which doesn't explain much of anything. However, something a Russian cosmologist told me struck home. This thing, whatever it's made of, must be a transducer of some sort. But that doesn't answer the question either."

"Transducer?"

"Yes, like something that can capture one form of energy and convert it to another. Like water pressure turning a turbine, which generates electricity. The turbine is a transducer, is it not?"

"Of course, but I don't see the connection," the NASA engineer said.

"To overcome gravity you must either have a gravity shield, which probably doesn't exist, or expend energy."

"Yes, but with no fuel, what energy?"

"Dark energy."

"That's a non-answer. It may not exist either."

"Well something has to exist. The damn things levitate, and propel themselves into space. And to me, dark energy is a viable candidate since theoretically it is everywhere. Even the apparently empty space between galaxies has dark energy. If you can transduce that energy, then you can power an antigravity ship, and take it wherever you want."

For a moment there was complete silence in the room.

Then the engineer smirked and asked, "But what transducer?"

Parker shrugged. "Have no idea, except we rode in one. Two hundred years ago we couldn't imagine an electrical generator or motor, or a nuclear reactor that can transduce the power of radioactivity to propel a ship or submarine. Now we take them for granted. And considering how old the Frog's civilizations must be, they must have figured out how to transduce dark energy."

"But how would they control it?"

"Child's play, at least for Frog children. That's what we call psychokinesis."

"And the lights?"

"From what I've read, light does not interact with either dark matter or dark energy. But it can perhaps control the transducer by modulating the thrust from the transducer."

"How?"

"It seems to me that if all the lights are on, the force on the ship is just enough to levitate it. And if you want to move in a particular direction, you dim some lights in that direction, which increases the buoyant force, producing a force imbalance which then leads to motion. If you turn all the lights off, then you get full thrust upwards. If you de-energize the ship, the lights go out, but no thrust results. The transducer has switched off."

"Why would you think the lights inhibit the force rather than increasing it?"

"First, there's observation. If you watch the video, you'll see what I mean. Secondly, the human body is a living example. Inhibitory neural pathways are extremely important in regulating human physiology. If it weren't for inhibition, our bodies would remain uselessly energized, until we burn out."

"Like a seizure?"

"Perhaps."

"Where might the different colors come in?"

"Once again, it's just a guess, but different colors have different wavelengths and therefore differing energies, and therefore varying efficiencies at muting the overall anti-gravity effect. By varying colors, intensity and orientation along the periphery, you can have an almost limitless number of options for altering force, and therefore altering course and acceleration."

Every man and woman there, including Laura, was staring at Parker, not sure what to say.

Finally, the NASA engineer voiced what they all may have been thinking, but he did so in a skeptical, sneering manner.

"That is certainly an … imaginative explanation."

He looked around the room, apparently looking for recognition for his clever rebuke.

That was a mistake. The man did not know Parker well.

Parker was quick to respond. "Have you ever been for a ride in these things?"

"No, of course not."

Parker was not about to be patronized by an armchair pilot, if even that.

"When you do, let me know what your pet theory is."

Parker was not through with him. "Have you ever been to the moon?"

"Uh, no. I was too late for that."

"Well, did weird shit ever happen on those missions?"

The man looked nervously around the room. "I can't say."

"Well, you get my drift. When you see things, you try to rationalize it. This is what I'm doing right now."

The Air Force General asked, "Do you think you could produce a computer simulation of what you were talking about? The dark energy transduction and, what did you call it?"

"Light-induced inhibition would be a good term."

"Yeah, that."

"Given a little time, it should be doable."

The General responded, "Next week maybe? I've never seen anything like that before."

"Me neither, but I can visualize it, and that's half the battle. But a week, that's kind of tight."

"Well, we've got this rock sitting in Pascagoula, and I need to brief Congress on what we plan to do with it. How can I help you?"

"Give me access to your best programmers, physicists, and cosmologists, and we'll see what we can do."

"Keep in mind it doesn't have to be reality. It mostly has to look good. We've got a sales job to do."

"Got it," Parker answered with some well-deserved cynicism of his own.

The man who Parker assumed was CIA based on his demeanor, asked, "What else did you take away from your experiences?"

Parker thought a moment and then smiled. "I would sure love to have a car made of that spacecraft hull material. Not because it can fly, but because it doesn't rust, ever. And think what a great submarine it would make. Hell, imagine a submarine that can fly, or stay in the deepest bottom trenches for thousands of years and not rust, or have any biofouling. And there's no machinery inside so it's maintenance free. Just imagine."

The man said nothing, but from the cryptic look on his face, it seemed to Parker that he was indeed imagining. A Navy Admiral, who had been invited as an afterthought, started taking notes.

Parker turned to Laura. "Do you have anything more to contribute?"

"Just one thing, and it's more philosophical than anything. Remember the message the Frogs gave us? It covered ten years into the future. We're now at year three, and we still don't know what it said. But I'm just wondering if the Frogs were thinking we'd need their abandoned ships. And if so, why?"

A man and woman of unknown identity leaned close to each other and whispered something.

Godfrey followed up Laura's comment with discernable interest. "You don't think it's a coincidence that we found these ships?"

Laura shook her head gently. "Where the Frogs are concerned, I'd be surprised if there are any coincidences. Serendipity, maybe. Synchronicity, perhaps."

The General asked, "What do you mean, synchronicity?"

"It means what has happened may be a meaningful coincidence. It happened for a reason."

"And what would that reason be?"

"Well, we certainly don't know, do we? But the Frogs may have known. And their parting gift may be meant to help us."

One of the unidentified said, "I looked it up just now. Carl Jung used it in a paranormal sense. Sorry folks, but we can't sell paranormal to Congress."

Parker leaped to his feet. Turning to face the presumed Agency man in the top row, "Mister CIA, I'm throwing the bullshit flag on that. Wouldn't you say your remote viewing program was paranormal? How

324

much money did you get from Congress for that? We had a troll, our friend Truman Baltazar, download a flight plan for our escape from Russia, with his mind. What is that? Paranormal perhaps? Laura and I communicated with the Frogs only through our mind. Isn't that pretty freaking paranormal? We also activated a UFO containing nothing inside, again with our minds. It can't happen, but it did."

People in the audience looked stunned.

Laura wondered if it was humanly possible for Parker's voice to get any louder, or for his face to get any redder, but it did, right in front of her. "Frankly, I wish that word had never been invented. It just means we don't understand how the universe works. These events are not paranormal. We're just stupid!"

Parker paused to catch his breath. Still standing, he continued, "Dark matter. It's not paranormal, it's science. We have no idea what it is, yet our brightest scientists tell us the universe is filled with it. Dark energy, the same thing. We have no clue, but Congress funds millions in research to find out what it is. So don't tell me an indestructible spaceship or bottom-of-the-ocean submarine can't get funding because of a word. If you believe that, don't use the damn word. It doesn't mean a thing."

Laura could not resist jumping in to support her colleague.

"Do you know what the Russians are talking about now? The Noosphere, the collective consciousness. They take it seriously, and if you don't want to be caught with your pants down, you better start thinking about this stuff. I suggest you look that word up, while you're at it."

Godfrey attempted to calm things down a bit. "You two have been through a lot these past few days. I understand you're emotional."

But Laura wasn't through. "And here's another thought. The trolls that saved our lives and brought an alien ship to you have a word for Jason Parker. It's Ta'veren. That's a fictional word, but then again, if you realize things happen for a reason, you have to wonder what is fiction and what is truth? So you don't have to look the word up, I'll tell you what it means. It means that Jason Parker causes things to happen. He's the source of the synchronicity."

Parker looked at her, then at those gathered before them, then back at Laura. He seemed just as shocked as they were.

Parker said, "Well, then, uh, can we answer any more questions for you?"

Gina Godfrey stood up and said, "I think you two have given us plenty to think about. What I would like to do next is get you two back to Pascagoula, while I'll be calling together some in the National Academy of Sciences so we can review your dark energy theory."

"It's not a theory," Parker said. "It's just a guess."

"Whatever it is, we need to study it, and see if we can come up with alternative explanations."

Laura started looking agitated when the word "Pascagoula" was mentioned.

"About Pascagoula, that concerns me. If you're planning on us opening up that thing, and then flying it, well, things could go badly for us. Last time we did that, we were sent unconscious into outer space, with no plan for landing safely."

The Air Force General had a ready answer. "We've got that covered Laura. You'll be perfectly safe, and Parker will get to do what he loves to do, fly. And if he's whatever word you said he was, then I guess things will turn out just fine."

Parker did not take much solace in the General's confidence.

CHAPTER 58. OVAL OFFICE

The sun was streaming through the windows of the Oval Office, reflecting off two spinning wheels on the President's desk. The wheels sent spots of reflected sunlight whirling around the room, distracting all in the room except for the man with the power to move wheels, and Armies.

Those wheels were his playthings, occupying his hands while his brain was forming the words that just might change the course of history.

"Martha, we have got to get every damn one of those Trolls out of the Yucatan and into that cave in Florida, or wherever else they want to go."

The Secretary of State was not going to be easily convinced. "Mr. President, they are in Mexico. We can't just roll in there and yank them out."

"We can if we declare them U.S. citizens, members of a sect that illegally entered Mexico. The Mexicans didn't even know about them until some damn reporter talked to a Marine in Marianna. As far as the Mexican President is concerned, they are not Mexican citizens."

"Well actually Sir, genetically they're not even human. They may look like us, but they're not human. It's going to be a tough sell to give non-humans the rights of American civilians."

"Considering what Baltazar did for us, he and his kin deserve to be U.S. citizens."

"Mr. President, could it be that your logic is being clouded by your not wanting the Russians to get hold of these people?"

He looked at her by peering over his reading glasses. "From what I've been briefed, these creatures have a neural connection to two Frog ships in our possession. And I want every neural connection we can get. If Baltazar croaks from old age or some cave virus, I want another one standing in the wings to take over."

"He may be the only one."

From the expression on his face, the President wasn't buying it. "And they may all have that skill, bred into them. Look, I'm afraid sooner or later the U.N. is going to force us to give the Baikal ship back to the Russians. If the Russians figure out what we know, and grab one of the Trolls, then we're screwed. And you know they'll try since they already nabbed Parker and Smith."

"Well, maybe they should get their ship back based on what we're learning from our De Soto Canyon Codex."

"Martha, if there is disaster coming, I'm not going to give the Russians an equal footing with us."

"Sir, at some point we have to look after the human race."

"Right now I want you to look after the Troll race. Do your diplomatic magic, lie to the Mexican government as much as you need, and get transport vehicles on the beach as soon as possible. I want every one of those people on a ship headed to Miami by the end of the month."

Madam Secretary paused, having been given a tall order. However, order it was, without a doubt. She could tell from his body language that he wasn't budging.

"Mr. President, I will do my best. Is there anything else?"

For a long moment, he said nothing but was apparently not ready to dismiss her. He was waiting for the two spinning wheels to wind down in their usual erratic, bumpy finale.

"I'm surprised you've never asked me about these wheels. I thought they would be a conversation piece, but no one mentions them. I wonder if they think I'm eccentric. Is that what you think Martha?"

"No, not at all Sir. That's not you."

The President looked up to the ceiling where the sun's reflections were whirling dizzily over the Oval Office.

"It's all math and physics, these wheels. But very educational. You see, you take both hands and spin them, and then you watch what happens."

To illustrate, he spun both wheels clockwise.

The wheels weren't really wheels, but each had a central hub riding on a low friction pin, and from each hub extended three spokes. Instead of a wheel rim connecting the spokes, each spoke had a bulbous end. The spokes were only connected to the hub.

"You see, everything is moving fast and smooth, just as I'd intended. But watch as the wheels begin to slow down."

The Secretary moved closer to the desk to better watch the demonstration.

"For me, these wheels are symbolic. One wheel is me, and the other can be whatever I'm thinking about. It can be Congress, or the media, or the American people, or President Dmitriev."

As friction began to slow the spinning wheels, their motion started becoming less smooth, and then it became erratic. Eventually, the two wheels began batting each other, to and fro in opposite directions. And then they stopped.

"Why did they do that?" she asked.

"Something tiny and invisible, magnetic fields."

"Those are magnets on the ends?"

"Yes. Sometimes when the magnets get close, they repel each other. Eventually, they end up pushing each other around."

"I've never seen that before."

"Oh yes you have. It's in politics and public policy making. We politicians always start off with the best of intentions, but it's the weak little forces we can't see that can do us in. We start a program with a big push and at first, things seem to be great. But then when the inertia begins to die down, the invisible forces begin to play a dominant role."

"Do the wheels always end like that?"

"No, and that's the point. The final result is unpredictable. You see, this is a chaos demonstrator. Each time you spin the wheels you get a different result. It's controlled chaos, but chaos nevertheless."

"You're implying governing a country is chaotic?"

"By this definition, absolutely. Weak invisible forces can affect wars or Presidential elections. I may try to force a particular outcome, but the final outcome may not be at all what I had intended."

"That's dreadful."

"No, that's life. Of course, when a campaign fails I'm tempted to blame generals or politicians or state enemies, but if the truth be told, the culprit may be mathematics. The net unpredictable influence of tiny invisible forces can do us in."

"I guess it's good to be mindful of that," she said, "but is there a reason we're discussing this now?"

"I woke up this morning with an idea. With your past ties to the Agency, you or they may have already thought about it."

"About what?"

"Wouldn't Baltazar make the perfect spy?"

The Secretary raised her eyebrows in disbelief. "The Troll Baltazar?"

"He can read minds. He can remote view wherever he wants. He requires almost no care and maintenance. And on top of that, I heard that one of them beat the crap out of two armed Marines without them even knowing he was there. Shoot, if I were in that business, I'd be fighting to get him in my employ."

"Are you serious?"

"Sure. The only thing is, I cannot predict the outcome if we tried to recruit them, or put them in the field. My little wheels tell me that I have no idea if that would have a good outcome or a disastrous outcome."

"That's thinking pretty far out of the box Mr. President. But since the Trolls rebelled from the Frogs, I'm not sure they'd be willing to turn right around and swear allegiance to us."

"But we're not the same as the Frogs. Are we?"

"With all due respect Sir, I think that's yet to be determined."

The President smiled. He'd found that as far as the Secretary of State was concerned, there was usually more meaning in her words than first meets the eye.

"We'll worry about that when we get them all safely stateside. We'll let them decide where their allegiance lies."

"Yes, Mr. President."

.

CHAPTER 59. PASCAGOULA ROCK

Jason Parker, sitting alone with his thoughts, was staring at the inanimate object shrouded in metal and mystery at the Naval Base in Pascagoula. Parker had finally received the DNA report on the yellow hair-like strands that J.R. had managed to yank out of whatever was in the De Soto Canyon cave. He still had no understanding of how J.R. could return from an out of body experience with tangible, material substance, but the DNA report did little to explain either what J.R. had seen, or what he and Laura had seen in the medical freezer at the Russian mining site. The only thing the report had done was rule out plausible explanations.

The genomic material in the hair shaft had been minimal, but there were just enough hair roots pulled out of the creature that mitochondrial DNA was available for limited genotyping for species determination.

For sure, it was not filamentous algae like he had first assumed. Nor was it from a human, nor any known hominid. As for aquatic species, it wasn't from a fish or shark, porpoise or whale.

The report had a checkmark in the box for "adequate sample size," but it also had a checkmark in a box labeled "indeterminate."

And it sure as hell was not one of the frogs.

As Parker kept replaying the vision of the creature in the Russian freezer, and imagined the scene described to him by Oleg Kiselev in the hangar when the Russian craft's door finally opened, he found himself filled with a growing terror. What if that happens here?

What if he manages to open the door to the craft before him, and a guard, or whatever that creature is, blocks the entrance? Parker theorized that the Russians inadvertently disabled him by not having enough oxygen in the hangar, and then killed him by giving him too much oxygen through the medical oxygen mask. What about here?

There is no oxygen control. Everything's sitting in air, with maybe ten times the safe dose of oxygen for the Frogs, and perhaps as well for the unknown creature encountered by J.R. A door opening might

John Clarke

cause the death of the last living ... oh hell, I might as well call it what it looks like ...merman.

Parker's growing anxiety was interrupted when Joshua Nilsson was led into the floating hangar.

Responding to the subtle sound of Parker rising from his seat, Joshua turned to face him.

"I hear they've taken your partner in crime away from you."

It was true, ODNI was not about to risk their top alien expert, Laura Smith, on more Frogship test flights.

"Without her special connection to anything Frog-related, I can't even open the door to this thing. That's why I asked for reinforcements."

"So the cavalry is arriving, with one horse, and a very blind Californian," Nilsson said. "I wouldn't get your expectations up if I were you."

Parker guided Nilsson with his hand, leading him slowly to a chair in full view of two of the triangular sides of the craft.

"I heard you and Laura flew one of these home, stealing it from under the noses of the Russians."

"We were passengers. But that bird is in seclusion somewhere, being poured over by our scientists and engineers in case we have to give it back. But this thing in front of us is all ours. Our divers risked their lives to find it, and it's up to us, you and me buddy, to make it work."

"So why did the Frogs leave the Russian ship behind?"

"It wouldn't pressurize. Riding in it was like going for a spacewalk. There was no pressure and no appreciable oxygen inside it at altitude. If I had not forced the Russians to give us Cosmonaut suits to wear, we'd be dead."

"But you don't know what's wrong with this one," Nilsson said.

"Nope. We haven't even been able to get inside it."

"But if Laura was here, you think you could?"

"I'm sure of it. She's freaky powerful."

"And you want _me_ to help?" Nilsson emphasized the word "me." He was seemingly skeptical of Parker's logic. "Why do you think she's so powerful?"

"She thinks it's because she was one of the Frogs in a previous life. I don't believe that, but belief can be strong medicine. She has so

332

much power that I call her my *hyperdrive.* And she is certainly a strong believer."

"What about you?" Nilsson asked.

"The Frogs claim I was also one of them in a previous life, but I think they were lying. I'm certainly far weaker than Laura is."

"Well, there you go. Maybe you're weak because you're not a believer."

"This is what I believe. The Russians have bought fully into the *mind over matter* business. They want to weaponize it, from what I can tell."

"You're kidding?"

"Not at all. After all, they started the remote viewing efforts. I'm not a bad remote viewer, but you are one-of-a-kind, the best there is."

"So they tell me."

"I've been telling people for a while, that the fact that a remote viewing program works is proof that the Russians may be on to something. Remote viewers like us are using mind over matter, or at least mind over time and space."

"There's only one way to find out. Let's try to open this thing. How do we begin?"

"Before we do that, there's one thing I want to discuss with you."

"What's that?"

"I've tried RVing into this thing, and consistently come up empty. But you're way better than I am. When's the last time you took a mental look inside it?"

"Funny you should ask. I explored it again just this morning before coming over here."

"And?"

"Like you, I came up empty," Nilsson said.

"So you detect no lifeforms?"

"No. Are you expecting any?"

"Not really. I just wanted to be sure."

"Keep in mind, RVing is not a sure thing, so we might be in for a surprise."

That was an honest answer, but it was exactly what Parker did not want to hear.

"So, like I said," Nilsson reminded Parker, "how do we begin?"

Parker had been putting off this moment, but now the time had come. He had to pray that no one, or no *thing*, died from their actions.

"Visualization. That's how we do it."

Nilsson winced.

Parker continued. "We imagine in our minds a door opening."

"You've seen the door on the Russian ship," Nilsson said. "What does it look like?"

"It's basically the size of a cargo loading elevator. I'd say it's at least fifteen feet wide, and ten feet high and opens to an airlock which is maybe 15 feet deep. Apparently, the trolls used it to load minerals they'd mined for the Frogs."

"Can you see an outline of it from the outside?"

"No. It's undetectable from the outside."

Nilsson reached out to Parker. "I'm ready if you are."

Parker took Nilsson's hand, which was warmer than he'd expected. "I'm ready," Parker said.

After no more than ten seconds, a large cargo door opened in the lower portion of the triangle, below the row of bulbous lights. And much to Parker's relief, nothing was standing in the doorway.

Cued to subtle mechanical sounds coming from in front of him, Nilsson asked, "Did something happen?"

Parker stood up, with a big grin on his face.

"It sure did."

Apparently, the Russians were wrong. A hypoxic atmosphere was not needed for the door to open.

Parker had not dropped that trick from his playbook. If all else had failed, he'd planned to brief that option. However, it was an expensive option, and Congress was becoming increasingly disenchanted with spending boundless sums of money on a gamble. Now it wasn't necessary. All that was needed was a couple of strong minds.

Two weeks later, the first air-sea trial of the newly commissioned U.S.S. Canyoneer was about to begin. Both Parker and Nilsson, dressed in spacesuits with life support backpacks, were seated as comfortably as they could, in the pilot and copilot's seats. The troll Truman Baltazar had downloaded the air-sea plan to the already activated craft under the watchful eyes of Laura Smith, Hans Richter, the NSA remote viewing spook, Gina Godfrey from the State Department, and Parker's often challenged and frequently terrified wife, Sandy.

Being married to Jason Parker was enough to test the limits of any marriage, especially one where the man had a habit of mysteriously disappearing with a beautiful, bright and powerful young woman.

Also on hand were the two deep sea divers who had risked everything to make this day possible. J.R. and Tom gave Parker two thumbs up through the now transparent windscreen of the cockpit, but secretly they both were second-guessing the wisdom of sending Parker off with a blind copilot. The government does some strange things sometimes.

Navy and Air Force strategists had estimated that when the flight plan involved long distances, like from Siberia to Nevada, a near parabolic, high-altitude, near-space excursion must be preferred by the craft, rather than a flatter, lower altitude route. To minimize the risk of very high-G acceleration, or destruction on reentry, the first downloaded test flight plan would cover only a short distance, taking it to the De Soto Canyon cave entrance, 2500 feet below the Explorer Platform 100 miles away. There, the Canyoneer's water entry and descent could be observed by cameras and instruments.

Since the ship had come from that location, it was considered safe to allow it to return to that depth.

The final leg of the flight plan was for the craft to return to the surface once it had reached the bottom.

Some, like Laura, were concerned that once the craft returned to its home at depth, it might not want to come back to the surface. Her attitude reflected the worry of a few others in the government who were slowly coming to recognize that the ship was, as Baltazar described it, "alive." Like a horse racing back to its stable, no one could guarantee it would willingly return to the surface.

When Laura expressed her concern to Parker, all he said was, "A good rider has to convince a horse to do what the rider wants, not what the horse wants."

Secretly, Parker did harbor a little concern about his ability to control this alien craft, but he also knew that shadow of concern was not about to stop one of the most interesting test flights of all time.

Nilsson reached out his left gloved hand to hold Parker's right gloved hand and smiled inside his helmet.

"Are you ready?" Parker asked.

"As ready as ever. Let me know what I'm missing."

"Sure thing. Now let's do this."

John Clarke

And with that final word, the craft lifted vertically to clear the local obstructions, then accelerated up and to the southeast at an easily manageable three Gs. Within seconds it had shrunk to the size of a speck downrange, rising to a maximum of ten thousand feet and a speed of Mach 0.9 before beginning a curving descent towards the water. Instruments and cameras on the Explorer platform watched its steady approach and splashdown. The Canyoneer entered the water at 250 miles per hour and at a 45° angle a half mile from the platform.

Thirty seconds later, a signal was received by those on the platform and onshore that the craft was on the bottom.

Parker turned to Nilsson. "Did you feel the splashdown?"

"I only felt deceleration."

"Yeah, me too. I can't believe how gentle supercavitation is."

"Have we stopped moving?"

"Yep, welcome to the bottom of this part of the De Soto Canyon. And don't worry, I can't see anything either."

"Now what?"

"Now we wait for the rest of the flight plan to execute."

Laura was sitting beside a Navy sonar technician on shore who had a relayed signal from the sonar on the platform.

"Anything happening?" she asked.

"Nothing. No movement."

"It's been ten minutes."

"Nine minutes 47 seconds to be exact."

"I was afraid this would happen," she said.

"You think we're stuck?" Nilsson asked, sounding concerned.

Before Parker could answer, they heard a thud inside the craft. It sounded like metal crashing into metal.

"What the hell?" Nilsson said.

Then they heard another impact, and another. It became a crescendo, almost sounding like hail hitting a car roof, with the sound resonating within the air-filled passages internal to the craft.

"Topside," Parker called. "We're getting a lot of metallic noise down here. Do you see anything happening?"

Parker's primary concern was that the hull might be wrinkling, the first step in an imminent implosion resulting in instantaneous death for the two helpless occupants.

"We hear it too Jason. But we can't see any deformation from here."

The noise continued.

"That's not very comforting Topside. Something is sure as hell happening."

The outside lighting got brighter, followed by another call from Topside.

"Jason, remember the drones? They seem to be swarming the craft like they're trying to get inside."

"You have got to be kidding me," Parker said. "There's no way that can happen."

Before the words fully left Parker's mouth, a seeker, maybe a foot long, attached itself to the transparent portion of the hull directly in front of the men. From their vantage point, they could see pleated suction cups like those on a remora.

"At least I don't think that can happen."

Parker wondered for a moment if the seekers could drill their way into the craft. If the bastards penetrated the pressure boundary that would be just as deadly for the men as an implosion.

"Topside, we're getting the heck out of Dodge."

"How do you plan to do that?"

"I don't know. Sheer willpower I guess."

Remembering that an upward motion required the visualization of rising, with no other directional component, Parker began imagining a slight rising in the water column.

"I'm getting something," Nilsson said. "We're no longer parked."

"I agree. Now let me concentrate."

Trying to tamp down any rising excitement, Parker maintained his concentration.

"Slow and easy," he said to himself.

A minute later, Parker announced, "I see some light in the water. We're definitely rising."

On the platform and shore, a report came back that the craft was now at 800 feet and rising. Richter, Laura, Sandy and two dozen other people cheered.

It was anybody's guess what the Canyoneer would do when it reached the surface. Would it fly or float, or God forbid, sink again before Parker and Nilsson could get out?

On the platform, all hands were ready to secure the craft as best they could, and extract the pilots. A loudspeaker was calling out the depth. "Two hundred feet, one eighty, one fifty, one twenty, one hundred, eighty, sixty, thirty, surface."

Once on the surface, the ship lifted out of the water, and Parker and Nilsson in their EVA suits could be seen through the transparent cockpit portion of the hull. The ship rose to the main observation level of the platform and stopped.

"Jason, you're not going to believe this, but you are covered with drones. They look like remoras attached to a shark."

"Yeah, I can see one, and I agree with that description. They're actually called seekers, and I think I know why. I'm not stopping here fellas 'cause I want to get this baby to the shipyard. I don't want to risk it sinking here."

"Well good luck with that. I'd keep it slow. I don't know if they'll spoil your lift."

"Roger that, quarter speed ahead it is then."

The Canyoneer circled the platform once as Parker tested the ship's controllability, then it rose to two thousand feet and headed off towards Pascagoula at the leisurely pace of two hundred miles an hour. The seekers were tenaciously holding on.

Parker's return to a water landing at Singing River Island was not the most graceful approach and landing Parker had ever made, but it was by far the most momentous.

Once on the platform, the two men quickly got their door open, exited the craft and then turned to see what everyone was staring at. There must have been several dozen of the elongated seekers plastered to the hull of the ship, everywhere except for the magic lights.

Before disconnecting his comms and removing his helmet, Parker announced, "New toys for everyone. But be careful, they may bite."

Perhaps because of the risks her husband had taken, Sandy had been granted escorted access to the facility. As soon as he had been helped out of his spacesuit, his wife planted a slobbery Southern kiss on his lips.

Then she asked, "Did you really go into space?"

"Not this time," he said. "But it should still make for an interesting entry in my flight log."

Having logged a few flight hours herself, Sandy asked, "You going to log it as aircraft or submarine time?"

He thought about that for a moment, then looking back at the triangular craft he quipped, "I'll just call it Triangle time."

Simultaneous with Parker and Nilsson's return, Dr. Harry Kincaide from the Stanford Research Institute, father of the CIA's Remote Viewing program, was funded under strict secrecy to start training future Frogship pilots. The pilots were to have Laura and Parker's skill at activating and controlling the colored glass training aid left behind three years ago by the departing Frogs. It was believed that particular skill was a prerequisite for eventually commanding the U.S.'s one and only Frogship, assuming the Russian Frogship would eventually be returned.

For the time being, the U.S. would be dependent upon Trolls to upload navigational flight plans to the ships, while hoping that Truman Baltazar was not the only Troll with that ability. Soon, over three hundred of them would be available for evaluation.

The National Academy of Sciences was hard at work trying to understand both antigravity ships and mind control of those ships. Laura, being the DNI's expert on aliens and alien technology, was working overtime to find out if the "collective consciousness" and the Noosphere have any credibility or applicability to alien technology. If it did, then mankind might be on the cusp of a technological revolution.

CHAPTER 60. U.S. CITIZENS

The U.S. Citizenship and Immigration Services, falling under the Department of Homeland Security, was about to take the oath of allegiance from over three hundred trolls. It was certainly the first time that the genetic boundaries of humanity had been stretched this far. Argxtre, who refused to be called Truman Baltazar once his cave mates had arrived on American shores, had a concern that he shared with his friends, Parker and Laura.

"I've heard that some in your government are questioning how we can be sworn in as citizens if we are not even human."

Laura looked at Parker, obviously perplexed. "Who's saying that?"

"I don't know them."

Argxtre continued, "What does it mean to be human? Our former Masters used to say they were humans. I don't know why this is being said about us."

Parker dived into that question, being a biologist at heart.

"What is a human? It may be self-centered of us but we say a human is a member of the species Homo sapiens. And what is a species? A group of individuals that can successfully breed with each other, but not with another species."

"Were Neanderthals Homo sapiens?"

"No, they were not."

"But we now know they did breed with Homo sapiens," Argxtre said, "and the proof is in your genes. You have Neanderthal genes."

"You are quite well read for a man who lives in caves."

Argxtre said, "You don't have to be so delicate. I know what a caveman is, and I probably do fit the description."

"But still, distinct species rarely if ever exchange genes," Parker said. "Do you know if any of you have ever mated with Homo sapiens?"

"No, I don't know," Argxtre said smiling, "but I'm looking forward to trying."

Parker glanced at Laura to see what her reaction would be.

Her reaction was immediate and directed towards Parker. "What are you looking at me for?"

"What you're telling me is, we don't know if we're humans or not," the Troll said. "And by your definition, we won't know until we have babies with you. Is that right?"

"I guess so," Parker said. "Until then, we're giving you the benefit of the doubt."

"Maybe if we weren't so good at programming Frogships, as you call them, we would not be given that benefit."

Laura complained. "I think that's unfair. We want you to have a good, safe home."

Argxtre seemed to be giving that some thought. Then he said, "Let me ask you, what does it mean to be a U.S. citizen? Does it mean we get a good, safe home, as you say?"

Laura answered, "We will certainly do our best to make sure your people are safe and happy."

"But what does it really mean?"

Parker thought that was an amazingly insightful question, one that he wasn't sure he could answer. However, Laura did.

"It means you are allowed to be yourself, as strange as that might be, without fear that the government will persecute you. Of course, that strangeness does not mean you can hurt people, but if you want to worship a Pie Plate God, you can worship freely, without fear of persecution from the government.

Pie plate God? Parker had never heard that one before, even from Laura.

"It means if you want to share a story about your life, you can without fear the government will burn your books. Again, as long as no one else is hurt by it."

"Does it mean everyone will like us?"

"No, it does not mean that. It means the government has bestowed upon you the rights and recognition of citizenship. You will soon belong to a very special club."

"Please understand, after repelling our Masters who enslaved us for thousands of years, we do not want to be enslaved by another Master."

"The United States government is not our Master, and we are not its slaves. The government works for its citizens. We are the Masters."

"So then it is a good thing to be a citizen."

"Yes, a very good thing."

Apparently satisfied, Argxtre turned to go back to his people, but Parker caught him by the shoulder. The Troll turned back around.

"On behalf of the U.S. Navy, I want to thank-you for returning the body of our ex-Navy Chief, Wayne Brinson. I know you don't understand the significance of that, but the family and we greatly appreciate it."

Argxtre nodded his head.

Taking Argxtre's hand, Parker said, "This is one way we show our appreciation."

Parker shook his hand, while Argxtre watched carefully what was being done to his hand and arm.

Touching his hand to his head, Argxtre then said, "We think our appreciation."

He then moved his hand from his forehead to Parker's forehead, touching him.

At the same instant, Parker clearly heard a voice inside his head say 'thank-you.'

And with that Argxtre went back to stand with his people, all three hundred of them.

Parker turned to Laura and patted her affectionately on the back. "Laura, you are one amazing gal. I had no idea how to answer his questions."

"Well thanks, I guess. Maybe working in D.C. has had me thinking about such questions. You know, about who the true Masters are."

"Knowing you, I suspect you're thinking about who the Masters of the Universe are."

She laughed. "Well, that is my job you know, but I can't talk about it."

A short time later, the assembled trolls were repeating the Oath of Allegiance as it was read to them, one phrase at a time.

"I hereby declare, on oath, that I absolutely and entirely renounce and abjure all allegiance and fidelity to any foreign prince, potentate, state, or sovereignty, of whom or which I have heretofore been a subject or citizen;

that I will support and defend the Constitution and laws of the United States of America against all enemies, foreign and domestic;

that I will bear true faith and allegiance to the same;

that I will bear arms on behalf of the United States when required by the law; that I will perform noncombatant

342

service in the Armed Forces of the United States when
required by the law;
that I will perform work of national importance under
civilian direction when required by the law;
and that I take this obligation freely, without any mental
reservation or purpose of evasion; so help me God."

After the celebration was over, Argxtre returned to Parker and Laura who had been watching on the sidelines.

"Jason, I have a question for you, since Laura answered all my other questions."

"OK, I guess it's my time."

"That last thing we said, 'so help me God.' Who is God?"

"Uh, that's a really hard question. Don't you want to answer it, Laura."

"No, it's your turn." She was smiling.

"Uh, well you see, we believe …"

Argxtre interrupted Parker, laughing like Parker had never seen him laugh before. "You don't need to answer. I just wanted to see you get nervous."

"Well, that really is a hard question."

Argxtre winked. "I know."

Parker had never seen Trolls wink before.

Maybe they really are human.

The trolls began boarding buses headed to Andrews Air Force Base where C17s were waiting to fly them to Tyndall Air Base in Panama City, for final relocation to the Marianna Cavern.

Argxtre lingered at the back of the line and then approached Parker one last time.

"Tell me, Mr. Parker, would your government be willing to make citizens of more of us?"

"I'm sure. But I thought there were no others."

"We were not the only group to rebel against slavery. A smaller group in Siberia did the same thing. They mined minerals for the ship in Lake Baikal, but now they are under control of the Russians. When they learned how you treat U.S. citizens, they asked to join us."

"You talk to them?"

"Of course."

"Are there any more groups out there?"

343

"No. All the rest left with the Masters."

"Really? I thought the Frog's low oxygen atmosphere would kill you."

"That is not true. The Frogs are pressure tolerant, and we are not, but we are oxygen-tolerant, and they are not. We can switch our metabolic need for oxygen as needed. If it gets too low, we go to sleep, but we do not die, as long as it doesn't change too quickly. Our bodies need time to adapt."

"Really?" Parker exclaimed.

Parker saw Laura watching from across the room, and he motioned for her to join them.

As she stood next to Parker, he told her he was about to ask an interesting question. And he truly was.

Addressing Laura he said, "I was just told there are more Trolls, in Russia, who wish to join these new citizens."

Laura raised her eyebrows. "That's interesting."

"But what's more interesting," Parker continued, "is that the two groups are in telepathic communication. Which brings me to a question you need to hear."

Laura looked at him with a quizzical look on her face.

Facing Argxtre, Parker said, "Before we knew you and your people existed, both Dr. Smith and I had a dream where a human killed a Frog-child on a Frogship, and the Frogs in turned killed most of the humans. Were those two dreams merely a coincidence?"

Parker expected him to say something like, "How would I know?"

But he didn't. Instead, Argxtre stared at them for a moment, then looked around the room. Finally, he moved close to both of them so he could speak softly and still be heard.

"No coincidence. That happened, but they weren't humans. They were my people."

"What?"

"Like my Russian friends, they knew that if they had stayed here, they would have been given freedom. But they were angry that their future, and that of their offspring, would be one of servitude. They did not know freedom until we knew freedom."

"But the timing was off," Laura said. "We hadn't met you yet."

Argxtre smiled. "True, but the future is more knowable than you think."

Parker was incredulous, and his scrunched up face showed it.

"Do not doubt us, Jason Parker. Thanks to you, in our time you had already found us. We had already gained our freedom. But those who left with the Masters will not know freedom. Just anger."

"But, in our dreams we were there," Laura explained, "in the ship. We can't be in two places at once."

Argxtre pointed to his head. "You have two minds."

Laura and Parker looked at each other in disbelief.

Argxtre said to Parker, "When you're remote viewing, your mind is in two places at once."

"That's ridiculous," Laura said.

"One day you will understand," Argxtre replied.

Then, as easily as flipping a coin, Argxtre's tone changed from that of a transcendental mystic to that of a garden variety Troll.

Well, maybe not so much garden variety.

"On a more practical level, you may be interested in knowing we can fly the ships."

"You?" Parker asked, still disbelieving what he was hearing from this surprising Troll.

Argxtre smiled at Jason. "Actually, I'm a much better pilot than you. But then, I've had more practice."

"Then you can't leave just yet," Parker said.

With that, Laura walked away to call her boss on a secure phone, and after a few minutes of nodding her head, she pulled aside the Secretary of State.

An hour later, the Secretary of State was briefing the President, the Secretary of Defense, available members of the National Security Council, and Homeland Security.

"We recommend we maintain the secret that these guys are now U.S. citizens," she said. "We have a plan to use them, and in the event of capture, it would be more convenient for us to have plausible deniability."

The President cocked his head, wondering once again where the Secretary came up with her ideas.

She continued. "The Russians want their craft back, and we want the Russian trolls. We can kill two birds with one stone, just as I've already briefed you."

"What's the downside?" POTUS asked.

John Clarke

"Not much. At least no American pilots will be at the controls, as far as the Russians and the American public know."

The President smiled. "I like it. Let's make it happen."

CHAPTER 61. RESCUE

A combination of human and Troll ingenuity was about to play out on the large screens in the White House Situation Room. The Russian Frogship had just taken off from its storage facility at White Sands, New Mexico, headed on a parabolic profile to the edge of outer space over Alaska, then down to Lake Baikal. Two Trolls were piloting the ship, wearing American spacesuits to protect them from the low pressures encountered during the apogee of their flight. To no one's surprise, Argxtre was one of them.

The Russian government, alerted by the President of the United States, was expecting their craft to land near the Baikal mining facility. However, the U.S. Trolls had a different plan. The ship was headed for a site about 285 miles northeast of the so-called mine, a rugged site near Lake Uokinda, that gave every appearance of being accidentally short of the intended landing site.

Unknown to the Russians, their entire contingent of Trolls had traveled silently through the night from the surrounding mountains to the true landing site.

From the Situation Room, the U.S. President called the Russian President as the craft set down on its intended remote site, bustling with Trolls.

"My apologies Mr. President. We seem to have misprogrammed the craft. We are recalling it, and will send it right back to you as soon as we download the correct coordinates. You have my word; it should be back to you within two hours.

By the time the Russians figured out exactly where the craft had landed, all of the nearly two hundred Trolls had been loaded on board. When the ship took off again, it flew in a low-altitude profile that would not kill the Trolls who were not wearing spacesuits.

That flight plan was a gamble. It would keep the Trolls safe from hypoxia and decompression but would expose them to enemy fire if the Russian President gave the order.

But he didn't, knowing full well that it would be idiocy to shoot down his own Frogship. He passed the word to stand-down anti-aircraft batteries, and to keep his fastest fighters on the ground.

And then he laughed with his inner circle and ridiculed the Americans for their ineptitude with simple navigation.

"No wonder we put a man in space first," he laughed. "They are idiots made more idiotic by their mind-numbing television."

The American subterfuge worked.

From the Situation Room, the President's Security Council and Cabinet Officers watched the craft land back at White Sands. Within minutes of landing, the Russian Trolls were whisked away by buses while Argxtre mentally downloaded the correct navigation course. With that completed, and his feet firmly planted on American soil, he sent the ship the following message.

"It's time to fly away home."

The U.S. President called the Russian President back. "As I promised, it's headed back your way, with the correct coordinates this time."

"Well, Mr. President, like your people say, *If at first you don't succeed, try try again.*"

"You got me there Andrei. Let me know when it's safely down."

Thirty minutes later, Dmitriev made the call. "It is back without a scratch. You are a man of your word."

"Of course, Mr. President. We are an honorable nation."

By the time evening came, the keepers of the Russian trolls were in a panic. Every last troll was missing.

Of course, Andrei Dmitriev would never mention the trolls to the U.S. President. It would be an international human rights violation to admit that you had a group of captive slaves; not entirely human-slaves at that.

It would probably never occur to the Russians that their troll slaves were the only ones who could program the flight data for the Frogships, other than the Frogs.

The U.S President was thinking about the day's events before he finally turned back the covers to his bed.

He thought to himself, *An interesting end to an interesting day. The Russians have their ship back, but they have no way to enter a flight plan. Without that, it's just a toy.*

I think this is going to work out well!

CHAPTER 62. EPILOGUE

Two months after the rescue of the Russian trolls, the President's inspiration about using trolls as intelligence assets had gained some traction among the various communities. At least it had attracted some analysts with enough curiosity to meet with the lead troll and test his supposed telepathic abilities.

Argxtre was becoming one of the most widely traveled trolls, and this time he'd been transported by private jet up to the seat of American intelligence, Langley, Virginia. And now he was seated in a windowless secure briefing room facing six carefully selected questioners.

Laura Smith was the only one of them that Argxtre knew. She smiled warmly at him as he entered the room.

To cover the paranormal side, Nilsson was there as well. Nilsson seemed vaguely familiar to Argxtre, although he could not place why.

The other four, two men and two women, represented diverse intelligence agencies and were selected due to their open-minded nature. When it came to trolls, an open mind was imperative.

The most senior of the group, judging from his lush but completely white hair, opened the meeting by addressing Argxtre.

"I begin this meeting with an apology. Since we will be speaking about personal and sensitive things here, I hate to affront your sensibilities by not using your real name, but as a matter of record, I'm required to call you something we can all pronounce. So following the convention started by Dr. Jason Parker, I'll call you Truman Baltazar. Again, my apologies in advance."

Argxtre smirked but nodded his head in acceptance of the artificial requirement.

The leader continued. "In just a moment we Panel members will place an image in our minds. Truman, I would like you to attempt to tell us what those images are. Is that something you are willing to do?"

Argxtre smiled. "Let me know when you are settling down. Your imagery is all over the place right now."

The leader turned to the others and asked, "Are we ready?"

They all nodded silently.

"OK then Truman, you can begin anytime."

Argxtre smiled. "Starting from left to right, first is a white elephant, a pink rhino, a triceratops, the Washington Monument, the American flag, waving, and a garbage truck."

There was a long pause before the leader spoke.

"Well, folks, I think he did amazingly well. He missed only one, the garbage truck."

One sheepish looking man raised his hand. "I'm sorry, I forgot to put out the garbage this morning, and this is garbage day."

"Correction," Argxtre said, "Now he's thinking of a sandy beach."

"Wow, very impressive. That is 100% correct, plus extra credit for the garbage truck."

The panel members smiled, nodding their heads in approval.

"And from now on, I'd like the panel to try and remain focused. We have serious work to do."

The other five panel members whispered to each other. They seemed astonished. Laura certainly was astonished, but she was mostly proud.

"Now we're going to think about policy topics of national and international importance. Is the panel ready?"

Again they nodded.

"OK, Truman, you can start."

Again Argxtre did not hesitate. Sweeping his head from left to right, he said, "Nuclear proliferation, terrorism, bioweapons, space wars, population control, and climate change."

"I'm dumbfounded," the leader said.

Argxtre continued, "But I also see those things you hope I don't see. Your wishes and fears, your secret thoughts. I shall name them."

"No, that's not part ..."

"One of you was raped by an older Boy Scout at camp, in a tent. One of you wonders what it would be like if the baby you gave up when you were sixteen contacted you, one tied a string around the neck of baby birds and threw them over a balcony until their heads popped off, one of you slapped a screaming child."

Then turning to Laura Smith, he said, "As for your thoughts, I think it's highly unlikely we are related."

Nodding in the direction of Nilsson, Argxtre said, "And this young man seems to be fixated on a girl's butt with a gun and holster tattoo."

John Clarke

No one on the Panel said anything, but the expressions on their faces confirmed their shock.

The facilitator spoke up. "OK, I'm not going to ask the Panel about the accuracy of those comments, which by the way, will be stricken from the record."

With the facilitator seeming to be floundering, now fully off-script, a matronly looking woman took over.

"OK, Truman, I think we can confirm that your mind-reading skills are the best we've ever seen. But now I want to know more about you as a person."

"And as a U.S. citizen," he said proudly.

"Yes, that too. On a personal level," she continued, "what happens if you meet someone you have a deep philosophical disagreement with? How do you handle interpersonal conflict?"

"With our ability to understand their thoughts, we are quite capable of knowing their motivations. We either accept their point of view, or we find the flaw in their logic."

The lady smiled, looking around the room to make sure everyone was aware of the importance of what had just been revealed. "That sounds like an admirable and peaceful way to resolve conflict."

Someone else asked, "What if you don't win them over?"

Argxtre shrugged. "Then we kill them and eat them. We Trolls are very spiritual that way."

"Oh my God," Laura said under her breath.

At that very moment, the room went dark as a squirrel exploded itself on a local electrical transformer.

As was his nature, Argxtre began removing his clothes.

Coming Next

The adventures of Jason Parker, Laura Smith, and the Troll named Truman, will continue in the next volume of the *Jason Parker Series*. Look for it as early as 2018.

GLOSSARY

1MC – U. S. Navy shipboard announcing system

CNO – Chief of Naval Operations

Collective consciousness – the set of shared beliefs, ideas and moral attitudes which operate as a unifying force within society. The term was introduced by the French sociologist Émile Durkheim in his Division of Labor in Society in 1893.

Cosmologist – a scientist who studies the structure and history of the universe

Deep dive – 1) a technique used to immerse a team into a situation for problem solving or idea creation. 2) a dive using divers to depths greater than normal scuba and commercial diving; typically 300 to 2000 feet.

EmDrive – A nickname for an Electromagnetic propulsion drive, properly called a radio frequency (RF) resonant cavity thruster.

EOD – Explosive Ordnance Disposal, a special operations branch of the military

Fortean Times – a British magazine of news, reviews and research on strange phenomena.

Genomic material – the genetic material of an organism

Genotyping – the process of determining differences in the genetic make-up (genotype) of an individual by examining the individual's DNA sequence using biological assays.

Head break – restroom break

High frequency oscillation – a method of mechanical ventilation especially effective on newborns.

John Clarke

Hominid – any of various primates of the family *Hominidae*, which includes orangutans, gorillas, chimpanzees, and modern humans, and their extinct relatives.

HPNS – high pressure nervous syndome, a stimulation of the central nervous system caused by high pressures encountered in deep diving (600 feet or deeper). It can produce tremors and psychosis.

Inert gas – a gas which does not undergo chemical reactions. The noble gases (helium, neon, argon, krypton, xenon, and radon) are the least chemically reactive. Nitrogen is considered an inert gas in diving, but can react under certain conditions.

MARSOC – United States Marine Corps Forces Special Operations Command

Metabolic need – the whole range of biochemical processes that occur within us (or any living organism), but usually referring to the amount of oxygen required for a given work load.

Noosphere – a postulated sphere or stage of evolutionary development dominated by consciousness, the mind, and interpersonal relationships (frequently with reference to the writings of Teilhard de Chardin).

ODNI – Office of the Director of National Intelligence

OIC – Officer in Charge

OPNAV – Office of the Chief of Naval Operations

Perfluorocarbon – fluoronated hydrocarbons (PFCs). Some have been used in liquid breathing experiments due to their ability to dissolve oxygen.

Phalanx CWIS gatling gun – a 20 mm close-in weapon system for defense against anti-ship missiles.

Photophores – a light-producing organ in certain fishes and other animals.

POTUS – An acronym for President Of The United States

Pressure swing absorption – (PSA) is a technology used to separate some gas species from a mixture of gases under pressure according to the species' molecular characteristics and affinity for an adsorbent material.

Quantum encryption – or quantum cryptography is the science of exploiting quantum mechanical properties to perform cryptographic tasks. The best known example of quantum cryptography is quantum key distribution which offers an information-theoretically secure solution to the key exchange problem.

Quarterdeck – The quarterdeck is a raised deck behind the main mast of a sailing ship. Traditionally it was where the Captain commanded his vessel. In modern usage, it is the secured entry to the offices of Commanding Officers.

Remipedes – Remipedia is a class of blind crustaceans found in coastal aquifers and caves which contain saline groundwater. Cave remipedes tolerate very low dissolved oxygen levels.

Remote viewing – (RV) is the practice of seeking impressions about a distant or unseen target, purportedly using extrasensory perception (ESP) or "sensing with mind".

ROV – Remotely Operated Vehicle

SCI – A security rating above Top Secret, standing for Sensitive Compartmented Information.

SECDEF – The Secretary of Defense, sometimes shown as SecDef

SERE – An acronym for Survival, Evasion, Resistance and Escape

SETI – An acronym for the institute for the Search for ExtraTerrestrial Intelligence, cofounded by Carl Sagan and Frank Drake. The Institute is located in Mountain View, California.

John Clarke

SF6 – Sulfur hexafluoride is an inorganic, colorless, odorless, non-flammable inert gas which is five times denser (heavier) than air.

Sick call – United States military parlance for "a daily lineup of military personnel requiring medical attention."

Skua – a large brownish predatory seabird related to the gulls. Some species breed in the Antarctic. The eggs and young of other birds are an important food source for most skua species during the nesting season.

SOCOM – Special Operations Command

Sorb – Carbon dioxide absorbent used in diving rebreathers, closed circuit underwater breathing apparatus.

Supercavitation – the use of cavitation effects to create a bubble of gas inside a liquid large enough to encompass an object travelling through the liquid, greatly reducing the skin friction drag on the object and enabling achievement of very high speeds.

Synchronicity – a concept, first explained by psychoanalyst Carl Jung, which holds that events are "meaningful coincidences" if they occur with no causal relationship yet seem to be meaningfully related.

Ta'veren – people who cause events to happen that would likely not have otherwise, and people to make decisions that they likely would not. The Pattern and the Wheel both protect ta'veren jealously, making them almost-immortal. A ta'veren can be almost destroyed, but somehow will still complete their task.

TCAS – An aviation acronym for airborne Traffic Collision Avoidance System

TS – Top Secret security clearance

Visual cortex – the region of the human brain responsible for vision. Damage to the back of the brain where the visual cortex resides can cause "cortical blindness," the inability to see, even though the rest of the visual apparatus is intact.

Zero-point energy – the lowest possible energy that a quantum mechanical system may have; i.e., it is the energy of the system's ground state. Zero-point energy is the energy associated with the ground state of the quantum vacuum. The concept of zero-point energy was developed by Max Planck in Germany in 1911 as a corrective term added to a zero-grounded formula developed in his original quantum theory in 1900.

ABOUT THE AUTHOR

John Clarke is an adventure-loving scientist and aviator who challenges preconceived notions about mankind and the universe. He has been a diving scientist with the U.S. Navy for thirty-eight years, conducting research specializing in the adaptations of people and animals to the deep-sea. That research began at the Georgia Institute of Technology (Georgia Tech) and Florida State University, culminating in research in the Puerto Rico Trench and participation in the U.S. Navy Scientist in the Sea Program. The University of Florida School of Medicine provided NIH-funded postgraduate training in human medical physiology. His Navy research began at the Naval Medical Research

Institute, Bethesda, MD and continues at the Navy Experimental Diving Unit in Panama City, Florida. He has conducted diving research in both Antarctica and the Arctic, and aviation research for the Navy and Air Force. He is a Physical Scientist, and holds a Ph.D. in Physiology.

Clarke lives in Panama City, Florida, USA. His website is http://johnclarkeonline.com.

Made in the USA .
Columbia, SC
16 June 2020